ALTERNATE GENERALS III

Edited by
HARRY TURTLEDOVE
and ROLAND J. GREEN

ALTERNATE GENERALS III

This is a work of fiction. All the characters and events portrayed in this book are fictional, and any resemblance to real people or incidents is purely coincidental.

A Baen Book

Baen Publishing Enterprises
P.O. Box 1403
Riverdale, NY 10471
www.baen.com

ISBN 10: 1-4165-2114-3
ISBN 13: 978-1-4165-2114-3

Cover art by Jeff Easley

First paperback printing, March 2007

Library of Congress Control Number: 2004029942

Distributed by Simon & Schuster
1230 Avenue of the Americas
New York, NY 10020

Pages by Joy Freeman (www.pagesbyjoy.com)
Printed in the United States of America

CONTENTS

A Key to the Illuminated Heretic
    by A. M. Dellamonica......... 1

The Road to Endless Sleep
    by Jim Fiscus............... 39

Not Fade Away
    by William Sanders 71

I Shall Return
    by John Mina.............. 101

Shock and Awe
    by Harry Turtledove 127

A Good Bag
    by Brad Linaweaver......... 151

The Burning Spear at Twilight
    by Mike Resnick 171

"It Isn't Every Day of the Week..."
    by Roland J. Green......... 193

Measureless to Man
    by Judith Tarr 253

Over the Sea from Skye
    by Lillian Stewart Carl 297

First, Catch Your Elephant
    by Esther Friesner.......... 323

East of Appomattox
    by Lee Allred.............. 349

Murdering Uncle Ho
    by Chris Bunch 375

A Key to the Illuminated Heretic

A. M. Dellamonica

Frontispiece: Joan of Arc stands chained in a horse-drawn wagon, wearing a black gown. Leaning against a pair of nuns, she seems almost to swoon. Her right arm is portrayed as bones without flesh. The horses' ornate curls and gleaming teeth lend a ghastly note, and blackened angels border the image.

The scene is easily recognized: the Maid's debilitation, the nuns, and especially the cloud of larks above serve to identify it as Joan's journey to the trial that ended her thirteen-year imprisonment for heresy. It was at this "Exoneration Trial" that she encountered Dulice Aulon, the Jehanniste artist responsible for the holy pictures on which the codex illuminations are based.

✵   ✵   ✵

"We mustn't face the king in battle." Joan had the light, clear voice of a young woman, even after her years in prison and the hard decade since her release. She'd asked one of the new archers, a girl of perhaps seventeen, to cut her hair, and a few broken strands of silver hair clung to her neck. The rest lay at her feet, bright in the glow of dying fire.

"Not fight Charles?" Hermeland was incredulous. He was a badger of a man, with a dramatic, pointy face and remarkable speed with a sword. "We must turn his army back before it unites with the force of mercenaries coming up from Rome. If you can't see that—"

"Can't see it? Who ordered us to turn north, days before anyone knew the king had pursued us into Burgundy?"

"You—" he began, and as her brow came up he corrected, "your Voices."

They were nearly of a height, less than perfect subjects for a drawing. From her seat in the shadowed corner of the tent, Dulice tried to capture the dirt on Joan's blue tunic and leggings, her sheathed knife of a body. She was all deadly intent, a knight with a lined face and too many scars. Her eyes blazed—it was a wonder Hermeland did not flinch from the heat there!

"What I do not see is why Charles is coming at all," she said. "He's an old man. He never led men-at-arms before."

"Politics," he replied. "So says Marcel Renard."

"He would bring that filthy word into it." She waved off the archer gently, shaking out her shorn locks as the girl left.

"We can win this battle, Joan," Hermeland said.

"We *would* win." She dismissed the issue as she took up her sword. "But God did not have me crown this king only to tear him down."

She had no doubt at all, and it was plain Hermeland was surprised. Misunderstanding Joan as usual, Dulice thought—he thinks she fears defeat, but it is victory that worries her.

Dulice herself didn't share their belief in the small Jehanniste army—or even, sometimes, in the Maid's heretical faith. Her uncle had been Joan's squire, years ago, in the fight against England and Burgundy. He had brought Dulice with him to the Maid's Exoneration Trial, and Joan spotted her in the crowd. She'd been drawing the scene on a scrap of vellum. Perhaps because Joan couldn't read, the image had captured her as firmly as the making of it gripped young Dulice.

Joan had adopted the girl on the spot, keeping her close ever since. Her need for a record of her doings was so strong she never questioned whether her handmaiden's truest love was for God or merely for pen and page.

"If we stay this course we will meet Charles," Hermeland pressed. "Then we'll fight, ready or not."

"I'm telling you, we must pray for—"

"Joan, an army that does nothing but pray is just a moving monastery!" he thundered.

Her chin came up. "And an army that never prays?"

"Emerges victorious, probably." He strode from the tent, stomping off into the sound of men breaking camp—low conversations, the snorts of horses and the groans of wagons being loaded. Birdsong rose above the murmur of preparation. The air was mild and damp; it had rained the night before.

"No time for Mass this morning," Dulice said, making herself noticed for the first time.

"We'll say a quick one now, just us two." Stretching, Joan raised her sword in an attack pose, spearing an invisible enemy through the chest. "Will there be churchbells ahead?"

"We might hear Autun. And there's a monastery east of there . . . Saint Benoit? If we keep this direction, you might hear one or the other ringing Vespers tonight." She was happy to give the answer—Joan loved bells, for they often brought her Voices to her.

"Of course we will march," Joan said. For just an instant she sagged, and the younger woman saw the chasm of years between them. "God set us on this path, not me."

Dulice teased out the piece of paper, translated the words into Latin, and wrote them at the bottom of the page as Joan gathered up the cut hair on the ground and tossed it into the fire. The tent filled with black, stinking smoke, making them both cough.

Joan smiled apologetically. "It's the only way to keep the soldiers from making talismans of it."

Or selling it to relic makers, Dulice thought, nodding her understanding as she roughed in the lines of a portrait. There would be time to add the details later.

"First Communion." The Maid emerges from a shop, wearing men's clothing and carrying bread and wine. A faintly sinister Saint Catherine hovers behind her, seeming to whisper in her ear. The passersby surrounding Joan all have their eyes turned in her direction.

The inscription and the spires of Saint Ouen in the background make it apparent that Joan has just suffered her famous rejection at that church, turned away on her first attempt to celebrate Mass as a free woman. Now she will perform her own variation of the sacrament. Contemporary accounts differ on the issue of whether Joan knew, in that moment, that she was about to create a new faith that would shatter Rome's hold over Europe.

Hermeland raised a crumb of bread and his glass of wine. "This is my body," he intoned in Latin with the other worshippers. "This is my blood."

Riding all day had blackened his mood. In the months since Pope Calixtus had decided to expunge the Maid's followers from the soil of France, Joan had kept them moving, choosing small battles and defending Jehanniste villages against mobs from neighboring Catholic towns. They might have kicked out the Pope's teeth earlier if they'd moved with more certainty. Now his jaws were closing on them.

" . . . in remembrance that Christ died for me. I feed on him in my heart." His eyes roamed the congregation, looking for Dulice. She fancied she could make herself invisible, but he found her easily enough. There—wearing the gray dress and standing in the corner. She was between two of the men, praying unobtrusively and watching Joan. Her voice did not carry to his ears, but seeing her warmed him. She was beautiful and passionate both, an irresistable lure to his thoughts.

"The body of Christ, the bread of life." Prayer complete, Hermeland laid the bread on his tongue.

It was no great surprise that the Host still felt like what it was—a lump of bread. There were times when it was subtly different, exalted somehow; those were the moments that bound him to this faith bone and sinew. As for today . . . he shrugged inwardly. This was hardly his first failure to transubstantiate mere bread into the body of Christ. Perhaps tomorrow he would find the peace of mind required for true piety.

Ahead in the field they had blessed as a temporary church, Joan swallowed her Host, face lit with joy. There was nothing of the warrior about her now. As far as he knew, the miracle had worked for her every time since she had remade the sacraments for them all.

Today's Latin lesson had been given by a wounded former monk from Bordeaux. Now, at his urging, Joan strode to the front of the assembly and they repeated the words she spoke at her heresy trial. It was their movement's signature prayer: "If I am not in God's Grace, may he put me there. If I am, may he keep me there."

The congregants' voices rang with conviction. They all believed that clergy could block the path to Heaven. Even so, it strengthened their faith when their Maid led them in prayer. Here in church she was a holy woman, a mystic—you would never believe that come dawn she would strap on a sword and ride to war.

As the crowd broke up, she sank to her knees in the turf, face turned toward the churchbells tolling in the distance. She would be there for hours, and in the morning rise as if she had slept heartily.

I should ask her Voices where to trap the coming army, Hermeland thought sourly, and turned away.

Young Marcel Renard fell into step beside him. "I've been thinking about our problem," he declared.

"I wasn't aware that *we* had one."

Marcel was the younger son of one of the army's sponsors, a merchant-born knight with finer armor and manners than the few nobles who had been swept up in the Conversion. He was a great friend of the Maid's scheming brother, Jean, and perhaps the closest thing to a courtier that Hermeland had encountered in the ranks of his new church.

Marcel's thoughts moved as if they were oil, always seeking the easiest path to what he wanted. It was a turn of mind Hermeland sometimes admired.

"Of course we have a problem, you old skunk! We cannot fight Charles."

"I see no way to avoid it."

"You look for no way. Come, Hermeland, it'll just toss him into the Pope's lap."

"Your pardon, but he is already there."

"So far all he's done is march. Charles hasn't molested any of the Jehanniste—"

"Listener," Hermeland corrected urgently. They were still close enough that Joan might overhear.

"Listener towns, yes. They've passed through several now without burning them."

"A king can't afford to massacre his subjects at will."

"I think Charles is undecided, my friend. He may not mind having the Pope's hand on France's shoulder . . . but he doesn't want it around her neck, either."

"Pretty words," Hermeland grunted. "Do they mean anything?"

Marcel pointed at the moonlit figure of their praying leader. "Why did the English want the Church to condemn her? To prove the king illegitimate, that's why. Why did Charles have her retried?"

"He thought her all but dead." He didn't try to keep resentment out of his voice.

"To prove his rightful claim to the throne!" Marcel's face was aglow with excitement, the certainty of youth that everything could be fixed, that great fires could be put out—like candles—with breath alone. "If Charles opposes her now, he makes himself a bastard again."

"What would you have us do—convert him?"

"Give him a way to come to us honorably. Dispense with teaching Latin to farmers and translate the Bible into French. Let that be the text we preach from. The crown prince will strengthen ties with Rome when Charles dies. But if the old king has established an independent church . . ."

Hermeland stared at the merchant's son.

"You think it is impractical," Marcel said finally, a hint of uncertainty in his voice.

"I think it is obvious and elegant. It could solve, as you say, our problems." He said it with funereal solemnity.

Marcel scratched his head. "You do not think she will agree?"

"Her Voices tell her to say the Mass in Latin, to teach us to memorize the Bible as it is written."

"She didn't think that part through. This is much easier, and God won't mind . . ."

"There is no chance, my son," Hermeland said. "Not in heaven, not on this earth, and not in hell."

"Follow God, not me." A young girl kneels before Joan, who tries to raise her to her feet. Behind the

Maid's shoulder a winged infant with a halo hovers, its whole being outlined in silver light. Larks nest in the grass in the bottom corners.

Most scholars analyze this scene in the context of Joan's characteristic rejection of special status within her own cult. It should also be noted, however, that the kneeling girl is said to be the sister of a stillborn infant Joan allegedly revived from death in a village called Lagny. (The child survived just long enough to be baptized.) Unlike the many conflicting accounts of Joan's miracles during the Jehanniste holy war, this earlier event was well documented, and Joan spoke of it herself at the heresy trial in 1431.

There were only six soldiers in the maidens' tent this evening, one merry farmgirl-turned-lancer having been crushed by a cannonball in their last battle. The new archer tried hard to fill the hole in their chatter, but she was better suited to the crossbow than conversation. Every time she spoke up, she merely drew attention to the loss.

Dulice was sitting with them when she heard Joan return, soft footsteps and a rustle of fabric that should have been imperceptible, was she not as attuned to it as a mother was to the faintest movements of her babe.

She excused herself, stepping carefully over muddy ground toward the tent she shared with Joan. Low fires burned across the camp. The smells of wood smoke and cooking pork teased her nostrils, spiced—when the wind shifted—with a hint of latrine. The breeze made the night cold, even for springtime. Hunching her shoulders and hugging herself, Dulice quickened her pace.

Joan was sitting on her pallet, cross-legged in a

plain shirt and breeches, as unaffected by the chill as she was by all other bodily complaints. A single candle burned beside her, playing golden light over the sword resting across her knees. She gave no sign that she knew Dulice was there.

Dulice touched the bottle of ink she kept on a chain at her throat. "I have been thinking about drawing a picture of you in prison," she said. "Marcel says nobody will prefer a plain picture—"

"They will if his father stops selling the one with the angels."

Dulice licked her lips. "You said you had visions, when you were locked up in the castle of Philipe Auguste."

"Hush." Joan's face hardened.

"Your story brings people to our faith. Joan, if you had visions . . ."

"When I talk of such things, Dulice, they get bent into tales I don't recognize."

"You can't control what people say," Dulice wheedled. "All you can do is make the truth known."

She was sure she had gone too far, that she would get nothing. But Joan shifted slightly, expelling a long breath. "Two visions, yes. In the first, I never recanted. Cauchon took me to the stake and they lit the fire . . . and can you guess? It wouldn't catch. They tried so hard they burned the ropes binding me. I stepped away from the pyre. The crowd there had come to cheer me off to Hell, but when the ropes fell away from the stake the people's hearts opened. They spirited me away and I went back to war. I drove the English out of France . . ."

Dulice reached for her pen, but a look from Joan

stopped her. The Maid patted the ground at her hip and she sat, conscious of the knotted muscles of her heroine's shoulder pressing against her shawl, of Joan's heat against her cold skin.

"You said there were two?"

"In the second vision, I recanted," Joan said. "My jailers did all the things you heard: took away the dress I was to wear, so I was naked. Sent that soldier to rape me. Left my men's clothing handy as a temptation to relapse."

Dulice's teeth clenched. The ordeals had gone on for months before the false priests had put out their torches and resigned themselves to having the Maid as a prisoner instead of firewood.

"In my dream I bore it for three days. Then I found my courage, put on my clothes, and told them I was done. They burned me in Rouen, as they'd planned all along." Her voice was matter-of-fact. "I was brave, I think, at the execution."

"You're always brave."

"I gave in to fear when I recanted, didn't I?" She darted her hand through the candle flame, leaving a fat smear of soot on her fingers. "But fire burned away that sin. It hurt terribly—"

"You felt it?" Dulice interrupted.

"Like I was there. Oh, don't look like that. All suffering passes, is it not so?" Despite her words Joan shuddered faintly.

"It's still suffering."

"It was a faster penance than prison. And when I was purified, Saint Catherine and Saint Margaret carried me away. Up."

Dulice's breath hitched. "You saw Heaven?"

"A glimpse. So wonderful I sometimes can't believe I have remained down here so long."

"But how unfair to feel the fire, and not to fully taste the reward!"

"It's a pleasure delayed, that's all." Joan pinched wax drippings off the candle and smeared them on her fingers. "If I'd burned then, I'd be forgotten now, don't you think?"

"No! You crowned Charles."

"Pah. People could say anything once I was gone. They made me a witch at my trial, when I was standing right there!" She scowled. "You guard me from those lies now, Dulice. You take what's real and pin it to the page. If I'm tried again . . ."

"God forbid!"

"It's all caught in pictures, just as it happens. No lies, no foolish rumors . . ."

Joan flipped the sword lightly, fingering its blade. It was a poor substitute for her first, or so she'd often claimed. That had come from the monastery at St. Catherine de Fierbois, and she'd broken it over the back of a camp follower. "God waited thirteen years to take me into His heart again, Dulice. He's sending me toward Charles, and yet I know we must not fight."

"What will you do?"

Tears welled in the Maid's eyes. "I won't break with my Voices, not in the tiniest way. They say to go forward . . ."

Dulice picked at her toenail, feeling sullen. She might never admit it, but there were times when she disliked God so much she wanted to cut her own heart out, to feed the pieces to pigs. "I know you hate praise . . ." She swallowed, forcing herself to continue, "But it took strength to stay in prison all that time."

"It takes no strength to lie where you are chained, dear Dulice."

"You were *strong*," she said fiercely, staring at the steam of her breath. Then Joan's arms came around her in a crushing hug, so suddenly she nearly cried out.

"Come on, let's sleep," Joan said. They curled up in the blankets like sisters, and the chill finally forced itself out of Dulice's bones.

It was waiting for her later, though, when her bedmate's breath finally loosened into sleep and she could creep out again, driven to capture by candle flame the images of the two dreams.

"A little brawl at Neufchateau." Knights and men at arms brawl with peasant Jehannistes near a Franciscan monastery. The Maid is in the foreground, dressed in a partial suit of armor and brandishing a shortsword. Behind her is the abbot who summoned the knights; Joan is defending him from her own people. Enraged Jehannistes burn the monastery, framing Joan's form in flames. In the lower left corner, a newly converted Brother Hermeland battles the Duc D'Alençon, leader of the Church forces.

D'Alençon was very close to Joan in the days before her trial, and it was believed he would take the Maid into custody with no difficulty. Instead he found himself at the center of a riot that even the Maid had difficulty quelling. While she would later speak of this first battle dismissively, the Testament of Hermeland reports she was heartbroken at the Jehanniste destruction of the monastery and the death of her friend.

✸   ✸   ✸

"To arms, to arms!"

Hermeland was half dressed when Joan's voice rang through the camp. Her words were clear and carrying, and captains took up the call, scrambling to rouse the men. A few early risers had been setting up for worship, and the ribbons that marked off the place of consecration were knocked down and trampled as people ran back and forth, shouting and seeking their weapons.

The Maid, already armored and mounted, was galloping away, placing herself between the confused encampment and whatever danger lay ahead. Puffing, Hermeland rushed to join her.

They had camped near the ruins of a Jehanniste village, a town that had been burnt by a band of the Pope's mercenaries early the previous winter. To the east, he could see the graves of thirty families. The makeshift crosses that marked their mounds had been kicked down by vandals or weather.

Ahead, abandoned fields and vineyards were growing wild. A stand of trees blocked any view they might have had of the road. Reining hard, Joan stared in that direction, though everything seemed calm enough.

Hermeland was about to ask why they were all in a panic when she pointed her sword. There—a glint of light on armor.

"An ambush?"

"Not anymore." Her smile was broad, almost predatory. She was all warrior today.

"Is it Charles?"

"No."

He didn't know if he was disappointed or relieved.

"We'll—" Suddenly a small force of knights came charging out of the thicket, crushing his plan unformed. Driving forward smartly behind a red banner adorned with a golden cross, they came quickly into bow range. The Listener archers were unprepared, though, and the advance was opposed only by a thin volley of crossbow bolts.

Joan spurred her horse and a small company of men-at-arms—twenty, maybe twenty-five fighters—followed her lead. It was all they had mustered, so far, to protect the chaotic camp behind them.

Cursing, Hermeland joined her, while Marcel Renard closed in on Joan's left side. The three of them became the center of the thin defending wall.

The two sides met in the middle of the overgrown meadow with a crash of weaponry and armor. Catholic or Jehanniste—it ceased to matter to the dead as they fell. Shrieks filled the air as blades clashed against shields.

Joan, as always, drew more than her share of enemy attack. With Marcel and Hermeland fighting fiercely on either side of her, the odds were just barely fair. Cutting at would-be assassins, Hermeland found his arm muscles aching with familiar soreness. Sweat rolled inside his armor; breath steamed out of his visor in gusts.

A sudden pocket of quiet fell on the three of them as the fighting moved elsewhere on the line. Joan drew herself up instantly, scanning the enemy's rear. "There!" She shouted so loudly her voice rasped. Heads turned to see where she was pointing, a spot about twenty feet away. The faithful, knowing her keen eye for cannon placements, scrambled away.

Moments later an explosion ruptured the runaway

grapevines. Hermeland's horse staggered, perhaps struck by a clod of dirt from the blast. He dropped his shield, fighting for balance . . . and a knight with a shortsword came straight at him, weapon high, screaming a prayer.

Marcel shouted a useless warning. Hermeland bellowed too, as if his voice alone could block the fatal blow.

But a single swipe of the Maid's sword saved him, knocking the attacker onto his back. His helmet fell loose, showing a young face gored with a mortal wound.

Now she'll start to weep, Hermeland thought, heart skipping at the close call as he gathered himself at last.

As the battle wore on, soldiers from the camp fell into companies, swelling and strengthening the line. They showed a discipline they had lacked in their early months together, and though the Churchmen tried twice to push past them, Joan had the numbers now, and she turned back the charges easily.

Their herald was one of the last to find his place, pushing to the fore nearly an hour into the battle. He bore up the Listener pennant, a white banner ornamented with an unlit torch and a lark. Cheers broke out among the army as they saw it, and the enemy faltered.

"Marcel, gather up a company and get behind them," Joan ordered. "Take their supplies."

By now the Listener army was fully deployed, their would-be destroyers routed, but the assurance of victory did no more than it ever did to quicken the end. The battle played itself out to a bloody conclusion. When it was finally over the Jehannistes had captured two *couleuvrines*, along with some cannonballs and a few hundred pounds of gunpowder. Only fifty or so of the enemy had escaped.

"Too many," Hermeland told Joan as they left the field. "They must have been going to meet up with His Majesty. Now he'll know to expect us."

"I'm sure he has spies in Burgundy, just like you. He must already have known."

"Better that it be probable than a certainty."

"Cheer up, friend." She squeezed his arm. "If they'd caught us at Mass, we'd be at Judgment now. One whole army, praying forever." Her eyes sparkled, teasing him.

Hermeland was nodding when he spotted Dulice. She sat exposed on a hill, too near the fighting. Imagining herself unseen, she drew furiously. His face reddened, and he snapped at Joan. "I suppose this victory means God wants you to fight the king?"

Joan's face tightened, and the color raised by the battle drained away. "We drove the English out of France, and now we'll drive out the Church. This is our mission."

Which was no answer, but he reined his temper with difficulty. "And do we march through the afternoon, or rest?"

"We consecrate the graves in the village," she said, striding away. She left Hermeland to strip the prisoners of their arms and regret that she wouldn't order them hanged.

Conversion at Orleans: In 1429 Joan led the troops that relieved the English siege of Orleans. Now, in 1450, the city's gates stand open to her and her converts.

Joan is upright on a black stallion, brandishing an unlit torch. Behind her, the Listener troops straggle, bleeding and in apparent despair. The townspeople are rapturous: girls dressed as men beckon Joan, holding up the pieces of a full set of armor. Larks fill the sky, soaring on the town's high spirits. At the gate, four priests and the Bishop of Orleans clutch at their throats.

Folklore has it that the Catholic clergymen were struck dumb as they tried to convince the city fathers to close the gates to the Jehannistes. The Testament of Hermeland states unequivocally that they were merely shouted down and turned out of the town. Historians do agree that the Listener movement would have died out without the support of Orleans at this critical juncture—their army was ill equipped and half starved.

The bourgeoisie of Orleans were mad for Dulice's illustrations of Joan. So wrote Marcel's papa, anyway, in his monthly lament about the restrictions their dear Maid was putting on the process of producing the paintings in quantity: the insistence on Latin for the inscriptions, the hard condition that the illustrators refrain from adding to Dulice's simple scenes, and the insulting requirement that he send each completed illustration back to be checked for inaccuracies.

Meanwhile Papa's competitors translated the Roman texts back to proper French and threw in as many angels and ghouls as they chose . . .

"Yes, Papa, yes, Papa." Marcel grinned, murmuring the words as if he was home receiving the sermon personally. "Is it my fault the Maid is mad to keep her every stroke of fortune from being counted a miracle?"

A dozen copyists Papa had in his shop, filling vellum and imported paper with portraits of the Maid and her deeds. Their paintings might not be as lurid as their paymaster would wish, but they were bringing in plenty of gold. From Dulice's dirty and bloodstained originals, they made gloriously colored pictures, bordered with silver flowers and bright stars.

Their images of the Maid were never old or plain enough to please a Joan who had come forth from prison shorn of her pride and legendary boastfulness. That was a pity, in Marcel's opinion—it had given her a much-needed flair.

If only she had lost her stubbornness instead!

He winked at the wagon driver who'd brought in the supplies. It was Jean d'Arc, who was slipping back into his sister's penumbra after an exile stemming from a scheme so old neither of them remembered its details. Grinning furtively, Jean hefted a long, heavy satchel from underneath the sacks of grain.

"The sword?" Marcel whispered, though the cool iron inside the fabric made the answer obvious.

"Sword *and* flag," Jean murmured, pulling his hat low over his eyes. "Nobody's seen them."

"Dear Papa. He turns paper to gold and gold to food." Jean nodded, looking at the other wagons and the hard-driven horses that had caught them up to the army. "And this time . . ."

"Yes, this time?"

Caught in his reverie, Marcel was unpleasantly surprised to find Dulice at his side. "Ahh, the alchemist herself."

"Alchemy is witchcraft," she said.

He bore her displeasure happily, since it gave Jean time to slouch away. "Shall I call you our little Latin tutor, then? The one who somehow never teaches our Maid any Latin? Most unfair, since we have to mouth it psalm by onerous psalm."

"She learns when she may," Dulice said.

"She prefers to study war. Who will she drive from France next, do you think, if we win?"

"What do you study, Marcel, besides nonsense?"

"Only the provisioning of our company." He pointed at the supplies. "The finished pictures are in that wagon. If they portray the true doings of our Maid, perhaps you would write to my father so he can spread our message?"

"What's this?" She poked his bundle, discerning, no doubt, the shape of the weapon within.

Marcel did not blush. "Gifts from home."

Dulice had only been in a convent two years, but she had the penetrating gaze of a mother superior. It had quite marred her—despite the round body, cornflower eyes, and golden hair, she could never be a woman with whom a sane man would lie comfortably.

"Private gifts," he amended, but by now the damnable woman's fuss had summoned Joan.

How did they manage it, this art of seeing the unseen?

"What is it?" the Maid asked peremptorily. "The French Bible Hermeland mentioned?"

"No such thing," Marcel said stoutly. There had been no time yet for anyone to translate, let alone copy, such a book. "Food for the army and paintings for you and Dulice to examine." Pretending he'd forgotten she was as unlettered as a farm animal, he showed her a scrap of vellum—Jean's inventory of Papa's wagons.

She batted it away, and the mule was hard in her features. "You must—"

A shriek from the east interrupted her. A girl ran toward them, one of the scouts, coming from a distant Roman edifice called the Temple of Janus. Legs pumping in her breeches, her pale face was a blot of white amid the landscape of green and brown. Hoofbeats beat behind her, a knight galloping in hard pursuit.

Marcel felt, rather than saw, Joan's movement. He flung himself blindly at the nearest horse, just reaching its bridle as she mounted.

"No!" Between them, they startled the animal into a kick. Joan lost her saddle and came off, landing half atop him. His arm jerked painfully before he thought to release the reins. As he hit the ground, the animal's back hooves whistled past their heads. The pair rolled away fast in opposite directions, gaining their feet in the same instant.

"You aren't even armed," he protested.

Joan crossed the space between them, slapping Marcel hard enough to knock him down again, then calming the horse with a single murmured word.

Rubbing his jaw, he saw Dulice was oblivious to both the animal and the fleeing girl headed toward them. Transfixed by Joan, the artist was memorizing the scene. *No market for this*, he wanted to tell her. *Papa couldn't sell two copies of a picture of the Maid striking a follower.*

"Oh, now it's too late!" Joan cried.

The knight had indeed caught up with the fleeing scout. Instead of cutting her down he snatched her by the arm, heaving her up across the horse and then galloping away.

"Captured, not killed," Marcel said, tasting blood as he probed loosened teeth with his tongue. "You'll get another chance to save her."

She ignored him, pacing like a caged dog and eyeing the bend in the road where the knight had vanished. "That knight—do you know who he is?"

"Who?"

"He's the son of Georges de la Trémoïlle." Her voice was harsh as she spoke the name of the man who had probably prevented her ransom, years before. "Just when I think I've outlived all my old enemies . . . There's always someone new, isn't there?"

"It's your gentle nature," Marcel muttered, earning himself a glare.

"Joan!" Hermeland bustled to her side, glancing quizzically down at Marcel. "Autun has announced they are with us. The whole town's converted, and the king's army demands they return their churches and souls to the priests of Rome. Charles has stopped vacillating—he'll burn anyone who resists."

Joan scowled, scraping mud off the heels of her hands.

"We must go to Autun," Hermeland suggested. "Their walls are strong, but . . ."

"The king has cannon enough to break them," Joan agreed. "We will assess the town's defences and leave them some help if need be. The army will place itself between Autun and danger."

"We'll meet Charles soon, then." Hermeland spoke mildly, the old anarchist, as if he wasn't lusting after a little king's blood.

She nodded, not hiding her pained expression, and waved him off toward one of the more reliable captains. Then she extended a hand to Marcel, yanking him to his feet.

"I'll see your gifts from home now."

He didn't argue, but reached for the bundle and unwrapped it carefully. Perhaps he might just slide out the sword—

Reaching past him, Joan grabbed the wrappings and yanked them upward. Then she gasped.

White boucassin fringed with silk unfolded in her mud-smeared hand—a pennant. It showed a field strewn with lilies, and two angels on either side of the world. The words *Jhesus Maria* blazed across it.

"My standard . . ."

She pulled it to her face in a doubled fistful, and Marcel thought she would smell it. But she kissed it instead, tears streaming down her lined face as they so often did.

"I haven't seen it since my capture at Compiègne." She stretched it out for a look. It was perfect: faded, soiled and then washed, its fabric worn.

Marcel waited, face a blank.

Then Joan's face stilled and her tears dried up. He felt a pain like gas in his belly as her head turned, piercing him with the look an owl might use to freeze a field mouse. "Where did you get this?"

Pretend ignorance and blame Papa? No, those eyes dragged forth the truth even from him. "Hamish Powers lives yet. He remembers the original well."

"You made a copy," she said, dropping the banner like the corpse of a dog. She rubbed at her mouth, dirtying her lips, and then she dumped the satchel from Orleans with one violent heave. The sword dropped out. It was a replica of the holy blade she had broken over a whore's back all those years before. "Marcel, what are you up to?"

He swallowed. "I thought . . . if Charles saw you with your pennant restored, your broken sword whole . . ."

"You would *stage* a miracle." Marcel could see she was on the verge of throwing him away, and all Papa's resources with him. "Have you no faith at all?"

"I confess my mistake," he said, forcing himself to look down. "I want to help . . ."

"By doing wrong?"

"I'm sorry." Each humble word was singed by the rage rising in his throat. If she would just allow them to read the Bible in French! "I want to bring the king to our side, that's all."

"You must try harder to believe!" A silence then, while he looked at his toes and endured the stares of common soldiers who lurked at the sidelines. Intolerable, after all he had done—but he tolerated it. At length, the Maid sighed. "But you are confessed and I forgive you."

Relief flooded him, and he dared a glance up. Joan was testing the sword's weight without realizing it, raising it in that dangerous way of hers so the point was aimed at his throat.

Then, suddenly, she smiled. "Nobody will mistake this for the original—that had five crosses, and this has three." With that, she slid it into her scabbard.

Marcel indicated the banner, still lying on the ground. "And this?"

"Burn it." She spared the pennant not a glance. "The Lark banner will do good service tomorrow."

★   ★   ★

"Jump, for this time we are with you." Joan, in full armor, leaps from a burning church steeple. Saints Catherine and Margaret grasp her arms, bearing her slowly to the ground. Below, Jehanniste soldiers watch in wonder.

It is interesting to note that the original Dulice Aulon sketch for this plate has survived and is available for comparison with the final Orleans illumination in the codex. The sketch calls for columns of smoke from the church fire to surround Joan's body and makes no mention of the saints. It also notes that Joan's foot should be bare and bloodied but does not say what this signifies.

The inscription, it is generally agreed, indicates Joan had achieved a renewed state of grace by the time of this dangerous leap. In a 1430 attempt to escape her English captors, Joan jumped from the sixty-foot tower at Beaurevoir. Though she survived, the escape attempt failed. She said later that her Voices had told her not to jump.

They were moving to it at long last, and after so much waiting for a decisive battle, Hermeland should have been relieved.

Instead, he was too aware of his mount. His old horse, Rust, had been lamed in the skirmish the day before. He'd found him limping this morning, favoring a bloodied pastern. The young black stallion he rode now was poorly trained, fighting the bit and trying to crop grass every chance he got.

They moved with deadly purpose, racing past Autun. By meeting Charles beyond the town, they left themselves a place of retreat. If it came to that, though, they and Autun would probably come to ruin.

It won't come to that, he thought. They had won small victories before, and now they would show their strength and the righteousness of their cause.

As they neared the walls, they spied a band of soldiers scouting its gates, a force so small it fled at their approach. The knight—de la Trémoïlle—who had captured their scout was the last to retreat, turning twice to glare at Joan before galloping away.

Nearer the cheering town, they found the scout herself. She was lying in a shallow stream with just her head and shoulders on the bank. Blood ran from her mouth.

Shooting a murderous look at Marcel, Joan dismounted.

"Someone else can give her Last Rites," Hermeland said, and then regretted it. It would take but a few minutes. What was the difference?

"She's breathing," Joan said indignantly.

And she was, he saw. The Maid bent, murmuring prayers, the sun glinting off her silver hair as she dipped a hand in the stream and rinsed blood off the scout's pale face. It roused the girl—she coughed, spraying red droplets over her own wet chin.

"Have her carried to town," Joan ordered. She lifted the injured girl, straining to raise the slack body and water-sodden clothes as well as her own armor-weighted limbs. Two young men-at-arms and one of the fighting women rushed to relieve her of the burden.

There was a receding bustle, and then they were under way again.

It was a warm, sleepy day. The sky was dotted

with small clouds, and a firm wind cooled the lancers, ensuring a steady and comfortable march. Despite the tussles with his horse, Hermeland scanned the edges of the army for a blond head. Dulice must not come near the fighting again. She could have been killed or captured yesterday, up on that hill in plain sight with her pen and ink bottle.

The thought brought a rush of confused feelings: pain, desire, fear for her safety and a wistful longing. He shoved it all aside. The girl would never leave Joan, and that meant she would remain unmarried and chaste. Unless they won, there was no point in wondering if the artist might take a once-monk to wed.

No point either if they lost, but he would not think of that.

At length they reached a floodplain run through on one side by a shallow river that must have been the Arroux. Larks nested in the grass by the water.

On the other side of this plain was the massive, glittering army of Charles VII.

Hermeland felt a small flutter in his belly, a feeling like hunger that was really just shock. *No word from the other scouts*, he thought numbly. *They must all be dead or captured.*

The two forces halted well out of bow range, weighing each other. The Jehanniste army seemed tiny and tired in comparison to the company arrayed across the field. Hermeland thought of the battle the day before, the Listener numbers overwhelming its foe easily, even when the camp had been unprepared for a fight.

Finally the silence grew too long. Clearing his throat, he spoke: "The king has more knights and better weapons."

Marcel laughed. "What a great and unnecessary understatement."

"Here's another, then—we have God," Joan said, staring at the king. Her voice was threadbare.

Here was the real army he had wanted to fight for so long. What arrogance! For the first time Hermeland appreciated Joan's tactics—how she had kept them on the move as she trained the men, why she had always chosen the smaller battles, the most defensible towns. There might have been five thousand men out there across the valley, well drilled, well fed, and fresh.

"Should we advance," he asked, "or let them charge?"

"I always advance," Joan said. "But . . ."

A movement to their left brought his head around. Dulice Aulon was edging toward a low rock, no doubt thinking to crouch behind it and record the carnage.

Joan's gaze followed his. "Dulice," she called.

The girl startled. Then she headed toward them as if she'd meant to come that way all along.

"Get to the rear, woman," Hermeland growled.

She ignored him. "Joan, please. I must see what is going on."

"We will tell you everything later."

"That's no good!" Blond brows drew into a fierce scowl. "They're already saying there has been a miracle here. I can't draw rumors—I must *see*!"

"What miracle?" Joan raised her visor. "Marcel?"

He puffed up indignantly. "Am I to be accused of fraud every time God is kind to us?"

"It's not true, Dulice," Hermeland said. "We've been riding together all morning. I'm sure I'd have noticed the hand of God if it came down and pointed our way. Please, go before you're trampled."

Dulice's bright eyes sought out Joan's, unrelenting. Her back was stiff with determination. "They're saying our scout was dead and you raised her."

"They could charge any second," Hermeland interrupted. "Dulice is unarmed and on foot. Our own soldiers will run over her if battle's joined."

"Your brothers are in the camp, spreading tales," the artist protested. "This is what you want me to prevent!"

"Joan," Hermeland said. "Please. She'll be killed."

Joan sighed. "Marcel, bear Dulice to the rear. Order my brothers turned out of the company . . ."

"No," protested Dulice.

"The fight is upon us, Joan. Surely I'm needed—"

"Yes, Marcel—needed at the rear." Her voice was iron. "And please tell everyone the scout was alive."

Sulking, Marcel drew Dulice up onto the horse, seating her in front of him. She had to flap her arms, birdlike, to balance her drawing board and papers without losing them to the wind. Hermeland sighed, and the knot in his belly untied itself. She would be safe with Marcel. And now . . .

"Will you advance?" he asked the Maid again.

"Yes." With a brisk move, Joan plucked her banner from the standard bearer. "And you will charge too, Hermeland . . . if this falls. Not before."

He knew what she would do. "You think Charles won't kill you now? That sick old man left you to the Church once already! It would be a miracle if you made it back."

Her voice was furious. "Everything I do is a miracle, haven't you heard? I'll speak to the king one more time. No attack unless this falls, do you hear?"

"And if they take it from you?"

"Destroy them," she said carelessly.

Banner held high on its ash shaft, Joan urged her white horse forward at a walk.

A whisper ran through the army. Hermeland heard its echo, a surprised rise and fall of voices, from across the valley. Then larksong was all he could hear. The Maid rode well beyond his protection: twenty feet, fifty, a hundred. Soon she was across the field, and even the birds fell silent.

Hermeland realized he was praying.

Marcel had not ridden a step. He wasn't ignoring orders—he was simply stuck, staring at Joan with the frozen expression of a man who expects to see disaster. So did they all, all except Dulice. *She* was twisted awkwardly on his horse, writing board pressed into her stomach, thumb mashing a page to its surface while she scratched with her pen as if possessed.

When Joan was twenty feet from the enemy army she dismounted. Banner raised, she slapped her horse's rump. The animal loped straight to Hermeland, eyes reproachful. *She is all alone now*, it seemed to say. Beyond rescue.

"Perhaps we could steal forward a little," Marcel murmured.

Dulice paused in her drawing just long enough to crane around, giving him a look that would sour milk. "There's no saving her now if he strikes."

"And no saving him if he harms her," Hermeland said.

His voice challenged Marcel to laugh, to point out the odds were against them. Instead he heard his own words spreading like fire, warming the gathered men as Dulice's eyes met his with a jolt.

The gusty air around them seemed to thicken. If the battle came, Joan's men would make it an expensive one. Marcel had become a knight, Dulice an artist, he a general. The Listeners had been transubstantiated through God's grace from a band of cross-bearing bandits into a true army. Now, perhaps, their day had come.

He was strangely content to wait and see.

Across the field, Joan of Arc knelt before her king.

Wedding in the Loire: In the center of the image, a young couple kneels before an outdoor worship assembly. The girl's white dress befits the occasion, but her lowered head and expression speak of a grief that is absent from the face of the groom. Joan and a group of well-wishers stand in the right corner of the image, bearing farewell gifts—food and travel necessities.

Despite attempts to place this image after Autun and to claim it as the wedding of Brother Hermeland and the martyr Dulice Aulon, the evidence clearly favors another interpretation. A crossbow sits in easy reach of the bride's hand, marking her as a member of the army. Further, the "Forbidden Marriage," as it is known, took place in secret so that the rigidly prudish Joan would not be faced with turning the no-longer-chaste Dulice out of the Listener ranks.

It was cold up there at the front line, drawing with a board wedged against her belly and Hermeland's concern sending chills through her bones. Dulice drew anyway. A quick image of the Maid raising the banner, her orders written in French—no time for translation now. Then a figure of her riding toward the king, covered with more notes: horse does not gallop. Wind strong, banner fully extended.

And now, on one knee before old Charles, her neck bent. Dulice had to squint to make her out clearly. When she did, fear pushed the breath out of her in a moan even as her hand shakily unstoppered her ink bottle, spilling black drops onto the neck of Marcel's cream-colored horse.

A motion from the king and Joan rose, bending backward stiffly so she could look up at him. Clad in armor, the distant figures gave no clue as to their mood. They might as well have been statues, dolls.

"What do you think she's saying?" Marcel asked.

"What else but the usual?" Hermeland's voice was reverent. "The Lord God wants me to drive the corrupt Church out of France. Stand down or die."

"She wouldn't say that to Charles."

"She'll say anything," Hermeland said. "Will she do it? That's the question."

The men's voices were faint, far away. Dulice pressed a new page to her writing board, inking her pen to draw the Maid standing in front of the vast array of armed men. So small and alone against the force of Charles!

Now the king-doll was shaking his head, so stiffly his shoulders moved with him. Joan bowed again, turning on her heel and starting back. Her gait—angry steps Dulice knew well—said the parley had not gone well. She still held the banner aloft.

When she was halfway across the plain, de la Trémoïlle could contain himself no longer. He spurred his mount and galloped after her, a charge of one.

Both armies jerked forward. Shouts from Hermeland and Charles VII cracked across the field, and the twin advances halted raggedly. Marcel's armored hands tightened around Dulice, jostling her pen so that a thick black line scratched across Joan's figure.

"I'm safe," she said furiously, but Marcel wasn't listening.

Raising her eyes from the page, Dulice saw the knight bearing down on Joan. Her safe world of picture-making burned away, and she screamed.

Joan had needed no warning. She did not draw her sword, just turned with her banner and waited for him to come. The knight twirled a flail overhead, swinging as he galloped past her. The blow struck hard, its crunch sending another shock through the army. It lifted Joan off her feet. She landed on her back, and did not move.

Hermeland's armor creaked as he raised his hand to signal a charge . . .

. . . but the Lark banner did not fall. It remained in Joan's hand as she lay there, dead for all anyone knew. The staff that held the standard remained perfectly upright.

Wiping her nose, Dulice pressed her pen against the page. She drew Joan, lying beside the banner. Her eyes were wide and she could hear herself sobbing. She turned her head whenever a tear fell to keep it from further smearing the ink.

"Brother . . ." Marcel said breathlessly, but Hermeland did not signal a charge. He moved his head slightly and a girl archer stepped forward, firing an arrow at the knight as he wheeled back to Joan. The shaft caught his horse, striking it in the haunch. The animal screamed and danced sideways, forcing the knight to dismount.

Raising his weapon, he strode toward the fallen Maid.

"She moves!" A cry went through one army, perhaps both. Joan sat bolt upright and then stood, as if it were no effort at all, as if she were wearing nothing heavier than a nightgown. Her hand fell away from the standard pole as she drew her sword.

Again the banner did not waver.

And that was wrong. The wind blew still, strong enough to unfurl it fully, and yet it stood upright, as if planted deep in the ground. *Perhaps it is*, Dulice thought, *perhaps Joan's weight as she fell drove it into the soil . . .*

"But the ground is dry and hard," she said, not sure who she was asking. "Isn't it?"

The knight looped his flail up, bringing it down toward the Maid's head. She skipped back, uncommonly fast, and raised her free arm in defence. The chain wrapped around her wrist. Metal screeched against metal and Marcel hissed as if in pain.

Around her pen, Dulice's fingers were white.

The knight yanked on his flail, but Joan did not fall. She jerked her captured arm backward sharply, closing her fingers around the handle of the flail and pulling it from her attacker's grip. Her sword was at the ready, but Joan drove the butt of the flail against de la Trémoïlle's helmet, once, twice. The blows were so loud they echoed back from the other side of the meadow. The knight staggered back a few paces.

"Turn aside. I would not fight today." Her words rang across the field.

Bellowing, the knight charged.

Joan was ready. She drove the sword home, piercing de la Trémoïlle's collar with shocking force. The man crumpled without making another sound.

Turning her back on the body, Joan marched lightly back to where her standard was waiting. She lifted it as easily as if she took it from a waiting herald.

"The ground is dry, Dulice," Marcel whispered urgently. "You must write of this. Joan told me yesterday the Lark banner would . . ."

"Now, of all times!" Dulice rounded on Marcel, furious.

"I'm telling you—"

"Don't speak to me." She twisted, sliding down from the horse, and lost her last clean page to the wind.

Marcel snapped his mouth shut. Then he turned his horse.

"Where are you going?" Hermeland asked.

"To expel Jean d'Arc from the army."

Dulice stared, dismayed, at her ink-wet paper. It would smudge if she turned it over now. With the other page lost, she would have to draw miniatures next to the image of the Maid on her back.

When Joan had almost reached her army, she turned to face the king. Tearing off her surcoat, she revealed the bare crumpled armor over her heart. Then she raised her open hand, apparently indifferent to the flail caught in the joint of her gauntlet. The whole of the Listener army strained against its leash.

But one by one the gold-crossed flags in Charles's army fell to the ground. Soon only the king's personal banner remained upright on the other side of the field.

Joan lowered her own hand slowly and turned to face the troops. "Save your strength. We will not fight the king."

Dulice scribbled the words in the margin of a picture as the army gentled.

"We're going to win," Hermeland said softly. "Charles will ride with us."

"With God," Joan said.

A smile twitched at the corner of his mouth. "And in Latin, too."

She nodded, looking at the crushed, blood-weeping gauntlet. "I don't think I can get this off. The flail's stuck and it's all bent."

"We'll see to it." Hermeland slid to the ground, holding out the reins of her horse and offering to help her mount.

"Thank you," Joan said, passing the staff and flag to her herald as she mounted. She reined the horse awkwardly with her good hand, her path taking her right past Dulice. Her shadow fell on the hodgepodge of ink on that last page.

"You've made me too brave again," she said, but she smiled, and Dulice felt her whole soul open up. Had she once had reservations? Not she: she would be here with the Maid and Hermeland forever. She would blaze the truth of their fight: its small wonders and the miracles that weren't, that were just good fortune and life's merciful accidents. Her drawing was God's work indeed, not false pride. Could she ever have doubted?

But . . .

"What of that?" she said, pointing to the Lark banner. "How will I show that so nobody says it was a miracle? It stood when you fell. It stood when you walked away."

An impish, youthful smile crossed the Maid's face. "What was it you said? 'If it's truth . . .'"

"Then it should be made known," Dulice said. She fought back a tremble in her voice.

"Good, sensible advice," Hermeland said, and his tone was warm.

"Just give us whatever you see, Dulice." Spurring her horse, Joan rode, bleeding, in the direction of Autun.

Wet-eyed but with a steady hand, Dulice scratched out the Maid's instructions, word by word, in Latin, filling up the last clear space remaining on her page with bold letters and certain words.

Three Miracles at Autun. Gauntlet raised, Joan stands between the supine figure of an armored girl and the corpse of a knight. A stylized puddle of water surrounds the girl, who takes up the largest part of the center of the page. Blood seeps from the knight's armor and the two fluids mix at Joan's feet.

One of the most confusing and controversial images of the Jehanniste holy war, Three Miracles is said to depict holy works by Joan that convinced the famously indecisive Charles to throw his favor to the Maid's cause. The first miracle was defeating Georges de la Trémoïlle in single unarmed combat; the second was the resurrection of the girl, who had been drowned by de la Trémoïlle earlier that day.

As usual, attempts have been made to identify the girl as Joan's favorite, Dulice Aulon. It is far more probable that the figure is her standard bearer, for Aulon was neither a combatant nor given to self-portraiture. Further, the woman holds the Lark banner.

Despite the title of the image, the nature of any third miracle to take place at Autun in the spring campaign of 1456 has been lost to history.

The Road to Endless Sleep

Jim Fiscus

Caesar's ghost stalked the Forum Romanum, but it was only the dictator's stern face staring down from his statue. Marble columns and facades glowed white under the sun beating against the broad stones of the Forum and the crowd filling the great plaza. The temples and basilica, hung with red and gold banners and garlands, enclosed the civic center of Rome. Fourteen years before, Marcus Antonius stood on the wide marble platform of the Rostra and rallied the people against the murderers of Caesar. Now, he would pass in triumph before the great speaker's platform. But even in victory, Antony knew that the people of Rome did not love him as they had loved

Caesar. My troops lined the Via Sacra as it passed through the Forum before the Basilica of the Aemilii and Caesar's senate house, guarding against a surge from the crowd.

I am Quintus Petillus Celsus. My father was a centurion with Caesar in Spain, where I later joined the legions and fought with Sextus Pompey, the son of Pompey the Great. When Octavian's admiral Agrippa defeated Pompey, I was called a pirate. Facing slavery, I fled to the East and joined Antony's legions. Standing on the edge of the Rostra, I watched the crowd that packed the Forum, jostling to move closer to the route of the triumphal parade. I glanced behind me, where Cleopatra sat surrounded by courtiers and attendants. My quick glance turned into a stare as I noticed a woman of the court, whose dark hair and striking beauty held my attention. Our eyes met and she smiled. I turned from the unattainable back to the crowd.

Legion had fought legion in civil war and no triumph is awarded when Romans slaughter each other, so Antony claimed his Triumph was for victory over foreign princes allied with Octavian. Everyone knew it was Octavian's defeat he celebrated. Most citizens said Antony's victory meant the final death of the Republic. Half the Senate fled as his army neared Rome while others cowered in their country villas waiting for the political winds to calm.

Hundreds of carts laden with the arms and treasure captured by Antony had rolled over the broad stones of the Sacred Way on the first day. Hundreds more, filled with treasure donated by Cleopatra as proof of her friendship with Rome, followed on the second day. On this, the third day, wagons carried the broken remains of Octavian's fleet captured at Actium. Dancers and musicians clanging cymbals and blowing small horns pranced beside Octavian's shattered glory.

The triumphal parade had started from the Field of Mars as the first hour of the day began with the rising sun and wound through the city, through the Circus Maximus and on to the Forum. From the Forum, it would climb to the Temple of Jupiter on the Capitoline Hill. Crowds lined the route. The long hours of late spring had passed slowly. I stared across the crowd to the newly enlarged Basilica Aemilia, two stories of grand marble columns and arches, its bronze roof gleaming under the afternoon sun. The crowd filled the space between the street and the columns of the basilica, pushing back against the booths of the merchants. The arches of the upper floor were crowded with more people watching the Triumph. Except, I realized, for the third archway which stood empty but for vague figures in the shadows. It might have just been a rich man and his sycophants wishing to avoid the crowd, but I could not tell.

I jumped to the paving stones. The scales of my armor clanked as I landed and the hobnails of my heavy sandals clicked on the stones as I pushed through the crowd to the Via Sacra. A legionnaire snapped to attention.

"Centurion!"

"Getting a closer look," I said, not ready to sound the alarm till I knew something was wrong.

Trumpets called for the attack and drummers beat the rhythm of the oars. A low wagon, so wide that it barely passed along the route, was pulled into the Forum. Atop the wagon, a model of Agrippa's flagship sailed to meet Antony's fleet. Dwarves in the tiny ship rowed at the air. A second wagon entered, also with a model of Agrippa's ship, its dwarf rowers moving their oars desperately as the beak of Antony's flagship appeared to crush its side. Dwarf legionnaires hurled golden-tipped javelins at their attackers and fired miniature catapults, but the weapons bounced off the armored shell of the testudo navalis and fell to the street. Members of the crowd darted out to claim the gold spear points. Scores of prisoners followed the wagons. Antony would arrive next.

I sprinted across the street. I could not tell how many men were in the alcove, but they held bows. Four legionnaires watched the side street between the basilica and Caesar's new curia.

"You men, with me."

We pounded into the basilica, the crowd parting before us, and turned toward the staircase. I drew my sword and took three stairs at a time, the legionnaires behind me. Glancing through the first arch, I saw Antony's golden chariot entering the Forum.

A heavy curtain covered the third archway. Three thugs waited, as if protecting a wealthy client. They pulled swords from beneath their tunics. The leader lunged toward me. I blocked his thrust and slashed across his neck, opening his throat to the bone. His blood spurted across the scales of my armor. Two legionnaires hurled their pila, the javelins driving into the remaining thugs, who staggered back. Dying hands gripped the curtain, tearing it free.

Three archers stood overlooking the Forum. One spun, releasing his arrow. It sliced across my left arm below the mail. He dropped his bow and twisted, reaching for a dagger as my sword plunged into his side. I pulled the blade free against the suction of his organs. Between his companions, I saw Antony's chariot on the Via Sacra, the crowd cheering. Concentrating on their release, the remaining archers tracked the general. A pilum thudded into the back of one man and his arrow flew toward the crowd. I kicked the second man in the back as he released. He staggered and fell from the window. His arrow missed Antony by a hand's breadth. The imperator stared upward at the basilica. His hand rose and the procession stopped.

The archer I had kicked from the building lay unmoving on the flagstones. Turning from the window, I glanced at the archer who had taken a javelin in the back and asked the legionnaire standing over him, "Is he alive?"

"Not for long, Centurion."

I knelt beside the man. The stench of his released bowels filled the alcove. "Who sent you?"

"I fight for Agrippa."

"Agrippa's head decorates the Rostra."

"His honor lives."

I stood slowly, aware suddenly of the deep gash in my biceps and the bright blood that ran down my arm. I nodded to the fallen archer. "We caught them flat-footed. Tear me a piece of his tunic." I wrapped the cloth around my arm. A tribune from Antony's guard clasped my shoulder. "The general wants to see you."

Antony stood in the golden chariot, using its height to study the crowd that surged forward to catch sight of the disturbance. Antony was fifty-four, his broad face puffy after years of dissipation. His thinning hair was marked by streaks of gray beneath a triumphator's golden laurel wreath. He wore a purple toga and his face was painted vermilion to match the statue of Jupiter on the Capitoline.

Antony stared at the prisoners who stood in chains before his chariot. Certain they would be led to their deaths from the Forum, most were broken men. One stood alone: Octavian, who would have followed Caesar as dictator of Rome. Antony pointed his ivory scepter at Octavian, who looked even thinner than when I had last seen him. "Octavian, I understand you planned to call yourself Augustus when you ruled Rome as king. Your rule shall be limited to the cell of the Tullianum, until the cord tightens around your throat."

The prisoner stared back at Antony, yielding nothing. He called out, speaking more to the crowd than to Antony, "You cannot hold what you have seized, Antony. You and your whore will follow me soon."

"Take Octavian," Antony said to the tribune beside me. "Place his head beside Agrippa's."

"Quintus Petillus Celsus, you have saved me again." Antony spoke softly, so only those near us could hear. "Come to me tomorrow at the end of the eighth hour. You will select and command the queen's bodyguard in Rome."

"Imperator," I said, already thinking of men I trusted who would be loyal to Antony—and to me.

Cleopatra had remodeled her mansion on the Palatine, turning a large dining room off the garden into a study. The house was her refuge. She kept the sycophants of her court at a country villa north of Rome that she seldom visited. I had served as head of her bodyguard for five years since Antony's triumph, protecting her when she was in Rome, as she was for most of the year. The queen spent mornings dealing with affairs of state, as she did today, even though Republican legions marched on Rome to overthrow her rule with Antony. I stood in the doorway waiting to give my daily report. Two days past the Ides of May, I was glad I wore a cloak over my military tunic to hold out the morning chill. The queen wore a heavy white robe studded with gold and jewels. She had pushed an unfinished plate of cheese and bread aside. She worked at a small table, reading a scroll recently arrived from Caesarion in Alexandria. I don't know if Caesar actually was the father of the queen's son, but the boy acted as Cleopatra's regent in Egypt. She dictated instructions to a secretary, speaking first in Greek, then added a few words in Egyptian. I understood the Greek.

Cleopatra's reputation, fostered by Octavian's propaganda, was of a whore and megalomaniac. She was forty-four, but her body had not gone to fat as many do. Still, the queen was no beauty. She had a long face with wide-set eyes and a high forehead. Her nose and chin were far too prominent and her features seemed heavy and thick in profile. Her dark hair was put up in tight rolls. Despite her lack of beauty, she bound people to her with the force of her presence, not with sex. The queen could also charm any man or woman with her grace and laughter, though I had not heard her laugh in months. She had captured Caesar, but not held him against his drive for power. Antony was a weaker man. He had tried to use Cleopatra for his own political goals, but had fallen in love. As commander of her bodyguard, I knew of everyone she saw and visited. She had lived as chastely as the most proper Roman matron during her five years in Rome. Antony was her only lover, and he spent more time drinking than loving.

Cleopatra set the scroll down, then gestured for me to enter and her secretary to leave. She spoke in Latin, her voice suddenly sounding exhausted, "I am tired of life in a land I do not understand." Her voice fell to a whisper. "Antony brought peace and closed the doors of the Temple of Janus. Why do the Romans reject him?"

I was a professional soldier and not party to the politics of Rome, and the queen had decided some time ago that she could speak to me in confidence and trust my answers. "In Egypt, you call yourself Queen of Kings. Romans fear kings, and reject them."

"Antony is dictator, not I."

"You and Antony are seen as one."

"Perhaps we are, and perhaps had we pretended to maintain the Republic and not taken power openly, we would have succeeded."

"No, Majesty. Romans would allow no woman to rule them, and the people see Antony as merely another strong man, a weak copy of Sulla or Caesar. After three generations of dictators and civil war both plebeians and patricians finally seem ready to truly reform and revive the Republic."

"Do the fools really think that the legions will allow that? If Antony falls, another general will replace him." Cleopatra closed her eyes a moment, then asked, "You're a soldier, Celsus. Can Antony defeat our enemies?"

"The Republicans bring eight legions against him.

He has only six near the city. Still, the enemy is divided and Antony defeated the army the Republicans sent against him two years ago, but his legions have not been paid for two months and may go over to the enemy."

"His legions will be paid. Yet are we not like Pyrrhus, winning victories in a war we cannot win? I am pharaoh and must protect Egypt," Cleopatra said. She added, speaking so softly that I barely heard her, "But I will not desert him. Not while victory is possible."

"You would have fled Actium," Antony's voice bellowed from the door, "had we not quickly killed Agrippa and shattered his fleet."

I snapped to attention, but he ignored me.

"I gave you the world and you plot to desert me."

"I do not." Cleopatra stood and stepped toward him, returning without passion to an argument I had overheard before.

The five years since his Triumph had turned Antony into a pudgy old man. He wore a black loose-fitting tunic to hide his blubber, and failed. It had rained yesterday and washed some of the black dye from his hair, leaving blotches and streaks of gray.

"My love, I rule here with you. I also rule Egypt. I must be ready should the war not go well for us. I must protect my people," Cleopatra said. "We do not need Rome. Our power is in Egypt and the East."

"I tried staying in the East, and Octavian nearly destroyed me. Rome is the world. Flee home to Alexandria."

"Those who rule can't afford love, but I love you, Antony."

"Even though I am not Caesar?" he asked, for he

had become obsessed with comparing himself to the Divine Julius.

"Caesar loved power. He did not love me and I did not love him. How often must I tell you?"

Antony's voice softened, and was filled with despair. "I can't lose you." Even in early morning, he stank of wine. His anger returned. "You expect me to lose and prepare for defeat."

"I prepare to save us both."

Anthony spun and stomped from the room.

Cleopatra watched him cross the garden and enter the main building. She looked at me, and I saw that her eyes were moist. "Even if he wins this battle, I fear that he will fall. Sometime, and suddenly. Go, and close the door, Celsus."

As I left the room, I saw one of Cleopatra's women, Neferet, waiting in the garden. She had been in Egypt for six months, and the moment that I saw her again, I understood Antony's greatest fear. Truly, the soul of a lover rests in the body of his beloved. Neferet held my soul, and I hers.

Neferet was Egyptian, not Greek. Black hair fell to her shoulders, framing large eyes, and a small, straight, nose. The sun had darkened her skin. She was thirty-two, six years younger than I. She walked with the grace of a dancer, which she had been when she first served Cleopatra.

I led her back toward the front of the garden. "The queen wishes privacy," I said, speaking softly. "I didn't know you were back from Alexandria."

"The Tiber is at flood, and the captain had the ship rowed all the way to the old docks at the Forum Boarium. We arrived at dusk, and stayed aboard last night rather than risk traveling through the city after dark." Neferet's Latin carried a slight accent of Alexandria. "I hoped you would be here, Quintus."

I led Neferet between low shrubs to a colonnade that circled the garden. A painting in bright blues, red, and gold captured the rising sun over the Nile delta. The deep shadows of the colonnade gave only the illusion of privacy, but I could wait no longer and kissed Neferet, holding her tightly. After a moment, she pulled away.

"Perhaps the small bath is available? I am caked with salt spray and road dust." She smiled. "Would you, as a citizen and soldier of Rome, help a foreign slave? And we must talk." I had first seen Neferet standing beside the queen at Antony's Triumph, and had thought her a lady of the court. We met, and she infatuated me with her beauty and quickly captured me with her intelligence. Only after infatuation turned to love did I realize she was a slave.

The main bathing room with its hot and cold pools was attached to the mansion, but a smaller chamber opened onto the garden. Hot and cold water from the main baths flowed into a small granite pool, and could be mixed to give the temperature wished by the bather. Diffuse light filled the room from windows high in the walls. Warm air passed from a furnace through the channels of the hypocaust under the floor and on through channels in walls, making the room pleasantly warm.

I walked ahead of Neferet to make sure the room was empty and began letting hot water into the pool. I tossed my cloak onto a marble bench and turned as I heard the door close.

Neferet wore a dark brown cloak for travel. I

stood, and she came into my arms. "Quintus, I missed you." She held me tightly, her face pressed against my shoulder. "I feared the queen would not call me back to Rome."

"Then I would have had to travel to Alexandria to find you." We stood holding each other for what seemed an instant but might have been many minutes before I pulled away. "Cleopatra doesn't send ships for the convenience of a slave, however favored. There is more behind the timing of your arrival."

"I obey the queen's will." Neferet shook her head slightly. "More than that. She has earned my loyalty with her kindness. But the real news is not the loyalty of a slave. I brought enough gold from Egypt to pay a dozen legions."

"You may have just saved Antony from defeat." I crossed back to the pool and checked the temperature of the water, adjusting the flow to warm it slightly. I heard the rustle of cloth behind me and turned. Neferet tossed her cloak aside. Underneath, she wore an Egyptian dress of nearly transparent white linen that showed the soft curves of her slim body as she came to me.

My hands gently stroked her back, then slipped the dress from her shoulders. She stepped back and it fell from her body. I felt my passion, my need for her, overcoming me. Even more, I wanted to protect her, though I knew it was folly to love a slave, especially the slave of a queen.

Spring had turned hot in the past week, and the morning light filtering through the walls of Antony's tent seemed harsh. Three days before, I had escorted two chests of Cleopatra's gold to Antony to pay his men. The impending battle and the presence of an enemy had restored Antony's vigor.

"Letting you serve me was my wisest act, Quintus Petillus." He motioned to his slaves, who quickly strapped on his bronze breastplate.

Antony walked to the open flap of his campaign tent, glancing out at the remains of the camp that sat on a low hill overlooking narrow plains a day's hard march southwest of Rome. The four and a half legions of his army had formed across the valley, blocking the Via Latina. Five cohorts, half a legion, stood in reserve behind the line. Five Republican legions under Lucius Munatius waited behind a ditch and low rampart. Wide ditches topped with a palisade curved to the rear, guarding their flanks.

"Imperator." A short, stocky man limped toward us. A dark red cloak covered his armor. Canidius served as consul with Antony. His limp was the result of a wound he had received the day we defeated Octavian's army at the River Luro. Today, he commanded the reserves.

Antony acknowledged Canidius with a nod. "Any news of Marcus Titus?"

"Nothing since yesterday's report that his army was closing on Rome from the northeast, along the Via Salaria. The Twelfth Legion will try to slow his advance. Imperator, once more I say that we should withdraw to Rome, where we are strongest. The enemy does not have enough men to storm the city and has no siege equipment. If we attack Munatius behind his defenses, we waste our strength.

"No. We will destroy Munatius here, then turn north and crush Titus."

A slave set a stool beside Antony's horse, a beautifully groomed black mare. Antony pulled himself onto the horse, helped by a push from the slave. "Canidius, join your men." Antony kicked his horse into a trot.

Canidius studied the hills around us. "I wish I knew where Titus was." He stepped to his horse. "Stay here until you know how the battle goes. The queen will want a full report."

I watched the battle from the camp, angry that I could not join in the fight. At the same time, I feared that I betrayed Cleopatra and Neferet by not riding immediately to Rome. Below me, Antony's army stood in cohorts ready for battle. Suddenly, a red banner flew above Antony's command group. Moments later, the silver and gold standards of the legions, cohorts, and maniples raised, flashing, in the sun. Trumpets sounded, and Antony's legions swept forward, the leading units forming wedges to penetrate the enemy line. The ditch, and the hurled javelins of the enemy, stopped the advance. The battle raged along the entire front, a constant shifting and jerking of tiny figures. From time to time, the rear lines moved forward to replace the men in contact with the enemy.

The armies fought for over an hour, deadlocked. I saw that Republican troops were moving from the flanking ditches to support their front. I called a messenger, but before I could send him three cohorts of the reserve moved left. They seemed to crawl across the ground, but I knew they were nearly running. They swung around the flank and formed alongside the ditch before they charged. The attack swept the weakened flank guard aside. The enemy line tried to curl back to meet the attack, and failed. The line broke into small segments that were quickly surrounded by Antony's forces. A few groups surrendered. Most formed squares and fought on.

Something tugged at my cloak, and I turned, my gaze following the pointing hand of the messenger. A widening stream of men poured into the shallow valley from tracks across the hills to the north. They had already formed into maniples and cohorts on the valley floor. I knew that Titus must have marched cross-country to reach us.

I was the senior officer in the camp. I grabbed the messenger's arm. "Tell Canidius the enemy is behind us and to bring the last of the reserves. We will hold till he arrives." I sent a second rider to inform Antony.

About three hundred legionnaires were in the camp. I ordered them into a line facing the new enemy, each man with as many pila as were available. Antony had taken all the archers, but left many slingers who waited for the enemy well in front of the line.

The weak enemy cohort, about four hundred men, I estimated, rushed up the low hill. If they had taken a few extra minutes to form properly they might have smashed through our line, but they attacked raggedly. Our slingers hurled heavy stones, smashing skulls and breaking limbs. The Republicans closed to fifty yards, and the slingers retreated behind the legionnaires. The tall, curved shields of the enemy matched our own scuta. Their mail shirts and bronze helmets mirrored those of my men. They reached twenty yards from our low rampart. I called, "Now," and my single trumpeter signaled attack. The men standing in line hurled their pila as the enemy cast theirs. Our extra javelins, three or four for each man, fell on the enemy in rapid volleys, and we drew our swords.

"Stand and gut the bastards!" A legionnaire fell back from the line, his face ripped open, blood pouring from slashed vessels. Another fell where he stood, a gladius stabbing through his mail. I rammed my swagger stick into my belt and drew my sword. Grabbing a fallen scutum, I stepped into the gap in the line.

A javelin smashed into my shield. The heavy point of the pilum jabbed through my scutum near its top. The weight of the point and shaft pulled the shield away from me, and I dropped it and drew my long dagger. A gladius stabbed toward my groin. I deflected the blow and countered with a thrust toward his chest. His shield knocked my arm down and I used the force of his blow to drive my sword into his groin. He fell, and others took his place. The man before me swung the edge of his shield toward my face, thrusting his gladius at my chest. I ducked under his shield, sweeping his sword aside with mine and plunging my dagger into his body. I twisted it free and sliced his throat. The world became a sea of sound. Above the clash of metal on metal rose the grunts and bellows of the soldiers and the screams of wounded men. I don't know how long we fought, but we held. We held ground red with blood.

Behind me, I heard the blaring of a trumpet. I stepped back as the first maniples of the reserve strengthened our line. The standard bearers, tall men cloaked in the skulls and skins of bears, ran forward, the golden palms and medallions of their standards held high for the men to see. The reserve rushed to fight before their standards, and the enemy fell back. I heard Canidius shouting to hold firm.

The enemy charged again. They crashed against us, as if a wave shattering on a rocky headland. As with the sea, they withdrew slightly only to attack again and again before finally retreating to the bottom of the hill.

"Quintus Petillus, to me," I heard Antony call my name.

Antony was directing men into our line. I glanced toward the main battle. The enemy was withdrawing in good order. Half of our army moved to our relief while the others guarded against a counterattack. On the hills north of us, the paths were covered in bronze and red as more troops flooded toward the battle. I counted fifteen Republican cohorts forming and several moving around our camp toward the earlier fight. I recognized the standard of the Twelfth Legion, and knew they had gone over to the enemy. Soon, Antony would face the enemy's full strength, and I knew he would fail.

"Imperator." Jogging to stand before Antony, I felt a sharp pain in my left leg, and saw blood running from a gash on my thigh.

"Celsus, your duty is to protect the queen. Tell her we won. Her resolve must not weaken." He saw my wound, and turned toward a wound dresser, "You, bind this man's leg."

I sat on a rock beside a capsarius who worked on a gaping wound in a legionnaire's side. I looked to the wounded man's face, recognized an old comrade as he died, and cursed again that Roman fought Roman. The capsarius paused only an instant before turning to examine my leg. "Deep but clean. I'll stitch you up and bind the wound. You won't feel a thing."

A messenger who knew the region led me south across country. We reached the Via Appia as sun set at the end of the twelfth hour. The moon was nearly full, and gave good light so that we were able to push on to Rome. The commander of the guard at the Capena Gate passed us through at the start of the fourth hour of the night and we entered Rome near the Circus Maximus. I gave the messenger my horse and he rode to find the tribune commanding the city. I threaded my way up the slope of the Palatine. With every step up the steep hill, pain knifed through my leg.

Two of my men guarded the door of Cleopatra's mansion. Others, I knew, waited on the roof and in a neighboring house. Light shined weakly through a small window in the door. "Is all well?"

"Bit of a riot down in the Suburia earlier in the day, sir, but we've had no trouble here." One of the soldiers knocked twice on the door. "Open for Quintus Petillus Celsus."

I blinked against the light, and saw Gaius Decius, my second in command, walking down the long hall from the atrium. I handed my cloak to a slave.

"Celsus, you let some bastard stab you."

"Only one of the many who tried."

"And the battle?" he asked as we walked down the hall toward the atrium.

"When I left, Antony was trapped between two armies. The battle may be over by now. What happened in the Suburia?"

"Antony left orders to seize the few Republican senators still in the city. They hid in the Suburia."

"Senators hiding in the slums? How the pompous have fallen."

"The people welcomed them and fought the troops sent to seize them. The city has not felt this way in my lifetime, Celsus, with all the citizens standing together. The troops withdrew."

"Put the men on alert."

"They already are."

"Good." I spoke so only he would hear. "There is an Egyptian quinquereme at the dock near the Forum Boarium. Before I left, I made Gordian her captain and ordered him to replace the Egyptian crew with men he trusts. I sent the ship's Macedonian marines to guard the queen's villa."

"Then they're cut off from Rome by the enemy."

"Just as well. Send for Gordian."

"Centurion." Cleopatra's chief clerk, an old Greek slave, stood just inside the atrium. "The queen wishes to see you."

I followed the slave up the stairs leading to Cleopatra's private quarters on the second floor, his shock of white hair a beacon in the dim light. Two of the queen's Macedonians guarded her door, tall men with oval shields, spears, and gilded breastplates and helmets. Antony allowed a handful of them to remain in the city. The clerk tapped on a door and stood aside when it opened. I tried not to limp as I entered.

Cleopatra lay on her couch, wearing a white robe, her long, dark, hair in disarray from sleep. A small table had been pushed against the couch. Several of her women waited across the room. I saw Neferet, and

wanted to take her in my arms, but instead inclined
my head slightly to the queen. "Majesty."

"Celsus, you look as if you need some wine." The
queen held up her hand, and Neferet brought a tray
with dark blue bottles holding wine and water. Neferet
again wore the thinnest of linen dresses, this one of
dark yellow.

Neferet mixed Cleopatra's wine, her gaze coming
back again and again to the bandage on my leg. I
glanced down, and saw that it was lightly stained
with blood. Neferet filled my goblet, mixing my wine
half-and-half.

"All of you, out."

Neferet and the other slaves left by a side door.

The first sip of wine rushed through my body, and
I felt myself sway slightly with exhaustion and silently
cursed my weakness. The queen nodded toward a stool.

"Thank you, Majesty." Quickly, I reported Antony's
battle with the first Republican army and the arrival
of the second in the moment of his victory.

"Is Antony dead?" Her voice nearly trembled.

"Majesty, I . . ."

"No." She was again in command. "Do not specu-
late. We must wait for news. You have two hundred
men in my bodyguard, I believe."

"I command a maniple, two centuries, of legionnaires and a century of archers and slingers. We are
close to full strength, and have nearly two hundred
and fifty men."

"Will the men remain loyal?"

"They will. Most have served you since I raised
your guard five years ago."

"I should not have asked, Celsus, but thank you for

the reassurance. Get some rest, and send in Neferet as you leave." Cleopatra smiled, showing for a moment the charm that events had driven from her. "No, have Neferet look to your wound."

Neferet lay with her head on my shoulder and I gently stroked her hair. The musky scent of her recent arousal enveloped me. She rolled over, and I felt the warmth of her breasts on my chest. "Celsus, my love, tell me again of how you gave Antony and my queen victory over Octavian?" She grinned and kissed me.

"No, love, I'll not waste my energy talking." But I remembered. After joining Antony's legions in Alexandria, I was sent to help guard the shipyards. One day, I saw children from the East playing with toy boats. They had placed the shell of a turtle on one. I realized a shell could protect a warship, as the raised shields of the legions formed the testudo and protected the men. I told my idea to a ship builder. He was an honest man, and told Antony. Antony promoted me to centurion, restoring the honor I lost when I fled from Agrippa. At Actium, our testudo navalis broke through to Agrippa's flagship, bringing victory. As the memories slipped from my mind, I realized just how cleaver Neferet had been. She had reminded me of a victory when I needed the confidence the memory would bring. The room was hot, but I held her to me for a moment longer.

"Quintus," her voice was serious, "are you as different from other Romans as you seem? Does your passion really include love?" Her wide, dark, eyes stared into mine. "I am foolish to hope so, yet I pray to Isis that it does."

"Most men would call me weak for loving as I do. They say that of Antony," I said. "I used to agree with them, but life changes us all, and it has changed me. You have changed me. The world believes slaves are only for pleasure and not for love." I felt her tense, and knew I had spoken her fears. "For most Romans, the opinions of the world count for everything. I have learned that a man's honor, his worth, has little to do with the views of others. Fortuna was with me when I met you, and I want you with me, always.

There was a loud knock on the door. "Centurion, the ship captain is here."

"I'll be there shortly."

"Our time is over, isn't it, my love?" Neferet asked. I saw that she was trying to hold back tears, and I knew she meant more than our time of rest.

I felt an overwhelming sadness that I pushed from my mind. "Perhaps. But perhaps not. Neferet, you are a slave bound to your queen. I am a soldier bound by honor to my general. We must help each other." I stood and started dressing.

Neferet dropped her long, gauzelike dress over her head and put one foot up on the couch. "Perhaps, Neferet, a more practical dress for travel, as lovely as it is on you."

"I'm a pharaoh's slave. I don't have anything more practical." She hiked up the dress and strapped a dagger high on her right calf. Neferet grinned when she saw my surprise. "How can I help you, my love, if I am defenseless?"

Gaius Decius and I stood over a map of the city that we had spread across a table in the atrium. "The enemy is outside the Coline Gate northwest of the city. One attack has been repulsed already."

"Give each legionnaire a hundred denarii and each auxiliary fifty. Tell them there will be twice as much at the end of the day. Send seven sections to guard the ship."

"Seven sections, Centurion?" I turned to a short, compact man standing near the door who had spoken.

"Sailors!" I mumbled, and said, "Eight men to a section, Gordian. Ten sections to a century."

Gordian had spent two decades on the seas and a third piloting barges on the Tiber, and his face reflected every storm he had faced and every day he had stood beneath the broiling sun. He could also tie more knots than any other man I knew. "I understand the river has fallen nearly a foot. Will you be able to take the ship back to the sea?"

"Yes, Centurion. I know Father Tiber. Sir, I have a request. May I bring my family aboard: my wife and three children, and a slave who has been with us for twenty years? I do not want to leave them alone in Rome."

I needed Gordian's loyalty, and we could endure the extra crowding. "They can bring only what they can carry. What about the families of your crew?"

"I chose good men, Centurion, but I also chose men without families."

I left the atrium and crossed the garden to Cleopatra's study. "Majesty, we must leave now to reach the river safely."

"We wait for Antony." Cleopatra looked up from her desk. "I thought I could leave before I knew if he lived or died, but I can not." She pointed to six chests, each about a foot square. "Celsus, if I die in Rome, the gold and jewels must reach Alexandria. Caesarian will need them to buy the loyalty of the legions in Egypt."

"I promise you that the gold will not fall to the enemy." I saw a legionnaire hurrying across the garden. "Excuse me, Majesty."

"Centurion, trouble in the street."

I hurried to the roof of the mansion, pain ripping through my thigh as I climbed the ladder. I stared at smoke rising above the Suburia and from farther north near the Coline Gate. A dozen thick, gray columns roiled into the sky, blending with the low, heavy clouds. The stench of the burning city hung in the air. Automatically, I checked the readiness of the archers who lined the roof. Twenty legionnaires guarded the front of the building. South, the street was empty for the two blocks I could see before it curved. North, toward the Forum, a mob of several hundred filled the street between the walls of single story houses. They surged toward us. I called to the archers, "Fire," and the mob fell back under the impact of the arrows.

An archer pointed north. "Behind the mob, coming up from the Forum."

I saw several dozen legionnaires moving slowly toward us, and was certain Antony was with them. The mob kept him from reaching us, and he formed his men in line to repel attack. "If the mob comes into range, fire on them," I ordered the archers.

I skimmed down the ladder into the garden, and ran to the front of the mansion. "Four sections with me. You also." I pointed to our trumpeter.

I led them into the street. They were armed with

spears fixed with broad, sharp iron points. "Form two lines across the street."

"Remember your training. Advance in rushes of twenty paces. Cut them apart, but let them retreat. Ignore the trumpet and follow my commands." I glanced at the trumpeter, and said, "Sound Hold in Place," hoping that Antony would understand my tactics.

Advancing nearly shoulder to shoulder, the men would have been too packed together to fight effectively as swordsmen, but it was easy to charge forward till we contacted the mob, and to stab and slash at unarmored bodies with the long spears. The mob shuddered, fell back, and we charged again across the bodies of the fallen. Again, they retreated. Dozens fled into the shadows at each alley. We let them go, and I left a few men of the second line to guard against their return. Then, over the heads of the last, the bravest, of the mob I saw the helmets of Antony's men. They stood blocking the street, just past an intersection. Trapped between us, the last of the mob fled.

"Celsus, good man," Antony called, sounding for a moment the great leader he had wanted to be. "More men like you and we would have broken them all. I should have given you command of a legion." Blood and dirt covered Antony's armor and tunic. He grasped my right forearm in a tight grip with both hands, and his next words came from a man haunted by failure speaking in a voice that trembled. "Canidius is dead. We lost five legions, slaughtered or become traitors. These few men are all that is left of us."

"Then it has come to the triarii, and there aren't many of us," I said, hoping that the mobs had not circled the Palatine and blocked our escape.

In the guardroom, Antony held out his arms as slaves stripped off his gore-splattered armor. He took a cup of wine and drained it in a single gulp, pulled off his tunic and dropped a clean one over his head.

"Imperator, there is a ship waiting at the Tiber."

"Don't mock me with an empty title. The imperium, my command, is worthless without legions. You expected my defeat, didn't you, Celsus?"

"I expected neither victory nor defeat, General, but I prepared for both. We must leave now. Let me send for Cleopatra."

"Go."

The queen was in the room before I turned to fetch her, Neferet beside her. "I would not cry until I saw your body," Cleopatra said, touching Antony's cheek with her hand, "and now, I don't have to, for you are here. You are alive. We have legions in Egypt and gold to keep them loyal. We do not need Rome."

Antony nodded, saying nothing. Looking at the shattered remains of Antony, I took back my honor rather than leave it in his shaking hands. Then I looked again at Cleopatra. She wore a simple dress with Neferet's brown cloak over it. Her hair was down, and had been cut off to match Neferet's. Neferet was dressed as the queen, in a dress of the finest white linen boarded with golden thread. She wore a heavy gold necklace studded with lapis lazuli and jewels and golden bracelets on each arm. She wore a wig that matched Cleopatra's normal rolled hairdo.

We left the mansion in the middle of the afternoon. A third of Rome seemed to be burning. The clouds had grown even denser, forcing the smoke to settle over the city and turning the afternoon to twilight and streets into dark, shadow-filled corridors. My scouts reported that Republican troops were north and east of the Palatine. If they occupied the Circus Maximus and the streets around it, we could be cut off from the ship. I detached five sections of legionnaires in the lead and to guard the flanks, commanded by Gaius Decius. Three litters followed, each born by eight slaves. The first carried Neferet, dressed as Cleopatra, the queen dressed as a slave, and Antony. The second and third carried the queen's gold. The handful of men who had come with Antony followed the litters. I was angry, enraged that Cleopatra endangered Neferet with the disguise. I would, I knew, let the queen die to save the slave.

The air was hot and muggy. Within minutes I was bathed in sweat under my armor. Scattered members of the mob scuttled behind us, staying out of bowshot. Every time I glanced behind us, the mob had grown larger.

The rear guard formed in line, the archers and slingers firing from in front of the legionnaires, retreating behind the line when the mob came too close. Sensing loot but sill wary, the mob charged and retreated again and again, hurling rocks and the occasional spear or pilum. More and more, they attacked from our flank nearest the Tiber, and I ordered men to charge and drive them off. We moved slowly, leaving our dead behind us. At the back of the mob I caught sight of several men in armor, and knew they were directing the attack.

"Keep them back, but don't let yourself to be cut off," I ordered the senior section leader. I jogged toward the front of the column, wincing as I felt my wound tear open. Thunder crashed above us and rain fell in a deluge. Within seconds, I was soaked.

The advance guard neared the bottom of the hill. Gaius Decius saw me, turned, and I called, "They're trying to herd us away from the Tiber."

In that instant, a wedge of legionnaires charged from an alley and struck our vanguard. My men flung their spears at the enemy and pulled their swords. Decius and the flank guard charged the attackers as I called, "Antony's men, to the front. Rear guard, hold." The litter was on the ground, Antony standing, drawing his sword. Cleopatra and Neferet were beside him, protected by the queen's half dozen Macedonian guards.

A swordsman broke from the shadows. I parried and drove my sword into his chest. He twisted and fell away, wrenching the sword from my hand. I ducked low under a blow from another man and punched into his groin, staggering him back. He was taken in the throat by one of my men. I grabbed his fallen sword.

All of the Macedonians were dead, but they had driven off the attack on the litter. The men attacking the vanguard fell back as Decius and the flankers struck them. "Clear the way," I called, and rushed down the steep street toward Decius.

"Celsus . . ." Antony's call turned into a cry of surprise. I spun, my sword up to parry a blow. The image froze in my mind. Antony, feet tangled in the cloak of a fallen soldier, slipping on the wet cobbles, falling onto my gladius as I turned.

We both stared at his blood pouring over my sword. He stepped back, pulling himself free, his hands clasping the wide wound. He sat straight down, the slightest moan escaping his lips.

I knelt beside him, but was pushed aside by Cleopatra. "Antony!" She looked up at Neferet. "Bandages. Something to bandage him." Cleopatra pressed her hands against the wound.

"My queen, my love," Antony whispered. He leaned forward, weakening quickly. He looked up, finding my face. "Celsus, save her."

"Imperator." Around us, my men fought and the last attackers retreated. "Neferet, the queen." Neferet pulled Cleopatra back as Antony fell to the side, the rain already washing his blood from the stones.

Cleopatra mumbled something, an invocation I think, in Egyptian. She pulled free of Neferet and held Antony's head as he died. Legionnaires lifted Antony into the litter. The queen sat with his head in her lap with Neferet sat behind her, trying to console her.

"Decius, lead off."

We reached the bottom of the Palatine and turned toward the river. Rounding the end of the Circus, we angled east to pass south of the Forum Boarium.

I realized we were on one of the great avenues Antony had followed during his triumph as he rode toward the Forum, Octavian in chains before him. So he had entered Rome. So he left it.

The doors of a warehouse stood open ahead of us. I motioned Neferet to stay where she was and signaled the remains of the rear guard to close around the litters. Decius waved a section forward, and the men dashed through the doorway. I followed with Decius. Several legionnaires lay dead along with a dozen other men. Otherwise, the building was empty.

"Bring the litters inside and get those doors shut," I told Decius, and nodded to a section leader, "Your section with me." I led the way out the far door of the warehouse.

The dock was empty, the ship gone. I felt hope vanish.

"Centurion! Quintus Petillus!" I looked to the river. The quinquereme was about fifty feet off the bank, held against the current by ropes secured up-river and others running to the dock. It was nearly hidden by the pounding rain and the smoke haze that clung to the Tiber. Gordian stood in the stern beside the tiller, hands cupped as he called again, "Pull us in. Stern first." My men rushed to the ropes and began pulling the ship back to the dock. The quinquereme came into clear view, her single bank of oars raised to keep clear of the docks, she was large for her type, nearly one hundred and thirty feet long and eighteen wide. Five slaves, I knew, manned each oar on the hellishly cramped lower deck.

I called back into the warehouse, "Decius, bring the litters." I heard a crash from the building, but before I could react, I saw the mob closing along the dock from north and south. The ship nudged the dock and sailors leapt ashore to tie her securely as others pushed a wide plank to the dock. A score of legionnaires followed the sailors and formed a thin line between the river and the warehouse. My men formed a line protecting the other end of the dock.

"Decius, get the litters out here!" I stepped into the warehouse, and into chaos. The far doors were shattered. Men swarmed in battle in the cavernous building. The queen's litter lay on its side, Antony's body sprawled on the dirt floor. Cleopatra knelt beside him. Neferet stood behind her holding her dagger, her fine gown soaked with water, torn, and covered with dirt. The other litters were also tipped over. The slaves had fled.

A centurion leading the attack shouted, "Capture the whore. Don't let Cleopatra escape."

I charged across the floor, stabbing the centurion as I shoved him out of my way. An attacker spun to face me. I parried his thrust and slashed at his arm. He fell back, grasping at the stub of his wrist.

Two of my men fell. Cleopatra stared into the face of an attacker. His gladius struck like a serpent, stabbing into her breast. Cleopatra grabbed his arm, and Neferet drove her dagger into his side. The last attacker pushed past the queen and grabbed Neferet, pulling her toward the door. I thrust my sword into his back, sensed motion behind me, and spun. I just held back my blow as I recognized Decius.

"We're clear for the moment."

"Get those chests aboard the ship. Have the men ready to board." I looked at Cleopatra, who had fallen across Antony. "They have traveled the road to endless sleep. She died the descendent of kings and Antony as a general of Rome. Bring their bodies. They will have proper rites."

The mob held back, still fearing my men. I pulled Neferet aside. "The masquerade is too dangerous." Her eyes seemed empty and she was shaking, but she tossed the wig aside. I grabbed Antony's cloak from the litter and wrapped it around her. We boarded quickly, and I stood beside Neferet as we cast free of the dock and let Father Tiber carry us from the city. I held Neferet to me, and felt her pull away. She was crying. "Neferet."

"When I was a child and first her slave, I thought Cleopatra was the incarnation of Isis. Today, I would have died to protect her as we fought. If I still believed she were the Goddess, I would follow her in death even now." Her tears slowed. "I will mourn for her, but I will not die for her memory." She looked up at me. "It would take me from you."

I kissed her, then turned, and stared into the faces of my men who had survived. The smoke thinned as we moved down river, but I saw scarcely a century of them on the deck. I glanced down at the chests of Cleopatra's treasure. I called to a crewman, "Tell the slaves that if they pull us to safety they will all be free men with gold in their purses." Then, I shouted to the men on deck, "Legionnaires, sailors, you will all be wealthy."

Gordian stood beside the tiller. He grinned. "We don't sail for Alexandria, do we, Centurion?"

I kissed Neferet. "From this moment, you are free," then smiled at Gordian. "Spain is beautiful in the spring, Gordian."

〜

End Note:

My thanks to Plutarch for his comment that the soul of a lover rests in the body of another and to Propertius' eulogy of Cleopatra for my title.

Not Fade Away

William Sanders

It was around the middle of June that I saw him again, and realized at last that it was really true. Like everybody else on Corregidor, I'd heard the reports—first the rumors, which I ignored because you could hear all sorts of tales on the Rock; then the initial reports on the radio, which most of us put down as Japanese propaganda, and finally the official word from General Wainwright's headquarters.

But it didn't really register, somehow. I guess there was a tendency to denial, about that and a lot of other things, at that time. Even after the fall of Corregidor, as we sat around the old Spanish prison in Manila waiting for them to decide what to do with us, there were people who still refused to believe MacArthur had been captured. It was just a Jap trick, they'd tell you, the general was already in Australia getting ready to lead a huge force back to the Philippines and rescue us . . .

I wasn't one of the holdouts, but I have to admit it didn't fully sink in, wasn't quite real to me, until I saw him coming in the gate flanked by half a dozen Japanese guards.

That was a couple of weeks after they took us out of Bilibid Prison and moved us north to a former Philippine Army camp near the little town of Tarlac. They hauled us in trucks; nothing like the infamous forced march from Bataan, which had happened before Corregidor fell, and in fact we hadn't even heard about it yet. Anyway, they treated the senior officers a little better than the juniors and the enlisted men. We were of course worthless *gaijin* prisoners, permanently dishonored by having surrendered, but the Japanese obsession with hierarchy did get us a few privileges. You could still get slapped around by any Japanese private who didn't think you'd saluted him smartly enough, but serious beatings were fairly rare.

I got off even easier, in that respect, than the others; the guards would yell at me but rarely laid a hand on me, once they got a look at the freshly healed stump of my right arm.

"It's got nothing to do with sympathy or consideration, you know," Carl Norton told me. He was a Marine major who had been stationed in China until just before the outbreak of war, and had had a good deal of contact with the Japanese officers there. "It's just another of their quirks. Most Japs are uncomfortable about physical contact with anybody who's, uh, damaged, you know? They figure your luck must be bad, and it could be catching."

They might have had something there. After all, I'd lost my arm and my command a mere three days into the war, when a stick of Jap bombs blew my submarine to scrap metal at the Cavite dock. I wouldn't have wanted to get too near me either.

When we got to Tarlac we found other prisoners had gotten there before us, officers captured in the fall of Bataan. They'd been through the Death March, and then the filthy hell at Camp O'Donnell, not far from Tarlac, where disease and thirst and hunger had decimated their already pathetic ranks. We were appalled at their appearance; we'd thought we'd had it pretty rough, but obviously we had no idea. And these were senior officers like us; what it was like for the enlisted men, I didn't even want to imagine.

So Tarlac must have looked pretty good to them; and it wasn't all that bad, really, by the standards of Japanese prison camps—not, God knows, that that's saying much. The food was monotonous and tasteless and not very nutritious and there was never enough of it, but they didn't actually starve us, and the living quarters weren't too squalid. We actually had bunks to sleep on, and blankets; at Bilibid most people had had to settle for the concrete floor.

The original commandant was a colonel named Ito, and he seemed a decent sort, but a few days after we arrived he suddenly left. His replacement was another colonel named Sakamoto, a heavy-set son of a bitch with a permanent scowl. Sakamoto made it clear right away that he intended to run a tight ship and didn't give a damn for his prisoners' exalted rank. But at least he wasn't a brutal sadist or a screaming nutcase like some of the commandants you heard about.

The real hardship for most of the prisoners at Tarlac was mental. This was a camp for colonels and generals, after all, with a handful of lower ranks—as a mere Navy commander, I was pretty close to the bottom of the totem pole—and promotion had been slow in the peacetime years. So what you had was mostly a bunch of middle-aged and even elderly men; many of them had served in the last war, in France. The physical privations were rough enough on them, but the humiliation—having to salute and bow to teenaged Japanese privates, getting slapped like unruly children for trivial offenses—was far worse.

And then there was the shame of defeat. Especially this particular defeat. "They got their asses handed to them," Carl Norton said, "by a bunch of people they'd always looked down on as ridiculous little monkeys who couldn't do anything right. That's what's really eating them."

"But not you?" I asked him, grinning. We were good friends; we'd known each other since Corregidor.

"Not me," Carl said. "I saw the little bastards in action in China, remember? I knew the minute the war started we were in deep shit."

There was a lot of arguing among the Army officers, too, about the reasons for the defeat, a lot of recrimination and blame-swapping, some of it pretty bitter. All that frustration and anger had to find some sort of outlet, after all . . . and anyway, there really wasn't much else to do. The senior officers didn't have to pull labor details, and the supply of reading matter or writing materials was nearly nonexistent, so squabbling like a bunch of old ladies was just about all there was left. That or simply sitting around staring silently off into nowhere.

General Wainwright arrived a few days after the rest of us, in a car from Manila. As senior American officer he might have been expected to do something about the state of morale, but his own obviously wasn't so great either. He looked and moved like a man in tremendous pain, even though they hadn't harmed him; and it wasn't hard to understand why. He'd been the one to surrender—not just Corregidor, but all the American forces in the Philippines. That was one of the things people talked and argued about, though not within his hearing.

Anyway, that was what things were like at Tarlac when they brought MacArthur in.

He wasn't wearing his trademark cap; I guess he'd lost it when Bulkeley's PT boat was sunk. He was bareheaded and his uniform was a stained and rumpled ruin, and he wasn't wearing his stars—none of the prisoners were allowed to wear rank insignia—but it didn't matter; he'd have been recognizable in a jockstrap. He still carried himself tall and straight—he towered over the Japanese guards like an Oregon cedar—and he still moved with that long-legged stride, so that they had to hustle to keep formation around him.

But God, he looked old . . . he wasn't a young man, of course, but he looked ten years older than when I'd seen him last.

"He looks like hell," Carl Norton said. We were

standing maybe twenty or thirty yards away from
the gate; we'd just happened to be walking across
the compound when the motor convoy drove up in
front of the gate. No one in the camp, even General
Wainwright, had been told MacArthur was coming.
Maybe the commandant didn't want us holding some
kind of parade or ceremony to welcome him. More
likely it just didn't occur to the Japs to tell us, any
more than you'd bother telling the stray mutts in the
pound that you're bringing the big dog in.

"Still got that presence, though," Carl mused.

"It's about all he's got left," I said.

"Yeah. Poor devil."

We watched as they escorted him toward the headquarters building. Colonel Sakamoto had come out
onto the porch and was waiting. A Japanese lieutenant came up and saluted and handed Sakamoto some
papers. Then he shouted a command and the guard
detail stamped to a halt.

The commandant stood staring at MacArthur. I
couldn't see MacArthur's face from where I was standing, but I was pretty sure he was staring back.

And then, after what seemed like a long time,
MacArthur saluted. It was an absolutely West-Point-
correct salute, but it was as if he had enormous
weights lashed to his arm.

Colonel Sakamoto didn't return the salute; they never
did. He just turned and walked back into the building, gesturing for MacArthur to follow. The lieutenant
screamed at the soldiers again and they about-faced
and headed back toward the gate.

Carl Norton let his breath out in a long ragged
sigh. "Jesus," he said.

And after a minute: "I never liked him, you know. I always figured him for a show-off and a glory hound. I still think he handled the defense of the Philippines like somebody trying to stick his dick in his ear. But you can't help feeling for a man who's been knocked down that hard."

We still didn't know, though, just how hard this particular man had been knocked down. We found out a couple of days later, when Sergeant Watanabe, the chief interpreter, told us MacArthur's wife and son had been lost when the PT boat was sunk.

"There's no question about it," Watanabe said. "The bodies were found, washed up on the beach, the next day. The torpedo boat was literally blown out of the water, you know, by the destroyer's guns. The only survivors were the general himself and an ordinary sailor who died of his wounds on the way back to Manila."

He spoke in a clear, flawless English with only the faintest touch of an accent; four years at Princeton had left their mark, and not just on his language skills. He wasn't happy about the war and he'd tell you privately that it was going to end catastrophically for Japan.

"I know Americans," he would say. "You seem so easygoing, but under the surface you are a violent and vengeful people. You also think life is like your Western movies, in which the hero never draws first. An attack like the one at Pearl Harbor was the surest possible way to enrage the American people beyond all reason. You will not stop now until you have had your vengeance, no matter what it takes."

☆   ☆   ☆

Now Watanabe said, "It was a strange business in Colonel Sakamoto's office. General MacArthur stood there looking straight ahead, without expression, while the commandant spoke and I translated. He only spoke in reply to direct questions, and when he did speak his voice was hoarse and indistinct, as if it hurt him to talk."

He raised an eyebrow. "How has he been behaving, since his arrival?"

We both shook our heads. "We haven't seen him," I said, "except at a distance. The generals don't mix much with us lower orders."

Which was true, not that we'd have told Watanabe if we had known anything. The Japs made a point of not recognizing distinctions in rank among the prisoners, but even so, the generals had their own barracks, and had their meals together and so on.

And MacArthur had stayed out of sight; as far as I knew he hadn't left the barracks except when he had to. We'd seen him at the morning roll-call formations, when we all had to bow in unison to the emperor, who was represented by a white post at the end of the parade ground. Really, I'm not making this up; you should have seen us, over a hundred middle-aged-to-elderly men lined up in ranks, bowing respectfully to a wooden post. Carl kept saying he was going to sneak out some night and piss on it, but he wasn't suicidal enough to do it.

We'd seen MacArthur at mealtime, and a couple of times on the way to the latrine. But we hadn't been close to him, and it wouldn't have mattered if we had; there was a wall around him that was almost visible. It wasn't just the traditional isolation of the man at the top; MacArthur seemed to be on another planet. One of the outer ones, cold and dark and with crushing gravity.

"They say he doesn't talk to anyone," Carl reported, later that evening. He was friendly with a couple of artillery colonels, and they in turn knew some of the generals, and so from time to time he heard things. "They say he just sits around, or lies on his bunk looking at the ceiling."

MacArthur not talking? There was a thought to shake your faith in the immutable laws of the universe.

"Some people are worried he might kill himself," Carl said.

"It's possible." On Corregidor it was common knowledge that MacArthur had said openly that he intended to shoot his family and then himself if capture was imminent. He probably meant it, too. "In some ways," I said, "he thinks a lot like our beloved captors."

"Yeah," Carl said. "He'd have made a great samurai. Ironic as hell, huh?"

But then the following day, as we were walking across the parade ground, there he was, striding briskly toward us. He was wearing an old-fashioned campaign hat someone had given him—you didn't go bareheaded in the Philippine sun if you could help it—and the brim shadowed his eyes, but there was something different about the set of his jaw and the way he held his head; or rather something more like the MacArthur I remembered. We stopped and came to something resembling attention, while Carl snapped off a salute. The stump of my right arm came up reflexively before I could stop it.

MacArthur ground to a stop in front of us and returned Carl's salute. I suppose I looked embarrassed, because he turned to face me, still holding the salute, and said, "That's all right, Commander. It's fitting that I salute *you,* in view of the sacrifice you have made for our country."

Then, lowering his hand, he added in a lower voice, "I too have lost my right arm . . ."

I couldn't think of a damn thing to say.

After a second he said, "Well, Commander, I haven't seen you since Corregidor." His voice had changed again; now it rang with a kind of strained heartiness. "How's the arm? Healing well?"

"Yes, sir. Seems to be."

"Good, good." He nodded energetically. "And Major Norton, you're looking well. I want you to know," he said, "how much I appreciated the Marines' contribution to the defense of these islands."

I still couldn't see his eyes clearly in the shadow of the hat's brim, but there was something truly terrible in the lines around his mouth. It was as if the skin of his face had been stretched too tight.

Carl mumbled an indistinct thanks. MacArthur said, "Well, gentlemen, I'm afraid I haven't time to stop and talk. But don't hesitate to come to me if there's any way I can be of help. We all have to help one another get through this time of trial."

He turned, or rather did a parade-ground about-face, and strode away. We watched as he marched across the parade ground, somehow giving the impression of being followed by at least a division.

Carl said, "What the hell . . . ?"

"Don't ask me," I said. "I'm in shock, too."

"Well," Carl said, "at least he's got the line of bullshit back. Wonder what the story is?"

I said, "I doubt if we'll ever know."

But in fact we did find out the following day, by way of Carl's artillery colonel buddies. "It was Bluemel," he told us, and right away things started to make more sense.

General Bluemel was a monumentally tough old infantryman who had commanded a Philippine Army division in the Bataan campaign, and from all accounts he was absolutely fearless. His own subordinates had been terrified of him; there were rumors that he had personally shot men trying to retreat. "Son of a bitch should have been a Marine," Carl Norton often said, bestowing his highest accolade.

"I wasn't there," the colonel said, "but what I heard was that Bluemel just walked up to him in the barracks, while he was sitting on his bunk staring at the wall, and laid into him. Chewed him out like an awkward recruit, right there in front of the other generals. They couldn't hear all of it, but everybody clearly heard the phrase 'sitting on your ass feeling sorry for yourself.' "

"No," I said, and Carl said, "You're kidding."

The colonel shook his head, grinning. "I tell you, Bluemel's something else. On Bataan he was up front with a rifle leading counterattacks like some young lieutenant. His men held their positions when everybody else was breaking and running, just because they were more afraid of him than the Japs."

"So what did he say to MacArthur?" Carl prompted.

"From what I heard, he told him to pull himself

together and start exercising some leadership. Said, 'You're not the first general to lose a campaign, or even the first man to lose his family.' Asked him if he thought his son would want to know his father had turned out to be a quitter."

It was like hearing that someone had gone up and kicked God in the ass. No, that would have been more believable; God, they tell us, forgives, which MacArthur never did.

"Bluemel told him he had a responsibility to the men in this camp," the colonel went on. "And that it was time he started fulfilling it. Then he turned and walked away, without even giving MacArthur a chance to reply."

"And?" I asked.

"And MacArthur just went on sitting there, still without speaking, the rest of the evening. But then the next morning he was up before anybody else, and he was—" The colonel spread his hands. "As you've seen. He's been like that ever since. I'm not sure whether I want to thank Bluemel or kill him."

In the days ahead there were times when I felt the same way. MacArthur was back in full force-of-nature style. He reorganized the mess and somehow persuaded Colonel Sakamoto to improve the food allowance. He instituted a series of classes in which officers lectured the rest of us on their various subjects of knowledge, from military history to Shakespeare. Christ, he even started group singing sessions in the evenings!

None of which went over all that well with the men whose morale it was supposed to restore. For one thing, they were veteran professional soldiers; they didn't appreciate being hustled like a lot of homesick Boy Scouts. For another, a considerable number of them—probably over half the officers in camp—blamed MacArthur for the military debacle that had put them behind barbed wire to begin with.

Still, they went along, if only from boredom and because resistance would have taken too much energy. And the additional food, and the other small concessions MacArthur managed to get from Sakamoto, did a lot to improve his popularity.

Watanabe asked us a couple of times whether we knew anything about the sudden change in MacArthur's behavior. I wouldn't quite say he tried to pump us, but he was pretty persistent. Needless to say we didn't admit to knowing a thing.

"Very strange," Watanabe said. "His earlier despondency, I can understand. After all, to become a prisoner is bad enough, but to be captured while trying to flee—the humiliation must be all but unbearable." He shook his head. "The fortunes of war, as they say. If that destroyer hadn't happened to be where it was that night, if General MacArthur had made it to Australia, he would be a great national hero now."

"After getting whipped the way he did?" Carl Norton snorted. "I don't think so."

"Oh, but you forget your country's admiration for brave losers. The Alamo, Custer's last stand, and all that. It is one of the aspects of your culture," Watanabe said, "that we Japanese find most baffling."

"Something phony about that son of a bitch," Carl said after Watanabe was gone. "Somebody that smart, that well educated, and he's just a buck-ass sergeant at a prison camp? Bullshit. I'd bet my rapidly diminishing ass he's with Jap intelligence. All these senior officers here, they're a gold mine of information on the U.S. military. A man like Watanabe, with his good-guy act, could pick up all sorts of valuable information."

"Or he's playing some kind of private game," I said.

"Could be," Carl said. "In my experience most people are."

A week or so later the camp had a visitor.

He didn't arrive with any sort of fanfare; he just rode up in an unmarked car, unaccompanied except for the driver. I happened to be passing nearby as he got out of the car, and I got a pretty good look at him. He got a look at me, too, and his face went dark and he started to open his mouth, no doubt to yell at me for not saluting him; but then he saw the stump of my arm. While he was registering that I threw him a quick bow—I had a feeling this was somebody I better not piss off—and when I straightened up he was standing there staring at me, the way you'd look at something really disgusting you'd just stepped in.

He wasn't much to look at; he was short and squat even by Japanese standards, with a bristling black beard and mustache and thick glasses—none of which hid nearly enough of his face; he really was an ugly little bastard. He wore an ordinary field uniform, badly rumpled and a little too big for him; his collar bore the three stars and three red stripes of a colonel.

He stood for a moment giving me that hating glare, and then suddenly he turned and headed toward the headquarters building, walking very fast, with an odd, almost loping gait. And I hauled ass away from there before he could change his mind; I didn't know who the hell he was, but he had *bad news* written all over him.

Sergeant Watanabe was standing near the fence, watching the visitor as he stalked across the HQ porch and disappeared inside. "You are a lucky man," he said to me. "I thought for a minute you were in big trouble. You don't want to attract Colonel Tsuji's attention."

"Tsuji?" The name was a new one on me.

"You don't know, do you? You should. All of you should know about Colonel Tsuji." There was no one anywhere near us, but Watanabe's voice was very low. "Because he wants you all dead."

"I thought that was what you all wanted." I held up my stump. "You sure try hard enough."

"It's not a joke." Watanabe looked serious, even scared. "When Bataan fell, he tried to have the prisoners executed, and in some cases he succeeded. General Homma gave orders that the prisoners should be treated humanely, but Colonel Tsuji countermanded them."

"What the hell?" I said. "Since when do colonels countermand orders from generals?"

"There is a great deal General Homma does not know about what goes on in his command. Perhaps he chooses not to know."

Watanabe grimaced. "I'm afraid our army isn't quite like yours. Your officers form cliques to advance your careers. Ours form secret societies for the purpose of changing the nation's destiny, and terrorize and even assassinate those who stand in their way. Colonel Tsuji," he said, "is the leader of one of the most radical groups. Even his nominal superiors are wary of crossing him. In Malaya he once stormed into a general's bedroom and harangued him for not being aggressive enough."

Watanabe certainly seemed to know a lot, for a mere sergeant. Carl Norton's theory was beginning to look more credible. I said, "And he got away with it?"

"Colonel Tsuji gets away with things. Don't misunderstand, he's a brilliant officer—they call him the God of Operations; in his way he really is a genius—but he's also quite mad."

He looked off toward HQ again. "I don't know why he's here today, but it worries me. I think he was responsible for having Colonel Ito replaced, because he was too soft on you prisoners."

"Sakamoto belongs to Tsuji's secret society?"

"I don't believe so. But I'm afraid he's under their influence."

"But what's this about executing prisoners? I mean, why?"

"If all the prisoners are executed," Watanabe said, "then there will be no turning back for Japan. There will be no more possibility of a negotiated peace, as some still hope for. It will be all or nothing."

"He wants to kill us," I said incredulously, "just to burn the bridges?"

"Yes. And also," Watanabe said, "because he hates white people."

Tsuji left the same day, and despite Watanabe's fears, there were no immediate changes in our lives. MacArthur continued to organize new projects to improve our lives if it killed us.

Then one morning, as Carl Norton and I were standing in the shade of our barracks talking about this and that, MacArthur appeared in front of us. "Good morning, gentlemen," he said. "Would you come for a little walk with me?"

There was another man with him, an Army Air Corps lieutenant colonel named Fannon who had been on the staff at Clark airfield. He was close to my age, maybe a little older. That was all I knew about him, except that he was one of the more devoted MacArthur loyalists.

We fell in with them as MacArthur led the way out across the compound. "Look casual," he said, "as if we were merely out for a walk. We don't want to look conspiratorial."

That wasn't altogether realistic, since we were now well into the hot season; strolling casually under the Philippine sun was not something many people cared to do. But it was still early and the sun wasn't high yet, so I didn't say anything.

MacArthur clasped his hands behind his back. "Robert E. Lee often said that duty is the sublimest word in the language. And no one can deny that every man in this camp, during the recent campaign, did his duty with exemplary devotion."

He glanced in the direction of the generals' barracks, where General Wainwright was standing in the doorway. "Perhaps some of us . . . had different concepts of where our duty lay," he said, "but that is neither here nor there. Gentlemen, we all know the duty of a soldier who has been captured."

I realized suddenly where this was going. *Oh*, I thought, *shit*.

"Of course," he continued, "this camp poses special problems. Many of the officers here are, to put it baldly, too advanced in years for feats of derring-do. Others, especially the survivors of Bataan and Camp O'Donnell, are badly weakened in health. Still, I confess I am disappointed that there has not been a single escape—nor even an attempt—from this camp."

He looked at Fannon. "Until now. Colonel Fannon proposes to change that. Don't you, Colonel?"

"With your permission, sir." Fannon looked at Carl and me. "I don't know if you've noticed, but every afternoon about the same time, there's a Filipino who rides in on a carabao cart bringing fresh produce for the Japs' mess. The guards never search it, coming or going, and he parks it around back of the kitchen where it isn't clearly visible from any of the guard posts."

"And you're figuring to hide in the back of the cart," Carl said, "and hitch a ride out of here? Okay, what then?"

Fannon shrugged. "I know my way around the Philippines pretty well. I've dealt with Filipinos, too, and I know how to handle them. I'm confident I can find people to help me work my way down to Mindanao, and from there maybe I can find someone with a boat who'll take me to New Guinea or Australia. I'll have to play it by ear, but I'm not worried about it."

"The ability to improvise is the hallmark of a good soldier," MacArthur said approvingly. "However, I've got one problem with your plan. I don't like the idea of your going alone. You should have someone with you, for help and support."

I said, "General—"

"No, Commander." MacArthur almost managed

a smile. "I'm sure you're not afraid to go, and I'm sure you'd try your best, but—well, please don't take offense, but taking you along might pose problems, surely you can see that?"

Actually I'd been about to say it was a damn fool idea, or words to that effect, but if MacArthur chose to believe I was a hero I wouldn't disillusion him.

"I'm afraid," he added, "that I'm exploiting your misfortune, and for that I beg your forgiveness. You see, your presence will keep our captors from suspecting anything, should they notice us talking together. A group that includes a one-armed man, they will think, cannot be up to anything very serious."

He turned to Carl. "Major Norton, on the other hand, strikes me as the ideal candidate. Possibly the youngest man in camp, almost certainly the fittest. What do you say, Major?"

Carl said, "Sir, are you ordering me to escape with Fannon?"

MacArthur paused in mid-stride. "You're refusing?"

"I won't refuse if it's a direct order," Carl said. "If it's my call, though, then with respect, I think not."

MacArthur was looking seriously pissed. He never did like it when people didn't want to go along with his ideas, and it was obvious that this one meant a lot to him. For a minute I thought he was going to lay into Carl.

But all he said was, "If that's your choice, Major, then I won't make it an order. I must say I'm disappointed," he said very stiffly. "I thought the Marine Corps produced a special breed of men. Apparently I was misinformed."

✯   ✯   ✯

"What the hell?" I said to Carl after MacArthur and Fannon were gone. "You've been talking about escaping ever since we got here. I'd have thought you'd jump at the chance."

"I'm still planning to do it," Carl said. "In fact I ought to do it right now, tonight, before that fool Fannon makes it harder. That's what's going to happen, you know. Even if they don't catch him, and ten gets you one they will, the shit's going to come down big time."

"You don't think his plan will work?"

"Oh, he can get out that way, sure. Anybody could get out of this camp right now. I don't know why he's making such a fancy-ass production of it."

That was true enough. The security at Tarlac was ridiculous; the guard force was inadequate and the physical setup was laughable. The fence around the compound consisted of half a dozen strands of ordinary farm-and-ranch barbed wire that wouldn't have stopped a determined range cow.

"The real problem," Carl said, "is going to be surviving in the mountains and the jungle, and finding friendly locals who won't turn you in for Jap money. And Fannon hasn't got a clue how to do any of that, hasn't even thought it out. If MacArthur had asked me to go alone, all right, but no way in hell am I going to hook up with that asshole. If the Japs didn't kill him I probably would."

He made a face. "But it's going to be a bitch around this place after he makes his try. You'll see. Even Ito warned us we'd all be penalized if anybody tried to escape. God knows what Sakamoto's liable to do."

★   ★   ★

I don't know if MacArthur made any further efforts to find someone to escape with Fallon, but if he did he wasn't successful, because when Fallon went out the following day he went alone. Just as he'd said, he went out in the back of the carabao cart, and sure enough, the guards didn't look.

He wasn't alone when they brought him back, though, two days later, right after roll call. He was surrounded by guards, stumbling along being half carried by a couple of them, while the others encouraged him in various ways, mostly involving their rifle butts and bayonets. His head hung limp on his chest; his eyes appeared to be swollen shut. His feet were bare and bleeding, and his clothes were so ragged he was for all practical purposes naked.

Everyone gathered up near the gate to watch, and for once the guards didn't break it up; probably Sakamoto wanted us to get a good look. There was a certain amount of angry muttering, though not as much as you might think. Life had been very hard in the last couple of days; Sakamoto had handed out mass punishments like Captain Bligh, cutting off the extra food supplies MacArthur had arranged, outlawing any sort of group gathering—even religious services—and conducting a surprise midnight shakedown in which a couple of bad-tempered lieutenants confiscated most of the pitifully few personal possessions we'd been able to hang on to. The guards had turned mean, too, slapping and punching for any reason or none—one of them gave General Wainwright a black eye for not saluting quickly enough; I even got kicked a couple of times myself.

And Colonel Tsuji had been to see Sakamoto again, the next day after the escape. Nobody else knew who he was, though, and I kept my information to myself. I got enough criticism as it was, for being too friendly with Watanabe.

Anyway, a lot of people were pretty annoyed with Fannon, for bringing all this down on us with his half-assed little glory play, and maybe they felt he deserved whatever he got. But you couldn't help feeling sorry for the poor silly son of a bitch, seeing what they'd done to him and wondering what more they were going to do.

We learned the answer soon enough. That afternoon they called a second roll-call formation, and after we had been counted and bowed to His Imperial Japanese Post, Sakamoto came out on the porch of the head-quarters building and delivered a speech. Watanabe stood nearby and shouted the translation:

"Colonel Sakamoto says you were all warned against attempting to escape. He says he attempted to treat you well and deal justly with you. Now you have all had to suffer because of this one stupid man. This is how it is. Anytime one of you does wrong, everyone will pay. This was the first time, so the punishments have been very light. Next time he will not be so lenient.

"Now he wants you to see what awaits those who try to escape."

He turned and said something in Japanese and a lieutenant shouted an order. A moment later a pair of guards came out the door of HQ with Fannon between them. This time there was no question about it; they were carrying him, dead limp, between them. His bare feet dragged helplessly in the dust.

Sakamoto began talking again; Watanabe resumed his translation:

"You think this was done to him by our soldiers when he was captured. In fact this is essentially how he looked when he was found, wandering in circles in the forest. Colonel Sakamoto says this just goes to show that you white men don't belong in this part of the world."

Sakamoto's voice rose higher; he seemed to be working himself up to something. "Now," Watanabe said, "this man is going to pay the penalty for what he did. The same thing will happen to anyone else who tries to escape, or anyone who helps him. The Colonel says you should all be glad this man was captured. Otherwise some of you would have to be punished in his stead."

And while that was sinking in, Watanabe added, "He says that is all. You are dismissed."

Sakamoto turned and stomped back into HQ. While we stood there, too shocked to move, the two guards began dragging Fannon toward the gate. A truck had driven up in front of the compound, with half a dozen armed soldiers in the back.

Carl Norton said softly, "Oh, my God."

The two guards loaded Fannon into the truck, with some help from the soldiers already on board, and then climbed up to join them. The truck pulled away in a cloud of dust and a clatter of badly shifted gears.

Somebody nearby said, "They wouldn't."

Somebody else said, "Yes they would. They're going to."

And a little while later, from somewhere down the road and out of sight, the sound of a volley of rifle fire drifted to us on the afternoon breeze.

*   *   *

"I hope everyone understands," Watanabe said to me the next day. "I hope everyone realizes that Colonel Sakamoto is serious. He is under great pressure, you know. Colonel Tsuji already tried to persuade him to execute the senior generals, on no grounds at all, and then in reprisal for Colonel Fannon's escape. If there is any further pretext—"

He shuddered visibly. For once I didn't doubt his sincerity; he looked genuinely worried. "I think something terrible is going to happen. I hope I'm wrong."

That was the following morning after they shot Fannon. When I got back to the barracks Carl Norton was sitting on his bunk looking through his gear. It wasn't much; like everybody else, he'd lost most of his belongings in the shakedown.

He made a little gesture with one hand, beckoning me closer. I went over and sat down on the bunk beside him and he said in a low voice, "I'm going out tonight."

And, when I started to speak, "Keep it down, okay? I don't think anybody here would rat me out, but the way things are going you never know."

I said, "You can't be serious. Now of all times—"

"Now's the best time. They won't expect anybody to try, this soon after what happened to Fallon. Besides, it's the last night of the dark moon. I've been keeping track."

He looked at the little pile of odds and ends at his feet and sighed. "God damn it, they even took that old beer bottle I found, that I was going to use for a canteen. I had more stuff than this back when I was a kid riding freights during the Depression."

"But you saw what happened to Fallon—"

"Fallon was a silly jackass who didn't know shit. I can take care of myself in the jungle," Carl said. "That's one thing I know how to do. Hell, that's how I got my start in the Corps, back when I was an enlisted man, chasing around Nicaragua with a crazy bastard named Lewis Puller."

"How are you planning to get out? They're strengthening the fence, you know, and posting extra guards."

"No sweat. There's a drainage ditch out back of this barracks, runs past the cook shack, goes right under the fence. They've stuck in some bamboo stakes to try and block it, but nothing I can't get through."

"You do know," I said, "what this is going to mean for the rest of us. If you make it."

"Yeah. I know." He looked at me and shrugged. "What can I say? I'm sorry."

I said, "Does MacArthur know?"

"Oh, sure. I already talked to him about it. He actually apologized for what he said before. Said if I made it he'd see to it I got a medal, after the war. Like I give a shit for that."

"Carl," I said, "there's something you need to know."

I told him what Watanabe had said about Sakamoto and Tsuji. At the end he blew out his breath in an almost-whistle. "Damn. I don't know, then . . . well," he said, "only one thing to do. Take it to the man, see what he says."

MacArthur listened quietly to the whole thing, not interrupting. At the end he nodded. "Thank you, Commander. You did right to come to me with this information. Please let me know if you learn anything more."

Carl said, "General, what about tonight? Do I go or not?"

"Well, of course. Why—oh." MacArthur actually smiled. "You think Colonel Sakamoto might retaliate against me. I am moved by your concern."

He reached out and put a hand on Carl's shoulder. "Don't worry about me, Major. They're not going to do anything to me. Nothing I can't handle, anyway."

Watching his face as he said it, it hit me what he was really saying. I could almost hear it, clear as if I were reading his mind: *Nothing they haven't already done.* And I knew then that it was useless to say any more. Watanabe was right; it was going to happen. If ever a man's fate was written on his face, MacArthur was wearing his. I wondered why I hadn't noticed before.

Carl went out that night, sometime after midnight—I didn't know the exact time; they'd taken my watch in the shakedown—and I stood in the deep shadow of the barracks and watched him go. He moved quickly and silently across the open space and vanished into the ditch.

I couldn't see him any longer, but I continued to watch, trying to estimate his progress, picture it in my mind. By now he should be passing the kitchen . . . only a little farther to the fence . . .

Then I saw the guard.

He wasn't moving in any purposeful way; he was just ambling along in the starlight, a skinny little man with a long rifle slung over his back. He went up to the edge of the ditch, looked quickly around, and began undoing his fly. A moment later I heard the sound of trickling liquid.

I choked down a hysterical urge to cackle, picturing Carl lying in the ditch not daring to move, maybe getting pissed on. But then there was a startled grunt and the guard took a jerky step backward. "*Nan desu ka?*" I heard, and he started to unsling his rifle, while my heart slid down into my stomach and stopped.

And there, by God, was MacArthur! To this day I don't know where he came from; lurking somewhere in the shadows, I guess, like me, watching to see if Carl made it.

He came up behind the guard, moving incredibly fast for a man his age, and piled into him with a shoulder block. For a moment the two dark shapes merged in the dim light, and then MacArthur stepped back and I saw that he had the rifle.

He didn't try to fire it; he just held it by the barrel and forestock with both hands and swung it like a baseball bat at the guard's head. The guard got an arm up in time to take part of the impact—I was certain I heard bone snap—but it still knocked him off his feet. It must have stunned him; he lay on the ground for several seconds before he began to scream.

By the time the other guards got there MacArthur had thrown the rifle away. That was probably the only thing that kept them from killing him on the spot, but it didn't stop the other things they did. Or so I heard; by then I was back inside, in my bunk, trying to look as if I were sleeping, wondering if I ever would again.

And Carl was long gone. They never caught him; he made it to the hills, hooked up with some friendly Filipinos, got a ride south aboard a fishing boat, and eventually became one of the most famous guerrilla leaders on Mindanao—but of course I didn't know anything about that till long after the war.

They did it the following Monday morning. They marched us out onto the parade ground and had us stand in a kind of big hollow square, facing the center, so we could all see.

When they brought MacArthur out he had his hands tied behind his back. He was blindfolded, too; the soldiers on either side of him were holding his upper arms and steering him. Watanabe walked beside them. A young lieutenant I'd never seen before led the way. He was carrying a long sword.

Somebody—I think it was General Bluemel—called sharply, "Atten-*shun*!"

Standing on the HQ porch, Colonel Sakamoto looked around angrily as a hundred-and-some-odd scarecrows snapped to a ragged attention. But he didn't say anything.

The guards led MacArthur to the middle of the square. The lieutenant said something, not loudly, and Watanabe translated, though we couldn't hear the words. MacArthur nodded and started to kneel. He lost his balance and the guards caught him and helped him down, very gently and solicitously.

Everything got very quiet.

MacArthur bowed his head. "Ready when you are, Lieutenant." he said. He didn't raise his voice; he might have been requesting a subordinate to hand him a map. His voice carried in the silence, though, like an organ chord.

The lieutenant took a step forward, raising his sword. He brought it down slowly, turning it to touch

MacArthur's neck with the back of the blade. Then he swung it up again. The steel caught the sun for an instant before it flashed down.

I confess I closed my eyes then; but I heard the sound, and that was enough. And when I opened my eyes again, what they saw was still something no man should ever have to see.

"Such a tragic thing," Watanabe said. "Such a waste."

We were standing near the gate, almost exactly where Carl and I had been standing that morning when they brought MacArthur in. It was late afternoon, almost time for dinner. You'd think no one would have had any appetite after what we'd seen that morning. You'd think that if you'd never been a prisoner of the Japanese.

"Just a little longer," Watanabe said, "and none of this would have happened. They're going to close this camp down, you see. All the senior officers are going to be moved to a camp on the island of Taiwan, which you call Formosa."

He looked off across the now-empty parade ground. They'd spread earth over the stained spot, but you could still see where it had happened.

"And General MacArthur—there were plans for him, because of his high rank. He was to be confined on the mainland of Japan, in a special facility which was being prepared for him. In my own hometown, as it happens." Watanabe looked wistful. "So much better than this place . . . a beautiful city, I think you'd like it. I don't suppose you heard of it."

He cocked his head to one side, seeming to think

of something. "Although—you know, when I was at Princeton, there was a silly little ragtime song the boys used to sing around the piano—"

And he began singing, in a high uneven tenor, the ridiculous words contrasting strangely with the deep sadness on his face:

"Nagasaki, where the fellows chew tobacky,
And the women wicky-wacky-woo!"

I Shall Return

John Mina

Manila, December 8, 1941 3:40 A.M.

Brigadier General Dwight D. Eisenhower was shaken from a deep sleep by a relentless cacophony. He sat up instantly when he realized it was the telephone on the nightstand. "What is it?" he barked, trying to sound more annoyed than alarmed.

"It's the Japs, General!" screamed the reply. "They just hit Pearl Harbor!"

There was a brief pause as the general tried to absorb the full impact. "Spence, is that you? Settle down! Is it confirmed or just another one of those bullshit rumors going around?"

General Spencer B. Akin of the Signal Corps tried to respond with some composure. "It's on the wire service and one of my boys heard it announced on a Los Angeles radio broadcast. Also, Admiral Hart confirms it. Seems the Navy lads knew about this twenty-five minutes ago."

"Christmas! Why is it that when we don't want news to travel it moves faster than a fly towards buttermilk but when there's important information . . . anyway, thanks, Spence. Stay on the horn and keep me posted." He hung up the phone and picked it back up again. "This is General Eisenhower. Put me through to General MacArthur immediately."

About three maddening minutes later he heard a voice on the other end. "Who the hell is this?"

"It's Ike, General. The Japs just hit Pearl."

"Pearl Harbor?" MacArthur exclaimed in astonishment. "But that's our strongest point! They must have gotten their tails whipped!"

"We don't have any damage reports yet. In any case we need to put the men on alert."

"I agree, Ike, but don't initiate anything without my orders."

"No, sir. But I do need to have Doolittle and Patton prepare for possible invasion."

"Just have them put their men on standby. I doubt we'll be attacked. If we go off half-cocked and this turns out that a few Jap reconnaissance planes were shot down over Hawaii we'll be a laughingstock."

Eisenhower's head was swimming as he struggled pulling his pants on. *How the heck did I get into this mess?* he thought. Then he recalled his friend back in DC. "Marshall! When I get home I'll have to kick his butt."

Ike had known the situation here, in the Philippines, for many years as did any of the military personnel who had spent as much time here as he had. They were the obvious strategic target for an ever more aggressive Japanese empire, as most military experts agreed. However, local politics, the distracting behavior of the Germans, and MacArthur's innate ability to alienate everyone in Washington had placed them in a position of almost hopeless vulnerability. Back in '38, he went, on behalf of MacArthur, to Washington to try and drum up support for the Philippines but the emotional climate there had been less than favorable. This was due to the fact that the Filipinos were clamoring for independence. As far as the War Department was concerned, as long as they were pushing for independence, they could "jolly well look after themselves." After a campaign of unsuccessful begging, he finally bought a few planes on his own and returned to Manila.

Then in '39, when the Germans invaded Poland, he had asked, and had been granted a transfer back to Washington. As he worked feverishly to prepare for the inevitable war in Europe, his conscience had been nagged by feelings of guilt over having deserted his friends in the Pacific. In an effort to clear his mind he once again pleaded MacArthur's case to Marshall. "That was my mistake," he muttered to himself as he finished tying his shoes.

To his shock, Marshall had agreed with him. "You're right, Ike. We do need to bolster the Philippines. And you're gonna take charge, personally. I need a workhorse out there, not just grandstanding. Plus, you're the only one that can get around MacArthur's ego. As long as you humor him, he'll give you free reign. You know what to do."

Eisenhower was too stunned to respond. Before he could formulate a tactful refusal, Marshall was standing and giving instructions to his secretary to write out the orders. Of course Marshall was right, but Ike wasn't expecting this sudden change of plans. "I'm going to need some good people, George. I can't go it alone," he shouted as Marshall reached the door.

"Whatever you need, Ike. Just get the job done."

So here he was, getting the job done. Unfortunately he hadn't been given whatever he needed. But he did manage to get a lot more than otherwise would have been sent to MacArthur, as well as George Patton and Jim Doolittle.

He had completed making himself presentable although he knew his appearance would fall well below what MacArthur considered appropriate for a commanding officer. However, he couldn't spare the time for even a shave. He grabbed the sentry and ordered the confused soldier to drive to headquarters.

When the jeep pulled up there were already some officers present, hurriedly trying to straighten their uniforms. *How could everyone know so fast?* he thought. A cup of hot coffee was placed in his hands as he entered the building. "Call a general meeting for all available senior officers in one hour," he commanded to the nearest of his staff.

"Should we order an alert, General?"

"No! No alerts. Not yet," he replied too angrily and went into his office. Before he reached his desk, the phone was ringing. He grabbed the receiver and sat down. "Yes?" he said.

"Is that you, Ike?"

Eisenhower recognized Patton's voice. "Yes, George. Where are you?"

"Where the hell do you think I am? I'm in bed. What the hell's going on? I got a call from my chief of staff who says the whole place is buzzing. Is there some kind of fire or something?"

"The Japs just hit Pearl. That's the word. Could be a hoax but I'm not taking any chances. Get down here as soon as you can."

"Jesus Christ! I'll be right over. Don't start the war without me!"

Five minutes later Eisenhower was on the line with Colonel James Doolittle. "Jimmy, have you heard?"

"Sure have, Ike. Is it real?"

"Don't know yet but I don't want us to get caught with our pants down. I want you to send up some reconnaissance."

"Already ahead of you. I've got my boys on rotating patrol covering the ocean in a hundred-mile radius doubling up from here to Formosa. Of course we're spread pretty thin. We're using every available plane, even those damn Buffaloes. I'd have another fifteen fighters ready if we had the goddamn spare parts!"

"I know, I know. They've been promising us the moon . . ."

" . . . And don't even send us moonshine. We have to make our own."

"Well, whatever we have now is all there is. We have to make due. What about the bombers?"

"Most of them can be ready to fly in a few hours," Doolittle replied.

"I mean what about their safety? What if the Jap fighters slip through?"

"Not likely. Just in case, do you want to move them to Del Monte field?"

"What do you think?"

"I'll move them. I'll be at Clark if you need me."

By the time Patton arrived, Eisenhower had finished briefing his senior officers. "Good to see you, George."

"What's the scuttlebutt? Did they hit or not?"

"I just had a screaming match with Admiral Hart. The louse got word from his buddy Kimmel in Honolulu. Then he just sat on the information."

"Those swabbos can be real assholes. So it's for real?" Patton was leaning forward in his seat.

"I think this is it. There was definitely an attack of some sort but we don't know too many details. Hart thinks we got creamed but MacArthur called me and said he heard that the Japanese had suffered a setback. He said he heard it from the War Plans Division."

"Well, whatever the outcome, the bastards attacked us. I'll mobilize right away. Any news from the fly-boys?"

"Hold off on mobilizing, George. The Old Soldier doesn't want us to do anything the Japs might consider 'overtly hostile.' It seems that he's getting a lot of pressure from the local governor to keep the Philippines neutral and MacArthur doesn't think the Japs will attack us, but if we become too aggressive he thinks we might force them to."

"Christ Almighty! They just bombed the shit out of an American city. Sounds pretty damn 'overt' to me. What the hell's he waiting for; some Nip to blow up his garden? Let that little shit of a governor squawk. Who do you think he'll come whining to if there is an invasion?" Patton was now pacing furiously.

"Settle down, old friend, I agree. But there's a lot we can still do without directly violating orders. We can call it a drill or maneuvers. Get everyone ready to move and start sending detachments north. If they hit us, that's the direction they'll come from. Just try to keep it low-key."

Patton stopped and thought, then smiled to his commander. "Low-key it is," he said and without another word was out the door.

About an hour later Doolittle was back on the line. "I just got a call from Hap Arnold. We did get hit at Pearl pretty bad."

"Any more details? What about orders?" Eisenhower was hoping for a green light from Washington.

"No details. He just said, 'Step up patrols and move the bombers south,' and I said, 'Yes, sir. Good idea. Thank you, sir.'"

"You know, Jimmy, you can be a real—"

"I know. All my friends tell me that. So what now?"

"Anything in from your men in the air?"

"Still too dark. But the sun will be up in about an hour. By then I'll have a squad over Takao Harbor."

It was only forty minutes later when Doolittle reported back. "Reports are coming in, Ike! Seems Formosa's fogged in but there's a shitload of Jap troop transports heading our way. There's also been a few skirmishes with enemy fighters that are probably from carriers. We lost some planes, General."

"Damn! Get all the B-17s that are already fitted

out in the air as soon as possible. I don't care what MacArthur says now. We're moving. Got it?"

"Yes, sir. It should take about an hour and a half."

Eisenhower called MacArthur but was told that the general was in a meeting with the Filipino governor.

Patton was next on his list and, fortunately, was easier to reach.

"To heck with low-key, George. There's an invasion force on the way, most likely headed for Lingayen Gulf."

"I'm glad you said to drop the 'low-key,' Ike, because the whole island is buzzing like a hornet's nest. The locals are all heading south in droves and there have even been some reports of looting. So far the Filipino soldiers are sticking around but we'll see what happens when the shit starts to fly."

"What's the armor status?"

"Crappy. As you know, the five Grants they sent keep bogging down in the soft ground so they're pretty useless anywhere but the roads. Of the twenty-six Stuarts, we've had to cannibalize three for parts and another five are off-line until the goddamn parts come in. I wouldn't hold my breath. One platoon is too far south to do us any good. That leaves us with fourteen to try to repel a full-scale invasion."

"How about infantry?"

"We should be able to bring up about thirty-five hundred of our boys and two thousand locals."

"Why so few Filipinos?"

"Listen, Ike. I had to go through about twenty for every one that I kept. For one thing, they speak about a hundred different languages. And most of them just don't get it. I'd rather have a thousand soldiers than a hundred thousand pack bearers."

"What are your thoughts?"

"I think the Old Soldier is right. Looks like the bastards will hit the beaches at Lingayen. He's also right about stopping the Japs there. Once they get a beachhead they'll go through the rest of the island like crap through a goose. I'm moving out right away along with my men. Wanna come?"

"Actually I do plan on moving my headquarters north. What are our chances of stopping them?"

"I can't make any promises, Ike. But I will tell you that our boys won't run until they get the order. They're damn good men, every one of them, and the Japs are gonna have to pay a lot of blood for beachfront property."

It was ten o'clock before General Eisenhower got a call back from MacArthur. "This is Eisenhower, General. Do you have any more updates?"

"What the hell's going on, Eisenhower? My aides tell me the whole island is in an uproar. I told you not to sound an alert! You may have just single-handedly brought this whole country into the war."

Ike knew he was getting bawled out in that unnerving way his superior had of screaming without raising his voice. "But, General, the enemy is attacking. We've already lost some planes!"

"You think I don't know what's going on? You think I'm just sitting here sipping tea? Of course we lost some planes. That hot dog Doolittle sent our boys buzzing over their base like a swarm of bees. You think the Japanese aren't going to react? That act of his may have been enough to incite the enemy to attack. I'll have his hide when things settle down!"

"But, General. There have been reports that an invasion force is crossing the strait."

"Listen, Eisenhower. We don't know what's going on. It could be maneuvers or routine patrols. It would not be in the interest of the Japanese to invade here. I want you to prepare all air and ground defenses only. Do *not* bomb their bases on Formosa. That's an order, General. Do you read me?"

"Yes, General. But . . ." He heard the click of the receiver being slammed down. Ike cursed silently. Immediately, the phone rang again. Eisenhower quickly picked it up. "We must have been cut off, General MacArthur. I was going to ask . . ."

"Hold on, Ike. It's Jimmy. You sound like you've been getting your ass chewed!"

"That's an understatement. We've been ordered not to bomb Formosa. Can you believe that?"

"That's not gonna be a problem, Ike." Doolittle's voice was on the edge of hysteria. "From the reports my boys have been sending in we're in no position to attack their bases. The fog cleared and ever since, their airfields have been busier than a two-peckered goat. Our pilots claim the skies are black with Jap planes. I'm sure some formations are being reported more than once but from what we can figure, there's probably a couple hundred planes on the way. Sounds like an equal mix of bombers and fighters. Our patrols have been ordered to get the hell out of there and prepare to defend our coasts."

"What about our bombers?"

"All but three B-17s are in the air. It took longer

than I promised but most are loaded with bombs and waiting for orders. The three on the ground are gonna stay there because we don't have the parts to make 'em fly, dammit."

"I'm afraid all we can do is order the flying ones to safer fields in the south while the Japs tear up whatever is in their range. Let's get every fighter armed and airborne, Jimmy. We can't stop them but at least we'll make sure they don't have a cakewalk."

"Listen, Ike. If we just sit here and wait the whole country will be overrun in no time. We've gotta try and stop the invasion force."

"I agree, but how the heck are we going to do it? Patton doesn't have enough men and tanks to do more than slow them down for a little while. I'm afraid we have to start getting ready to pull out."

"You know this position is the key to the Pacific. We have to hold out at all costs."

"You have a suggestion?"

"Well. We do have the bombers."

"I told you. We can't touch Formosa."

"We don't have to. What about hitting their ships?"

Eisenhower paused for a few seconds. "You're talking about using B-17s to attack troop transports. Can that be done?"

"Why not? We'll have to come in real low, maybe fifty feet, and most will miss, but if any hit . . ."

"Their fighters will be all over us."

"I didn't say it would be a free ride, Ike. I don't know how many of ours will make it back. But what else can we do?"

"I don't know. It's a pretty big sacrifice."

"I'll take that as a yes. And listen, Ike. I'm going

up to direct the whole thing personally. I'll take my own squadron as part of the escort. If it looks too hopeless I'll call the whole thing off."

"Carry on, Jim. And may God watch over you."

Colonel James Doolittle eased up on the throttle of his personally modified racing P-38 and signaled for the other eleven planes in his squadron to do the same. He was anxious to try the new planes in combat. Because of his aviation record he managed to get the first dozen P-38s made for himself and his hand-picked squadron. The rest of his fighter pilots had to fly the P-40s except for the poor bastards stuck with the P-36s. Below the sparse cloud ceiling he could see the entire Jap transport fleet. He picked up the radio transmitter to contact the lead bomber pilot. "Eggbeater. This is Thunderbird One. Over."

A clear voice responded. "I got you, Thunderbird. Any luck?"

"I'll say. The whole school of fish! Their position is about twenty-three miles from you at heading one-four-niner. No sign of mosquitoes yet but I know they're out there. Signal the others to begin their approach. And be prepared to abort if things get too hot."

"Yeah, sure thing. We'll just fly home, sit in the cabana and guzzle beer, while the doughboys get plastered all over the beach."

"Just keep an ear open for my orders, smartass."

Doolittle held his squadron back, not wanting to alert the enemy before the bombers came into view. It wasn't long before he could see them down below, diving even lower. "All right, boys. It's off to the races!

Thunderbird Seven through Twelve, break right. The rest, follow me." With that, he pressed the throttle and sped toward the fleet.

It wasn't long before the action started. The excited voice on the radio squealed out, "Thunderbird One. This is Thunderbird Seven. Looks like about six mosquitoes heading right for our bombers."

Doolittle responded with a calm voice. "We'll get 'em Thunderbird Seven. You just keep your eyes peeled for the main flock. Now that we've been spotted they'll be showing up any minute." He wobbled his plane to signal the rest of the squadron, then put it into a power dive heading straight for the lead enemy fighter.

Four minutes later he was circling to gain altitude. He tried not to feel too invincible as he watched the last Jap plane crash into the sea. "Thunderbird Seven. This is Thunderbird One. Enemy planes have been neutralized."

"This is Thunderbird Seven. You guys could have left some for the rest of us. Hoooweee, they sure do burn bright when they catch fire!"

"Don't worry, Thunderbird Seven. That was just a scouting patrol. There'll soon be plenty for everybody. Just keep your eyes . . . holy shit!"

Doolittle could see two large groups of Japanese fighters coming in low from the north. "All pilots. This is Thunderbird One. We got about forty Zeros coming in. Try to stay in formation but from here on we're pretty much on our own. Protect the bombers! Let's go!"

The first group of enemy fighters dove for the bombers while the rest broke into smaller groups to attack the American fighter escort. He ignored the second group and dove straight for the first. He intercepted them just before they hit the lead B-17. A short burst from his guns started a Zero smoking; he pulled up fast to avoid a pair of enemies on his tail. He would have been a goner but at the speed he was traveling he quickly outpaced them.

Doolittle turned his plane and saw the first two B-17s being swarmed by Japanese planes. One of the American bombers already belched thick black smoke from one of the engines. He did a quick barrel roll to the right to elude the new fighters on his tail and swooped right into the thick of the fray, taking care to stay out of range of the bomber's tail gunner. He sent another Zero plummeting toward the ocean before he was able to catch his breath and assess the battle.

His fighters seemed to be doing okay so far. Although they were badly outnumbered most of the Jap fighters were concentrating on the B-17s. Of course the Zeros going up against his squadron were shocked at the speed and maneuverability of his expert flyers. The American bombers were also knocking down a few enemy planes but, for the most part, were getting hammered. At least two were down and two more were in trouble. But they were making their final runs now and it looked like most would get to drop their loads.

He gunned his engine and raced to protect the lead B-17. He shot down another Zero but three more closed in and the bomber exploded. Doolittle watched the next well-escorted B-17 drop its bombs. Great geysers erupted in front of the Jap troop ship but it remained undamaged. "Dammit!" he cursed. Then, as he watched the bomber begin to regain altitude, he realized what had to be done.

He screamed into the radio, "All Thunderbird and Blue fighters. This is Thunderbird One. Cease escort after the birds lay their eggs. Repeat. Protect only loaded bombers!"

"Jesus Christ, Colonel! Do you know what you're saying?" came an unidentified voice.

"Just do it!" He turned his plane around and headed for the B-17s that were still making their bomb run. He could see some of the Jap fighters going for the now unescorted American bombers. He knew they wouldn't be able to resist.

A series of loud explosions drew his attention downward and he saw a troop ship break in half. The dogfights were still furious but, with a number of the enemy drawn off, the odds were a lot more even. Again and again bombers were able to score hits which were always kills on the light transports. Doolittle watched in horror as a dying B-17, hounded by Zeros, made a lumbering turn and crashed right into an enemy ship.

The colonel downed another plane before the last B-17 dropped its load, scoring a direct hit, instantly demolishing a troop ship. "All planes back to base!" he screamed into the transmitter. "All Blues and Thunderbirds. Cover bombers. Come on boys, let's discourage them from chasing us." He then led a savage attack on the Zeros continuing to harass the bombers. *Oh, Christ!* he thought as he scanned the sky and counted the few survivors.

☆   ☆   ☆

General Eisenhower paid no attention to the bouncing jeep as his driver negotiated the potholes. He welcomed any distraction to keep his mind off Doolittle's suicide run. When they approached the next checkpoint he could see a sergeant waving him down and his heart started pounding.

"Message for General Eisenhower."

Five minutes later he was on the phone. "Jimmy. This is Ike. Thank God you made it!"

"Yeah," came the somber reply. "But I don't have a lot of company."

"And the mission?"

"I think we knocked out about half their troops. There were a lot of smoking wrecks in the ocean when we left, Ike, but they weren't all ships."

"Well done, Colonel," Eisenhower offered.

"You might not think so when you hear the bill."

There was a brief pause. "How bad?"

"We lost fourteen fighters. Most of the P-40s from Blue squadron. But we downed between thirty and thirty-five fighters."

"And the bombers?"

Now Doolittle paused. "The B-17s took eighty percent casualties, General."

"Dear God," came Eisenhower's reply.

The pilot continued. "I take full responsibility. I ordered the fighters to protect the planes that hadn't unloaded."

"You did what you had to do to get the job done, Jim."

"But was it enough?"

"We'll know by tomorrow. Things have been pretty hectic here while you were gone."

"I heard. Reports are still coming in."

"Bring me up to date. I've been on the road," the general said as he took out his pen.

"Most of our fighters accounted well for themselves, Ike. Except the poor bastards in those worthless Buffaloes. They went down faster than the Hindenburg. Overall we lost about twenty-five planes that were defending the island. Plus the three grounded B-17s. But we dropped over forty of their bombers and at least a dozen more Zeros. The Jap pilots must have had a few mixups. Probably because they had so many targets. Whatever the reason, some of their bomber squadrons had no escorts and we just slaughtered them. Also, those antiaircraft batteries you let me install at the airfields were pretty effective."

"And the airfields?"

"Pretty chopped up. There's only two runways still operational for fifty miles. We'll have at least two more cleared in about forty-eight hours. But Clark is just a big trashpile. Also, there are dozens of buildings and installations burning. I'll tell you, Ike. First chance I get, I'm gonna take every plane I can get my hands on and bomb the hell out of Tokyo!"

"You do that and you'll have me cheering loudest, Jimmy. Salvage what you can and keep the remaining fighters ready for additional attacks. If the Japs are following through with their invasion the assault should start in about thirty-six hours. And . . . thanks."

"Yeah. Sure. Anytime, General," came the dejected response.

It was 2:00 P.M. the next day before Eisenhower finally met up again with Patton. He returned the salute, then shook his hand. "How's it going, George? You look like hell."

"Well that's a damn shame, Ike, because I was planning on entering a beauty contest tonight."

"What have you got for me?"

"Assuming they land where their planes hit the hardest, we should be in good shape. As long as they don't attack us with more than half a dozen old ladies."

"That bad?"

"Not quite. But most of the roads to the supply depots are torn to hell. A lot of our shit has to be brought up on foot and oxcart. Is it too late to get those hundred thousand pack bearers I turned down earlier?"

"What about the defenses, George? What are we looking at?"

"Of course everything depends on where they hit and how many there are. But I think we'll be able to give them a run for their money. The tanks will help a lot. We lost some Grants to the Jap bombers, but the Stuarts all made it, being able to go off-road. By the time the Japs hit, I'll have men and tanks spread out far enough to cover the main area but close enough to support each other. Plus I'm holding back some reserves to cover any breach in the front line. Any chance of the Navy pitching in?"

"No chance at all. They're getting harassed by a small carrier group and MacArthur wants them to stay in the south in case we have to abandon the Philippines."

"Figures. How about some cards?"

December 11, 1941

Eisenhower stood up in the makeshift sandbag bunker and watched the approaching enemy ships through his binoculars. An aide had come to wake him up at dawn that morning but he was already awake, fully dressed, and finishing his second cup of coffee. "Enemy ships approaching, General," was the awaited announcement that set the day in motion.

Now it was two hours later and he was about to witness the invasion. His staff pleaded with him to make his headquarters in a safer spot but he refused. "I'm not going to sit blind in the bushes and try to guess the outcome." So here he was, gazing out over the beautiful Gulf of Lingayen. A spot he had enjoyed picnicking at years before. The American light artillery pieces had already started taking ranging shots. Enemy plane activity was surprisingly light. *No time to wonder about it now*, he thought as he focused in on the ships. So many. *Thank God half were destroyed or we wouldn't stand a chance. But do we?* He looked around and the heavy vegetation gave the impression that only a handful of defenders prepared to meet the assault.

He watched the ships spread out and slowly form two lines facing the shore, coordinating to hit all points at once in two waves. "They seem pretty organized," he commented to his aide, who nodded in agreement.

Once they formed up they began heading toward the beaches at full throttle. That's when Eisenhower noticed the planes. Enemy fighters started strafing runs while two squadrons of bombers held back, waiting for the defenses to reveal themselves. He heard the sharp reports of the tanks opening up on the approaching vessels, saw the splash of the near misses and the bursts of the hits as they ripped through the hulls.

He watched the lead ships ground themselves and the troops pouring over the side. One ship must have hit a reef in deep water because the soldiers jumping in were over their heads. Some were swimming, many never came up. The defending machine guns were now in full swing, mowing down men as they approached the beach. My God, what a slaughter, he was about to exclaim when the world around him erupted.

The next thing he knew he was lying on his back trying to rub sand out of his eyes. He was aware of a heavy weight being lifted off his chest, then saw the bloody, lifeless face of his aide.

"General! Are you hurt?" cried a voice.

"I don't think so. Somebody get me a canteen so I can wash my eyes out. What the heck hit us?"

"Jap bombers. They're pounding the shit out of our defenses."

Eisenhower managed to clear his eyes enough to look around and assess the situation. Heavy attacks from the air had subdued the defenders enough for the enemy soldiers to establish multiple beachheads. While still taking heavy casualties, the enemy was slowly, successfully advancing and his own men were forced to pull back. He saw the smoking wreck of a tank a few hundred yards down the beach. "Get me Patton on the phone!" he screamed to no one in particular.

"George," he yelled into the field receiver. "They're breaking through. We need to counterattack!"

"Jesus Christ, Ike. I'm not just picking my ass. I

know what's going on. I've already got the reserves on the move. You just watch the show and let me do the generaling. That's what you brought me here for, remember?" He abruptly hung up.

Sure enough, the jungle behind him came alive. A Stuart tank raced up, spraying the enemy with machine-gun fire to deadly effect. Dozens of Japanese fell less than a hundred yards in front of him. Behind the tank came American GIs; their youthful faces displaying grim determination. He saw a screaming group of Filipino soldiers charge right into the enemy line. The ferocity of the counterattack first staggered, then stopped the advancing line of the invaders. Eisenhower was beginning to cheer as the enemy broke and raced back toward the water, then noticed the other squadron of Japanese bombers closing in. At the same time, the second wave of infantry was massing on the beach, preparing to finish off whatever was left after the bombs hit.

Again he managed to get Patton on the line. "More bombers, George!"

"I see."

"What are our chances? Any more reserves?"

"I think we're screwed, Ike. Anything that can do more than spit is on our front line and the bombers are about to plaster us."

"Do we retreat?"

The roar of the first bombs exploding confirmed Patton's reply. "Too late, Ike."

General Eisenhower stood paralyzed as he watched the earth-shaking explosions getting closer. Then a blast of a different type of explosion drew him out of his trance and he glanced curiously upward in the direction of the new sound. There he saw a Jappanese bomber burning as it plummeted toward the sea, trailing great gouts of black smoke. Then he noticed two more enemy planes going down.

"Ike! You still there?"

Eisenhower had forgotten to hang up the field phone. "Yeah, George. What the heck . . . ?"

"It's Doolittle! That crazy bastard and the rest of his squadron are taking on the whole Jap air force. And you know what? They're winning!"

Ike could see the small P-38s buzzing around the enemy bombers with Zeros hot on their tails. There were still some bombs falling but most had been neutralized. Just as the last attacking bomber exploded in the jungle to his left, a single P-38, flying about thirty feet off the ground, strafed the invading infantry along the entire beachfront. It then disappeared over the jungle before the three pursuing Zeros could close.

The inspired allies responded as if it were a signal and advanced, pinning down the Japanese soldiers; turning attackers into defenders. From where he stood, Eisenhower watched pockets of desperate invaders try to charge up the beach but all were killed or driven back. At last the remaining attackers began to lay down their arms. First in small groups, then whole platoons. He heaved a great sigh as he realized that the invasion had been repulsed.

December 25, 1941

General Eisenhower glanced out the window of his personal car then gave a cynical smile to General

Patton, who had just gotten in and sat down next to him. "Merry Christmas, George. Wouldn't you just know it: perfect weather! I think MacArthur must have a direct line to God."

"That's one school of thought, Ike," Patton replied. "Personally, I think his master comes from the other direction. Though, if you spend enough time around him you get the feeling God takes orders from him. Merry Christmas to you, too."

"Congratulations on your promotion. We're gonna miss you around here."

"Thanks. I'll miss you and the guys but not these jungles. No place for tanks."

"You did all right, George, jungle and all. It's not so bad here."

"No. I suppose you're right, Ike. Could be worse. At least it's not the Sahara Desert. 'Course, it doesn't really matter how I feel, I'm bound for Europe either way. Wish you were coming, too. Helluva thing. I'm not surprised about MacArthur taking and getting all the credit . . ."

Eisenhower laughed, "Not surprised? C'mon, George. We'd have all been shocked if he didn't!"

"Sure would. But why in the hell is he playing me up so much? You and Jimmy did most of it."

"Don't kid yourself. You did plenty. The Old Soldier knows he'll need you right there with him when he goes up against the Germans in Europe. That's where the real war is going to be. That's where they're gonna need a tank commander." Eisenhower paused and sized up his friend. "You know, George, you're a hero now. Everything you do will make the news back home. Try not to slap any more soldiers."

Patton laughed defiantly. "I don't give a shit about any goddamn reporters. I'll train the men the way I want to." Then he met Eisenhower's gaze and gave him a comradely smile. "You know, Ike, you'd be going with me to fight the Germans instead of MacArthur if you hadn't left Washington to come back here."

Ike looked at the surrounding countryside that he had come to love so much and drew a deep breath. "Yeah, but then what would have happened here to these good people?"

"I don't even want to think about it," Patton answered, then sat straight up and looked out the front of the car. "Holy shit! Is the circus in town?"

Eisenhower again smiled and shook his head as he stared at the scene they were about to join. There were hundreds of soldiers, American and Filipino, wearing their dress uniforms and standing at attention. There had to be thousands of locals waving American flags and holding up MacArthur banners. Some were cheering and many, weeping. On a raised platform stood MacArthur himself, surrounded by reporters and cameras. There was a band playing but it was being drowned out by the crowd.

After the speech and ceremonial "passing of the reins" to Eisenhower, MacArthur waved to the screaming crowd, descended the steps, and climbed into a waiting car. Just before the door closed, Ike looked him in the eye and asked, "Think you'll be back, General?"

After a brief pause to look around, the response came quietly, "Not even if Hitler makes this his summer home."

☆   ☆   ☆

Admiral Isoroku Yamamoto glared disapprovingly at the younger officer who had directed the invasion of the Philippines. "You bring me news of this failure after such a great success in Pearl Harbor? You should be filled with shame. The enemy forces were so much greater in Hawaii than those that you faced, yet our victory there was beyond our greatest hopes. And you, facing resistance less than your own numbers, dare to tell me of your defeat?"

"We accomplished much to weaken them, my admiral. It was not a complete failure."

"And we lost even more!" screamed Yamamoto.

"We also learned a great deal from our attack."

"Oh? So what do you now suggest?"

"To take what we learned and use it effectively. I made a vow on the blood of my ancestors."

"A vow?" The admiral looked thoughtfully at his officer. "Tell me this vow."

As we left the island, I looked back and swore: "I shall return."

Shock and Awe

Harry Turtledove

The lowlands are soft. The hills are hard. The rule is as old as time. The lowlands yield. The hills resist. So it has ever been. The lowlands welcome. The hills shun. So it will always be.

And when the soft lowlands yield and welcome, the hard hills have to punish. For the hills and the lowlands are locked together in unbreakable embrace; they are two halves of one flesh, even if the lowlands have a wandering eye.

Down came the raiders to burn and to steal and to scourge out those who had been welcomed and to chastise the faithless ones who had welcomed them. The lowlands had cozied up to the latest conquerors.

The hills raised up the latest rebel chieftain to try to push them into the sea.

When he had made a scourge of small cords, he drove them all out of the temple. The garrison soldiers tried to take him then. They discovered, as others had before them and yet others would in centuries still to come, that the only thing worse than not trying is trying and failing. He rose against them, and his followers with him, and tried to drown the lowlands in blood.

Lowlanders knew what to do in times like those. It was not as if they had not seen them before. The rich and the accommodating fled their farms and took refuge in the cities, where the conquerors they had been accommodating would protect them from their unloving upcountry cousins. For the conquerors needed collaborators—almost—as much as collaborators needed the conquerors. This too is a rule oft seen in other lands and other times.

Some of the rich—fewer of the accommodating—did not run fast enough. Few crimes are worse than bad timing, and few more harshly punished. How the hillmen howled! "Generation of vipers!" they cried. "Who warned you to flee from the wrath to come! Repent, you—for the kingdom of heaven is at hand!"

And they sent those they caught to heaven, or wherever they went, with the sword and the axe and the rope and such other tools as an aroused ingenuity might suggest. And their chieftain looked at what they had done, and he saw that it was good. "Follow me," he said, "and I will make you reapers of men."

They howled louder and harder after that. They reaped men and burned fields and vineyards and cut down olive groves. "Now also is the axe laid unto the root of the trees!" they cried. "Thus every tree which does not bring forth good fruit is hewn down, and cast into the fire."

Trees were not all that went into the fire. So did many of the rich, and their wives, and their mistresses, and their children—legitimate and otherwise. "Happy shall he be," sang the hillmen, "who takes and dashes your little ones against the stones." By that measure, many hillmen were happy indeed.

They came down on a city, there in the plain. It was closed against them, of course. Its walls rose up five or six times as tall as a man. Up at the top of them, the defenders pointed out at the ragtag and bobtail force that presumed to stand against *them*, the greatest power in the world. Some of the defenders laughed. And why would they not? Those walls were thick as well as tall. The hillmen had no siege train. A siege train was the mark of a civilized army, not hairy, unwashed, circumcised barbarians.

The rebel leader—the Son of God, some of his fanatics named him in their madness and arrogance— called up to them, "Judge not, lest you be judged." Hardly any of them understood him. He spoke only the guttural local language, not the civilized tongues, the tongues of the West. If he grunted and brayed like that, how could anything he had to say possibly matter? Even the handful who could follow his worthless jargon laughed at his presumption.

A few of his men, wild with rage, tried to storm the frowning walls. The defenders' weapons smashed them. They were brave. Indeed, they were wild to give up their lives for the greater glory of their leader's

Father. But courage would take even the bravest men only so far. It would not take them to the top of that wall.

He called them back. "I came not with peace but with a sword," he told them, and he drew one, and he brandished it. "He that is not with me is against me. For we wrestle not with flesh and blood, but against principalities, against powers, against the rulers of the darkness of this world. Take to yourselves the whole armor of God so that you may be able to withstand them in the evil day."

"How shall we go up?" they cried.

"Many that are first shall be last, and the last shall be first," he replied, and added, "Narrow is the way, and few there are that find it." And he met with his twelve chief followers, and they talked till after the sun went down.

Everything was quiet in the night. When day came again, the hillmen raged against the city—raged against it and were beaten back. Quiet returned on the second night. On the third day, the rebels once more surged like a restless sea. On the third night, quiet came again—and the defenders relaxed something of their vigilance. Quietly still, hillmen thrust stakes in between the stones of the wall, and used the ladders they thus made to mount to the very top.

Yes, on the third night they were risen, and they gained the wall, and they gained the city, and great was the slaughter therein. "This is the day the Lord has made!" they cried, and they killed the defenders, and they killed the collaborators, and they killed anyone else who happened to get in their way, and they put the place to the torch. And then, with a shout of, "He has scattered the proud in the imagination of their hearts. He has put down the meat from their seats, and exalted those of low degree," they—and the Son of God—melted back into the hills.

The transport made its slow way into the harbor. Gulls wheeled overhead, skrawking for a handout. More transports followed the first. Warships flanked them, ready to pounce in case fanatics in small boats tried to hurl fire into them, killing at the cost of their own lives.

On the deck of the lead transport, Marcus looked ahead with interest. The green plains seemed reasonably familiar. The forbidding brown hills beyond them? No. Marcus had joined the army when he turned eighteen. It was that or spend the rest of his days staring at the north end of a southbound mule. He was still a good-natured, smiling kid . . . unless you happened to be the enemy, in which case you were in more trouble than you knew what to do with.

One of his buddies bumped up against him. "Watch where you're putting your big, smelly feet, Lucius," he said.

Lucius told him something that had to do with his mother. Lucius had got a girl in trouble, and gone into the army instead of facing her father. He was short and stocky, where Marcus had half a head on him and was on the lean side. Apart from their build, they both could have been stamped from the same tough mold. Lucius looked out toward the hills, too. "It's not much like Europe, is it?" he remarked.

"Gee, no shit," Marcus said. The two of them laughed again. Why not? They were young, they were strong, they were well trained, they had the best equipment in the world, and they were confident nobody but nobody could measure up to them. Considering the imperial reach, they had a point. Marcus added, "I was just thinking the same thing. Different kind of country."

"At least the sun's out," Lucius said. "That's something, anyway. When we were in Germany, you wouldn't see it for days at a time."

"We'll see it here, all right. We won't be so glad to see it when we're on the march, either." But Marcus laughed one more time—he really was a happy-go-lucky fellow. "We've been doing this for a little while now. We can complain no matter what the weather's like."

Thud! A gangplank smacked down onto the quay. Marcus slung his pack on his back, shouldered his weapon, and tramped down onto solid ground. After so long at sea, terra firma felt as if it were shifting under his feet. "Come on! Come on! Come on!" his company commander shouted. "Form up, then head for the market square. Once we're all there, the general will tell us everything we need to know." Quintus had been in the army a long time. His bass rasp said he'd seen and done everything. It also said nothing had been able to kill him yet, and he didn't think anything he ran into ever would be able to.

The soldiers roared out a dirty marching song as they quick-timed it to the square. Bearded locals in long, funny-looking robes gaped at them as they went by. The locals muttered to one another in their incomprehensible language. Even their writing looked peculiar to Marcus: strange squiggles that could have said anything. He'd heard the letters ran from right to left instead of from left to right. He didn't know, and didn't much care; he couldn't have read them either way.

None of the locals did anything more than murmur. Nobody shouted an insult in a language the soldiers could understand. Nobody threw a stone or tried to mix it up with the troops, either. Keeping a low profile was sensible of the locals. You didn't want to mix it up with people with body armor and the finest weapons and training in the world, not if you wanted to go on breathing you didn't.

Marcus had heard that some of the locals didn't care whether they lived or died, as long as they could take out their enemies as they went. He'd heard it, but he didn't believe it. You could say that, but meaning it once you got out on the battlefield was a different story.

That fierce sun beat down. He took a swig from his canteen, which held a mix of water and wine. When he got to the market square, he wondered if it would be big enough to hold all his buddies. He shrugged, and his body armor clattered about him. That wasn't his worry. He took his place, his company took its, and more and more units took theirs.

The general strode forward and stood on the rostrum. "Men, we are going to disarm and pacify this country," he said, pitching his voice to carry. He knew his business; he had no trouble making himself heard all over the square. He went on, "The fanatics here have given us too much trouble for too long. We are going to root them out this time. They don't respect Western values. They've made that very plain. They think their god and this so-called Son of God count for more, and they can do whatever they please as long as it fits in with their religion. They think they'll get a happy afterlife on account of it. What *I* think is, they'll change their way of thinking pretty quick if we send enough of 'em to the afterlife. So that's what we're going to do. Have you got it?"

"Yes, sir!" Marcus shouted along with the thousands of other young men who'd come from the West to restore order to this miserable place that kept flouting the authority of the strongest nation in the world.

"Are those wild-eyed maniacs going to stop us?" the general inquired.

"No, sir!" Again, the shout from Marcus and his comrades filled the square and echoed from the walls.

"All right, then." The general made his smile extra broad, so all the soldiers could see it. "These people are going to find out they don't know who they're messing with. Isn't *that* right?" The roar of agreement that went up then dwarfed the other two.

Word soon reached the hillmen that the Western soldiers were coming after them. The rebels had spies and sympathizers everywhere. One of the invaders couldn't step off the road and squat behind a bush without their knowing about it right away. But knowing about it and knowing what to do about it were two different things.

One of the rebel chieftain's most trusted counselors was a man they called the Rock. "We ought to just disappear for a while," he said as the rebels' leaders squatted around a campfire. "Take off our helmets, throw away our weapons, vanish into the country-side. All they'll see when they get here is a bunch of farmers digging up weeds and trimming vines and pruning olive trees. How can they fight a war if there's nobody to fight?"

Several others from among the twelve nodded. The Rock was a practical man, a reasonable man. He'd given practical, reasonable advice.

But, as their chieftain saw it, they were not in a practical, reasonable situation. They were in a war. When men went to war, they threw practicality and reason on the rubbish heap first thing. Shaking his head, the chieftain said, "I told you before—I come not to send peace, but a sword. He that finds his life shall lose it: and he that loses his life for my sake shall find it."

The Rock exhaled heavily. "I am not sure this is a good idea. I am far from sure it's a good idea."

"Is it not lawful for me to do what I want with my own?" the chieftain demanded, growing angry in his turn. "You will hear of wars and rumors of wars—see that you are not troubled, for all these things must happen. And, I remind you again, he that is not with me is against me." He fixed the Rock with a stare of messianic intensity.

Against that stare, even the stalwart Rock had no defense. He bowed his head, murmuring, "Your will be done."

His will was done. The hillmen gathered. To the Son of God, their numbers seemed as far beyond counting as the grains of sand by the sea. "Though I walk through the valley of the shadow of death, I will fear no evil," they sang, "for you are with me." The Son of God inclined his head. The hillmen marched.

☆   ☆   ☆

Some of Marcus' buddies grumbled as they moved toward battle. He didn't mind getting there. Most of the time, he just stopped thinking about anything in particular and let his feet do the work. That way, the miles unreeled behind him, and he hardly even noticed they were gone.

Every so often, he had to cough. So many men and animals and vehicles on the move kicked up an ungodly amount of dust. He couldn't keep it out of his eyes, either. It was just one of the things you had to put up with.

Mobile troops and scouts went ahead to make sure the main body of the army didn't run into any nasty surprises. Then came a division to back them up in case they found trouble, the vehicles and the artillery, the high command and the rest of the supply train, the main body of the army, and the rear guards—more mobile forces, also stiffened by heavy infantry.

Trouble didn't take long to come. The locals thought they could shoot at the advancing army from the side of the road and get away with it. They caused a few casualties, but only a few. Body armor saved several men's bacon. And the soldiers deployed with practiced efficiency, hunting the locals down like dogs going after hares. Any one hare could usually get away from any one dog. But when the dogs outnumbered the hares and worked together better than they did . . . Not a lot of the bushwhackers who tried to harry the army on the march had joy of the outcome.

"They want to trap us," Lucius remarked after helping to get rid of another small band of raiders.

"Good luck, assholes. Pretty sorry-looking traps after they try and close on us," Marcus answered. He had a bloody rag rapped around one hand. The wound wasn't worth seeing a physician about, but it annoyed him just the same. Worse, it embarrassed him. Yes, the raiders would stand and fight when cornered, but that one skinny fellow had had no business whatsoever getting through on him, none. The bandit was dead now, dead with his blood soaking into the dirt, his guts spilled out on the ground, and carrion birds squabbling over his eyes and tongue. *Plenty for everybody, birds*, Marcus thought.

When night came, the army made sure trouble didn't come with it. The soldiers quickly built a camp with a fortified perimeter surrounding it. The square encampment conceded nothing to the local geography. Entrances were set in the middle of each side. The streets that ran from each entrance to the one opposite met in the center of the camp. The general and his leading officers were quartered there, at the heart of things. Heavy infantry, light infantry, mobile forces, artillery, logistics—all had their assigned places. They were the same here as they would have been in Spain or Germany. Marcus entrenched his stretch of the perimeter, strengthened the works with stakes, and then lined up for supper.

Come morning, the men would tear down what they'd built the night before, fill in the entrenchments, and go on their way. The locals wouldn't be able to take advantage of what they'd made. That, too, was standard operating procedure.

As he and Lucius got ready to sack out after eating their rations, Marcus said, "You know, I'd just as soon fight the battle and get it over with. I swear we don't work as hard going up against the enemy as we do when everything's routine."

"Yeah, I think you're right." Lucius wrapped himself in his blanket. "Tell you something else, too—I don't think we're gonna have to wait real long. Do you? . . . Do you?"

Marcus didn't answer. He was already snoring.

From a hill not far away, the rebel chieftain looked down on the Western imperialists' camp. In his own mind, he contrasted its good order to the straggling hodgepodge of tents and huts he'd left behind. The Rock stood behind him and, by his frown, was doing the same thing. "They are formidable," the Rock said, reluctant respect in his voice.

With a shrug, the Son of God replied, "Truly, I say to you, there will not be left here one stone upon another that will not be thrown down."

The Rock had a mind of his own, and a wry sense of humor. "Of course not," he said. "They'll take down the camp themselves."

"God is not mocked," the rebel leader said sternly. The Rock bowed his head again. If his chieftain thought he'd gone too far, he accepted the rebuke. The Son of God continued, "The word of God is quick, and powerful, and sharper than any two-edged sword. It pierces even to the point of dividing soul and spirit and the joints and marrow. It discerns the thoughts and intents of the heart. Without shedding blood, there is no remission."

"I understand. The great Satan made me speak so," the Rock said. "I will be sober and vigilant, for my foe Satan is like a roaring lion walking about and seeking those he may devour."

"Watch and pray, that you do not enter into temptation: the spirit indeed is willing, but the flesh is weak," the chieftain said, and the Rock bowed his head yet again. The Son of God added, "The children of that kingdom shall be cast out into outer darkness. There shall be weeping and gnashing of teeth."

"You have seen this?" The Rock looked up with regained hope, regained vigor.

"I have seen all the works that are done under the sun," the rebel leader said. "If you faint in the day of adversity, your strength is small."

"I will not," the Rock vowed. "Lead me. For it is better, if the will of God is so, that we suffer for doing well than than for doing evil."

"We shall smite them hip and thigh," the Son of God declared. And the Rock believed every word he said.

Horns blared, calling the army out of column and into line of battle. Marcus was glad to get off the road—which was no more than a dirt track anyhow—and get ready to fight. "Now we'll settle these ragheads once and for all," he said.

"You bet your butt," Lucius said. "They think they can stand up to us, they've got another think coming."

"Silence in the ranks!" Quintus yelled. The company commander was a stickler for doing things by the book. He added, "If you've got to talk about it, you're probably no stinking good when you really do it."

That stung. Marcus hurried forward, clutching his

weapon. He'd show Quintus! That Quintus hoped to make him think that way never entered his mind.

Little by little, as the army spread over an ever wider front and less of its dust obscured Marcus' vision, he got a look at the enemy. He had to peer through the dust the locals kicked up. What he saw signally failed to impress him. They didn't keep good order, and not many of them looked to have much in the way of body armor. Even helmets were few and far between.

Lucius had hit the nail on the head. If these raggedy fools thought they could beat the best in the world, they needed to think again.

But evidently they did think so. There were a lot of them. Maybe that made them confident. They started yelling something—Marcus had no idea what. He hadn't picked up any of the local language, and didn't want to. It sounded more like choking than talking, as far as he was concerned.

"They're shouting about how great their god is," Quintus said. "Talk is cheap, boys. I don't have to tell you that. Any minute now, we're going to show them just how cheap talk is. Keep your eyes open, help your buddies, and don't do anything dumb."

Marcus found himself nodding. He'd been in skirmishes in Germany, but nothing major. This wouldn't be a skirmish. This was the real thing. He glanced over at Lucius and at the other men with whom he shared a tent, shared the march, shared food. Quintus knew what he was talking about. Marcus couldn't imagine letting his friends down. Better to die than to do that. If you died, nobody would turn his back on you afterward.

Horns squalled again. "Are we ready?" Quintus asked—an unnecessary question if ever there was one. The company commander waved. "Then let's go!" With a cheer of their own, his men—and the rest of the army—advanced.

"The Lord is one! The Lord is one! The Lord is one!" the hillmen shouted as they swarmed toward the soldiers from the West. The rebel chieftain watched from a hillside. His right hand held a sword. The calluses there weren't all from the hilt; some had come from carpentry before he went into rebellion.

"Here they come," the Rock said as the enemy moved forward.

"Yes." The chieftain left it at that.

"They have good order," the Rock said. "Our own men—well, they're fierce enough and more than fierce enough, but they fight with passion, not with skill. That's a wave we have rolling toward them, not a line."

"I shall fear no evil, for the Lord is with me. How should one chase a thousand and two put ten thousand to flight, unless their Rock had sold them" —the rebel leader smiled at his comrade— "and the Lord had shut them up? Cursed be the man who trusts in man, and makes flesh his weapon, and whose heart departs from the Lord." He pointed toward the foe. "They have sown the wind, and they shall reap the whirlwind. The Lord is my light and my salvation. Whom shall I fear? The foe is my washpot. Over them I cast my shoe."

Nodding, the Rock watched the fight unfold. His countrymen swarmed to the attack. The enemy moved more deliberately. And then, all at once, the air was

full of missiles. They all flew at the same time; a single
man might almost have cast every one of them. And
when they struck home, the rebels wavered. Some
went down, shrieking. Others threw up their shields
to save their gore. But the shields did them less good
than they might have. The long, thin iron shanks of
the javelins bent when they hit, fouling the shields
and leaving them next to useless.

When another volley of missiles flew from the
enemy, more hillmen fell. Now they could not raise
those fouled shields. The foe's artillery began to punish
them as well. Great darts pinned one man to another.
Flying stone balls smashed heads from bodies without
even slowing.

A new cry rose up from the hillmen, not ecstasy for
their god but a sort of pained astonishment. They had
taken a town from the soldiers of the West. They'd
harassed them in skirmishes. They had confidence they
could beat the invaders when and where and as they
chose. They had confidence—but the Westerners had
weapons and doctrine and a relentless, driving preci-
sion that let them use both to best advantage.

After the volley of missiles, the enemy soldiers drew
their personal weapons. The horns rang out again.
The men of the West hurled themselves forward, not
breaking ranks. Their big semicylindrical shields and
body armor protected them from the rebels' swords and
spears. And they used those shields not only as wards
but as weapons in their own right, knocking down the
hillmen and leaving them dreadfully vulnerable to a
thrust in the belly or the chest or the throat.

The battle was decided before the hillmen realized
as much. Instead of breaking off and saving what

they could for a new fight on a different day, they kept pressing ahead into the killing zone—and the Western soldiers obligingly, methodically, killed and killed and killed.

"We are undone!" the Rock cried, no less astonishment and no less pain in his voice than in those of the men ahead of them, who were running up against something they did not understand and that taught understanding only through death. The Westerners' weapons were superior, but not overwhelmingly so. But marry superior weapons to superior doctrine . . . Here, the term had a meaning altogether untheological. And the weapons and the doctrine were married, and the hillmen burned.

In agony, the Son of God looked up to the heavens and raised his hands in reproach. *"Eli, Eli, lama sabachthani!"* he cried—*My God, my God, why have You forsaken me?*

As if to give him an answer of sorts, or at least to complete the rout and destruction of those he led, mobile forces thundered against both the rebels' flanks. After that, not even the most fanatical survivors could imagine anything but disaster had overtaken them. They turned and tried to flee.

But they had waited too long. By now, the Westerners all but surrounded them. Cavalrymen slashed them with swords. Archers stung them. The artillery still smashed men at long range. And the foot sloggers, the men who took ground away and held it, chopped them to pieces like a butcher chopping meat to stuff in a sausage skin.

Here and there, single men and small bands did manage to break free of the enemy. They ran. They threw away weapons and helmets and shields to run the faster. A couple of them saw the Rock and the Son of God on the hillside. "Flee!" they cried. "Flee from the wrath to come!"

"We should," the Rock said, setting an urgent hand on the rebel chieftain's arm. "If they catch us . . ." He shuddered. "If they catch us, they have no reason to love us."

"They shall deliver us up to be afflicted, and kill us," the Son of God agreed sadly. "We shall be hated among all nations for my name's sake."

"Even if I die with you, I will not deny you," the Rock said stoutly.

"Do you think I cannot now pray to my Father, and he will give me more than twelve legions of angels right away?" the chieftain asked.

"I see legions," the Rock said. "They belong to the Westerners, and they will take us if we do not flee." The enemy mobile forces had drawn very near. Even the fearsome enemy foot soldiers approached. The Rock shuddered. "They are liable to take us even if we do flee."

"Every one that has forsaken houses, or brothers and sisters, or father or mother or wife, or lands, for my name's sake, will receive a hundredfold and inherit everlasting life," the Son of God said.

The Rock cared little for everlasting life just then. Preserving what life he had in the world suddenly looked more urgent to him. He shoved his chieftain, and the leader of the revolt reluctantly began to move. By then it was too late. The Westerners' scouts were ahead of them, the main body close behind.

☆   ☆   ☆

"We've got all these stinking prisoners," Quintus said. That was literally true: the swarm of rebels the soldiers had captured did stink, not only because they hadn't bathed in much too long but also because fear had an odor all its own, a rank, wild stink that filled the victors' nostrils.

Marcus eyed the scrawny, dirty captives. They were so beaten, so demoralized, he would have pitied them—if they hadn't been trying so hard to kill his pals and him till the moment they threw down their weapons and threw up their hands and shouted, "Friend!" in as many languages as they knew. He didn't feel any too friendly toward them now. Neither did his buddies. Not all the locals who'd tried to surrender had succeeded.

Quintus held up a list. "We've got the top thirteen to sort out, see if they're alive or dead," he said. "Big reward for all of them, double reward for the rebel leader. With a little luck, some of us'll earn it."

"How are we supposed to know who the bastards are, sir?" Marcus asked. "One of these miserable, hairy assholes looks just like another one to me."

"The prisoners'll know who's who," Lucius said. "Some of them speak languages a civilized man can understand, too."

"Those are the ones who really piss me off," Quintus said. "They've got a good Western education, some of them, and they're still religious fanatics underneath." But he nodded. "Using the prisoners is just exactly what we're going to do. Either the leaders are hiding in among 'em, or else they'll know where the big guys are likely to have run off to. Do what you need to do to find out. Whatever it is, I don't want to hear about it." He made a production out of turning his back.

"Come on," Marcus said to Lucius. "Let's do it. I could use some reward money. How about you?"

"I wouldn't mind," Lucius agreed. "I wouldn't mind working out on the ragheads a little more, either." He had a small wound on one arm, and another on one leg. If he wanted to get a little revenge while he was interrogating, it was no skin off Marcus' nose.

Before long, they caught a break. They found a man named Bar Abbas. He wasn't one of the Big Thirteen; he looked like a thief. But he could understand them if they talked loud enough and thumped him a little, and he could talk to them some, too.

He pointed them at another man, a foxy-faced fellow with a red beard—uncommon even in the West and almost vanishingly rare here. Red Beard tried to deny everything, but Marcus saw the terror that stole across his face when he got pulled away from the rest of the prisoners. Lucius had fun persuading him that bullshit at a time like this wasn't a smart plan.

"All right! I'll talk! Don't get cross with me! Please don't get cross with me!" he said after a while. He talked funny, but you could make out what he was saying. He went on, "If you let me go afterwards, I'll take you to . . . him." He named no names, but he didn't need to.

"I think I'd sooner—" Lucius began.

Marcus grabbed his arm before he could. "You want the Senate to start investigating us or something? We need to find this guy. Besides, remember the reward."

"Oh, all right." Lucius still sounded sulky, but he went along. He nodded to the red-bearded local. "You got yourself a deal, pal. Take us to Mister Big and you go home free. Better than that—we'll even pay you a little something." He glanced over at Marcus. "There. You happy now?"

"I'm fucking jumping up and down," Marcus said, which made Lucius laugh. Marcus turned to Red Beard. "Come on, pal. You told us you were gonna do it. Now you better come through. If you don't, I'll just hand you to my buddy here and walk away. Nobody'll give a rat's ass what happens after that."

The local got the message, all right. He got it big time—he almost peed in his robes, in fact. "Let us go. If he is among the prisoners, I will show him to you."

"Uh-*huh*." Marcus and Lucius both said the same thing at the same time. They were both thinking the same thing, too. Marcus would have bet on that. If Red Beard tried to say the rebel honcho wasn't anywhere around, he was history. Extremely ancient history, too.

Red Beard went to and fro in the prisoner compound, and he went up and down in it. Marcus and Lucius tagged along behind, not too close but not too far. If the foxy-faced fellow tried blending in with the other captured rebels, that wouldn't work out so well for him, either, not considering what sorts of things were likely to happen to them pretty soon.

But he didn't. All of a sudden, he came on point like a truffle-sniffing pig getting a whiff of some of the juiciest goodies it had ever smelled. "Hey, hey," Marcus said to Lucius.

"Yeah," Lucius said to Marcus, and then, "I wonder if we ought to have some backup."

They weren't the only soldiers going through the

compound looking for the worst of the bad eggs. Marcus thought about waving to bring some of the others over. He thought about it, and then he shook his head. "They're liable to try and split the reward with us," he pointed out. "Let's see if we can extract this guy all quick and smooth-like. If we have trouble, *then* we yell for backup."

"Deal," Lucius said.

They hurried after the guy with the red beard. He stooped by a prisoner who didn't look much different from any of the other bedraggled locals and gave him a kiss on the cheek. Then he pointed to the fellow next to the one he'd kissed and said, "And this is the man they call the Rock."

The Rock didn't seem to care anything about himself. He pointed to the rebel Red Beard had kissed and he gabbled, "This is not the Son of God. It is not. It is not!"

Marcus and Lucius looked at each other. They both knew lies when they heard them. Their swords cleared their scabbards at the same time. "Come along," Marcus said. "Both of you, and make it snappy."

Red Beard had to translate for the rebel chief. Marcus wondered if there'd be trouble, but the man just wearily climbed to his feet. He knew it was all over, then. He said something guttural. "What's that?" Lucius asked.

"He said to give Caesar what belongs to Caesar, and to give God what belongs to God," the red-bearded local reported.

"His ass belongs to Caesar—and so does the Rock's," Marcus said. "Let's get moving."

They got the big shots out of the compound without the prisoners trying to mob them, which had worried Marcus. As soon as they made it outside, the guy with the red beard said, "You told me you'd let me go."

"Yeah, fine. You held up your end. We'll hold up ours. So long. Get lost," Marcus said. "Get lost and stay lost, in fact. We catch you making trouble again, we'll bury your sorry bones in a potter's field."

"My reward," the local whined.

"We haven't got ours yet," Marcus pointed out. Red Beard looked put upon. Marcus was tempted to scrag him. He didn't quite. He and Lucius hauled out their wallets and split the damage. "Here's thirty," Marcus said, handing the local the money. "Now fuck off, and be thankful you got this much."

Red Beard bowed almost double, like a slave. Then he disappeared.

The Rock eyed both the enemy general and his own chieftain. The enemy had not an ounce of give in him anywhere. The hillmen had rebelled, and they'd lost, and they were going to pay for it. They were going to pay for it in ways as nasty as the general could imagine, and he looked like somebody with a good imagination for that kind of thing.

His own chieftain, by contrast, still looked as if he didn't know what had hit him. The Son of God had been in shock since the men from the West shattered his army. The last betrayal only added insult to injury. The Westerners' awesome and awful display of power in the field would have made almost anyone doubt.

"What do you have to say before it's curtains?" the general asked.

"For myself, nothing," the Rock answered, and translated for the Son of God.

"Tell him he does not know what he is doing, and I forgive him on account of that," the rebel leader answered.

After the Rock translated that, the general laughed. "As if I need *his* forgiveness!" He pointed a stubby forefinger at the chieftain. "So you're the hotsy-totsy King of the Jews, are you?"

"You said it," the Son of God told him.

"Here's what else I say." The general turned to his aides. "Crucify both of them. One right side up, one upside down—I don't care which is which. Do it outside the compound. Let the prisoners watch before we send 'em to the mines and the arenas."

"Yes, sir, General Pontius!" the aides chorused.

"And fetch me a basin," the general added. "I need to wash my hands."

A Good Bag

Brad Linaweaver

Observing the general through a cloud of foul cigar smoke, the old woman insisted, "I don't care about other mediums and their pretenses at purity. The cosmic forces are indifferent to their petty little virtues. What matters is purity of the blood! I assure you that any manifestations we experience tonight will not be put off by my affinity for tobacco."

Her host laughed but ended with a cough. The old woman's taste in cigars was truly awful but if Sir Francis Younghusband, hero of the Tibetan-Chinese war, could prevail against the always testy declarations of Prime Minister Balfour, he would survive these vapors in his London study. Besides, if this woman was hale and hearty in her eighties, the damned cigars might have beneficial properties unknown to modern medicine.

"Forgive my bad manners, HPB," he said. "I only tease you because I wish you'd consider switching to my brand of tobacco."

Helena Petrovna Blavatsky, founder of the Theosophy movement, only allowed close friends to address her by initials. She had first taken a liking to Younghusband when he was a colonel with an uncanny ability to find himself in hot water—and that didn't mean teatime! He had the kind of male face she most admired. Under an imposing brow he sported a walrus mustache that set off the receding hairline. The gray hairs he'd acquired since becoming a general added a touch of distinction.

It was the right sort of face for a master at the Great Game; the game that Younghusband had changed for all time. Before he redrew the maps, the game was not so much for the Russians and British to seek mastery over Central Asia as to block each other's efforts in that regard. Now there was a new game.

"You and Tibet are tied together by destiny," she said. "You were the first military man I ever met who impressed me as a true mystic."

She made it sound more like a sentence of death than a compliment. Her piercing black eyes accented the pronouncement. Most people were made uncomfortable by her relentless stare but Younghusband found it exhilarating. Nothing impressed a spiritualist more than worldly accomplishment.

"I'm glad it stopped raining," he said. "Reminded me of those bloody downpours in Lhasa."

"We will have a still night."

"Would you like to see the room I've prepared for the séance?"

The black eyes danced in the old head. "I'd rather meet your wife first."

While they had been talking, Mrs. Younghusband began to play the piano at the end of the hall. That meant she had put the children to bed for the evening. Notes of Chopin beckoned to the warriors.

"This is a proud day for me," said the general, "the first time you'll meet my wife."

HPB took him by the arm in an uncharacteristically feminine gesture. "Will you tell her that I'm a notorious Russian spy?"

Neither laughed. Over the years she had been accused of everything. For a time it had seemed that she would not recover from charges by Richard Hodgson of the Society for Psychical Research that she had ingratiated herself with the Third Section of Russian intelligence. She was just too Russian for Whitehall to trust her! But with Theosophical chapters in every capital of Europe, she had been convincing when announcing herself as a citizen of the world.

Further complicating matters was that she was of mixed parentage, German as well as Russian. Various German admirers hinted that they, too, wished to play the Great Game. What side was she really on?

British doubts evaporated when Younghusband released to the press how information from Madame Blavatsky saved him from an assassin during military operations in Lhasa in '04. As he walked down the long hallway of his ostentatiously large house, the general reflected in this safe and secure year of 1910

how much he truly owed to this crazy Russian mystic
on his arm.

At the beginning of the Tibetan expedition, things
had not been going well. The thirteenth Dalai Lama
proved deficient as a political strategist. Only twenty-
eight years old at the time, he had paid too much
credence in the prophesy of one of his magicians
that 1904, the Year of the Wood Dragon, would
see a series of events culminating in the destruction of Tibet.

No stranger to the Great Game, the young leader
placed his hopes with the czar to protect him against
the British Empire. So when Colonel Younghusband
began his military entry into Lhasa, the Dalai Lama
and a small party escaped to the north. Their destina-
tion was Mongolia. Left behind was another lama to
negotiate as regent—a sharp operator by the name
of Tri Rimpoche.

Madame Blavatsky's intervention did more than
save an eager colonel's life. She saved his career and
changed the nature of the mission.

Her spy network was not part of Russian intelligence. The Theosophy movement had agents, too! HPB
had friends and allies among Buddhists and Hindus
because of the many points of convergence between
her system and the Eastern religions. Weirdly enough,
she even made converts from their ranks!

She learned that the Russians had no intention of
coming to the Dalai Lama's aid. Shouting Cossack
oaths at the British Empire was one thing; but close
scrutiny of a good map showed that the British only
needed a few thousand men to stop a Russian force of
any size emanating from Lhasa. So why worry about

Lhasa? The mountain passes were so narrow that it was a defender's dream.

And then the Chinese made everything really complicated. Ironically, the Russian agent Zerempil tried to kill the daring colonel as part of a mission to prevent China moving into eastern Tibet. The idea was that removing Younghusband also meant removing a challenge to General Chao Her-feng. Since Zerempil died instead, there was no way of testing his thesis. Zerempil never bothered to consider the possibility that Younghusband's death might just as readily embolden the Chinese.

As General Younghusband opened the door that would bring his wife face to face with the person who had done so much to shape his destiny, he appreciated that his honored guest's cigar had gone out. There were many small miracles and mercies in this vale of tears.

The pale young woman stopped playing the piano. "Dear, this is Madame Blavatsky."

The older woman took the younger woman's hands in hers and spoke softly. "You are a gorgeous creature. I'm not surprised to learn that the source of such beautiful playing is herself beautiful."

Younghusband had never seen his wife blush at the words of another woman before. Her long swan's neck turned ever so slightly as if she half expected HPB to kiss her. It appeared that Madame had made another conquest.

The general didn't need a séance to take him back to the day when Blavatsky convinced him that she did indeed possess occult powers. How else could she tell him where to find the exact place and moment in the

Tibetan wilderness where bandits had set upon the Dalai Lama and his party?

The leader of Tibet was enough of a mystic to recognize a good omen when it rescued him! The British expeditionary force changed history that day.

"My husband promises an interesting evening," said Mrs. Younghusband, bringing her better half back to the present moment.

Blavatsky allowed herself a chuckle and released her prey. "How else can it be when I am here?" she summed up with her usual modesty.

But HPB was in an expansive mood and left her favorite topic to return to complimenting others. "Mrs. Younghusband, you are a most aesthetic young lady. It could not be otherwise with your fine breeding. Blood will tell."

Unable to tear herself away from the old lady's devil eyes, she blushed again and said, "Thank you, Countess."

HPB winked at her host. "You've told her about my background. All true mystics have aristocracy in their past even if their modern circumstances are reduced to that of a beggar." As an afterthought, she added, "Great generals are reincarnations of earlier generals."

Before anyone could say Alexander the Great, they were all saved by a knocking at the door. The butler, Robert Weber the Silent, was as quiet as God's breath. The new arrival followed his example. So it was as if Tri Rimpoche materialized in the waiting room—a special envoy from the Dalai Lama.

There was a twinkle in the man's eye as he took the general by the hand and said, "Sahib."

The general laughed. "My house is honored by your presence."

HPB shocked all present by speaking words never vouchsafed by her Secret Masters: "Thank you for coming such a long way."

He bowed. "I could not deny you, Madame. Are we all here?"

"Two more are expected," volunteered their hostess.

Tri Rimpoche's dark complexion seemed to draw in more of the shadows from the flickering candles than his companions. Perhaps he had an affinity with the flame.

Slowly he removed his green gloves and passed them to Weber. "I must say, HPB, you are looking remarkably well."

"Blame it on Tibetan barley," she replied. "I once had a premonition that I was to die in 1891 but my Master spoke to me and said I had a duty to live until 1910. So perhaps my life is the greatest proof of the supernatural I can offer."

"That, and your cigars," added Younghusband.

"How did you come to rely on such an unusual diet?" inquired the hostess.

"From Dorzhiev, a good Russian who loved Tibet. He died during the war, unfortunately."

"The war," echoed Mrs. Younghusband. "If we are going to discuss all that, it will be more agreeable with refreshments."

So saying, she ushered them past heavy curtains into the parlor proper. Suddenly she stopped, embarrassed. "Oh my, I forgot. Is it premature to show the preparations beforehand?"

Blavatsky waved away all objections. "No more so

than to serve spirits before I commune with the spirit world! It's all right with me. I've reached the point where I am past the rigamarole. The Secret Masters of Tibet taught me to see through the illusion of our immediate surroundings. I could just as easily conduct a séance out under the stars."

Soon everyone had a drink in hand except for HPB who availed herself of the opportunity to ignite another of her cigars. Apparently the spiritual vapors would not object to competition from more noxious mists.

Mrs. Younghusband counted herself fortunate that her husband did not have the bad habit of tormenting his spouse with particulars of his military campaigns. As her guests began to gnaw at strategy and tactics, she recalled the newspaper stories that first trumpeted his success. Her man had proven wiser than General Macdonald and saw the future more clearly than Curzon. At the crucial moment, he managed the alliance between His Majesty's government and Tibet that succeeded in pushing back General Wang Chhuk when the Chinese finally overreached.

The armchair diplomats went berserk right on schedule. Shifting Prime Minister Balfour was more difficult than allaying fears in St. Petersburg. Finally, Whitehall and the czarist government were so united in opposition to Chinese suzerainty over Tibet that it changed the nature of the Great Game.

For the lady of the house, the conversation in her parlor brought the past alive without benefit of séance. She surprised herself by wishing that conversation would provide the only journey into the past this evening.

Any such hope evaporated as she heard HPB

intone, "Mystical ties of the blood must transcend national borders if we are to build a future worthy of the past."

They were in for the long haul tonight.

The Tibetan was not to be outdone: "Madame opened my eyes to the truth that Aryan Civilization began in Tibet long ago, the beginning of the fifth root race. We must move beyond the narrow bounds of national thinking. There are great dangers in the future."

As if to prove that his fingers were on the pulse of someone's greater destiny, a tremendous pounding thudded through the house at that precise moment. There was so much noise that HPB dropped her cigar on the Persian rug. With a speed worthy of the finest lancers, Mrs. Younghusband retrieved the cigar and gave it back to the medium before anyone had the opportunity to choke.

Loud footsteps in the hallway suggested a cause other than a psychic disturbance within the house. Tri Rimpoche was pretty sure who had just arrived and couldn't help but feel superior regarding the silent manner of his own entrance. There was nothing adept about a thunderburst of noise announcing unsubtle men with crude plans.

Even the inner door sounded louder as Weber brought the guests into the drawing room and toward the curtains which finally parted to reveal the final two guests of the evening.

The butler made his announcement: "Guido von List and Sven Hedin." The German and the Swede had arrived.

Both were large men dressed incongruously in

ill-fitting tweeds as though a parody of English gentlemen. Both had oversized beards but the German's white whiskers seemed to explode from his head in a tangle worthy of a drunkard's vision of Father Christmas.

Now the introductions took on a more formal, even solemn, tone. Hedin, the famous Swiss archeologist and adventurer, was an old friend of the general. But the German was a new addition.

HPB stated bluntly, "I've always wanted to meet you, Hedin." She shook hands with him in a masculine fashion. "Your Tibetan expedition discovered much of value."

"But not your hidden valley of Secret Masters," he added. Everyone laughed but Mrs. Younghusband, who had no idea what they were talking about.

The German could have been telepathic the way he suddenly picked up on the conversation they'd been having before his arrival. Without preamble he threw out, "Hedin's work is vital in establishing Tibet as a cradle of the Aryan race."

Madame Blavatsky turned her gaze on the author of *Die Religion der Ario-Germanen in ihrer Esoterik und Exoterik*, recently published in Vienna.

"I am also familiar with your work," she said. "You build your thesis on the Hindu theory of racial purity and reincarnation."

List clicked his heels and bowed. Somewhere there was the sound of good English tweeds tearing. The man was too large for the suit. "I acknowledge a debt both to Theosophy and Darwinism, dear lady."

Turning to his host, he added, "We Germans take Darwin straight! In Darwin's home country, you English wrestle with Christian piety over whether or not evolution is true. We take survival of the fittest as our starting point and follow the logic to its ruthless conclusion."

"Oh, I don't know," said Younghusband, smiling over his brandy as he took a dislike to the German. "We British have our ruthless side. You should read the novels of Mr. H. G. Wells for a fuller exploration of the subject. Or consider what one of my officers said when he ordered a force of retreating Tibetans shot in the back by repeating rifles."

The only Tibetan present felt a duty to interject. "This was right before the Dalai Lama and our genial host formed their new alliance."

"Yes, yes," said the German impatiently. "I'm familiar with your campaigns, General. What did your officer say?"

Younghusband finished his brandy. "That's a good bag."

"I don't understand the idiom," admitted List.

Tri Rimpoche interjected again. "British slang for killing game animals."

An awkward silence was just what Mrs. Younghusband needed. "Herr List, your comment about taking Darwin straight reminds me that you don't have a drink. May I correct that?"

To General Younghusband's horror, the boorish German was actually rude to his wife! "I'm not here to drink before engaging in a magical ritual," he snapped. "I'm surprised you allow your other guests to indulge."

"Do as thou wilt!" HPB snapped right back, restoring a sense of decorum. The author of *Isis Unveiled* and *The Secret Doctrine* had her own manner of doing things.

"You know what stage magicians say?" she went on. "The more the audience drinks, the better the magic. Well, practitioners of the real thing don't worry over such trifles."

Mrs. Younghusband surprised everyone with, "If we are going to witness genuine magic, this might be a propitious occasion to take up serious drinking!"

Her husband came quickly to her side and held her hand. "You don't have to participate, dear."

With a nervous chuckle, his wife demonstrated how far removed she was from HPB's Invisible Brotherhood by committing an unforgivable faux pas. She actually admonished the gathering with, "Just so long as what we do is morally respectable."

Blavatsky guffawed so grotesquely that it seemed another manifestation. Sven Hedin cleared his throat and tried to explain as he would to a recalcitrant child, "Dear lady, morals are only a matter of geography."

"And cranial development," List added.

The Tibetan sighed. "This fine lady invites us into her home and we behave badly. She has even been serving the drinks herself!"

"We let the servants go for tonight," she thought to say. "We only kept on Weber."

"Is that wise?" asked the German.

The general recalled the narrow pass he and his men once negotiated to reach the flowery paradise of Tangu. He wished he was back there right now. The time had come to maneuver his loved one past needing to deal with these egomaniacs so that they might reach the paradise of the séance.

"Our butler will stay for the evening," he said. "He is well suited to these sort of events. The man used to be in the service of Aleister Crowley."

The Tibetan finished the transition: "Then we better commence before the first light of a golden dawn steals the night."

The small group of six gathered around a table that had already been prepared. Lighted candles dominated the center. Weber made a fire in the ornate fireplace and then extinguished the room's regular lights. Shadows danced them to their seats, comfortable armchairs carefully arranged around the perfectly circular table.

The general noticed that his wife sat next to HPB; the woman who gave his life meaning next to the woman who once saved his life. The faces of a saint and a gargoyle.

Younghusband announced that any who cared to search the room for devices were welcome to do so. A few snorts and shrugs made it clear that honor was satisfied.

Weber retired from the room to prepare a late-night cold supper for them when they returned from their journey into the unknown. It was half past midnight.

"You know why we are here," said Madame Helena Petrovna Blavatsky. "We won't be conjuring ghosts of the dearly departed. We have been instructed to be here by my Secret Master, a genius from ancient Atlantis who guided my actions back in '04. He has a message for us tonight but only if we are all together. I do not know the content of the message."

She laid out several pieces of blank paper. Her

normal procedure was to take dictation from her spirit guide who obligingly translated the ancient Atlantean language into standard mediumistic scribbling easily translated into modern tongues. Perfect mind-to-mind contact always managed to overcome language barriers, at least according to every medium worth her essential salts.

The Tibetan volunteered to read HPB's spirit writings and inform the others of their content. While in her trance, the medium had no knowledge of what transpired. Everyone knew that. Everyone who believed in that sort of thing.

They began by holding hands. Mrs. Younghusband was surprised at the frailty of Herr List's grasp. She expected a stronger hand from someone who blustered. In contrast, the general noted yet again the strength in the big Swede's hands. Meanwhile, Hedin couldn't get over how strangely cool and dry was the Tibetan's hand.

The candles began to flicker even though there was no breeze. Then there was a heavy knocking from underneath the table. HPB's eyes started to roll up in her head and she seized her pen.

That was as far as the séance got.

Or it might be more appropriate to say that was when the séance actually began! The candles blew out and the pen flew out of the medium's hand to break against the fireplace. The blank pieces of paper followed the example of the pen and whirled into the fireplace where they did not so much burn as explode.

By some miracle, Madame Blavatsky recovered from her "trance." Her black eyes widened at the spectacle before them. According to the rules of a proper séance, the manifestations should have ceased at that moment. They didn't.

Beyond their little inner sanctum they could hear Weber the butler pounding on the door to these rooms. He couldn't open it. His voice sounded as if it were at the bottom of a well as he shouted out their names.

"What is happening?" whispered HPB in an entirely new tone of voice. Mrs. Younghusband heard her and blurted out, "I think we're in for it."

That's when the humming began. It sounded like a machine revving up. A circle of canary-yellow light formed on the ceiling. They couldn't help but crane their necks and look up.

A vaguely human shadow began to form in the light. It was masculine with huge shoulders and a small head. HPB shrieked, "A Lemurian beastman!"

They had never heard her shriek before.

Then the head grew in size until it was larger than normal. A voice spoke from the ceiling:

"Sorry about that. Had a little trouble bringing myself into focus. I'm Madame's Atlantean contact, by the way. It's a bother appearing like this but it can't be helped."

This time Blavatsky moved up the scale to a full-throated scream and fell heavily upon the table. Mrs. Younghusband picked up where HPB left off and screamed, "I think she's dead!

"Damn!" said the voice from the ceiling. "Her ticker gave out. I suppose we'll have to finish this session without her."

"Excuse me," said the general, feeling weirdly in

control of his senses as he addressed the ceiling, "but if our medium is dead, how can we still be communicating with you?"

"Bosh," said the slightly celestial voice. "You don't believe in this spiritualistic nonsense, do you?"

At this point, the German decided he should get into the screaming act himself but the voice was stern: "Stop that, you silly man." List stopped.

The voice, which the general began to notice was pleasant and mellifluous, continued, "I've been guiding the Blavatsky woman for the last twenty years. She was running a racket before that but I set things right when I began putting ideas into her head. She thought my notions were her notions, and really didn't have the wit to notice how much more effective she became at predictions. She even misremembered her past and assumed she'd always been on top of her game."

"Are you truly from Atlantis?" thundered Hedin, who was no more afraid than the general.

"Yes."

"But isn't that every bit as fantastic as what you call spiritualistic nonsense?"

"Not at all. Unless you believe lost civilizations are fairy stories. I'm using a time projector with a Vril lens."

"Oh," said Hedin, furiously stroking his beard.

The voice continued: "You see, ladies and gentlemen, we have a problem with the time stream. I was trying to prevent a disaster in the twentieth century and things haven't gone at all well."

"Why would you care about the twentieth century?" asked Younghusband.

"Because of dire effects on the twenty-fifth century, of course."

"You're from that era?"

"No, I'm from 20,000 B.C. Shall we get on with it? This little experiment of mine was to prevent wars in your century between England and Germany. There were some unfortunate consequences of those wars. Unfortunately, we have recalculated the sequences and it now appears that the new time stream we have created will be worse than the one we were trying to correct.

"The problem is that as a result of your small occult activities, alliances will be formed between all the so-called Aryan races. Primarily, England and Germany will unite, leading to the mass murder of so many Europeans of unpopular creeds and ethnic identities that that it will cause worse results in your future than what would have occurred from the wars."

The German came out of his own trance and blurted out, "What do you mean so-called Aryan races?"

"They don't exist. Every human currently alive belongs to the same race, and there's much room for improvement."

"What is the point of your appearance here tonight?" asked the general.

"To prevent the alliance of England and Germany."

The general furrowed his brow. "And if we prevent that alliance, then millions of innocents won't die in Europe?"

"There's a certain irony to that. The victims that will come of war add up to a sizable number, but not as many as from the alliance."

Mrs. Younghusband remarked, "Then maybe

only thousands will die if the Aryan nations fail to unite?"

The shadow on the ceiling seemed to shiver, and then spoke quietly. "Far more than that, I'm afraid, but still not so many as to fatally change the course of Western civilization."

"So you admit that the West is the most important civilization?" thundered Hedin.

"For the weapons it will create, Sven Hedin. For the weapons! We of Atlantis know all about weapons."

"It's a trick," shouted List. "I don't believe a word of it. There's probably some Jew behind all this!"

The German jumped up and ran toward the curtains. It was a bad move. He was electrocuted by touching the heavy brocade material, resulting in a most interesting new style for his beard. It was as if he'd received a lethal dose of static electricity. He was dead before his body hit the floor.

Mrs. Younghusband had had enough and spoke sternly to the ceiling. "Would you please stop killing our guests?"

"Weber is going to have his hands full," muttered the general.

The shadow from Atlantis shook his head. "I do apologize. We are creating a new time stream tonight and I had no foreknowledge that Madame's heart would give out. As for List, I should have pointed out what would happen if any of you tried to leave this room before I shut off the time lens."

"It was remiss of you," said the Tibetan. "Are you certain there is no Aryan race?"

"Yes."

Tri Rimpoche frowned. "This comes as quite a

blow. A higher race consciousness seems a way of limiting national strife and pointless wars against one's brothers."

The shadow nodded. "There is a higher race consciousness, but you aren't ready for it yet."

"Will there ever be an end to war?" asked Mrs. Younghusband.

"No, but the human race's martial spirit will come in handy when you face the dragons."

"Dragons," echoed the Tibetan.

"Afraid I must leave you now," said the shadow.

"Is this the extent of the body count?" asked the general, regarding HPB and List.

"Once again, I'm dreadfully sorry about that," said the shadow. "Do what you can, General. Wars between Germany and England will prove salutary in the end."

"I always thought we would fight Russia."

"Everything in its time," said the shadow as it faded from the ceiling.

The Swede brought his fist down on the table. "Well, I'll be hanged if I believe any more of this than did poor List!"

Younghusband stood and walked over to the body of Madame Blavatsky. After trying her pulse and checking for any sign of breath, he sighed. "She was my favorite Russian," he said.

"Part German, as well," added the Tibetan.

"Then she was also my favorite German. Imagine her having the greatest success possible as a medium and not living through it."

Suddenly the curtains parted without another shower of blue sparks. Weber stood in the light from the outer room, regarding List's body. "What shall I do, sir?" he asked his master.

"A good question," said the general, patting the corpse of Madame Blavatsky on the shoulder. "What are any of us to do? War between England and Germany. What do you think of that, eh, Weber?"

His wife came to his side. "How bad will it be?" she asked.

The general wiped away a tear. "The world will enjoy good sport, dear. We'll do our part. It's our duty now."

"You can't believe it," said Hedin, shaking his head. "Not really."

Younghusband sighed. "List didn't know the meaning of a good bag. I'm afraid that we'll learn through our children."

The Burning Spear at Twilight

Mike Resnick

Jomo Kenyatta paces his cell.

It is seven feet by nine feet. There is a barred window, something less than two feet on a side. Along one wall is a metal cot with a thin ripped mattress. In a corner is a rusted pail, filled with his urine and excrement. He has worn the same clothes for seventeen days; laundry day won't come for another two weeks.

It is 97 degrees out, a cool day for Kenya's Northern Frontier District. The flies are out in force; usually even the insects lie up in the shade during the heat of the day.

Kenyatta has been in the cell in Maralal for just

over a year. He has six years yet to serve. He wonders how much of his sentence he will manage to survive before he dies. His British guards, those who speak to him, are betting he doesn't live for half his sentence, but he will fool them. He is a tough old bird; he will serve well over half his time, perhaps even five years, before he succumbs.

He thinks back to the trial. Someday, when Kenya is finally free of the British, they will print the transcript, and the world will see that he was railroaded on a trumped-up charge. King of the Mau Mau indeed! To this day, he does not even know what "Mau Mau" means, or what language it represents.

Suddenly his door opens, and he realizes through the haze of heat that almost melts the mind that it is Sunday already, and that it is time for the one weekly visitor he is allowed. This time it is James Thuku, a friend of his from the old days.

Thuku waits until the door locks behind him, then places his hands together and bows as a British guard watches his every move.

"Greetings, O Burning Spear," he says. "I trust all is well with you?"

"You may call me Jomo, or even Johnston," replies Kenyatta, for before he was Jomo Kenyatta he was Johnston Kamau. "And I am as well as can be expected."

"Let me shake your hand in the tradition of the white man, that I may feel your strength," says Thuku.

Kenyatta frowns. The Kikuyu do not shake hands. But there is something in Thuku's expression that tells him that today they do, and he extends his hand. Thuku grabs it, squeezes it, and when they part, Kenyatta is holding a folded note in his huge hand.

"How do my people fare?" he asks, pocketing the note until he is no longer under close observation through the little window in the door.

Thuku's face says, *How do you think they fare?* but his voice answers, "They miss you, Burning Spear, and every day they ask the British to release you."

"Please thank them for their efforts on my behalf," says Kenyatta. Then, "Are they well fed and fairly treated?"

"Well, they are not in prison," answers Thuku. "At least, not all of them."

Stupid, thinks Kenyatta. *Here I give you an opportunity to say what the British wish to hear, and instead you tell me this. I doubt that they will allow you back here again.*

"More farms have been attacked?" asks Kenyatta.

Thuku nods. He doesn't care if the British hear. After all, it is in all the papers. "Yes, and they have mutilated hundreds of cattle and goats belonging to the British."

"They are foolish," said Kenyatta in a clear voice, loud enough to be heard beyond the cell. "The British are not evil, merely misinformed. They are not our enemies, and mark my words, someday they will even be our allies."

Thuku looks at him as if he has gone mad.

"They are a handsome race," continues Kenyatta. "They have strong faces and straight backs." He switches from English to Kikuyu, which is much more complex and difficult to learn than Swahili, and—he hopes—beyond the abilities of the guards to understand. "And they have large ears," he concludes.

A look of dawning comprehension crosses James

Thuku's face, and the next ten minutes consist of nothing but a discussion of the weather, the harvest, the marriages and births and deaths of the people Kenyatta knows.

Finally Thuku goes to the door. "Let me out," he says. "I am done here."

The door opens, and Thuku turns to Kenyatta. "I will be back next week, Burning Spear."

"I wouldn't bet on that," remarks one of the guards.

Neither would I, agrees Kenyatta silently.

He waits until the evening meal is done, and the new guards have replaced the old. Then, while there is still enough light to read, he unfolds the message and reads it:

It has begun! Tonight we spill the blood of the British!

The news is slow to trickle in. For six months after Thuku leaves, Kenyatta is allowed no visitors at all. Finally he learns what has happened, not from the Kikuyu, but from the British commander.

Kenyatta has requested an audience with him daily since he learned that he has been denied any visitors, and finally it is granted.

The black man with the gray beard is brought, in chains, to the commander's office. The commander sits at his desk, fanning himself in a futile attempt to gain some slight degree of comfort in the hot, still air.

"You wished to see me?" he demands

"I wish to know why I have not been allowed to have any visitors," says Kenyatta.

"We're not about to let them report on their missions to you, or receive new orders," says the commander.

"I don't know what you are talking about," says Kenyatta.

"I'm talking about your goddamned Mau Mau, and the massacre they committed at Lari!" yells the commander, pounding the desk with a fist. "We're not going to let you black heathens get away with this, and when we catch Deedan Kimathi—and we will—I will take great pleasure in incarcerating him in the cell next to yours. I won't even care about your exchanging information with him, since you're both going to be here until you rot!"

And with that, Kenyatta is escorted back to his cell.

"What happened at Lari?" he asks his guard.

"You ought to know. You were in charge of it."

"I am a prisoner who is not even in charge of his own life. How can I possibly know what happened?"

"What happened is that your savages went out and butchered ninety-three loyal Kikuyu in the town on Lari," says the guard. "Chopped them to bits."

"Loyal Kikuyu," repeats Kenyatta.

"That's right."

"Loyal to who?"

The guard curses and shoves the black man into his cell.

Kenyatta knows what will come next. It will not happen to him. He's probably safer in his cell than any of the Mau Mau are in their hideouts. But the British cannot tolerate this. They will strike back, and in force. He has to get word to his people, to warn them—but how is he to do so when he is allowed no visitors?

He begins smoking, begging an occasional cigarette

from the guards. One day, months later, a guard gives him two, and he thanks him profusely, lights one, and explains that he's keeping the second one for the evening. Then, when the guards have changed, he unwraps the cigarette and scrawls *You must get me out of here!* in Swahili on the paper. He doesn't dare write it in English for fear the guards may find it, and by the same token he can't write it in Kikuyu for he is sure that the prison doesn't employ any members of the Kikuyu tribe now that they are at war with each other.

Day in and day out he stands by his window, watching and waiting with the patience of a leopard. Finally, almost two weeks after he has written his message and carefully folded it up, a black groundskeeper is trimming the bushes near his window. The man is a Samburu, and the Samburu and Kikuyu have never been allies, but he has no choice other than to hope the man realizes that the British are the blood enemy of both races. He coughs to catch the man's attention, then tosses the folded note out through the bars.

The Samburu picks it up, unfolds it, stares at it.

Can you even read? wonders Kenyatta. *And if you can, will you take it to my people, or to the guards?*

The Samburu stares expressionlessly at him for a long moment, then walks away.

Kenyatta waits, and waits, and waits some more. He has not seen the Samburu again, and he has been given nothing else to write on. Burning day follows freezing night, and he tries futilely to exercise in his nine-by-seven-foot universe. He begs for tidbits of information, but the guards have been instructed not to speak to him. He thinks it has been two years since James Thuku passed him the note, but he could be wrong: it could be eighteen months, it could even be three years. It is hard enough to keep his sanity without worrying about the passage of time.

And then one night he hears it: the sound of bare feet on the uneven ground outside his window. There are more sounds, sounds he cannot identify, then a *crash!* and a *thud!*, and suddenly four Kikuyu men, their faces painted for war, are in his cell, helping him to his feet. One of them strips off his prison clothes and wraps him in a red kikoi. Another brings his trademark flyswatter, a third his leopardskin cap. They gently help him walk out the door.

"Where is your car?" asks Kenyatta, looking around. "I am too weak to walk all the way to Kikuyuland."

"A car would be searched, Burning Spear," says one of them. "We have brought an ox wagon. You will hide in the back, under a pile of blankets and skins."

"Skins?" says Kenyatta, frowning. "The British will stop you, and once they see the skins, they will search the wagon."

Another warrior smiles. "The British are too busy fighting for their lives, Burning Spear. The Nandi or the Wakamba will stop us, and if we let them take the skins, they will look no further."

And it is as the warrior has predicted.

Kenyatta asks them not to announce that he is free. He will go to his village, regain some of his strength, some of the weight he has lost, and try to learn what has been happening.

"I do not know if we can spare you that long, Burning Spear," says one of the warriors. "The war does not go well."

"Of course it doesn't," says Kenyatta.

"They bomb the holy mountain daily, and some fifteen thousand of us are captives in the camps along Langata Road."

"Are you surprised?" asks Kenyatta.

"Did not you yourself tell us that we could not lose, that freedom was within our grasp?"

"It was. I only hope that Mau Mau has not pissed it away for all time to come."

They stare at the old man, dumbfounded, and then at each other, and their expressions seem to say, *Can this be the Burning Spear we have worshipped all these years? What have the British done to him?*

Deedan Kimathi stands with his back to the cave wall, high in the Aberdere Mountains, and faces the assembled warriors. They are truly a ragtag army, not half a dozen pairs of shoes between them, most armed only with spears and clubs.

If I only had a real army, he thinks. *If only we had the weapons the British have.*

Still, he is prepared to fight to the bitter end with what he has, and he has pinpointed the one way in which they might still defeat the British who are crawling all over the Aberdares and the holy mountain of Kirinyaga itself.

"We have suffered minor defeats," he says, shrugging off an increasing number of military disasters in a sentence fragment, "but now the time has come to assert ourselves."

"How?" asks General China. (Kimathi tries not to wince at the ridiculous names his generals have chosen for themselves.) "Every day the British planes drop bombs on us. Even the elephants and the buffalo have deserted the holy mountain. If we have proved anything, it is that we cannot fight them with sticks and stones."

"We will fight them with a weapon they are unprepared to deal with," says Kimathi with all the confidence he can project. "We will fight them with a weapon they do not have in their arsenal." He sees stirrings of interest in his audience. "We will fight them with barbarism and savagery."

"We already have," says General China. "And what good has it done?"

"This time will be different," promises Kimathi. "We will attack their women and their children, we will make Nairobi itself a place of unspeakable horror, we will kill and torture and mutilate, and against such an onslaught even the British will have to concede defeat and go home."

"Nairobi?" asks a dubious voice.

"Wherever they think they are safe, wherever they hide their most precious possessions—their women and their children and their elderly. We have been making a mistake. They brought them all in from the farms to the city, and yet we continued to attack the farms. This is *our* land, and we do not have to fight by British rules. They bring an army to the White Highlands, and we have met them in battle with spears against rifles. We have learned our lesson. We must go where their army isn't, must do our killing when there is no chance of retribution. When they finally realize that we are slaughtering them in Nairobi and move their army there, we will attack them in Mombasa, and when they come to Mombasa, they will find we are butchering their children in Lamu and Naivasha."

"That is the path to disaster," says a strong voice, and all eyes turn to the mouth of the cave, where Jomo Kenyatta is standing, surrounded by a small force of painted Kikuyu.

"Burning Spear!" exclaims Kimathi, surprised. "I did not know you were free!"

"It is not something the British wish to publicize," says Kenyatta as he walks forward. "But it was essential that I escape and join you, because this battle cannot be won by the methods you described."

"Then we will make them pay in blood for every Kikuyu they kill!" says Kimathi passionately.

"There are far more British than Kikuyu," says Kenyatta. "Is that really what you want—to trade a Kikuyu life for a British life until one side or the other runs out of lives, for I can tell you which side will run out of lives first."

"What have they done to you?" demands Kimathi. "You were the first to advocate independence!"

"And I still do."

"Then we must drive the British from our land!"

"I agree."

Kimathi frowns. "What are you saying?"

"The day of our hoped-for independence began in sunshine and fair weather—but we have already reached the twilight, and this Mau Mau war, these atrocities, have done nothing but guarantee that the British will not leave. Soon it will be dark, and the rays of hope will vanish as surely as the rays of sunshine."

"How would you get them to leave?" asks General China. "Ask them politely?"

Kenyatta shakes his head. "They will not go because *I* ask them. They will not go because *you* ask them. But when the right people ask them, they will go." He holds a book up above his head. "Does anyone know what this is?"

"A book," replies a warrior.

"Ah, but what book?"

"A British bible?" guesses the warrior.

"It is a novel called *Something of Value*, written by an American named Robert Ruark. Even as we stand here, it is the best-selling book in the English-speaking world."

"What is that to us?" demands Kimathi, aggressively hiding the fact that he cannot read.

"It is about the Mau Mau. It depicts us as savages, not fit to rule ourselves. In this book we do nothing but maim and torture and mutilate."

"Good!" says Kimathi. "That should frighten them."

Kenyatta sighs deeply and shakes his head. "I have lived in England. They will never abandon their colonists to face such savagery as this book has convinced them that we will commit. You keep expecting the Americans, who fought the British to gain independence, to help us—but I tell you that no American will help the Kikuyu that are depicted in this book."

"Then what would you have us do?" says Kimathi. "I swore a blood oath: I will never call a white man Bwana again. I will never rest while the penalty for killing a white man is death and the penalty for killing a Kikuyu is a twenty-five-pound fine. I will never pay a hut tax to the British, who force us to work on their farms—*their* farms on *our* homeland!" He pulls himself up to his full height and thrusts his jaw forward. "*Never!*" he roars.

"Never!" yell a number of the assembled Kikuyu.

"I agree," says Kenyatta. "I have been fined and beaten and jailed for my beliefs. They have not changed. But because I know how the world works, and you have lived all your lives in Kikuyuland, which in turn is only a very small portion of Kenya, you lack the experience to deal with the British."

"All your experience got you was a jail sentence!" says General Burma.

"Use your brain," says Kenyatta, suddenly annoyed that no one can intuit what he is trying to say, that he must carefully explain it step by step as if to a roomful of children. "Why do you think that I was the only one they jailed before Mau Mau? All your other leaders were fined, but only I have been kept away from you." He pauses. "It is because only I know how to drive the British from our land."

"We will not bow and beg," says Kimathi stubbornly.

"No one is asking you to."

"Then what?"

"You must trust me," says Kenyatta. "I know how our enemy thinks, how he reacts. I can still lead you to independence, but time is running out and you must do exactly what I say."

"*I* am the leader of Mau Mau!" says Kimathi. "We will do it my way!"

"I put it to you," says Kenyatta to the Kikuyu. "You have done it Deedan Kimathi's way for three long years and where has it gotten you? Twenty thousand Kikuyu, those loyal to us and those loyal to the British, are dead, and less than one hundred British have died. Once we owned the White Highlands, and our tribal lands extended to Nairobi in the south and the Rift Valley to the west. Now we hide in caves atop the Aberdares and the holy mountain, and that is all we have left. Will you continue to follow Deedan Kimathi, or will you follow me?"

As one, the Kikuyu jump to their feet and pledge their loyalty to the Burning Spear.

Kimathi turns to Kenyatta. "You have won," he says bitterly. "The army is yours."

Kenyatta shakes his head. "We are in the midst of a war, and the army needs a leader. It is yours."

Kimathi frowns. "Then I don't understand . . ."

"The army," says Kenyatta with a smile, "will respond to the commands of one general—you. And *you* will respond to the commands of one general—*me*."

"I hope you know what you are doing."

"I know exactly what I am doing," says Kenyatta. He raises his voice for all to hear. "I am not just the Spear, I am the Burning Spear—and what does a burning spear do?"

"It stabs!" cry a number of warriors.

"And what else?"

There is a puzzled silence.

Kenyatta smiles a confident smile. "It illuminates."

Kenyatta has set up his headquarters in the densest part of the forest on Kirinyaga, at an altitude of about nine thousand feet. He knows he would be safer in Mombasa, or even on the Loita Plains in Maasailand, but he thinks it is important that his warriors be able to see that he is here with them, and he understands the importance of symbolism, which is why he is on the holy mountain rather than in the nearby Aberdares, which cover far more territory.

He is sitting on a wooden stool—he finds he no longer has the energy he had before his incarceration, and can no longer stand for hours on end—and one of his generals, this one a General Tibet (Kenyatta is sure the man has no idea where Tibet is located), is reporting the latest disaster: a squadron of British commandoes has ambushed twenty Mau Mau warriors and killed every last one of them. It occurred near the Gura Falls, about thirteen thousand feet up in the Aberdares.

Kenyatta sighs deeply. "It begins," he says.

"I do not understand, Burning Spear," says General Tibet.

"The first true step toward independence," says Kenyatta.

"But our men were slaughtered. We did not kill a single white man."

"If you had killed ten of them, it would make no difference," replies Kenyatta. "There are fifty million more where they came from." He paused. "Listen carefully, and do exactly as I say. After darkness falls, take five men that you trust to Gura."

"And bring back the bodies?" asks General Tibet.

Kenyatta shakes his head. "No. Arm them with sharp pangas, and when you arrive, cut the arms and legs from the bodies."

"We cannot do this!" protests General Tibet. "They are Kikuyu, not British!"

"They are dead. They will not mind." Kenyatta stares at him. "If you cannot do this, tell me now, and I will get someone who can."

"I will do it," said General Tibet, frowning. "But I do not know *why* I am doing it."

"Trust me, and it will all become clear," says Kenyatta.

General Tibet leaves, and Kenyatta turns to an aide. "Bring them to me now."

Four white men and two white women, all blindfolded, are ushered into Kenyatta's presence.

"You may remove your blindfolds now," says Kenyatta in English.

They do so.

"Well, I'll be damned!" mutters one of them. "So the rumors are true!"

Kenyatta surveys them. The reporters and photographers from the *New York Times*, *Newsweek*, the *Chicago Daily News*, two more from the British tabloids, and a documentary filmmaker.

"Welcome to Kikuyuland," says Kenyatta at last. "I apologize for the blindfolds, but I'm sure you understand why they were necessary."

"Okay, we're here," says one of the Americans. "Now what?"

"I promised you exclusive interviews when my emissary made secret contact with you, and you shall have them," answers Kenyatta. "I will give each of you half an hour. Then we will have dinner, and you will spend the night. Tomorrow morning you will be taken to observe the battlefield, such as it is." He pauses. "You are free to wander around my camp here, but please do not take any photographs that might help the British to identify our location. Also, do not overexert yourselves until you have adjusted to the altitude. I do not want the British reporting that we kill journalists."

One by one, Kenyatta gives his interviews. He is the voice of reason, only too happy to cease the hostilities if the British would stop slaughtering his people and give them back their country.

While the journalists are fed their dinner, Kenyatta retires to his cave to catch up on the day's news. His spies have little to report: the British seem to have melted into the forests and vanished. They are getting to know the Aberdares and the holy mountain as well as the Kikuyu themselves do.

"We have killed no British today?" asks Kenyatta.

"We have not killed any this week, Burning Spear," says an aide.

"Just as well. When it has been dark for three hours, and the journalists are all asleep, take two men out with you. Find a clearing within a mile of here, and dig three shallow graves. Then fill them in, and put a cross at the head of each."

"But we have no one to bury in them," says the aide, puzzled.

Kenyatta smiles. "I won't tell them if you don't."

"I do not understand any of this," says Deedan Kimathi, and for the first time Kenyatta sees that his second-in-command is sitting at the back of the cave.

"You will."

"Why do you allow these journalists to see our camp?" persists Kimathi. "Even if they take no photographs, they will remember enough landmarks to lead the British to this very cave."

"But they won't," says Kenyatta.

"How do you know?" demands Kimathi.

"Because I have lived among the white man and you haven't. I know it is difficult for you to believe, but there is an entire segment of white men who are predisposed to believe only the worst of their own race and only the best of ours, and these journalists represent the publications that they read, that mold their opinions. When they see the mutilated bodies of our men in the morning, they will not ask who mutilated them; they will assume it was the British, because they have been taught to assume that their own race is morally flawed. And when they see the graves with the crosses, they will not dig them up to see if British soldiers are really buried there. They will see that we treat their dead with respect, that we mark their graves with the cross of the Christians, and they will never doubt the evidence of their eyes."

"But this is foolish!" says Kimathi. "I would not believe it!"

"You are not a white journalist who is searching for a story that fits his prejudices," said Kenyatta.

Within a week, the photos of the limbless Kikuyu corpses have appeared in every major newspaper and magazine in the Western world. Three Pulitzer Prizes are eventually awarded for photos and articles cataloging the descent of well-trained British soldiers into total savagery.

☆   ☆   ☆

Kenyatta has chewed the *qat* leaves for two hours. He feels his consciousness slipping away. It is almost as if he has broken free of his old, weakened body, and is looking down on it from a great height.

"You are sure, Burning Spear?" asks the *mundumugu*, the witch doctor.

"I am sure."

"If I hear you cry out, I will stop."

"If you stop, I will order you put to death," says Kenyatta placidly. The *mundumugu* cannot tell if it is the Burning Spear speaking, or the *qat* leaves.

Five minutes later Kenyatta is so far gone into his trancelike state that he can no longer respond to questions. The *mundumugu* rolls him onto his belly and picks up the leather whip.

"May Ngai forgive me," he mutters as he brings the whip down on the old man's back. Tears roll down his face as he whips the man he worships again and again.

"I was treated fairly by my captors," Kenyatta is saying to four British journalists.

"That's not the way I heard it," replies one of the journalists.

"I have never said otherwise," protests Kenyatta.

"But a couple of your men say we tortured you."

"You are British," says Kenyatta. "Would you torture a middle-aged man who did not have the power to do you any harm?"

"No . . . but I'm not in the military."

"I have no complaints about my treatment."

"They never beat you?" persists another journalist, whose face practically begs him to contradict her.

"If they did, I'm sure they had their reasons."

"Then they *did* beat you!"

"You are putting words in my mouth," says Kenyatta. "If I were beaten, then surely I would bear the scars." He spreads his arms out. "Can you see any?"

"Would you take your shirt off?"

"Are you calling me a liar?" asks Kenyatta with no show of anger.

"No, sir," answered the journalist quickly. "But I would like to report to my readers that I have seen you shirtless and that you bear no scars."

"And then what?" asks Kenyatta with an amused smile. "Will you ask me to remove my pants as well?"

"No," says the journalist, returning his smile. "I'm sure just the shirt will be enough."

"As you wish," says Kenyatta, getting to his feet and starting to fumble with his shirt. "But I want you all to remember that I told you I have no complaints about my treatment at the hands of the British. I bear them no malice. The day will come when England will be Kenya's greatest friend and ally."

As he speaks, he removes his shirt.

"You see?" he says, facing them.

"Would you turn around please?"

Kenyatta turns his back to them. He is glad they cannot see his grin of triumph as their gasps of shock and horror come to his ears.

In the coming months he invites *National Geographic* to see the death throes of elephants, rhinos, and buffalo that have been crippled and torn apart by the British bombs. A ten-week-old lion cub with one foreleg blown away makes the cover of *Life*.

Every Kikuyu child who receives a wound from anything—a thorn bush, a jackal, a stray British bullet—is gathered into a single medical facility (it is too primitive to dignify it by calling it a hospital), and an endless parade of Western aid workers and journalists is ushered through it.

Each Kikuyu who dies from a British bullet is mutilated and photographed. Any British soldiers killed by the Kikuyu—and a number who never existed—are buried and their graves marked with crosses.

The King's African Rifles and the British Army deny all the press's charges, but the journalists know better: they have seen the carnage with their own eyes. They know the British are extracting a terrible, barbaric revenge against the Mau Mau up in the forested mountains, they know that the Kikuyu are treating the dead of the enemy with honor, they know that the old Burning Spear has been tortured in a British prison, and they know that hundreds of innocent Kikuyu children have become victims of a British army gone mad.

Within six months the American government is pressuring the British to grant Kenya its independence. The French, the Germans, and the Italians follow suit within weeks. Even the SPCA has publicly condemned the United Kingdom.

"I cannot believe it!" exclaims Kimathi as word comes to them that the British have declared a ceasefire and are withdrawing from the holy mountain. "We have killed only four of them in ten months, and they have killed thousands of us, and yet we are winning the war!"

"Different times call for different methods," replies

Kenyatta, who is unsurprised by this turn of events. "There is a sentence in their Bible that says the meek shall inherit the earth. They should have read it more carefully."

Two months later the meek have inherited Kenya. It is a foregone conclusion that Kenyatta will become the first president; an election seems a waste of time and money, but of course they will hold it.

At the ceremony that makes independence official, Malcolm MacDonald, the last British governor of Kenya, introduces Kenyatta to Prince Philip, who formally invites him into the Commonwealth.

"It is a new era, and hence a time for new names," declares the prince. "Just as Kenya Colony has become simply Kenya, I think it is time to cast aside the sobriquet of Burning Spear—" he waits until a murmur of disapproval from the crowd dies down, then continues "—and replace it with *M'zee*, the Wise Old Man. Certainly," he adds with a rueful smile, "he is wiser than we were."

Kenyatta silently agrees that the name suits him better these days. He decides to keep it.

"It Isn't Every Day of the Week…"

Roland J. Green

Being selections from the correspondence of Joshua Parker, late mayor of Baltimore, and Thomas Parker, brigadier-general of the Tennessee militia

Joshua Parker to Thomas Parker, aboard frigate United States, at sea, November 30, 1812

Dearest Brother,

Everyone as far as the Mississippi will be talking of our work yesterday, but I suppose my personal account will be of some interest to you and our mother. It would have been of even more interest to William, had he not been lost aboard *L'Insurgente*. He certainly had more aptitude for the naval service than I do, but I shall do my best.

I suppose that word of *United States* leaving New York was spread abroad more widely than it would have been otherwise thanks to the accident that damaged our bowsprit and disabled our Purser. Certainly we drew the cover off the Azores to no effect, speaking no ships save neutral Portuguese ones.

As we had replenished our water at the Azores, we had in it our power to cruise off the West Indies or South America. However, Captain Decatur showed unwonted prudence, in declining to risk our bowsprit in those waters in the hurricane season. He resolved to strike at the shipping between Halifax and Bermuda, drawing British ships from the blockade of the American coast.

We met headwinds, however, which slowed our progress but drove into our arms the British ship *Appleton Brothers*, with naval stores for Bermuda, as well as hardtack, rum, and nearly a thousand pounds in specie. We took what we could out of her and burned her, learning from her crew that several more ships similarly laden were following in her wake. They said nothing about the ships being convoyed, but Lieutenant Allen spoke for many of us when he said the Englishmen knew more than they were telling.

We encountered the first of those ships the next day (November the twenty-sixth), but she was able to keep her distance and lose us in a rain squall. *United States* is a stout ship, but is named "The Wagon" for good cause. One wonders if every spare piece of timber that came into Philadelphia while she was building went into her, giving her stout scantlings and a lubberly manner of sailing.

Not all things come to him who waits, but to those who wait with a keen eye enough good may well come. At dawn this day we saw several sail to the NNW, on a course toward us, and Captain Decatur ordered us to quarters. Having no purser's business outstanding, I stowed my papers and came on deck, ready to help with the wounded.

So I heard Captain Decatur say that if the British were in convoy, doubtless the escorting frigate was running down to engage us while the merchant vessels scattered. It was my understanding that we intended to disable the frigate at the longest possible range, then ravage the convoy while the frigate made repairs. Then we would add a second British frigate to the score of the American navy, and much wailing and gnashing of teeth to the British papers and their Lordships' meetings.

The largest of the ships came down upon us with both courses and topsails set on all three masts, as though she expected *us* to fly. With the clouds hanging low, she had closed to within two miles before we recognized *Africa*, the one ship of the line on the American station. American eyes had last seen her, I believe, from the deck of *Constitution*, during Hull's masterful escape from Broke's squadron.

All eyes on the deck of *United States* were turned to Captain Decatur. He snapped his glass shut and grinned in a manner that would not have been agreeable for the captain of *Africa* to contemplate.

"If she was a seventy-four, I'd want another forty-four with us. But a sixty-four built before our Revolution ended—it's worth chancing. The British may already be afraid to let their frigates go out after dark alone. If they have to guard their smaller two-deckers the same way . . ."

None of us needed telling that His Majesty's Navy would thereafter, and therefore, find maintaining a blockade rather harder than they might wish. Too many ships of force in American waters could allow the French out of every port from Venice to Hamburg, privateers in swarms and warships in squadrons, to ravage British commerce in Europe while we ravaged it in American waters.

None of us needed telling, either, that for a frigate to fight even the smallest ship of the line promised a bloody engagement, with our chances perhaps good but surely not certain. No frigate afloat could stand against *United States. Africa* might at least drive us off.

The breeze freshened soon thereafter, bringing *Africa* straight at us like an eager bridegroom toward his bride's bed. Decatur chose to keep the leeward gauge, as we and *Africa* were equally matched in long guns and he judged our gunnery under Lieutenant Allen's direction to be likely even more superior to the British than usual. We would try conclusions with a ship of the line only with as many circumstances as possible in our favor.

Africa came on. She did not yaw even when she was well within long cannon shot.

Decatur expostulated. "Has her captain not the wits to even suspect a trap?"

"He has a British ship of the line under him, and sees only a foreign frigate," Allen replied. "When was the last time that situation was dangerous for the British ship of the line?"

"Then let us respectfully persuade him that we are not French or Dons," Decatur said, ordering the starboard broadside to open fire.

Our respectful persuasion took the form of fifteen twenty-four-pound round shot, flung all at once straight at *Africa.* I only wish we could have equaled the range with a double-shotted broadside, as we struck fair and hard.

Her jib boom vanished, the fore course suddenly took the appearance of a nutmeg grater, her bowsprit was in worse case than ours. Enough shrouds and stays parted to make the foremast quiver majestically, then sway like Cousin Edward's old mare in her last days.

A handful of men scrambled into the fore rigging, doubtless to at least take in the fore course. We also saw *Africa* yawing to port, clearly hoping to open her broadside and at the same time increase her chances of crossing our stern to rake.

Having failed to terrify the "fir-built American frigate" and her crew of bastards into scuttling off like a whipped dog, *Africa*'s captain was clearly prepared to make a proper fight of it. We thought he might have left the decision a trifle late.

However, Captain Decatur threw the fore topsail aback, so that we would not pass out of range of *Africa*, and likewise put the helm over so that our guns bore through three more broadsides. We could have fired faster, with all hands not tending sail helping the gun crews, but Decatur wished to fire on the upward roll. Once most of our shot went high, but twice they came down with notable effect on *Africa*'s sails and rigging. We all prayed silently to see a mast go by the board, but the worst was the mizzen topsail yard sagging in its slings. Again, *Africa*'s top men went swiftly to work.

"They're making better practice at repairs than I heard of aboard *Guerriere*," Decatur remarked.

"The *Africa* doesn't have *Constitution*'s broadsides coming aboard every two minutes," Allen said.

The two officers exchanged looks. Before they could say anything, *Africa*'s first full broadside came at us. Amid the clouds of spray and smoke, half a dozen shot came aboard and one ball bounced off our hull just below the main chains.

"Huzza!" Decatur shouted. "We've the same iron sides as *Constitution*! Now let's put *Africa*'s to the proof."

Lieutenant Allen's face split in a vast smile. He had a very delicate sense of honor, and this long-range dueling could not have been entirely to his taste. I would not say that he would have yielded the battle rather than win it at long range, but clearly a stand-up fight was more to his liking.

Decatur would hardly care to turn our stern to be raked, so the helm went over again and we bore off to the NW, opening the range slightly while keeping up a fire from each main deck gun as it bore. *Africa* also reduced her fire to single guns, and altogether for the next fifteen minutes neither of us did more than disturb the sleep of the fishes. However, we were double-shotting the forty-two-pound carronades on the spar deck and I presumed that *Africa* might well be doing the same.

During that time we were both also maneuvering to rake. This was an exercise in which a lighter frigate (or a faster one, like *President*) might have quickly gained an advantage. *United States* was as stout as *Africa*, but only a trifle faster or handier. Captain Decatur left the helm orders to Lieutenant Allen, the guns being for now in the skilled hands of the junior officers, and studied *Africa* so intently that he might have been a silversmith like Paul Revere examining a newly cast tankard for flaws.

Several times during this study he moved forward or aft. Moving, he looked more like a hound casting for the scent. At last he bounded up on to the quarterdeck, snapped his glass shut, and ordered us laid close under *Africa*'s lee!

The great respect all aboard had for Captain Decatur did not prevent a few wide eyes or gaping mouths. Decatur merely smiled, or frowned at a few too openly doubtful.

As we came about, I noticed that the breeze had freshened once again, shifting to the WNW. Our new course was NNE, and with *Africa* carrying less sail we were coming up on her quickly. Her stern chasers and our bow chasers dueled briefly, but our broadside now lay silent.

Africa obliged by holding her course, but not by holding her fire. As the range

diminished still more, she began a steady
fire by divisions, and as the range shrank
still more, we began to take shot aboard
in some numbers.

Helping with the wounded became serious
work, likewise throwing the dead overboard.
Soon I had no attention for anything else, not
even the fore-topgallant mast coming down
in promiscuous ruin, strewing itself across
the spar deck and disabling two guns and
several times that many men.

I missed the moment we actually opened
fire, because I was below decks, carrying a
wounded man to the cockpit. Then gunner's
mate Wiley told me to carry a charge of
grapeshot to the spar deck, and not linger.

"You'll never be a gunner, Mr. Parker, but
you'll be an honest purser and that's worth
three midshipmen any day of the week."

"Aye," someone said. "And four and a
lieutenant on payday."

Just then I heard the fearful crash of our
entire port broadside, discharged as it was
at a range of no more than fifty yards into
Africa's lee side. Every gun was double-
shotted, some of the round shot struck
between wind and water as the Englishman
heeled toward us, and more than one triple
charge of grape swept her waist.

I staggered on deck, carrying my burden, but the carronade's crew had already
reloaded with a ready shot. In the minute
before someone took my charge of grape,

Africa replied with a full broadside, then we fired again and the breech of the recoiling carronnade nearly broke my thigh for standing too close. Smoke swallowed both friend and foe; someone I hoped was a friend reached out of the smoke and unburdened me, then I heard a fearful squealing and cracking of wood as the two ships crashed together.

A score of Englishmen plummeted on to our decks, whether shaken from the rigging or trying to board I do not know. Most were slow to get to their feet, and our gun crews were quick to wield rammer, handspike, bucket, and cutlass. Then the two ships ground alongside one another, with still more squealing and the Marines on both sides firing over the heads of the sailors—a mere hair's breadth over, in my case at least.

I saw an Englishman's face appear in a gun port, above a gun muzzle. Another bullet shrieked past my ear, the Englishman's face disappeared, I turned to see Captain Decatur drawing his second pistol, then my gun threw its load of grape straight through the port. It cut a swath clear across the upper gundeck. Suddenly a twelve-pounder was loose, breechings shot away, rolling over the screaming wounded.

I leaped back again as a British shot made my gun ring like a bell and took off the handspike man's right leg. I knelt to put a tourniquet on him and found nothing to

make it save the breeches of an Englishman who had no further need of earthly
garments. Then more fearful crackling, as
Africa's mainmast and our foremast came
down almost in the same moment.

We were luckier than the British. Our
foremast fell to starboard and leaning aft.
Axemen, led by Captain Decatur himself
in his shirtsleeves, ran to cut it away. The
wreckage shattered railings and the captain's
gig as it went overboard, but it was clear
and we were able to maneuver again before
Africa had well begun her clearing away.

It did not help her that the wreckage
masked many of her remaining serviceable
guns. On the lower deck, even those still
serviceable could fire only on the upward roll.
Decatur had reckoned correctly that with her
lower deck port sills barely six feet above the
water, *Africa* could not use her lower-deck
lee broadside in a fresh breeze.

I saw also that *Africa*'s foremast was swaying ominously, that several of her gunports
had been knocked into one, and that from
two others blood was trickling. Meanwhile,
our spar deck battery played fiercely on
Africa's waist with more grapeshot. The
Englishmen who survived long enough to
work on the mainmast would be a hardy
or lucky breed.

We lumbered into a turn to port, closed,
and raked *Africa* with another double-shotted
broadside from dead ahead. Her bowsprit and

foremast went by the board. After three more broadsides I was summoned below—the messenger threatened to chase me there at the point of a cutlass. We had dead and wounded to record, twenty-two of the first and forty-five of the second, and the surgeon and his mates had much to do, as well as hands too bloody to hold a pen.

So I did my work while the gunners finished theirs. When I came on deck again, *Africa* had only a stump of her mizzenmast left and was rolling heavily. Our topmen were already aloft, tricing up the mainyard to keep it from adding more ruin to our spar deck and hauling out spare spars to begin repairs. Captain Decatur had one arm bare except for a blood-stained bandage, and was hailing *Africa*.

"Do you strike?"

The first English reply was for the mizzenmast to go the way of the rest. Then *Africa* fired an unshotted gun to leeward. Finally, someone found a piece of cloth on which one could see the white under the bloodstains, and hung it over the railing, to flap in the breeze.

Then, for the next several hours, we had as lively a time as we had during the fight, if less bloody. Two British merchant ships closed with us, perhaps hoping to find us in such a state that they could avenge *Africa*. We forced both to strike, dismasting one of them.

We put prize crews aboard both *Africa* and the less damaged merchant vessel, *Heather*. We then appointed *Heather* a cartel—a ship for transporting prisoners—and laid her alongside *Africa*, to take her crew back to Halifax. We could hardly feed five hundred prisoners all the way to Boston, so we contented ourselves with a few tokens—perhaps more than a few—embarked her surviving officers as prisoners, and set her on fire.

She blew up just before dark, and we set all possible sail to be clear of pursuers before dawn. We were no longer a match for more than your common British 38.

It was only when the last glow from *Africa* died that the cheering began. Was it only then that we realized what we had done? Certainly we'd had enough work for all hands, and a hundred more besides, and weariness slows thought.

The cheering brought Captain Decatur on deck, from where he had been entertaining the surviving British officers at dinner. He stood on the break of the quarterdeck for a moment, then pretended to glare.

"What is this? Are we going to have a riot aboard *United States* every turn of the watch, from now to Boston?"

That altered the cheering, from plain "Huzza!" to "Huzza for Captain Decatur." The captain did not seem to find this an improvement.

Finally he sprang on to a quarterdeck gun.

This drew attention and brought silence. "Comrades, I thank you. I admit, it isn't every day of the week that a frigate sinks a ship of the line. And I promise you—you have permission to cheer *every time we sink another one.*"

We are now three days homeward bound. I will seal and weight this letter, so that it can be posted at once when we land or even if we speak an American ship, or thrown overboard if we are not fortunate to return safely to Boston.

God keep you, and prosper all your endeavours.

Your affectionate brother,
Joshua

∽

Thomas Parker to Joshua Parker, in camp near Emmetsburg, Tennessee, February 1, 1813

Great God, little Joshua!

By now you've no doubt long since read the Boston papers that we found in the same bundle with your letter. It's not every damned *century* that a frigate sinks a ship of the line, and I don't suppose any foreign frigate has ever done it the British. Serves them right, and I hope your Captain Decatur means what he says about doing it again.

Although we wouldn't mind having a man or two like him, commanding on the Lakes come spring. We've lost Mackinaw and Detroit down south, which means the British hold both the straits. All they need is a decent fleet on Lake Erie and they can carve a trail of tears all the way across the Northwest as far as the Mississippi. They don't have the Prophet anymore, but they still have Tecumseh and General Brock, and that's like fighting one old wise bear and one young wise bear at once. There's no way of being so lucky you don't get clawed.

If they turn every outpost in the Northwest into a Fort Mims, that could be bad enough. Then they could pick up more friends among the Red Sticks and the Choctaws and finish going north everything they didn't finish going south.

They might have that decent fleet, too, if the British get spitting mad over what you Navy boys have been doing on their sacred sea. The Federalist papers weren't even sure you could tweak the lion's whiskers, but you've damned near gone in and yanked out a tooth!

We'll do our best, but that might not be too good. General Harrison has all the regulars, who aren't very many or very good, and General Jackson has most of the militia and thinks he outranks Harrison. I hope they can lead their men separately, because if they ever have to fight in the same battle, they'll likely enough fight each other before they fight the British.

With a really good war to fight against everybody he hates, General Jackson is about as happy as he ever gets. Don't take me wrong—he's brave and stubborn enough to deserve his rank. But you don't have to be an Indian to understand why people are scared of him. I wonder how *I* looked, a while back when I had a temper and killed Charles Shaxxon. If I looked half as mean as Old Hickory, maybe the people who said I ought to go West knew something I didn't.

Well, not much we can do, except pray the ice on Erie is real slow to go out. The Indians can raid across the ice, but the Redcoats can't, and nobody can haul artillery or a sledge of rations.

If you can get to Philadelphia and find Cynthia Shaxxon McKnight willing to receive *anybody* by the name of Parker, please be received and give her my humblest respects and apologies. I don't suppose what I wrote her before leaving ever got there.

Keep your feet dry and your gullet wet.

Wishing the best,
Tom

Joshua Parker to Thomas Parker, aboard frigate United States, Boston, May 14, 1813

Dearest Brother,

I hope there will be a victory to report on the Lakes before this letter reaches you. Certainly we have not been backward in sending everything needed to give Master-Commandant Lawrence a respectable force.

Our victory over *Africa* seems to have begun a chain of events that bodes well for the American cause, by bringing us all together. Before that victory, I would not have sworn that New England would stand with the rest of our noble Republic. But when we entered Boston, flying *Africa's* ensign under ours, the spectacle was a wonder. Captain Decatur was given the freedom of the city, a subscription for our dead and wounded raised seventeen thousand dollars in two days, and many other signs of public rejoicing were manifest.

The British replied to our victory by a close blockade of Boston, hitherto left largely free, and Captain Bainbridge, commanding *Constitution*, took her out to engage the British. Finding only one frigate, Broke's *Shannon*, he engaged, and after an intensely warm action, took her, Broke being killed and Bainbridge likely enough crippled for life. He has most certainly redeemed himself for the loss of *Philadelphia*, being the first American and perhaps the first captain of any nation in a long while to take two British frigates, *Java* and *Shannon*.

With Rodgers taking *Macedonian* and Lawrence taking *Frolic*, we now count six victories in single-ship actions since the war began. This is more than all the rest of the world has won against the British Navy in the last ten years.

Not able to strike back by sea, the British struck by land. General Brock won a smashing victory at Queenston. Afterward he let his Indians and Glengarry Scots, vengeful for their slain chief MacDonnel, swarm across the Niagara River. Which was more ready with the knife and the brand, the Indians or the Scots, there were few survivors to tell for a width of twenty miles inland.

This brought about a miracle. Would you believe two staunchly Federalist papers called for the militia to march, and stand shoulder to shoulder on the Canadian border until not a sparrow wearing a red coat can cross? Subscriptions for a frigate, the same plan as *Essex*, to be named *Plymouth*, and two sloops of war, *Salem* and *General Scott*? Donations of naval supplies? The fitting out as privateers of every fast vessel that can swim and some that I think may prove slow or leaky?

Well, I have read as all this and seen some of it with my own eyes. I have not read what I suspect to be the true reasons, that if New England could not profit from a separate peace she would profit from joining the war, and in the process keep the British away from her borders and coasts. (We have heard tales, that the British have a large naval force on the Penobscot, and are encamping troops behind strong earthworks.)

Not a tale, though perhaps another miracle, is what happened only two days ago. A *French ship of the line* and a frigate sailed through the blockading squadron and entered Boston Harbor.

It seems that Their Lordships of the Admiralty feared our attacking the convoys that feed Wellington's army in Spain. I believe this has happened, and certainly many New England merchant ships that were once licensed to carry cargoes to Spain have been withdrawn, captured, blockaded, or even turned into privateers to prey on the commerce that they once carried!

However, the French supposed that the British might be weakening the blockade off the French naval ports, and ventured to send out a squadron of ships of the line, to raid the West Indies convoys. The British met and engaged them a week out from Bordeaux, taking two ships of the line and the supply vessels. A frigate was lost at sea.

The two French crews we have with us are scurvy-ridden, and not in a good state of discipline. However, the ships themselves are sound, having been refitted thoroughly before being sent out. I know this, because with my knowledge of French, I am busy with interpreting.

So we have offered to the French, to rest and feed their crews ashore in Boston. Meanwhile, we will finish refitting our own ships, and in return for our care for the French crews, man their ships and take them out with our own squadron.

This is the sort of bargain I would expect to appeal to a Yankee. I am told it appeals to the French as well. Their only request is that we not change the names of the ships. It seems that even a navy founded by Jacobins keeps to a few traditional sailors' beliefs.

I hope all is arranged for the best.

Your devoted brother,
Joshua

P.S. Do not even mention Cynthia Shaxxon in a letter to our mother. And be warned: the Philadelphia McKnights are kin by marriage to Captain Decatur, who is almost as good with a pistol as General Jackson, if not quite as savage of temper.

Joshua

P.P.S. All is arranged, as of an hour ago. I am to repair aboard U.S.S. *Le Malin*, to begin translating as much of her ship's books as we may need.

Thomas Parker to Joshua Parker, a camp near the Virginia line, late June, 1813

Salty Brother,

It looks as if you are taking nicely to the sea and the Navy is taking a nice bite out of the British lion. Keep biting! Even General Jackson says good things about the Navy, now that Captain Lawrence won on Lake Erie. In the past Jackson would say that spending public money on anything larger than a gunboat was just an Eastern way to justify raising taxes and establishing banks.

Captain Lawrence kept us from being ground between the upper and lower millstones. With our hold on Lake Erie, the best Brock and Tecumseh can do is hold what they have at either end, Niagara Falls and Detroit. We can even pry them out of Detroit if General Harrison can get a few more regulars up across Ohio.

We could also use those regulars here against the Muskogee Nation (that's the Creeks and Choctaws), but maybe not. If General Harrison came with them, I don't know who would be fighting who. Harrison's regular commission outranks Jackson's militia one, but waving a regular commission in Old Hickory's face is like waving a lighted torch over a barrel of turpentine. You don't want to be anywhere close to where that's happening.

The word about what we might have to do to the south isn't good hearing. The British have taken Pensacola in West Florida, claiming to protect their allies (the Dons) from French allies (us). They've also been sniffing around Mobile. God help us if they take that and start landing shiploads of arms for the Red Sticks' warriors.

I'm sure we could still stand them off if they came all the way north to try us, particularly if the Cherokees hit them from behind. But the Red Sticks in black paint are likely as not to go for Georgia, where the militia is thin as ants in an empty jug, and the Cherokees would have to defend their own land.

We also just march south and pound the Creeks into the mud, because we don't have enough men to do that and hold Tennessee and Kentucky the way the people want us to. I don't know how many men would be enough for that, but we certainly can't do it with less than four thousand, not with Jackson thinking about his career after the war. He won't get elected governor if he lets Indians run wild in places that haven't seen a scalping since the Revolution.

I've suggested that we muster a couple of companies of Rangers, to strike across country into Georgia, make the Red Sticks wonder what's next, and encourage the Cherokees. If this happens, I might be a captain of, or at least in, one of those companies. I might volunteer anyway, and you likely won't hear from me for some time.

Still, it would beat sitting here, waiting to
see if you'll wake up with your scalp still on
your head and if the next load of whiskey
is going to be worse than the last one.

This goes off tonight, toward the Ohio.
I hope it reaches you before you become
even saltier, by sailing across the Atlantic.
Don't stay up so late working on the papers
that you don't learn any of the French for
charming the ladies, or wear yourself out
so that you can't charm even the ones who
speak English.

Joshua Parker to Thomas Parker, Nantes, France, September 19, 1813

Dear Brother,

Your letter made me hope your under-
takings prosper by land as mine do by sea,
although not all the news I send by this
missive is good.

Two squadrons broke out of Boston, only
days after your letter reached me. One sailed
under Commodore Hull with *Constitution*
and *Chesapeake*, to trail their coat toward
Halifax, and ours was the other. The British met Hull and drove him back to port
in an action where we took *Endymion* and
sank *Tenedos* but Hull was killed. Both our

frigates will also need much work, and Commodore Stewart now commands in Boston, with Captain Perry in *Chesapeake*.

We sailed straight for France, in the strength of a ship of the line, *La Legion* (which means "legion" although there is only one of her), four frigates, *Le Malin* (which means "crafty"), *United States*, *President*, and *Constellation*, sloop of war *Somers*, and no less than seventeen privateers. If our kin in Baltimore do not hasten fitting out their ships, the New Englanders will surely try to strip the seas bare of British sails.

Rodgers, being senior to Decatur, could not resist being the first American commodore to fly his broad pennant in a two-decker. The man stands much on his rank, and his dark and dour countenance well matches his choleric disposition. However, he is a sound seaman and somewhat eased in mind and purse by the award of prize money for bringing the *Macedonian* into New York.

It also helped to have two commodores, because we could thus form two Navy squadrons to attack the rich convoys, leaving the privateers to dispose of single ships. The British certainly had guarded their convoys rather well against frigates, but I do not think it was "dreamt of in their philosophies" to see a well-found seventy-four flying American colors. As a *ruse de guerre*, Rodgers also flew the British East India Company's house flag, some of their larger ships being easily mistaken for ships of the line.

Suffice it to say, we *demolished* a West India convoy, then we and *Constellation* feinted at the Irish coastal trade, being now well supplied with coffee and sugar from our prizes. For a gift of either, the Irish would gladly supply us with information as to the whereabouts of the British Navy, so we made a fine bag of English merchant ships and coast guard vessels, as well as burning several shore stations. Smugglers will go about their occasions unmolested for some time, in that part of Ireland.

Commodore Rodgers took his portion of the squadron into Nantes, nearly losing *La Legion* on a reef because the French were slow to send pilots. However, they at once made amends, and now we at last are all safe in Nantes. *La Legion* will need to be drydocked and refitted after her grounding. It is well that she met that accident in France, for there is not a drydock in America.

In truth, I have had no occasion to use my French to charm the ladies, and no wish to use my prize money on those whose charms may be purchased. The ladies of Nantes in any case mostly lack charm, and the French Navy is jealous of its position in regard to them. (At times I think they are jealous also of American victories over "Perfidious Albion.")

Few of us have as yet received much in specie, except for the division of the moveable goods taken aboard our *thirty-one* prizes (to the Navy alone; I have no count for the privateers) and is not being spent to repair the flagship. (Naval stores are terribly dear in France, after so many years of blockade.) All the prize agents in France could not command enough specie to pay what is owed us just for the prizes we sent in, to say nothing of what we burned.

However, we have agreed with the French that they will provide us with a lading of lace, silks, and brandy, sure to fetch a good price in America. They are sending it to America in two of their own frigates. I wish them all good fortune, and will entrust this letter to it.

～

Thomas Parker to Joshua Parker, somewhere in northern Georgia, December, 1813

Brother,

We are very far from any place where a letter can be posted, so for all I know this letter may be found on my body by someone who will burn it. If it's a Red Stick, I hope he thinks it's a curse on him. I wish it was.

But if you read this at all—I did become

captain of the First Company in Donelson's
Rangers. The Donelsons are close friends,
maybe even kin, to Old Hickory, but they
don't have any men of the right quality to
lead it, so the name is Jackson's way of
flattering them. I don't much care about
what name I fight under, and the Second
Company is under a man of Pennsylvania
stock, named Kleinschmidt. He's a fine shot
and there are plenty of Duchies in Pennsylvania, but from what I hear about him, his
father might have been a Hessian deserter,
so Old Hickory would never make him a
major. Not having a major doesn't matter
much anyway, seeing as how the moon will
turn blue before the two companies fight
in the same battle.

Anyway, we struck off across country,
keeping to the hills to have the high ground
but marking routes for larger columns with
heavier loads. We probably still left a trail
so that any Creeks who followed us got
short of breath only by laughing themselves
into a fit.

The white settlers had been pretty well
burned out or driven into stockades, and
the stockades themselves were running
short of food. We told people that if they
had guns, their best chance was to get as
far toward the Ohio as they could, and be
ready to eat fish and their last hardtack
all the way downriver. They looked at us
kind of the way Job must have looked at

the people who tried to comfort him after he'd lost everything.

We were two days beyond a place called Presley's Spring when we decided to send out a hunting party, thinking we were clear of hostiles and knowing we were in good deer country. Well, the hostiles—Choctaws, I think—had circled around wide enough that with the rain of the night and the early part of the day we hadn't heard them.

Then half of them came running out of the trees, making as much noise as they could, and the other half sneaked up on us like snakes, on their bellies and just about as quiet. They didn't have more than a single musket and I think their archers must have had wet bowstrings, or they'd have knocked a bunch of us down before rushing us.

We'd made a run for a hillside that would give us high ground with cover, but knew that it was maybe five hundred yards and we'd lose a man every hundred if we were lucky. I said my prayers, particularly thanks for having a tomahawk. It hits harder than a sword and reaches far enough.

Then suddenly we had about fifteen or twenty men running at the Choctaws, and without stopping *five* of them fired muskets. They shouldn't have hit anything, firing on the run, but the range was so close that they probably could have hit the Choctaws with a thrown pumpkin. Anyway, three Choctaws went down. A sixth man fired a pistol and hit a fourth Choctaw, who let out a terrible scream and grabbed his belly.

Then the newcomers were in among the Choctaws, using knives, tomahawks, and musket butts. We stopped running when the Choctaws got busy with the newcomers, and did the same, except that some of our men had reloaded and some of *these* had a clear shot. The range was fifty yards at most, and all of us could hit a man at two hundred.

More Choctaws went down. Others ran. Still others charged us while we were reloading. We were fighting them hand to hand in front, and the others were doing them same behind them, with everybody shouting and screaming.

The shouting and the war paint made me sure we had Choctaws against us and Cherokees on our side. I don't speak enough Cherokee to do more than be polite if I meet one of them out hunting. I did shout back what I hoped sounded like thanks.

After a while, there weren't any more live Choctaws, at least on their feet. The Cherokees were killing the wounded, but not taking scalps, so I told my men to do the same.

The Choctaw with the belly wound was singing or more like gasping some sort of death song. A slim Cherokee stepped up to him, let him finish it, then cracked his skull with an axe. It wasn't a steel trade axe, either. It was one of the old stone tomahawks mostly

used for ceremonies now, the handle all dark
with years, sweat, and blood.

I repeated my promise, and the slim
warrior nodded and said, "We are grateful.
Have you food?"

The English was good, and the voice
made me take a second look. Sure enough,
I was talking to a woman, in buckskins cut
loose enough to hide her figure, mocca-
sins, and a belt with fancy beadwork. Her
skin wasn't much darker than a white farm
woman's at the end of summer, and as for
her eyes—well, she had big fine ones, even
for a Cherokee woman.

"We have little, but what we have, we
will also share," I said, and I hoped that
the hunting party would come back soon
with enough deer and possum for seventy
mouths instead of fifty.

They did, after a while. Some of them
had been close enough to hear the shooting
and ran back, coming empty-handed but
too late for the fight. I told them to set
snares for rabbits. Finally the deer hunters
came back, enough to go around, including
a great big buck.

When we'd done eating, I handed the
buck's hide to the woman, whose name was
Caroline Pineraft Bearkiller. She looked at
it, and grinned. Her teeth weren't much
worse than mine.

"Do you want to court me?" Then she
turned to her war party and told them what

she'd asked, only she used a much ruder word than "court."

I'd heard that Cherokee women were plain-spoken, but I was glad it was twilight so nobody could see me blushing.

"Well," I said. "There are other ways of sleeping warm, beside that. A good buckskin is one of them." She nodded, took the buckskin, sat down with it across her knees, and began looking at it for holes.

I laughed, and then waved Lieutenant Goble and three of the four sergeants over to me. (The fourth was tending to the cooking, but I didn't worry much about him. He's fifty years old and has nine children and fourteen grandchildren.)

"Nobody even looks strange at Caroline Bearkiller," I told them. "If you do, her warriors might kill you. Or she might decide to change her name to Mankiller. Or *I* might kill you."

Brother, if you read this after I am gone, find Caroline Pineraft Bearkiller or her family and give them whatever a Cherokee warrior gives a woman he would like to *court*, in my name. I hope and pray that even if I don't walk out to Georgia, she will.

By my hope of heaven and my fear of hell,

Thomas

Joshua Parker to Thomas Parker, Nantes, France, January 12, 1814

Brother,

The English papers assure the world that the Indians are sweeping all before them in Georgia, as Wellington is in Spain and the allies in Germany. I permit myself to hope that if the part about the Indians is true, they have not swept you up.

We have reason to believe that the papers are telling the truth, about the fall of New Orleans. Whether they are also truthful in saying that the French inhabitants of the city would not fight to remain under American rule, is a matter for speculation. Can you add to our knowledge of these circumstances?

Any possession of that city gives the British a military advantage, through holding the mouth of the Mississippi and barring the commerce of the settlers in the great river's valley. They might also be able to carve out their dreamed-of "Indian homeland." Does anyone believe this reflects anything but a desire to use them as catspaws against the United States?

Indeed, by the terms of the original Treaty of San Iledefonso, by which the French gained Louisiana from Spain, the French had no right to sell the territory to President Jefferson and he had no right to buy it! When we were at peace and the Spanish at war with the British, this clearly mattered little. But now that Spain and Britain are allies, with the British using Florida, could the British Crown not find a pretext for "protecting" their allies' territory from the dreadful Yankees and so remain in occupation of New Orleans and other parts of Louisiana in perpetuity?

I fear that giving the British cause to fear our power at sea may not have served our national purpose as well as we thought it would.

I must set down my pen, as we have just learned that Commodore Samuel Barron has reached Nantes and wishes to embark for the United States, apparently with hope of reinstatement in the Navy and a command at sea! This also is an unexpected consequence of the course of the war at sea.

P.S.—We are hastily preparing for sea. It appears that the Alliance against Napoleon may be disintegrating. There is talk of a victory over Wellington in the south of France, and a separate peace with Austria. The French semaphore system sends messages with the speed of the wind, but of course it can send lies as easily and swiftly as truth.

If the French can then make peace with the British, they will face only Spain, Prussia, and Russia. Spain is weak, Prussia implacable but needing British subsidies, and the czar a weathercock whose armies in any case would be campaigning far from home. Since any peace with the British would surely require an end to French cooperation with the Americans, we wish to be at sea before the French can decide to throw us to the Lion as a gesture of goodwill.

This letter goes on the Baltimore privateer *Barrett*, although I hope to have time to make a fair copy.

In regrettable haste,
Joshua

∽

Thomas Parker to Joshua Parker, from the middle of Georgia, late March, 1814

This missive ought to find its way to Baltimore, and I hope onward to you. If the rumors about peace in Europe are true, the British will have ships and to spare for us, not having to blockade the French coast anymore.

Since the last time I wrote, we have marched a long ways toward Savannah, skirmishing with hostiles most of the way. We'd have been in a sorry muck several more times without Cherokee help.

It seems as if the Muskogee Nation Indians used a deal of their powder and guns from the British to settle old scores with the Cherokee. This puts the Cherokee firmly on our side, at least as long as we're fighting the British.

General Jackson's command is catching up with us. When it does, we will have about two thousand men in three columns, most of them from Tennessee and Kentucky. Even where the Georgians had enough settlers to make up a militia, the ones who've turned out were half armed, more than half naked, and hungry. If it wasn't for the Cherokee trying their best to feed us as well as their own people, we'd never have been able to advance.

We are now down in the lowlands, where it can be warm even at this time of year. The soil is all red clay, which sticks to you whether it's mud or dust. After a day's march, you can't tell who started off *white* and who *red*, because everybody has turned clay-colored.

Nothing seems to be happening on the Canadian border. I suppose the strengths on the lake and on land are too evenly matched. I begin to doubt that the War Hawks were as smart as they thought they were. A war they thought would win us Canada may lose us even territory we had under the Peace of Paris thirty years ago!

A messenger in—General Jackson will be joining us in two days, and is sending word ahead to Savannah. If I can pour enough whiskey into the messenger, he might take this letter to the coast and find a ship to take it to Baltimore. The British are watching Savannah, but I've heard there are lots of creeks where nobody who doesn't know the water can sail even a rowboat.

Caroline Pineraft Bearkiller wishes me to greet you in her name. I don't think this means anything but good manners, which she has more than many white women I've known. She also says that *Bearkiller* is from an ancestor's hunting, but *Pineraft* is when she rode a log down a flooded stream to rescue a child who'd fallen in.

Your dusty brother,
Thomas

∽

Joshua Parker to Thomas Parker, aboard United States, Norfolk, May 15, 1814

I am sorry to say that our respected mother appears to have opened both of your last letters to me that reached her and is somewhat distempered about Caroline Bearkiller. She certainly wrote me in strong terms on the subject. If she has not written in such terms to you, I will spare you knowledge of them for now.

It was easier for us to return than it was to go out, because of the odd sort of peace that has come to Europe. The Austrians and the Russians have recognized Napoleon's son as emperor, but since he is a baby, there is a Council of Regency that includes his mother, the Dowager Empress Marie Louise, who of course is an Austrian princess. There is also a Superior Council of War, with old Boney himself in the rank of Marshal as its Chairman and some marshal named Davout as the Minister of War.

The French would not have welcomed the Bourbons back unless that was the only way of winning peace. Monarchist sympathizers in Nantes (whom we suspect in the disappearance of some of our sailors) did not like the agreement. But in time they admitted that if it kept the Prussians and Russians out of France, they could live with the Little Eagle or even under him without too much pain.

The British were said to be very reluctant parties to the armistice, and may yet balk at a peace treaty on these terms. There are also rumors that the Austrians hope to push the British toward agreement, by letting the French hold on to Italian territories that they would otherwise be returning to the Habsburgs. The British do *not* want the French all over the Mediterranean.

It's not every day of the week that one sees so many shiftings of alliances and so many friends become foes and the other way around.

The British have of course abandoned the blockade of France. They have also withdrawn Wellington's army to just beyond the Spanish border, because the Spanish have *not* signed a peace with the French. I do not know whether Wellington's orders are to prevent a French invasion of Spain or a Spanish invasion of France!

With no blockade off France but little of fair winds in mid-passage, we were forty-one days from Nantes to the Capes of the Chesapeake. We took only two prizes, the British now having most of their trade between Canada and the West Indies in convoys too heavily escorted for our privateers. Even the close blockade now consists of squadrons of frigates with the occasional ship of the line, and they will scatter small craft up and down the American coast again only when they have taken or rendered useless all of our heavier ships.

We were able to run into the Chesapeake at night in bad weather, with only one exchange of broadsides. *Constellation* was not so lucky, being taken by the British 74 *Triumph*. As of this writing, *Legion* and *Malin* are also safe in Baltimore, which should make the place secure against anything but a major expedition. Of course, the only way the French crews in Boston can come down to Baltimore is overland, so it looks as if the ships will be flying the American flag for a while longer. We are also said to be launching two ships of the line of our own later this year.

Ships that come from the south say the British appear to be gathering an expedition against Savannah. If they succeed, it will mean a rich haul of prize money, and they will be able to march northeast against Charleston or northwest against the Cherokees.

Commodore Decatur has appointed me his secretary, as a new purser has come aboard. I also learn that the frigate armed *en flute* reached Philadelphia, and if the Quakers are honest I shall see a handsome sum in addition to my prize money.

This letter is going south in a coasting vessel, so that I shall not add to it anything that might be useful to the enemy if the letter should fall into the wrong hands.

Do be careful with your Cherokee wench. Even if her people do not practice scalping, they seem to have plenty of guns and to be good shots.

Your affectionate brother,
Joshua

∽

Thomas Parker to Joshua Parker, Savannah, August 20, 1814

Esteemed Brother,

Don't call Caroline Pineraft Bearkiller a wench. I've already knocked one man down for doing that.

I am leaving this letter where it will be

safe if we hold off the British but I do not survive the Battle of Savannah. I will hope and even pray that you come in time—your Commodore Decatur sounds like a good hand in a fight. We have only about three thousand militia that are of any use at all, and this includes Americans from the Floridas and the Indian territories. We also have practically no field artillery and not much in the forts around Savannah that would stand up through a good fight.

That's not enough to hold the city against an attack from the sea and a second one from overland by way of Mobile or the Floridas. The British are sending regulars and some Dons from the Floridas, with the Choctaws, Creeks, and Seminoles to make a bad bargain worse.

The Cherokees can't hold the land route all by themselves, either. If they stay away from their crops and villages too long, they'll starve during the winter. Or their white neighbors will try to take over their land.

At least Old Hickory will do something about ungrateful bastards like that if he catches them! Nobody could ever call him an Indian lover, but he can tell people who've helped him from people who've hurt him. And people who've hurt him are safe, maybe, in the next territory.

Brother, you seem to have come home from the sea with more money than anybody in the family has seen in quite a while. Do you think you could loan me some of that pirate's gold to buy land for Caroline and her kin? A proper purchase with a legal title and everything will make it easier for them to keep off trespassers. Also, if I don't end the campaign in this world, Caroline will have something to call her own. The Cherokee sometimes make all kinds of noise about one of their women going with a white man.

Now please don't ask any questions where you wouldn't want Mother to hear the answers, even if you find me alive and in a state to answer them. Just say yes or no, and we'll part friends as well as kin.

Your grateful brother,
Tom

⌒

Joshua Parker to his mother, Sarah Madsen Parker, aboard General Scott, *Norfolk, September 15, 1814*

Dearest Mother,

I write to you to hope that you are well. I also enclose a promissory note to Thomas, to pay him eleven thousand dollars out of my share of the prize money and cargoes from the European cruise. I expect that both of us shall survive the coming campaign in the south, I to pay him and he to be paid and to buy the land in Tennessee on which he has set his heart. However, God is the Great Disposer of all things, and not only in war.

You ask how I see the progress of the war. It seems to me that we have gained much in the north, with General Harrison besieging Detroit and Chauncey's victory on Lake Ontario. Neither the Northwest nor New England can have much to fear from British offensives. Indeed, if New England's embodied militia is sufficiently reinforced by regulars and by our victorious Lake Ontario squadron, they may be able to sail down the St. Lawrence and threaten Montreal, as well as the supply line of the British forces in the Lake Champlain country. General Brock will do all that mortal man can do with his men—but that will be little enough if the Richelieu River is closed to reinforcements and supplies.

On the other hand, we may yet lose enough in the South that the British will claim territory there, if not for themselves then for the Spanish or the Indians. We sail for Savannah tomorrow to "spike that gun," as Tom would say it, by seeing that the British effort against that city comes to nothing.

We are four frigates and five fast-sailing armed merchantmen, carrying among them a thousand men, five thousand stand of arms, and much else by way of military stores. Commodore Rodgers flies his broad pennant in *United States*, which Commodore

Decatur has given up in favor of the lighter frigate *General Scott*, fitter for work close inshore or even up the Savannah River. Other squadrons from New York and Boston will seek to draw the British blockaders north, by seeming to threaten their ships off Long Island and the Penobscot.

I understand that we have Secretary of State Monroe to answer for much of this scheme. I trust his share in the victory at Bladensburg has not given him a *folie de grandeur*, as I believe those reports you have, that General Smith did the greater part of the work. But we shall do our best, and pray that along with the efforts of those already around Savannah, it will be good enough to loose the British hold on the South.

Pray for us, Mother, for it is the hour of our need and our country's, and will be so for some while yet.

Your loving son,
Joshua

⌒

Thomas Parker to Sarah Madsen Parker, Savannah, October 12, 1814

Dear Mam,

I leave this for you in case we don't meet again in this world. Please know that I haven't

always honored my mother, still less my
father, so my days may not be long. But I
loved you both and I am sorry for all the dis-
appointments and heartaches I caused you.

Please, I beg you, don't take my bequest
to Caroline Pineraft Bearkiller as another
heartache. There is nothing about her you
could possibly object to, if she was white.
Also, please note that this and all other fair
copies of the bequest are signed by both me
and Joshua and witnessed by Commodore
Decatur. I didn't think this was the time to
ask General Jackson to witness that kind of
an agreement between one of his officers
and a Cherokee woman.

They are beating the Assembly, and the
signal guns are firing both to the south and
along the river. That means the British are
in sight in force in both quarters. God grant
that I can soon write of a victory.

With affection,
Your son Thomas

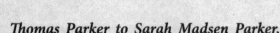

*Thomas Parker to Sarah Madsen Parker,
Savannah, October 14, 1814*

Dear Mother,
    I write in haste, so that this letter may go
with the first courier to leave Savannah for

the north. We have won a great victory, but at a high price. Many brave men are fallen and General Jackson is gravely wounded. The British not killed or taken are in flight by land and sea, the Seminoles mostly dead, and the Dons we could persuade the Cherokees to spare mostly taken.

I write this letter instead of Joshua, because he has a flesh wound in his right arm and cannot write anything a Christian could read with his left hand. His arm is in no danger, still less his life, and I am sure he will write the next letter at greater length.

But the prayers of us all for a victory *have been answered.*

Thankfully,
Thomas

Thomas Parker and Joshua Parker to their respected mother, Sarah Madsen Parker, Savannah, October 24, 1814

Dearest Mother,

We write this letter together, Tom penning and Joshua dictating. This is because Joshua understands more of the sea fighting but still cannot write a legible hand.

Shoal water made the British cautious about a close blockade of the mouth of the Savannah River, so the squadron ran in with only the loss of a Charleston privateer to the British. Several other privateers and one of the transports ran ashore and could not be got off, but we were able to take out their guns and gear and land most of the transport's stores. Then we set the ships on fire, placed the guns in battery to cover the mouth of the river, and proceeded up to Savannah in local boats.

A thousand men of Maryland and Virginia made a considerable difference to the American strength in Savannah, where General Jackson had been trying to hold with no more than three thousand. A quarter of these were the all but useless Georgia militia and a similar part the Cherokees. Those who knew of their fighting in the north thought well of the Cherokees but the Georgians had no faith in them. Nor did they care for French volunteers who came in the squadron, or for a company of free Negroes General Jackson organized.

Savannah lies on the south bank of its river. To the southwest is forest and farmland, to the southeast swamp with a few trails across dry ground. The city itself is well laid out for defense, with many of the houses arranged around squares. General Jackson proposed to demolish some of the houses outside the squares, to clear fields of fire and procure material for building revetments, but the citizens would not permit it until he threatened to declare martial law and *take* everything and everybody he needed.

The British came against Savannah ten days after the reinforcements arrived, enough time to let us arrange a warm reception for them. Half of the Cherokees scouted the swamps and kept watch from the islands on the river for enemy landing parties. The militia and a naval landing party under Commodore Decatur held the entrenchments around Savannah, with the Maryland and Virginia regiments in reserve. The rest of the Cherokees formed a skirmish line to the west. Upriver from the city, we hid *General Scott*, under Captain Allen. She was left with her rigging all a-cockbill and firepots burning on her deck, to let spies believe she had been abandoned.

General Jackson and Commodore Decatur were not fast friends, being rather too unlike in temperament. But they both believed that victory meant leaving none of the enemy fit to fight. They were resolved to do this even if we ran out of powder and had to finish the battle with bayonets and boarding pikes.

At the coming of the British, Thomas took his Rangers out to join the Cherokee skirmishers, while Joshua took a position beside Commodore Decatur, to record his orders. Soon we heard firing both on the river and inland, musketry and cannon both. Then the Cherokee guarding the trails past White Marsh Island came tumbling back, firing as they went, to report Seminoles approaching Augustine Creek.

The Georgia militia from the settlements along that creek immediately wished to advance against the Seminoles to save their homes. General Jackson said that homes could be rebuilt if Savannah held, but if they ran off now the Seminoles would kill most of them and he would shoot any survivors. Rightly enough, they took him at his word.

The British had two regular regiments, the 44th and the 71st, coming overland, and two more on the river, the 42nd and another whose number I never learned. None of them were at full strength, but add together Seminoles, Dons, West Indian Negroes, and a naval landing party as large as ours, they probably outnumbered us by half again.

They tried to land in the town of Gerardus on our left flank, but the citizens there had their wits about them. They fired several warehouses filled with combustible material and then fought the British in the streets, hiding in the smoke.

The British then tried another landing between Gerardus and Savannah itself, but we had two eighteen-pounders at the south end of the city, and a water battery of six-pounders on the island directly across the channel. We sank twelve boats and set fire to a brig. The Cherokees killed most of the British who got ashore, and they say that some of the ones in the water were eaten by alligators or bitten by snakes.

The British then dropped down the river and put their men ashore south of Gerardus, out of range of our guns though not of the Cherokees at the mouth of Augustine Creek. Our heroic Indian friends had to fight looking both ways, because the Seminoles were up past White Marsh Island by then, and not all of them came out safe. But they took a good toll of the enemy, with a particular delight in killing the Spanish. Again, they say that some of the Seminoles turned their coats, and added to the misery of the Dons.

General Jackson wanted to try to hold Gerardus *and* the river bank all the way to Savannah, but Joshua says that he saw Commodore Decatur persuade him to a different plan. Certainly the militia would never have stood except in entrenchments with naval guns, and we had nothing like that except at the city itself.

So the good folk of Gerardus and the Cherokees came tumbling back together, into the entrenchments, leaving Gerardus burning behind them. The Gerardus militia were so proud of the fight that they had made that we had several brawls between them and the Savannans.

So the British came up to Savannah and on the sixth day of the campaign launched their principal attack. They put three regular regiments and two of what the Dons called regiments against the entrenchments. Meanwhile, they tried to ferry the last regiment across the river to the island behind Savannah, along with some artillery to take the city in the rear.

It was not a bad plan, for we held the island lightly, with a few sharpshooters from the militia and some Cherokees, also a few South Carolina militia who had just come in the day before. They looked better than the Georgians, but Jackson and Decatur were agreed on not putting them in the forefront.

The British had two armed luggers guarding the river crossing. These beat down the water battery, or at least thought they did. (Joshua again says that Commodore Decatur gave the idea for the stratagem.) The British storming columns advanced, as the regiment in flatboats put out on to the water.

Then, relying on a favorable wind, *General Scott* swept down the river into the middle of the British. Most of her guns were ashore to lighten her and strengthen the batteries, but Captain Allen had twelve carronades and a hundred men armed with swivels, muskets, and thrown combustibles and was the man to know what to do with all of them. We do not say this to disgust you, Mother, or as a poetic figure, but the Savannah River did run red that day.

The three columns going against the city were British on the left and the right and

Dons in the middle. The Dons showed more stoutly than we had expected, nearly made it to the trenches, but fell back under our musketry and broke when we opened with grape.

The British on the right came along the riverbank, and of course expected the guns of the luggers and the river crossers to help them. They had no such help, as *General Scott* put both luggers out of action, then opened fire on the redcoats. They withdrew inland, losing a good half of the regiment.

The two regiments in the leftmost column were the most dangerous, as they came in at an angle that left them almost immune to artillery. Commodore Decatur and the sailors worked like Trojans to shift guns, but for nearly half an hour it was hand-to-hand fighting, with General Jackson in the vanguard taking the first of his wounds.

Thomas says that if it had not been for the Rangers and the Cherokees in the rear of the British on the left, they might have won. Of course, the Virginians and Marylanders also say it was their counterattack that saved the day.

Certainly, with neither foe against them, the British might have prevailed, or at least drawn off in better order. As it was, when repelled, they like the other enemies fled southward, to the banks of Augustine Creek. There Admiral Cockburn had prudently left boats and a few Marines to guard the line of retreat, but the Cherokee burned the boats and drove off the Marines.

The fighting went on into the night, to be ended more by the rain than by anything else. The Spanish surrendered as fast as they could to anyone who would let them, but the British regulars upheld their reputation. They fought us all the way to Augustine Creek, shooting from every kind of cover that they could find although not being the masters of open fighting that our best men were. We even had to bring up a six-pounder to blast them out of a farmhouse.

Our leaders were again in the forefront. General Jackson rode about, guiding his horse with his knees because he would not put down his sword and one arm was in a sling from a second wound. Commodore Decatur and the naval party held the river flank valiantly, and it was there that Joshua received his wound.

The British brought up four more luggers or large gunboats, to attack our flank and hold the mouth of Augustine Creek. Allen brought *General Scott* against them, but she ran aground in a shallow spot. The British tried to surround her and beat her into submission, but they did not reckon with the surviving privateers, who advanced under sweeps and fought the gunboats hand to hand. Eventually we took, sank, or burned all of the British craft, and when the rain came the river rose enough to float off our frigate.

By then General Jackson had taken his third and gravest wound, and there was not a standing building or an unbloodied plot of ground between Savannah and Augustine Creek. I think that if General Jackson had been killed, we would have taken no prisoners. As it was, Commodore Decatur mounted Jackson's horse and rode among the men, calling on them not to disgrace themselves in the moment of the Republic's greatest victory since Yorktown.

Then the rain started. By the time it finished at dawn, the British were holding a last-ditch position on the banks of Augustine Creek, which had gone out of its banks, was too swift to swim, and was threatening to drown the wounded. A few lucky survivors may have slipped down to the river under cover of the rain, riding on planks or driftwood. But near fifteen hundred unwounded British and Dons surrendered before noon, we took near four hundred wounded, and we have counted many more than a thousand bodies.

Our own losses were not light, being some two hundred killed and three times that many wounded, as well as being nearly out of powder. General Jackson lies on what may be his deathbed, but we hope that fear of his memory will keep the Red Sticks at a distance until we are fit to fight them.

Of the Red *Coats*, however, we need have no more fear.

　　　With affectionate respects, your sons
　　　　　　　　　　　　Thomas
　　　　　　　　　　Joshua (his mark)

Amendment

You may be altogether proud of your sons, Mrs. Parker, and be assured that they take less than the honor due them for their part in the battle. Joshua was at my side under the heaviest fire, never flinching, never failing to repeat an order accurately or write down an event the moment it happened. Thomas was not under my eye as much, but he helped carry General Jackson from the field, then led his Rangers through the rain to stand between the British and a disgraceful massacre.

　　　　　　　　　　　Your servant,
　　　　　　　　　　Stephen Decatur

〜

Thomas Parker to Sarah Madsen Parker, Savannah, November 11, 1814

I write with an equal burden of sad and joyful news.

General Jackson has died of his wounds. With almost his last breath, he urged Commodore Decatur to lead an invasion of the Floridas, to be sure that we will not have the Dons and Seminoles at our backs when we march west again. I can hardly write of the grief of all those he led to victory.

Also, Joshua's wounded arm had to be amputated. The amputation was done in plenty of time, by a skilled naval surgeon, who says that Joshua should recover completely. He has already tried to write with his left hand, and may succeed in writing something you can read before long.

Commodore Decatur has no plan to invade anybody or anything at the moment, although we have gravely hurt the British blockade off Georgia and South Carolina. They sent in a cutting-out party for the merchant vessels anchored at the river's mouth, while we were fighting in the city. But our men were alert and drove the British off, with more than a hundred men lost.

Then the British decided to bring a frigate and a ship of the line close in shore and try to bombard the anchorage. Well, the frigate ran aground, and then who should appear as the ship of the line was trying to tow her off but Commodore Rodgers with *United States*, *President*, and the new *Hull*. Commodore Rodgers proved what Commodore Decatur thought, that two of our big frigates could take a British 74. *Cornwallis* now flies the American flag, although we had to burn *Lydia* because we could not get her off before the British brought up the rest of the squadron.

We still have British ships roaming like stray cattle off the mouth of the Savannah, so news is slow reaching us and this letter will no doubt be slow reaching you. But it is not every day of the week that a British squadron has to look in all directions at once, like a cat in a kennel!

Your obedient son,
Thomas

∽

Joshua Parker to Sarah Madsen Parker, Savannah, December 1, 1814

Dear Mother,

As you can see, I am now writing with my left hand. At the moment it is somewhat of a burden, so this letter will be short.

I do assure you that I am out of all danger. The weather has turned moderate, reducing the danger of fevers. The British have sent a ship with provisions and medical supplies for those of their prisoners we still hold, and are negotiating with Commodore Decatur for a cartel to return them. We are

also sending a ship north under a flag of
truce and this letter will be aboard her.

> With affection,
> Joshua

⌒

Thomas Parker to Sarah Madsen Parker, Savannah, January 1, 1815

Esteemed Mother,

It can now be said of me as it was said
of Benedict, "Here may you see Thomas
Parker, the married man."

Yesterday I and Caroline Bearkiller were
married. I said the principal oaths in the
Cherokee tongue, Joshua was my witness,
her brother was hers, and we also had
Commodore Decatur standing up with us.
The marriage is legal and binding under
both Cherokee and Georgia law, and we
also feel that God has joined us and we
may therefore not be put asunder.

Joshua looked very fine in his new uniform, even with the empty sleeve. He will
be staying in Savannah for some time,
where Commodore Decatur intends to
leave a squadron of light vessels to guard
the river. The British are still blockading but they aren't raiding, so the only
enemy we have to worry about for now is

whatever Seminoles decided to stay behind in the hope of picking up some loot. The Cherokees are giving them a very short shrift, let me tell you.

Joshua says that the British victory off Cape Cod may not quite balance the Battle of Savannah. The British can't afford to lose that many ships while the Bonaparte dynasty still keeps a fair-sized navy. However, even if we take five of their ships for every one we lose, they will still have enough ships to fight the French, the day that we don't have a navy at all. By Joshua's reckoning, after losing *Constitution*, *Plymouth*, and *Columbus*, we have one ship of the line, three frigates, and five sloops and brigs ready for sea, with more ready by spring if the British don't burn them on the stocks.

So Joshua and I both advise you not to invest any more money in privateers. The British may capture them, the French will probably close their ports to them, and anyway we may have a peace soon. Pray that it be so. We can't win much more out of this war. Maybe the next one will be luckier.

Obediently,
Thomas

Joshua Parker to Sarah Madsen Parker, Savannah, February 12, 1815

Honored Mother,

You really did not need to call Thomas a hypocrite for subscribing his last letter "Obediently" when you disapprove of his "outrageous marriage." There is nothing outrageous about *my sister in law, Caroline*, and not that much that is outrageous about most of the other Cherokees I have met.

I cannot help noting, however, that you have taken to heart our advice about investments in privateers. This is as well, as we understand that peace negotiations have begun in New Orleans. I suspect that the British wish to hold them there, so as not to be under the eyes of spies from half of Europe.

The British seem willing to return that city and any portion of the Mississippi they hold, as well as making no claims in the Northwest. But rumors run, that they wish either part of northern Massachusetts given up to Canada, or the Louisiana Territory returned to Spain. They might also expect the Dons to make an independent Indian territory beyond the Mississippi, and of course they would keep Florida.

It is not every day of the week that we are put so neatly on the horns of a dilemma, by having the choice of either going on with the war or seeing New England set against the West all over again, as one of them will have to face a hostile neighbor close at hand. I suppose we should not be surprised, seeing how this came to be a much larger war than anyone had expected when we declared it, but I hope we can show enough wisdom to make an end to it before the British become totally implacable.

Tom and Caroline left for Tennessee before your letter arrived, so I will post it after them. He will not be returning to Georgia, I suspect, as he has been promised the command of a Tennessee militia regiment and his war is not over. It will take some while to reduce the Muskogee Nation to order, even with the help of the Cherokees and the leadership of General Harrison.

If you wish to write to them directly, you can post the letter to Colonel Tom Parker, Presley's Crossing, Tennessee.

Your respectful son,
Joshua

Measureless to Man

Judith Tarr

In Xanadu did Solomon Khan
The Temple of the Lord decree. . . .
—Samuel Mendel Cohen

The Temple of the Lord God was rising in Chengdu, on the long plain beneath the loom of mountains, under the endless sky. Its walls rose to the height of ten tall men. The breadth of it was as great as a city, and its nine courts advanced to the innermost shrine, the Holy of Holies, where the new Ark of the Covenant would come to rest when the Temple was complete.

The roof was on the fifth court, all but the last of it, a tracery of stone above the eastern edge. Abraham Han Li the architect stood beneath the soaring arches, frowning upward. "Perhaps after all," he said, "we should have built a dome. Nine domes in ascending order, sheathed in silver and gold, floating above the plain, would be a vision of divine sublimity."

"Surely, master," said Moishe his assistant, "that would be beautiful indeed, but these vaulted arches uplift the spirit in a way that even the most airy dome cannot quite manage."

The Great Khan's chief architect was in no way convinced, but whatever argument he might have begun was lost in sudden commotion. Moishe had felt the slight shift of the paving underfoot, as if the earth had shrugged in its sleep. An instant later, shouts and cries brought them all out of the court and running toward the western wall.

It was still standing, but long cracks ran through it. The earth had subsided visibly. Workmen milled about, babbling in a confusion of languages.

Abraham Han Li maintained a remarkable degree of calm. "You said," he said to the Great Khan's chief engineer, who stood gaping as foolishly as any of the rest of them, "that the caverns did not extend beneath that portion of the plain."

Moishe met the glance of the chief engineer's assistant. Buri was too circumspect to roll his eyes, but he could not quite control his expression. Whatever the chief engineer might have told the chief architect, the rest of the workmen and their overseers knew perfectly well how far the caverns extended. A river ran under the earth, cutting beneath the western corner of the

Temple. The great ones refused to know it because their plans called for the Temple to be just such a shape and just such a size, oriented in just such a way, and that required the raising of a wall above the hidden river.

"Can it be salvaged?" the chief architect demanded. "Can the earth be shored up?"

"It can," said the chief engineer. "Certainly it can. It will be a great undertaking, but if we commandeer men, requisition supplies . . ."

"The Khan has said it," the chief architect said. "Whatever is needed, it shall be supplied. Give us walls that will stand. This is for the glory of the Lord God."

The chief engineer bowed to that Name. His assistant sighed just audibly.

So too did Moishe. Khans and princes demanded the impossible. Assistants then had to do it—and pay the price if they should fail.

Moishe stood in a cavern of immeasurable size. Even lit by lamps and torches beyond count, it stretched far away into gloom. Pillars and columns rose into vaults overhead, touched with rose and cream and gold. The river ran black and silent through them.

The Great Khan's engineers and miners stood in a hush of deep reverence, and not only because the river had been holy for time out of mind. Sound could break; sound could shatter. Sound could bring down the roof that groaned already under the weight of the Temple wall.

"We'll need timbers," Buri said in a barely audible whisper, "and stone. And years—but we'll be given months. Days, if I know our masters. This is no mine, to be shored up as we go. This is a temple as wide as the one above, and infinitely more fragile."

"It's a pity we can't worship here," murmured one of the lesser engineers. He was still a pagan, Moishe suspected, although those who had not accepted the Covenant were wise not to confess it too loudly. "Open a gate, raise up a few pillars, and here's a temple to make any god proud."

"The God of Hosts is a god of the open sky," said Buri. "But more to the point, the Khan has commanded that the Temple be built on the plain of Chengdu. Therefore it shall be built there. And we will make certain that the earth will hold it up."

The engineer shrugged. It made no difference to him, his manner said, if the great ones chose to be fools.

Moishe could not be as censorious as he should have been. The priests insisted that the Khan's vision had been true; that the Lord of Hosts had commanded the Temple to be built in this place, to glorify Him in this age of the world.

And yet in this temple to the gods below, he wondered if there was war in heaven. Not every god yielded peacefully to the rule of the One God. The gods of this country were very old and had been strong before the Khan's father cast them down. They might not in fact have yielded to the conquest. They might simply have been biding their time.

It was difficult to think such thoughts in this cavern, in the silence and the sense of age-old peace. The Khan's engineers would break that peace. They would desecrate the temple below for the sake of the Temple above.

Or maybe the Lord had something else in mind. Time would tell, as it inevitably did.

"When Temujin was a boy," the rabbi said, "even younger than you, he was reckoned the last and least of his brothers. But the Lord sent him a sign and a guide, a slave taken from far away, a woman of a people whose ways were utterly strange."

"The Honored Deborah!" cried one of his pupils.

The rabbi was young and his pupils were princes. He did not rebuke the child for speaking out of turn. "The Honored Deborah, yes," he said. "She taught him a way and a faith such as he had never dreamed of before. She showed him a path that made him strong. She made him a warrior of God. She helped him to see his destiny: not just to rule the world, but to take the name of the Lord of Hosts wherever he should go, and bring the nations of the world to the Covenant."

"Amen," said the circle of pupils in the colonnade of the Temple. Here on the eastward side, the wall was complete, and the courts to the fourth of them, where the school was. The chants of Torah and Talmud had paused, a brief moment of silence, in which these youngest scholars had time to reflect on their lesson.

Just as the chanting resumed farther down along the colonnade, the rabbi went on, "So Temujin became Judah, the lion of God. First his brothers, then his cousins, then his clan, were moved in their hearts to accept the One God and to follow His servant. The Lord God made them strong and gave them victory in battle, until Temujin rose to be the Great Khan,

Genghis Khan, lord of the Golden Horde. The world lay down beneath his foot.

"After the Lord God had taken His servant to Himself, by the side of Abraham and Isaac, Jacob and Joshua, Moses, and the rest of the fathers of the Covenant, the Great Khan's son woke from a dream to the knowledge of what he must do. The world was his to rule by the Lord's decree. It well pleased the Lord that his father, and now he, had spread the Covenant so far, but one more thing the Lord required of him.

"'My Temple in the west of the world is fallen,' He said. 'The people of My first Covenant are scattered to the winds of heaven. That is My will, and so I have ordained. Now are you My chosen, My beloved. Build Me a Temple. Build it high and make it beautiful. Consecrate it to the glory of My name.'

"And the Khan, whose mother had named him Khubilai but whose father called him Solomon, bowed low before the Lord and consented to do His will. The Lord gave him the knowledge of the place in which the Temple was to be built, and the fashion of it, how broad and how tall, and what manner of beauty would adorn it. Two Temples there had been in Jerusalem, and both were long gone; but this would be greater than either, more holy and more beautiful. And so the Lord would be worshipped according to His will."

"This is it," said the prince who had spoken before. "This is the Temple that the Lord told Father to build. The Lord told him to build it in two times seven years, no more and no less—and now it's half done, and it's been ten years, and do you think the Lord is getting impatient?"

"The Lord has faith in His servant," the rabbi said. "It will be done because He wills it, and because your father is His loyal servant."

"Father can do anything," the prince said.

"Anything that the Lord wills," said the rabbi.

Moishe liked to listen to the lessons in the colonnade if he could. Sometimes he was called on to teach one, because he had somewhat of a reputation as a scholar. But today he should not have lingered as long as he had. Prince Subotai had spoken the very truth: that it was ten years of the fourteen ordained, and the Temple was not in fact half done, but less than that. The beginning was always the hardest; the end would be quicker. But would it be quick enough?

The western wall could not stand unless the cavern was secured. That would take as long as it took, which please God would not be too long. In the meantime there was more than enough to occupy a harried assistant to the chief architect. The goldsmiths needed gold to sheathe the pillars of the three innermost courts, and the masons needed stone of numerous kinds to build those pillars, and the caravan that should have brought these things had been expected for a month and more.

But more than this, or the thousand other troubles greater and lesser that vexed the building of the Temple, Moishe had to face the messages that waited in the ordered clutter of his workroom. There were half a dozen of them, written in various hands but sealed with the same seal. They had come in some days before, brought by an imperial courier. The first was years old, the last dated just after Passover of this year. They had come by a long road. One had dark stains that might have been blood, another was charred about the edges.

They all said much the same thing. The people of the first Covenant, the Jews of the west, had heard of the great work in the east. Their Temple was gone, their holy city occupied by followers of an upstart prophet. They were scattered to the winds of heaven. Yet they were still God's chosen people. They had in mind to see this new Temple, to look on its wonders and speak with its builders. Therefore a deputation had been sent from the Jews of the Diaspora, an embassy of scholars and descendants of the old priests. It was to arrive, said the latest and least battered message, sometime within the year—and if Moishe's calculations were right, in this very season, and probably within the month.

If the first message had come within a year of its sending, there would have been ample time to prepare. As it was, there was barely enough time to find accommodations for an unknown number of guests, with unknown needs or desires, for an unknown length of time. And what, thought Moishe, would they be thinking? Had they come to marvel or inspect—to worship or condemn?

He would know the answer to that soon enough. An escort had gone out under the banner of the Khan and the Temple, to find the westerners on the road and escort them in safety to Chengdu. That was Moishe's official action, in the name of the chief architect and the high priest of the Temple. He had also, on his own and in a moment of either wisdom or weakness, sent a particular friend to canvass for rumors that might be attached to the westerners. One never knew, after all, what people were saying, and anything he heard might tell him how to prepare for these guests.

He was not at all surprised, looking up from his hundredth rereading of the letters from the west, to find that same, very useful friend sitting peacefully in the corner that he had always favored. Chen was one of the invisible—a man of no distinction whatsoever, who could go where he pleased and do as he pleased, and no one took notice.

He grinned at Moishe, who was much too digni-fied to grin back, but he permitted himself a discreet smile. "You rode quickly," Moishe said.

"Mongol ponies," said Chen. "They may not run like the wind, but once they get going, they don't stop. If there's nothing else that you've brought to the Middle Kingdom, that one will gain you a nod or two from the gods."

"The gods who, of course, do not exist," Moishe said.

"Of course," Chen said blandly.

He was not going to say what he had come to say, not unless Moishe observed the rule of their discourse: no haste, no urgency, but Moishe had to ask before Chen would tell. The game should play on for a while longer; Moishe gambled and said, "It must be powerful news, if you came back so soon."

Chen's narrow eyes narrowed further, but he was too full of news to hold it for much longer. He shrugged, dallied, and in the end he said, "There are rumors spreading westward from here, stories that track to a hundred sources, but if you follow them closely, they come from a single place. Have you wondered why there has not been a bandit raid anywhere within reach of here, since at least the year before last?"

"I know why that is," said Moishe. "The Khan's armies—"

"The Khan's armies are halfway across the world," Chen said. "His grip on the Middle Kingdom is strong enough, I grant you that, but he's not here to see that every band of robbers is strung up along the road. And yet someone is doing it, or a succession of someones, advancing from the west and aiming toward Chengdu."

"A warlord?" Moishe asked. "A claimant to the throne? Or—"

"Or," said Chen, "an army of strangers. They're not challenging the Khan's men—they're traveling in secret, or pretending to be ordinary travelers. They scour out the nests of robbers as they come, and leave them for the ravens. It's a tribute of sorts, a gift to the Khan."

"That is very strange," Moishe said.

"Isn't it?" said Chen. "Here's what's even odder. The raiders are westerners. They have long noses and long beards, and eyes as round as coins. They rock when they pray."

Moishe's mouth was hanging open. He shut it with a snap. "They're— How many?"

"Rumor says thousands," Chen said. "Maybe there are hundreds. They're coming here, or somewhere within reach of here."

"An army from the west," said Moishe, "sweeping the lands clean as they come, but doing nothing to trouble the people who live in those lands. Are there scholars, too? Or only soldiers?"

"I wouldn't know a scholar if I saw one," Chen said, "but those are all fighting men. Middling good ones, at that. There is another company traveling here—a caravan. Maybe those are scholars. They're older, mostly, and softer, and they pray more often. They argue a great deal by the fire at night."

Moishe let go a long sigh. "Those are scholars. Are they connected with the others at all?"

"Not obviously," said Chen, "but sometimes a soldier comes to their caravan, stays for an hour or a night, then rides away."

A messenger, thought Moishe. He could see the shape of it, as odd as it manifestly was. An army was coming in fragments, meant to be joined together when it reached Chengdu. Its heart was the caravan, the seemingly harmless riding of merchants and scholars.

It was very clever. Had it been design after all that delayed the messages from the embassy until it was almost too late? Were they actually planning to invade the Temple?

Moishe sent Chen to a well-deserved bed. For himself, that night, there was no rest.

He did not have the authority to do the things that, if Chen was right, should be done. He was the chief architect's assistant and, when his duties allowed, a teacher and scholar in the rabbinical school. For this he needed a military commission, or a commander who both believed him and had the power to act on it.

His stomach had drawn into a tight and aching knot. When he went into the Temple, he had been running toward a calling—and away from altogether too much. He had prayed then that whatever the Lord chose for him, it would keep him far away from either acts or men of war.

The Lord had a way of humbling those who prayed too selfishly. Moishe bowed to the divine will. "And I do hope," he said with a touch of temper, "that You knew what You were doing when You chose me for this."

Naturally the Lord did not reply. He was never One to belabor the obvious.

The commander of the Khan's garrison in Chengdu looked Moishe up and down. Moishe resisted the urge to stand at attention, and the equally powerful urge to hide behind the nearest and burliest guardsman. He was not a child any longer, under the eye of a stern father. He was a man of some consequence, attached to the Khan's personal service.

With that to stiffen his resolve, he lifted his chin and regarded the commander with what he hoped was a sufficient degree of dignity.

"So," said Lord Ogadai. "You're the disgrace to the Red Wolf clan. How is old Batu these days? Still having babies for breakfast?"

Moishe gritted his teeth. He had been living in civilized places too long. He had mercifully forgotten what an old-fashioned Mongol was like. "As far as I know," he said as politely as he could manage, "he even enjoys the occasional toddler."

Ogadai bared his teeth in a grin. They were excellent—honed on saddle leather and nourished with mare's milk. "You look like him. He's uglier, but a sword blade across the face will do that to a man." He beckoned to one of the guards. The man brought a chair, a spindly confection in the Chinese style, quite unlike the sturdy object on which Ogadai was seated. "Here, sit. Sit! Don't stand about like a new recruit. *Kumiss?*"

Moishe had to take the chair, and could not in courtesy refuse the cup of fermented mare's milk. It was strong enough to make his eyes water, and rich with the memory of home: smoke, horses, stink of unwashed bodies, and the reek of *kumiss* fermenting in the skins or drying on the coats of his father's warriors after a drinking bout.

He had never been homesick for the camp of the Red Wolf clan. The Temple was home, with all its troubles and its half-finished glory. He took three sips of the *kumiss*, to be polite, then set the cup aside. A guard was there to take it, as he had expected. He folded his hands and looked the commander in the face and said, "I won't waste your time. There's something I need, and I'm hoping you can give it to me."

That caught Ogadai off balance. Moishe did not see why it should. He was clean and he was dressed in Chinese silk, but Ogadai himself had recalled Moishe's origins. "You— Your master in the Temple?"

"He doesn't know I'm here," Moishe said. He had gambled on directness, and that meant the truth, whatever it did to his cause. "I will tell him, of course, but he's a busy man. He prefers not to be bothered with possibilities—only results."

"I know the chief architect," Ogadai said. God forbid a Mongol should confess to respect one of the decadent Chinese, but he did not spit in contempt, which was accolade enough. "What possibilities are you not bothering him with?"

Moishe could not pause to think. That would look weak. He had to say it all at once, straight and clear.

"You know there's a deputation coming from the Jews of the Diaspora. It's a tour of inspection, I'm wagering—they can't be happy that we're building a Temple in our country instead of theirs. That's to be expected, and we're prepared for an onslaught of rabbis and scholars. But there's something else." And he told Ogadai what Chen had told him, word for word, exactly as he remembered it.

Ogadai heard him in silence. It sounded ridiculous when he said it in order: a threadbare fabric of rumor and speculation, delineating a plan that even a madman would laugh at. To bring a fragmented army all the way from the west into the heart of the Middle Kingdom, unseen and unremarked through the many divisions of the Horde, was outrageous—impossible. It would take a madman or a Sikandar to contemplate such a thing, still less to succeed in it.

He said so in Ogadai's continued silence, but he also said, "A small and determined force can infiltrate a stronghold and hold it against an army. Give that force hostages that matter, and make that fort so vital to the country or its rulers that its destruction would be an even worse disaster than its conquest, and you have the makings of an interesting situation. The invaders might actually manage to keep the stronghold, and to persuade the rulers of the country to accept it."

At least Ogadai broke his silence. "Supposing that this dream or fancy of yours can be true. What do they want, do you think? To destroy the place or take control of it?"

"I don't know," Moishe said. "I suspect even they don't. They'll know when they get here. We should be prepared for whatever they decide to do."

"If you are afraid," said Ogadai, "you could simply dispose of them before they set foot in Chengdu."

"No," said Moishe. "These are priests and scholars. Whatever their intentions, their destruction would offend the Lord."

"Even if you had someone else do it? Pagans?"

"Anyone at all," Moishe said firmly. "Will you help? Can you find the truth of the rumors? If they are true, the armies you can destroy—they come to threaten the Temple."

"If they exist," said Ogadai.

"Something is out there. The bandits—"

"Local defenses," Ogadai said. "Maybe a rogue raider or two, but I doubt it's more. I've heard your rumors, too, priest. I've done my own hunting. There's nothing there. People get restless when the Khan is so far away. Not all the conquered are honestly suppressed. We've put down uprisings and the threat of uprisings—there are always a few of those. That's all your rumors are. They've nothing to do with a caravan of barbarians."

Moishe should not give in to despair. Ogadai was an intelligent man. His rough edges had smoothed remarkably as he listened to Moishe. Of course he had heard the rumors; of course he had investigated them. His resources were considerably broader than Moishe's. If he said that Moishe was shying at shadows, then it was probably true.

But Moishe was stubborn—it was a trait he shared with his father, and it had brought him to the Temple instead of the khanate of the Red Wolf. He trusted Chen and he trusted his own instincts. However unlikely the prospect, he did believe, after all, that there was truth in the rumors.

"Tell me at least," he said, "that you'll put your forces on alert and increase the guard on the Temple. If you have scouts or spies, can they—"

"It has all been done," Ogadai said. He softened infinitesimally. "There, boy. You worry—that's not a bad thing. Pray; that's even better. But leave the rest to us. We'll keep your Temple safe."

Moishe had no choice but to accept that. He would have to pray as Ogadai suggested, that it would be enough.

One thing Moishe could do, and did. He prevailed on his master to speed the repairs of the western wall. By the tenth day after Moishe spoke with Ogadai, as the westerners rode toward Chengdu across the westward plain, Moishe looked out from the gate along the wall; it showed no outward sign of the troubles in the earth below. It had taken masons working day and night, and no little arguing with the chief engineer, to get it done, but done it was, thanks to Buri the able assistant. To those who came riding in their caravan, the wall was whole.

Abraham Han Li stood with the chief engineer and the chief of the priests and the master of the school and a large company of lesser lights of Temple and city. It was a great occasion to welcome the deputation from the Diaspora, and they were determined to do it proper justice. They were an impressive company, dressed in their best clothes and escorted by Temple guards. The gleam of silk and the flash of jewels must have dazzled the embassy from far down the road.

The caravan came on slowly. It was not a particularly large undertaking by the standard of the Middle

Kingdom, but it was not particularly small. It was well guarded, in keeping with its size, but Moishe would not have called its guards an army. The parts of that would not come in, if they existed at all, until the caravan was firmly established in the Temple.

Moishe effaced himself among the clerks and servants who escorted the chief architect. His gown was plain, his marks of rank unobtrusive: a silver button on his hat, a silken prayer shawl under his gown. He stood in Abraham Han Li's resplendent shadow and watched as the caravan approached.

His eyes were not on the nobly bearded men who rode on handsomely caparisoned mules, or even on the armed guards who flanked them, but on those who, like him, chose not to put themselves forward. They were in the second rank, even the third and fourth, and their coats were worn and their faces showed the ravages of care and cleverness. He was careful not to meet their eyes.

The chief of the embassy had the noblest beard of all, a cascade of white down his breast. His voice matched it: rich, rolling, made to carry through the sanctuary of a temple. He spoke Hebrew in an accent so pure that Moishe sighed in spite of himself.

Abraham Han Li appeared untainted by either envy or admiration. He answered the elegant phrases of greeting with phrases equally elegant if not nearly so perfectly accented. He presented each of his fellow notables by name and rank and position, at leisure and at length. That obligated the western rabbi to do the same, though the mules were fretting and the camels braying and the men looking strained about the eyes.

His name was Ephraim of a place with a barbarous name, like the grunt of a pig: York, which Moishe understood to be beyond the edge of the world. He had brought a good number of his cousins and relations from a number of places nearly as distant and nearly as outlandish. Moishe had heard of Salamanca and of Prague, but the rest were strange.

While Ephraim spoke, Moishe's eye found one whom he named all but last and apparently least: Barak, likewise of York. He was a big man, and young, and although he carried no weapon, he stood as if he were accustomed to a sword at the hip. His eyes were never still. They scanned the faces in front of him, pausing, measuring, flicking onward.

This was a mind that could conceive a wild and improbable plan. Moishe could see it in those quick eyes, that light and wary stance. If the man was a scholar, he was a remarkably martial and suspicious one. Moishe did his utmost to seem harmless and inconsequential, and not to draw Barak's attention.

Maybe he succeeded. If not, he would learn soon enough. By the time the introductions had wound to their interminable end, he had set a trusted clerk in his place and escaped to signal the guards and servants that the guests were coming in. The cooks were waiting, the feast of welcome prepared according to the strictest prescriptions of the Law. Not one compromise, not one variation—that was the order. Moishe made sure that they had been scrupulous in carrying it out.

Once the caravan was in and settled and placed under discreet watch, a sort of quiet descended. The guests were not obtrusive. They asked to see the

Temple, but they said little, and nothing that was not complimentary. Several of the scholars expressed a desire to visit the school; they observed in silence, neither smiling nor frowning, and for the most part even the students forgot they were there.

The first crack in the calm came on the Sabbath, which fell on the fifth day after the westerners' arrival. Workmen had come in that morning to lay the paving for the sixth court. The tiles for it had arrived the day before, and the men were eager to begin.

Moishe was just finishing his inspection of the work-men, briefly but happily delayed by a messenger with news that the caravan he had been awaiting most eagerly, the great one that the Khan had sent with gold and trea-sures, would come within sight of Chengdu by evening. He was in an excellent humor, therefore, and when he saw the cluster of men in western clothes standing on the rim of the court, he nodded and smiled.

They did not return the smile. There were half a dozen of them; all the westerners looked alike, but Moishe thought these might be the same scholars who had been attending classes in the school.

The oldest of them, whose beard was shot with gray, glowered at Moishe under his heavy brows. Nonethe-less it was not he who spoke but the man beside him, whom Moishe recognized as the man from the gate: Barak, the big man who looked more like a soldier than a scholar. Moishe had thought then that he was more than he chose to seem. The thought came back to him now as Barak asked, "You allow your men to labor on the Sabbath?"

Moishe's heart contracted. He did not know why it should do that. The man's voice was mild and he was unarmed. But there was an undertone, like a low growl. "It is for the glory of the Lord God," Moishe said.

"The Lord bade us remember the Sabbath, that He has made holy," Barak said.

"Indeed," said Moishe, "and what is more holy than the Temple that He has asked us to build?"

"Not on His Sabbath," said Barak.

The man had no humor, and no flexibility, either. Moishe mustered a smile, bowed as if in submission, and said humbly, "That may be. I am only a simple servant. Shall I present your complaint to the Khan's chief architect?"

"It is not a complaint," said the eldest of the westerners. "It is a statement of truth. You desecrate this Temple with the breaking of the Sabbath."

"Such strong words," Moishe said. "I shall speak to my master. Now come. Come and pray."

"How can we pray while men labor in the very Temple?" Barak demanded.

"Pray for us, then," said Moishe a little too sweetly.

"That, we can do," Barak said with no more humor than he had ever shown.

That was the first sign of trouble. The second followed all too quickly. Moishe had managed to divert the westerners from the horror of Sabbath-breaking, then after prayer they were invited to dine with the high priest. That should be a quiet and decorous gathering, and suitably scrupulous in its observance of the Law.

He had reckoned without a pack of young would-be scholars, a day of idleness, and rather more boredom

than was good for any of them. Almost he had yielded
to temptation and taken his supper in his room, but
that indulgence must wait for a more peaceful time. He
was hungry, he discovered, even under the cold eye of
the westerner who sat nearest—not one of those who
had been exploring the temple, but by now they had
all heard of his offense in the face of the Lord.

He had just finished a quite delectable dish of cold
roast fowl and reached for his bowl of noodles when
something small and fast burst through the door to
the kitchens. Several larger figures ran in hot pursuit.
The quarry was silent except for an occasional grunt,
but the pursuers were squealing as if they and not
the pursued were the pigs.

Prince Subotai led the pack. The piglet led them a
wild chase, darting under tables, veering around legs,
then in a feat truly remarkable for a pig, hurdled a
portly westerner, caromed off the elder beside him,
and skidded down the table in a spray of food, drink,
and shattered crockery. It came to an abrupt halt in
the lap of the chief of the embassy, and crouched
there, gaping up as he gaped down. Their expressions
were perfectly matched.

Moishe did not want to laugh. Nor, he was sure,
did any of the other easterners who were in the hall.
He succeeded—somewhat—in restraining himself, but
others were not so fortunate. The hall erupted in a
roar of mirth.

"Even if it had been a calf," Moishe said, "or a
foal, or even a dog, there might have been some way
to repair the insult. But a pig—Lord of Hosts, could
anything have been worse?"

"A pig on a platter," said Chen, "with an orange in its mouth." He licked his lips. "Gods! That makes me hungry. I don't suppose . . ."

"The pig's sentence is exile, not death." Moishe sighed deeply and knotted his fingers before they went back to tearing out his hair. "No, I won't let you eat him! He's unclean. Which is why—"

"He's as clean as a pig gets," Chen said. "The boys' servant has been looking after him. He bathes more often than the boys do, and eats better, too. What do you call that? Kosher—he's a kosher pig."

Moishe aimed a cuff at him, which he eluded with laughing ease. "He's a pig, pagan. That's all our honored guests can see. He defiled the Sabbath table—not to mention the Sabbath itself, and the Temple in which he was kept."

"How rigid," said Chen.

"Wars have begun for less."

"So they have," Chen said. "There's been no sign of the army we've been hearing of. No more bandits strung up by the road. Even the rumors have vanished into the earth."

Moishe shook himself. He rubbed his cheeks, then slapped them, in some small hope of bringing his mind back to order. This was what he had wanted to hear. Surely it was. His fears had been imaginary. The only threat he need face was the threat of disapproval from the Jews of the Diaspora, and God knew, that had already come to pass.

Chen watched him with a distinct edge of mockery. Moishe stared back hard and said, "If a signal has gone out, no one here has observed it."

"Certainly no one has," Chen said.

"Including you."

"Including me." For once, and abruptly, Chen was almost grim. "I can find anything anywhere. But these hundreds or thousands of men . . . I can't find them at all."

"So Ogadai is right," said Moishe. "They don't exist."

"They exist," Chen said. "Believe that. There isn't a bandit alive or raiding within nine days' journey of Chengdu. That's their doing. Now they've gone to ground."

"I don't think—" Moishe began.

"Do think," said Chen. "Forget pigs. There's an army out there. I'll wager it's coming here."

"I don't know if I can take your side of that wager," Moishe said in odd mixture of reluctance and relief. "Every sign points to this being an innocent caravan of priests and scholars. Some of them are more martial than one might expect, but that makes sense for a journey so long through so many wild countries. They'd want strong men to protect their scholars."

"The old Khan used to say," said Chen, "that no fort ever lost a war by overdoing its defenses."

"No small number of servants have lost their positions—and sometimes their heads—by crying danger when none exists."

"There is danger," Chen said stubbornly. "I trust my sources. You used to trust me."

"I still do," Moishe said. "But—"

"Don't give me 'but.' There's trouble brewing. I have as fine a nose for that as any spy in the Khan's service. That trouble is connected with your guests, and it's coming soon."

"They are looking for a fight," Moishe granted him. "We're managing rather handily to give them one."

"Why not?" said Chen. "Maybe a good fight is what we all need. It will clear the air."

Moishe glowered but did not try to cuff him again. Chen's impudence had a method in it, and Moishe had done well before to forget the annoyance and focus on the kernel of good sense. Chen was wise in his way. He could see, sometimes, what no one else could. And he had never yet, to Moishe's knowledge, seen what absolutely was not there.

"When your ancestors were worshipping stones in the desert," said the Rabbi of Huashan, "ours were a noble and cultured people."

"We are the chosen of God," said the Rebbe of Prague. "You are converts—and however old your country, your dedication to the truth is only as old as the barbarian who conquered you."

If these had been fighting men, they would have settled matters with swords. Since they were scholars, they slashed at each other with words. It had begun as a debate regarding certain finer points of the Talmud, until the Chinese rabbi had offered the possibility that his own ancient language might be better suited to such rarefied matters. The rebbe would hear no such thing.

"The Lord God set forth His Covenant in Hebrew," he said, "and in Hebrew it shall remain."

The rabbi sniffed in aristocratic disdain. "He matched His words, with some difficulty, to the limited tongue of a provincial people. It speaks well of His kindness and His supernal mercy."

"And where was Ch'in," the rebbe demanded, "when the Lord was forming His Covenant? Why did it come so late to His Word—and then at the hands of a barbarian invader?"

"He planted us like a seed in the rich earth of the Middle Kingdom," said the rabbi, "and when we were ready to bear fruit, He gave us His Word."

"A twisted and distorted Word in an outlandish tongue."

"That might be said," said the rabbi silkily, "of the Word as it was given to us."

Even his disciples gasped at that. The rebbe's followers surged to their feet. There might be no weapons in the hall of disputation, but fists and feet would do well enough—as many a tavern keeper could testify.

A battlefield bellow froze them all where they stood. Moishe, running toward the sound of battle brewing, recognized the voice when it spoke more softly, although it still echoed down the corridor. Moishe halted in the doorway and looked across the makings of a brawl to the men who stood above it. Barak had mounted one of the benches that ringed the room; with his height and bulk, that was enough. He raked his glare across the lot of them. "Sirs! Honored masters. This is a place of peace. Will you make it a house of war?"

Some of them most certainly would, but the sight of him cowed them into silence. "I think," he said with terrible gentleness, "that this discussion is over. We'll rest now, yes? And ponder the uses of restraint."

He had the gift of command. The brawl broke into a few dozen sullen men, going their separate ways under his stern eye. There would be no fighting today, though what might happen later, only God knew.

Moishe was drawn to approach him, though what he would say, or what would be safe to say, he hardly knew. But when he reached the place where Barak had been, the man was gone. Moishe found him after a long moment, wrapped in relative anonymity again, slipping out a side door.

It was too late to follow, and Moishe's wits had caught up with his impulses. He slipped away as Barak had, but in the opposite direction. It truly was best if only one of them knew what the other was.

The molds were made, the gold brought to the proper temperature and poured in a molten stream. Now the smiths were ready to unmold the newest and most splendid of the Temple's ornaments: golden lotus blossoms that would crown the gold-sheathed pillars of the sixth court.

In his preoccupation with the westerners both all too real and as yet all too imaginary, Moishe had barely noticed the passage of time. The fifth court, to his surprise, was nearly done. The sixth was rising with gratifying speed. The masters of the Diaspora were increasingly less pleased with the Temple and its builders, but the Lord, it seemed, did not share their opinion.

Work under the western wall was not going so well, but it was progressing. None of those involved had seen fit to inform the guests of that particular portion of the Temple's building. It was a tactical decision, made before Moishe could offer his own suspicions. An enemy who knew of the caverns and of the weakness that they represented could bring down the Temple.

Such summer heat as Chengdu knew had descended, and with it an influx of idlers and pilgrims from the lower plains. To them this heat was blissfully cool. They filled the city and crowded the Temple, gaping at its wonders.

The city's market had in past years shown a tendency to spill over into the first court of the Temple. The priests allowed it because the merchants paid a portion of their profits into the Temple's coffers. It was a useful arrangement, permitted by the Khan, whose treasury took its share of the profits as well.

In that crowd of gawkers and pilgrims, it was a great deal more difficult than it had been to keep watch over the westerners. The guards were in more difficulty than the watchers and spies—they were more obvious and therefore easier to elude.

The westerners, of course, were not even slightly amused by the sight of commerce in the Temple—and never mind that both the First and Second Temples had been markets in their day. This was a more righteous age, said the Rebbe of Prague. When by the Lord's will there was a Third Temple in Jerusalem—for he would not grant that this was the Third Temple itself—its courts would never suffer such an outrage.

He said this to Abraham Han Li, who so far had managed to leave these troublesome guests in Moishe's care. But there was no escaping the occasional press of duty. He had refused the Rebbe's invitation to dinner seven times already—Moishe had kept count.

"Accept once," Moishe said, "and the duty is done. I'll make sure you won't be asked again."

"Swear to that by the honor of your ancestral clan," said Abraham Han Li, "and I may—may—consider it."

"Agree to it, master," Moishe said, "and you won't have to look at them again until we celebrate the eve of their departure."

"May that be soon," growled the chief architect. "Very well. I'll waste an evening that could better be spent building the Temple, and you will waste it with me."

Moishe suppressed a sigh. Duty was duty, as he had reminded his master. Abraham Han Li would suffer duly for it: he would have to hear from his host that his entire great work and devotion to the Lord was a false construction, the child of a delusion.

He maintained a remarkable degree of calm in the circumstances. Moishe was proud of him.

"Tisha B'Av," said Barak.

Moishe had been seated beside him, an arrangement to which he would have objected strenuously if he had been on his guard. A place well down the table, among the least of the rabbinical students, would have suited him much better. But this was the westerners' banquet. They had seated him near the head of the table, between Barak and the assistant to the Rebbe of Prague.

It was a banquet in the western style. Its dishes were heavy and strange, its spices familiar but oddly combined. Guests were expected to bring a knife and a spoon to the table. There were no chopsticks; nothing so civilized. Moishe overheard one of the younger Chinese rabbis murmur to another, "Knives at the table—barbaric! I wonder how many banquets end in bloodshed?"

Thank the Lord, none of the westerners seemed

to understand the dialect of southern Hunan. In any case they had their own obsession, and it had nothing to do with food or the eating of it.

"*Tisha B'Av*," Barak said. "It's nearly upon us. Do you observe the rite?"

His expression was bland, his tone courteous. Moishe was careful to respond in kind. "Certainly we mourn the sorrows of the people, and the downfall of the First and Second Temples, each on the same day of the same month, half a thousand years apart. Is there any Jew in the world who does not?"

"I had wondered," Barak said, apparently unoffended to be lectured like a child. "So much else is . . . different."

"It's the same God," Moishe said, "and the same Books of the Law. Interpretations will vary even within the schools of the west—is that not what the Talmud is? Sacred argument that goes on for years, centuries—voices out of time, offering opinions and counteropinions. Ours is a lively faith, honored sir, and very much alive. And living things grow. They change."

"Not all change is desirable," said Barak. "Some in the west would say that the Christians are a radical sect of our own faith. We disagree. The Messiah has not come—though wars have been fought in his name, and nations have risen to oppress us because we refuse to accept their falsehood."

"Christians are harmless eccentrics in our part of the world," Moishe said. "We had one here not long ago, calling us heretics and condemning us for building a temple to an outmoded God. Our rabbis demolished his arguments. He ended the day a convert. You may

have seen him in the newest court. He has a divine
gift for working stone."

"Ours are seldom so easily persuaded," Barak said
with little pleasure. "The sad truth of the matter is,
they rule the world."

"Not our world," Moishe said. "And not yours,
either—not for long. Our Khan has taken his Horde
westward, and where the Horde goes, so does the
Covenant. Your Christians will fall. You'll take back
Jerusalem then, if you want it; the Khan has said so."

Barak's lips tightened. "We spoke with him," he said,
"east of Poland. He was gracious." And that was not
easy for him to admit. "He told us what he meant to
do. Some of us were deeply gratified."

"But not you."

"Outside of the Lord's Word," Barak said, "I believe
only what I see."

"Ah," said Moishe, and only that. He knew what
Barak had been seeing in Chengdu, and had a fair
sense of what he thought of it. He took care to shift
the conversation to less dangerous topics: the quality
of the bread, the flavor of the western wine.

It was, all in all, not the most pleasant banquet that
Moishe had attended, but it was useful. Somewhat to
his surprise, Abraham Han Li concurred. The chief
architect was singularly dedicated to his art, but if he
was forced to participate in mere human diversions,
he could be surprisingly and piercingly astute.

"*Tisha B'Av*," he said. "They were making particular reference to that. Almost as if we were being
taunted—or warned."

"The day on which both Temples fell—twice,"

Moishe said. A chill walked down his spine. "You don't think—"

"It's not my duty to think," Abraham Han Li said, "of anything but raising this Temple within the time allotted by God and the Khan."

That was manifestly true. Moishe bowed to it, and the man. "Master, *Tisha B'Av* is only half a month away. They're visibly hostile. What if they're plotting something? What if—"

"There is no army descending on us," said Abraham Han Li. He met Moishe's start of shock with a sardonic arch of the brow. "What, you thought I didn't know about that? I had a visit from the commander of the city garrison. He wanted me to know that he meant no disrespect to the son of the Red Wolf khan, and certainly none to my second in command, but what did I think of this obsession of yours? That forced me to depart from duty for a not particularly pleasant hour."

"And you concluded that I've far overstepped my bounds, that I've troubled a lord commander for nothing, and that—"

"Yes," said Abraham Han Li. "But I also reflected that you were never a man to start at shadows. If you see something, there must be a cause for it. Our guests are certainly not friendly. There are a hundred of them, most young, strong, and rather obviously of fighting age. They're inside the Temple, and by now have prowled over every part of it that we've let them into. I don't doubt they've found a portion or two that we would prefer they not see. If I were anything but an architect, and if I were a suspicious man, I might wonder if they were up to something."

Moishe regarded him in newfound respect. "I should have spoken to you first. Master, I'm sorry. I didn't mean—"

"You didn't want to trouble me," the chief architect said. "Nor did you. The lord commander and the westerners disrupt my work to no end. I can't give you troops, they're not mine to give, but if you're inclined to keep our guests thoroughly out of my way, you may do that."

"Imprison them?" said Moishe. "That's tempting— dear God, yes. But we can't do that. They're guests. We have honor, whatever they may be lacking."

"Certainly we do," said the chief architect. "Keep them out of my way. Deal with any of them who tries to start a war. That's simple enough, and within your authority."

Moishe bowed. Abraham Han Li had already forgotten him: he was deep the roll of plans that had been in front of him when Moishe answered his summons.

Moishe had thinking to do. He left his master to his work, and went to do it.

It was not easy to be given what he had thought he wanted. He could act now. But how? What could he do that any number of people in the Temple had not already done? He could send the westerners away—but that would not solve anything.

In the end he made a choice, the most difficult he could have made. He chose to let be. To wait and watch. To do nothing.

The westerners seemed also to have decided that quiet was preferable to a brawl. They curbed their disapproval and refrained from provoking arguments.

They also, and this Moishe made sure of, did not explore the Temple outside of those halls and courts which were both finished and safe.

Three days before *Tisha B'Av*, Chen was waiting in Moishe's cupboard of a room when he came late to sleep. That was unusual. Chen visited Moishe in his workroom or found him in the Temple in daylight; he never came in the middle of the night.

His impudence was untarnished. His greeting came out of the dark, startling Moishe almost into dropping the lamp he carried. "I see someone is suspicious," Chen said. "There's a guard on every rathole."

"My master noticed that too many of our guests are of fighting age and fighting fit," Moishe said as his heart slowed its hammering. He set the lamp in its niche. In the soft steady light, he saw Chen sitting on the end of his bed. He sat on the other end, yawned and stretched and said, "I hope I'll be able to sleep tonight."

"Tonight, yes," Chen said. "Maybe tomorrow. The night after . . . probably not."

"You found them?"

The answer was in Chen's eyes before he said the word. "Yes. They've been in the mountains. They're coming down, traveling by night. They're devilishly good at hiding—they've ridden right under the noses of the Khan's patrols."

"How many?"

"There's only one of me, and they're spread across a lot of country. I think maybe . . . half a thousand."

"Half a thousand? That many? How in God's name—"

"There may be more. We've seen caravans considerably bigger." Chen paused. "How sure are you that they don't know about the caverns?"

"Not sure at all," Moishe said grimly.

"I think you should let slip that they exist," Chen said.

Moishe opened his mouth to object, but for once his mind was working almost as fast as Chen's. "My master will howl."

"Which would you rather do? Lose the Temple or save the greater part of it?"

"I can't do this alone," Moishe said. "Neither can you. We need help. How well do you know the Lord Ogadai?"

"Well enough to cheer him in a procession," Chen said. "Should we be as close as brothers?"

"Find him now," Moishe said. "Bring him to my master's workroom. Make sure no one sees you."

Chen grinned. "You don't want me to have an easy night, do you?"

"When I have one, so shall you," said Moishe.

Chen was already gone. Moishe sagged where he sat. He was truly, deeply tired. He had been up since before dawn, doing things that had nothing to do with the westerners.

If he was not to sleep tonight, then so be it. He pulled himself to his feet and drew a deep breath, and went to lure the dragon out of his lair.

Abraham Han Li was awake, dressed, and scowling at the plan of the ninth court. He greeted Moishe completely without surprise. "We've done pillars of gold and pillars of marble and pillars of porphyry. We've studded them with jewels and inlaid them with fired glass and precious enamels. For the Holy of Holies, we need something else, but God help me, I can't imagine what it could be."

"Simplicity," Moishe said without stopping to think.

"Simplicity," said Abraham Han Li. His scowl deepened. "Simple—simple stone—something very pure, very clean: alabaster, or a veinless marble—everything as white as the clouds of heaven . . . yes . . . ah! Yes!" He bent over the plans, sketching feverishly.

"Master," Moishe said. Then louder. "Master!"

He had done it soon enough. Abraham Han Li looked up, more puzzled than, as yet, annoyed. "Master," Moishe said quickly, before he could fall back into the trance of creation again, "can it wait? Lord Ogadai's coming to your workroom. The rumor even I had stopped believing—it's true. There is an army of westerners. They're coming here and they're coming by night."

The chief architect sighed gustily. "You think they'll try to slip in unnoticed. You need me to tell you where."

"We need you to tell us how we can lure them to a particular place."

"Ah," said Abraham Han Li. He reached toward the rack of scrolls beside his bed and drew out one, then after a moment's hesitation, a second. He tucked them under his arm. "Lead," he said.

They did not wait long before they heard the soft scraping at the door. Moishe opened it carefully. Chen slipped through it, then the larger, bulkier shape of the lord commander. Ogadai, like the chief architect, was awake, alert, and looked as if he had not been asleep when Chen found him. Somewhat surprising, but most welcome, was the one who came in last: Buri the engineer, brightest-eyed of any, and visibly curious.

Chen looked like a cat in cream. Moishe would praise him for his initiative—later, when there was time for such amenities.

Abraham Han Li looked up from the plans that he had been examining, blinking at the newcomers. "This is where you want to go," he said, pointing with a long-nailed finger, "and this is where you should begin."

Ogadai leaned over his shoulder, with Buri close behind. Moishe had already seen; he had no arguments, though he had no few doubts. He had been living with them for too long; he could not believe that he was right after all.

Ogadai looked long at the course that Abraham Han Li showed him. Then he grunted. "We can't match their numbers—too much chance of giving the game away. It will have to be an ambush."

"Then you need to go here," said Buri, glancing at Abraham Han Li for permission. A glance granted it. Buri pointed to a slightly different place than the architect had.

"But," Moishe said, "that's—"

His master's cold eye quelled the rest of it. "Yes, it is. It makes a great deal of sense—though it tears my liver to say so." He turned to Ogadai. "You'll need to get your troops in place soon, and as secretly as you can."

"They'll be in by morning," said Ogadai, "if you'll give us a guide who knows the ways."

Moishe did not wait for them to turn to him. He said, "I'll go. I can still shoot—I hunt when I can. Can you spare me a bow and a quiver?"

Ogadai bent his head. "We'll get you a mail-coat,

too. Best you come with me. I may need you to make this clear to the men."

"I'll go with you when you do it," Buri said. "I built some of those ways. But I need to run another errand first. Swear you'll wait for me."

"We'll wait," Ogadai said before Moishe could take it on himself.

"Go," Abraham Han Li said. "All of you. What I have to do here, I can do myself."

For once Moishe did as he was told. No one knew better how little time there was to waste.

The caverns were the same by night as by day—perpetual darkness, and no light but what men brought into it. The shifts of workers were gone; they had finished shoring this weakest part and gone on to another, more distant and less vulnerable. Part of Buri's errand had been to see to it that none of them came back to explore or investigate. They were well and safely out of the way.

Moishe shifted in his coat of borrowed mail. It had been too long since he wore such a thing; it was heavy, dragging at his shoulders. On either side of him, Ogadai's picked men waited with soldiers' patience. Every second man was asleep, watched over by the man on his right hand. When this watch was over, the sleepers would wake and the watchers sleep. And if the enemy came—if it was not a delusion—they would all be up, wide awake, and ready to fight.

Ogadai was on Moishe's left hand, a breathing warmth in the gloom. There were lamps in the cavern, spaced far apart, to guide workmen in and out. They were not enough to read by and they cast deep shadows, but they struck random parts of the cave into sharp relief. From where Moishe sat, he could see the liquid flow of a column and the rough wood of the brace beside it, holding up that portion of the roof. Beyond it was the dark gleam of the underground river.

Ogadai's men were invisible in the shadows, spread with care around the inner edge of the cavern. Moishe had a sudden craving for open air—to be with Chen and another, smaller company, luring the invaders toward this place, or even to be with Buri and a certain very important company at the other end of the great cavern. But he had to be here; he was the soldiers' guide.

Chen would bring them. If, as Ogadai suspected, they were relying on someone from inside the Temple for guidance, Chen would discover who it was. He would make sure that they came here rather than through one of a number of more obvious but less useful entrances.

It was difficult to wait. The gloom was oppressive. One of the men nearest Moishe seemed to have been overindulging in either onions or garlic or both. Moishe was light-headed from trying not to breathe the stink.

Without sun or stars, there was no way to tell the passage of time. Counting breaths grew tedious. Ogadai's lieutenant had an hourglass, which he guarded jealously. By it they reckoned the turn of the watches.

Ogadai had waked twice and Moishe pretended to sleep twice. Shortly after Moishe's second waking, something set his hackles to bristling. He had felt it before he heard it: the softest possible scrape and a muted, barely perceptible thud.

Ogadai had not moved, but his eyes were open, glittering in the faint lamplight.

Very, very softly, he rose. Others followed suit, perceptible as shifts in the air. Moishe had his bow in his hand and strung, with no memory of having done it.

Barak led them—of course. He had shed his pretense of scholarly mildness and showed himself here for what he was: a soldier and commander, keen and deadly strong. Chen at first was nowhere to be seen—then Moishe saw the small bound figure stumbling between two tall westerners. He was alive and moving; that had to be enough, for the moment.

It had been a long while since Moishe went to battle. It was almost alarming to realize how well he remembered everything: the piercing alertness, the narrow border between terror and exaltation, the slowing of time to an endless, leisurely moment.

The invaders kept close ranks as they entered the cavern. They had scouts somewhat ahead, and a rearguard somewhat behind. The bulk of them moved as one, silent and sharply alert. But they had not marked the men now behind them in the darkness, nor seemed aware of any ahead.

All of the invaders were in the cavern before Ogadai gave the signal: a click of the tongue that sounded as loud as a shout in the silence. Well before the echoes died, Moishe had nocked arrow to string and loosed, just as the rest of the archers did the same. Hard on the hail of arrow-fire came a rank of men shrilling war-cries, swarming down from the niches and galleries upon the enemy.

A hand tugged at Moishe's sleeve. He loosed one last arrow into the gloom, slung the bow and scrambled behind the rest of the archers. He could not look back for fear he would fall, but he knew the plan as well as anyone could. The spearmen and swordsmen were driving the enemy into the center of the cavern, covering for the archers' retreat and the other, much more deadly activity near the entrance.

Moishe stopped short. There was no one behind him, to crash into him—and that was fortunate. He slipped and slid and scrambled down to the cave's floor, in among the fighting, with nothing but a bow, an empty quiver, and a knife meant originally to cut meat and leather on the march.

He was not thinking at all. He knew where Chen was—not too far from the front, and still surrounded by guards. They were big even for westerners. He darted in among them. They were slow and clumsy in his state of heightened awareness; he eluded them with effortless ease. He caught hold of the rope that bound Chen.

Someone moved in among the guards, as big as they but as quick as Moishe. He looked into Barak's eyes. They were calmly alert, and they knew him for exactly what he was.

Chen was on his feet and conscious, but Moishe was past caring. He heaved his friend onto his shoulder, groaning as his knees buckled with the weight.

Barak was closing in. Moishe had no words in him for prayer. He set his teeth and lurched into a run. Bodies caromed off him. He fell to one knee, poised for an interminable moment with the awareness of the man descending on him with drawn sword, and heaved himself up again. Almost—almost there. Almost—

Something large and heavy collided with him, wrenching Chen out of his arms. An instant later, he whirled through the air, coming to a bruising halt on top of something that cursed in gutter Chinese.

He stopped battering at his captor and lay as quietly as he could. It was one of Ogadai's men—and another had Chen. The motionless dark thing on the cave floor might be Barak, or might not; the glisten of wetness under its head might be water from the river that flowed perilously close, or might be blood. It was one of the things he might never know, not on this side of death.

His thoughts spun away in a whirl of speed. His rescuer had leaped into a flat run, bolting toward the far end of the cave.

The world shattered in a blast of terrible sound. Trumpets at Jericho. Thunderbolts in Gomorrah. Sea falling on Pharaoh's chariots, a roaring that went on and on, drowning out the shrieks and cries of the dying.

The silence was immense. There was light: daylight slanting down a steep passage. Slowly Moishe's rattled wits scraped themselves together.

Ogadai's man set him down with a grunt of relief. It sounded faint and tinny through the ringing in Moishe's ears. He reeled about, peering back the way he had come.

There was nothing to see but dust and rubble. The paving still rocked underfoot, gently, as the earth settled.

The cavern was gone. So were five hundred western fighting men who had come all the way from unpronounceable places to take the Temple of the

Lord by stealth, and Barak of York, who had led them unwittingly into the trap.

With an effort Moishe steadied his legs under him and made himself focus on the men about him. They all seemed to be there, which was a miracle. God willing, those on the other side, the sappers and miners with their barrels of blasting powder, and especially Buri who had been in command of them, had come out intact as well.

He nodded to Ogadai, who nodded back, and to Chen, who regaled him with a broken-toothed grin. Arm in arm, holding one another up, they ascended to the Temple.

Ephraim of York was not exactly a broken man, but he was considerably less arrogant than he had been before. He stood with Abraham Han Li and Moishe, Chen and Buri and Ogadai, on the edge of what remained of the western wall, and looked down into the pit that was his kinsmen's grave. His cheeks were wet with tears. "The Lord has made His will known," he said heavily, "and my people have paid the price for it."

"They were good men," Ogadai said. "They fought well."

"They were the best we had," Ephraim said.

Indeed, thought Moishe. There would not be another like Barak again, not in this generation.

Chen's mind ran along much the same path. "Your men fought well, no doubt of that," he said, "but for what? How long did you think you could hold this place against the massed power of the Horde?"

"We had thought," said Ephraim, "that the Lord

Measureless to Man 295

would provide, and that you would come to see the error of your doctrine. Then we would have the Temple, and you as hostages, and your Khan would be forced to accept us as his priests. Some of us indeed hoped that he would be persuaded to give up this labor here and take Jerusalem. Then there would be a Third Temple in living truth, and our faith would rule the world."

"That could still happen," Moishe said.

"But not for any of our doing." Ephraim shook his head, swaying a little as if in prayer. "Strange are the ways of the Lord, and incalculable His will. We will leave as soon as we may, and warn our kinsmen to attempt nothing of this sort again. Whether we can ever agree on doctrine—"

"Please," said Moishe. It was not what he had planned to say, and certainly it was not his place, but he had to say it. "Please stay for at least a while. We don't have to be enemies—and you don't have to be defeated. Surely we can find some common ground, and be allies if not friends. We worship the same God. We pray, for the most part, for the same things. Will you at least consider a compromise?

Ephraim seemed surprised, but he did not rebuke Moishe for speaking out of turn. Nor, and that was more to the point, did Abraham Han Li. The western rabbi said, "I don't think we have a choice. Do we? We're your prisoners. We have to do whatever you ask of us."

"You are not prisoners," Moishe said. "You can go if you insist. But I wish that you would stay. Are you so eager to go back to subjection under the followers of upstart prophets?"

"It is home," said Ephraim. "But . . . we will stay. For a while. This is the Lord's house, as unwilling as we may be to admit it. We will mourn our dead and make amends as we can. The rest is in the Lord's hands."

No one seemed inclined to take this out of Moishe's hands. His master and the Khan's general and his friends the engineer and the spy, and even the priests who had come to see what they were doing, all stood watching. None of them protested that he was getting above himself.

He bowed therefore and said, "Be welcome here, and be comforted. If you will, you can help us rebuild this wall yet again, for the honor of the men who died below."

Abraham Han Li nodded approval. Buri shrugged— he knew who would do the actual work, after all. Ogadai grunted. It was Chen, perched on a broken corbel, who said what they were all thinking. "Now that will take a miracle."

"Another one?" said Moishe. He thrust up his sleeves. "Well then, we'd better begin. We've a Temple to finish, and precious little time to do it in. Are you with me?"

"I am," Ephraim said, somewhat surprisingly even yet. But he did seem to mean it: his eyes were steady, his voice firm.

That would do, Moishe thought. Some might even count it among the day's miracles. When he went down to see what could be done about the damage, they were all with him, even Ephraim. They would find ways to work together, one way and another. In the end, who knew? They might even agree to worship their God together.

Over the Sea from Skye

Lillian Stewart Carl

From James Boswell's
Journal of a Tour of the Kingdom
of Scotland with Samuel Johnson:
Kingsburgh, Isle of Skye, September 12, 1773

We arrived late in the afternoon at the house of Allan MacDonald of Kingsburgh. He himself received us most courteously, and after shaking hands supported Mr. Johnson into the house.

Kingsburgh was quite the figure of a gallant Highlander. He wore his tartan plaid thrown about him, a vest with gold buttons and gold buttonholes, and tartan hose. He had jet-black hair tied behind, covered by a large blue bonnet with a knot of black ribbon like a cockade.

He conducted us into a comfortable parlor with a good fire, and a dram of admirable Holland's gin went round.

By and by supper came, and there appeared his spouse, the celebrated Miss Flora. She was a little woman, of a mild and genteel appearance. To see Mr. Samuel Johnson salute Miss Flora MacDonald was a wonderful romantic scene to me. Indeed, as indicated by Kingsburgh's garb, which was quite à la mode, time has healed the enmities between the kingdoms of Britain. In time I imagine the infant Prince of Wales will assume both thrones, as did his ancestor James VI of Scotland when he became also James I of England.

Mr. Johnson spoke to Mrs. MacDonald of the Duke of Cumberland's visit to Skye in 1746. "Who was with the duke? We were told in England there was one Miss Flora MacDonald with him."

Said she with a secret smile, "They were very right."

Armadale, Isle of Skye, April 18, 1746

Hearing the slow approach of hoofbeats to her stepfather's house, Flora threw her shawl around her shoulders and went out. Donald, the ghillie, was already waiting outside the stable door.

Sea birds called raucously above the Sound of Sleat. To the east the mountainous mainland faded into a pale spring twilight. The horse and man who appeared from the gloaming seemed so worn and weary they might have served as figments of nightmare. It was Allan, Flora saw. She stepped forward and held the bridle as he slid from the saddle with a groan.

There had been talk between their families, distant relations, that they should marry. As yet Flora evaded this notion, thinking Allan a man of great charm but little judgment. Now, though, she took note of the grave sobriety lining his features and raised her hand to his shoulder. "What of the rebellion, Allan? Is it over?"

"Aye," he said, "'tis over. Six days ago we made the crossing of the River Spey just beyond Ruthven, intending to catch Prince Charles before he gained the sanctuary of Inverness. But he turned, and the Highlanders came down upon us from the heights beyond the river before we'd had the opportunity to form up, let alone bring our artillery to bear."

Flora could see the scene: the flood of screaming men, unbreeked, unwashed, undeterred, armed with swords as tall as themselves. No surprise they overwhelmed soldiers bought by pay, not principle. Soldiers who had only the one shot before their muskets were rendered nothing more than props for bayonets. That tactic had defeated Generals Cope at Prestonpans and Hawley at Falkirk. Now it defeated William Augustus, Duke of Cumberland, King George II's third son and a general who had proved himself in the Continental wars.

"If only the prince had delayed his attack until we

reached smoother ground near Inverness. If only he had refused in his pride to take the advice of Lord George Murray, who is by far the superior strategist. If only two French ships had not slipped through the blockade and landed money and supplies . . ." Allan shook his head. "Well, such exercises in supposition are best left to historians."

With that Flora could only agree. "Cumberland and his army are retreating toward England, I suppose."

Allan's laugh was edged with bitterness. "The MacPherson levies denied His Grace the river crossing and the road south. He has fled west into the mountains, running like a rabbit rather than honorably surrender his sword to the victor."

"Perhaps he feared for his life."

"His life is hardly in so much danger as the prince's life would have been, had the situation been reversed. Charles has put a price on Cumberland's head, in a fit of mordant humor, I wager, but still he ordered his men to spare the wounded and release the captives. And so you see me here, at your mercy, cousin."

How have the mighty fallen, Flora told herself, thinking more of her crestfallen cousin than the English duke. Handing the reins of the horse to Donald, she guided Allan inside and sat him down before the aromatic warmth of the peat fire in the parlor. To the maid waiting in the hall she said, "Betty, bring bread, cheese, and porter."

Then Flora took the coat, its brave scarlet stained and torn, from Allan's shoulders. He folded his long, lean limbs into a chair and rested his head against its back. "The Pretender—the Prince Regent, I should say—has entered Edinburgh, to even greater applause than last year's acclamation. Strange, is it not, how many who kept back a welcome then are now flocking forward with one?"

"Is it so strange that few would commit themselves to Charles's rash enterprise until that enterprise became victory?" And rash it was, Flora told herself. Even if during the forty years since the Union England had dealt with Scotland as though it were a backward colony, to go to war seemed far from sensible. "Even supposing Prince Charles to have the right, it might have been very generous for one to support him at every risk, but it was not wise. Not until now."

"And now he has received the surrender of the castle, had his father proclaimed king at the Mercat Cross, and called a parliament. That will not last, he and his kind, they have little use for parliaments. Soon the old days will be back again, tyranny at home and a hostile neighbor assuring our poverty."

Betty brought food and drink. For several minutes Allan refreshed himself, whilst Flora admired the play of the firelight on his unshaven cheeks and the lock of black hair that hung forlorn over his brow. At last he set aside the empty cup, wiped his mouth, and asked, "Where are your mother and her husband?"

"He is commanding the government militia on Uist. She has gone to visit Lady MacDonald at Monkstadt and your mother at Kingsburgh and intends to return tomorrow."

"Ah." Allan summoned a smile, less radiant than his usual one, tense and uncertain.

She let him hold her small, clean hand in his large, rough, dirty one. It seemed the least she could do for a warrior so grievously disappointed.

Armadale, Isle of Skye, April 19, 1746

Marion MacDonald sat quietly, her hands folded in her lap, her countenance knitted in thought. "Well then. Did the prince proclaim his father James VIII of Scotland only, or James III of Britain as well?"

"Does it matter?" Allan asked. Cleaned, rested, and in a new suit of clothes—Flora's stepfather's shirt and breeks fit him tolerably well—he had reclaimed some of his usual ease of manner. Still, Flora sensed that her spirited cousin writhed beneath the unaccustomed mantle of defeat.

"Aye, it does matter," her mother said. "James might well overreach himself if he claims the throne of Britain entire."

"The Stuarts have never hesitated to overreach themselves. But perhaps the prince learned by his swiftly aborted incursion into England that he has little support outwith our own Highlands."

"Indeed, the present ruling family, of Hanoverian origins or no, has the possession of the united Crown and with it, perhaps, as much right as the deposed Stuarts. But this issue has been decided. It no longer concerns us." Marion's maternal eye moved from one to the other of the young people before her. "Now. Allan, I spoke with your parents at Kingsburgh . . ."

Flora's ear caught the sound of hoofbeats and voices from outside. Quickly she put down her sewing and went to the door.

Unlike yesterday's tender spring evening, this evening was coming on dark and swift. A cold chill wind churned the sea. White gulls looked like flecks of paper swirling up against the clouds massed in the

northwest, clouds colored the deep purplish-black of
a bruise.

One last fragile ray of sun illuminated the approaching party, a lad from the village walking before three
men on horseback. All three wore red coats like Allan's,
save these were decorated with bits of gilt braid. And
the heavy-set man in the middle was bedecked with
medals. " . . . the edge of the world," he was muttering, his face set in a supercilious scowl. "Beastly
country, savage mountain passes, not a decent inn to
be found . . ."

Allan's hand grasped Flora's shoulder and his voice
whispered in her ear, "I'll be damned—I beg your
pardon, Cousin, but it's the duke himself."

"Come here? To us? He must find himself in dire
straits, then, and in need of succor."

Behind them both Marion gasped. "The beds need
airing and the best china washing . . ." Her footsteps
receded into the house.

His errand completed, the lad sidled toward the
gate in the wall surrounding the house. Then he took
to his heels and disappeared toward the village. Flora
rendered her best curtsey and Allan his best bow.
"Allow me to make introduction. I am Allan MacDonald
and this lady is Flora, my cousin of the same name.
Your Grace is welcome in my uncle's house."

"Fort Augustus fallen to the rebels," grumbled the
duke, "and Fort William as well, garrisons incompetent,
should have hanged the lot of them . . ." He clumped
loudly to the ground. Again Donald came forward and
led the horses away, their hanging heads and rough
foam-flecked coats making of them a pitiable sight.

The men appeared in little better health, their

hats and the wigs beneath battered and worn, their chins unshaven, their clothing soiled—surely those were bits of heather clinging to the scarlet cloth. The taller of the two aides introduced himself as Felix Scott, the smaller as Neil Campbell. He added, "Are my kinsman Argyll's troop of men in the area, Mr. MacDonald? We must send a message to them as soon as possible."

Flora supposed Campbell of Argyll's militia was in the vicinity. It had been patrolling Skye for the government for some time now. So had His Majesty's ships been patrolling the Minch and the Inner Sound. She did not expect them to withdraw now, not when Prince Charles's victory would spur the French to even greater threats against the island of Britain.

Before she could answer Allan said, "I'll send the ghillie to make enquiries."

Flora contented herself by saying, "Your Grace, Captain Campbell, and Lieutenant Scott, please come inside and warm yourselves by the fire."

The young officers bowed politely and walked into the house. The duke eyed Flora in what she could only describe as an insolent manner. And yet the greenish tint of his jowls indicated that the crossing from the mainland had been rough. How indeed, had the mighty fallen, a king's son sleeping rough in the heather, his enemies pressing close behind. With a pang of pity she curtsied again.

The Duke of Cumberland thumped into the parlor, threw himself into Marion's best chair, and called loudly for brandy.

Flora and her mother hurried back and forth, bringing biscuits, brandy, and whiskey, and by and by serving a supper of roasted turkey, collops of venison, vegetables, bread, cheese, rum, and porter.

Allan played the host, and Scott and Campbell were as deferential to the ladies as to the duke himself. But as night fell, the candles were lit, and the claret and punch went round the table, Cumberland's face grew redder and more truculent. Even after Flora and Marion retired to the parlor and sat down with their sewing, they could hear his every blustering word.

"We faced genuine soldiers at Fontenoy and Dettingen. The Pretender's vaunted clansmen are but savages. I am told they live an idle sauntering life among their acquaintances and relations, and are supported by their bounty. Others get a livelihood by blackmail, receiving moneys from people of substance to abstain from stealing their cattle. The last class of them gain their expenses by robbing and committing depredations. And they have the uncommon gall to rise up against the hand that seeks to civilize them!"

"Better you should ask why our relations must live in such an unhappy state." Allan said. Her cousin was well into his cups, Flora realized with a sinking heart.

Cumberland asked nothing. "And the Young Pretender himself, what unmitigated cheek to place a price upon my head! Why your barbarian countrymen staged ambuscades from every hilltop!"

"King George placed a high price on Prince Charles's head," said Allan. "The very poverty that you deride, Your Grace, makes such a reward desirable, and therefore places your life in danger."

Flora frowned at her mending. Cumberland was also in peril from those who resented the heavy hand of allies such as Argyll, not to mention from those who would curry the favor of the new regime. By now half the island would know he was lodged at her stepfather's house.

Allan chuckled, but there was little humor in his voice. "You would have done better to have surrendered yourself to Prince Charles, who would have treated with you honorably and sent you home alive and whole."

"Surrender my sword to the Old Pretender's whelp, a puking boy barely out of the nursery?" Cumberland bellowed, overlooking the fact that he and the prince were the same age. "The Young Pretender is under petticoat patronage, I hear, his supporters stirred up by their women, wanton Jacobitesses. Like the lovely Miss Flora, perhaps? A pretty little chit, ripe for the taking, eh, MacDonald? Have you had the use of her?"

The needle stabbed deep. Flora thrust her wounded forefinger into her mouth and looked in horror at her mother. Marion was already on her feet. But before she could take a step toward the dining room came the sound of a chair crashing back and a glass breaking.

Allan's voice trembled with rage. "My family and I offer Your Grace hospitality, and this is how he repays it?"

Campbell's voice murmured of misunderstandings, Scott's of unwitting slurs and apologies on offer.

Another chair scraped. Cumberland snarled, "You call this hovel, this swill, hospitality? Why, I have banqueted with kings, you boor."

"You pile insult upon injury," said Allan coldly. "I have no choice but to demand satisfaction according to the *Code Duello*. Name your second, Your Grace."

Flora tasted blood. Her stomach went hollow. Marion

sank back into her chair, her complexion milk-white. "Oh, Allan, no."

"So the bumpkin plays at being a gentleman?" sneered Cumberland.

"My father is factor to Lord MacDonald, Your Grace. I have but lately served in His Majesty's militia. I am a gentleman."

"Then Captain Campbell will second me. And I offer you the services of Lieutenant Scott. They will provide us with their pistols."

More soothing murmurs came from Scott and Campbell, along with the clink of glass on glass. Flora suspected that additional punch and claret would not assist a peaceful resolution of the situation, but she had no idea what might do so. Should she try to persuade Allan out of his rash enterprise? Hardly. He'd look at her as though she'd lapsed into a tongue that he did not recognize. He could rightly claim that whilst he played the host here, this was not his house and he was not bound by hospitality to overlook such an infamous slur.

He was not bound by common sense, either, Flora told herself.

"As to duelling," Marion said weakly, "there is no case where one or other must die. If you have overcome your adversary by disarming him, your honor or the honor of your family is restored."

"Will either of these men stop at disarming the other?" returned Flora. "There is no rationality in dueling. Nor legality, come to that."

"No." Marion looked into her sewing basket, as though the answer were concealed there.

"For all his recklessness," Flora went on, "I do not wish Allan dead. But either the duke will kill him or he will kill the duke. And if he kills the king's son here, within reach of Argyll and the Royal Navy, then he is as good as dead. If the matter were tried in a Scottish court, with feelings running as they are now, he might be acquitted of the charge of murder. But not in an English court. They would inflict upon Allan the penalities they have been thwarted of inflicting upon the prince himself."

In the dining room Cumberland and Allan were still exchanging insults, somewhat slurred now but no less bellicose. Campbell's voice said something about dawn. Scott expanded upon the issue. "The wind may be in the man's face—he may fall—many such things may decide the superiority. In the daylight, though, such a matter of honor . . ."

Flora had little hope that in the morning the men would have forgotten the words exchanged in their alcoholic fever. "We must spirit His Grace away before he brings disaster upon us, unwittingly or no."

"He might be recognized upon the road by someone who has taken up the prince's cause," protested Marion. "Unless he is returned safely to his countrymen, we can expect reprisal. Better to have him wait here, and send his aides to Argyll asking for a troop of men."

"But then he would insist on settling his matter of honor with Allan, as Allan would with him . . ." Faintly but distinctly Flora heard shouts and the sharp discharges of firearms. She rose to her feet, but before she could peer cautiously out between the window shutters the rotund figure of Betty appeared in the doorway.

"What is happening?" asked Marion.

"A wedding party in the village."

"No one has married this week."

"Aye," said Betty, her voice dropping into a husky whisper and her eyes glancing toward the dining room. "I'm knowing that, and you're knowing that, but *he's* not knowing that, is he now?"

Flora had to smile, if half-heartedly. The villagers wished to celebrate the Pretender's—the prince's—victory without attracting the attention of Cumberland or any other Hanoverian supporters. How clever, to themselves pretend . . . Suddenly she knew the answer. Looking from Marion's sewing basket to Betty's furrowed countenance, she asked, "Has Donald returned from making his enquiries?"

"Oh aye. Argyll and his men are not to be found in these airts, but an English ship is sheltering in Loch Eishort."

"There you are, then!" Flora knotted her hands into fists. "Mother, I will convey the duke to that ship."

"How?" Marion demanded.

"To begin with, there are many ways of interpreting shouts and the discharge of weapons in the night. I imagine the villagers have a bonfire as well?"

"Aye, that they do," said Betty.

"Then this must be our strategy."

Mistress and maid shared a long speculative glance as Flora spoke, and offered more than a few words of dissent, but in the end they had to agree that of all their choices, Flora's plan was the only possible one.

The voices in the dining room rose. Chairs scraped. "I shall linger in this company no longer," said Allan. "Good night, Your Grace. Until the dawn." Uneven footsteps crossed the hall and mounted the stairs.

"Good," Flora said. "Allan has gone to his bed. May he sleep the deepest sleep of his life."

"Leave him to me." Marion slipped catfooted up the stairs, her passage marked only by the swish of her skirts.

Betty sat down, opened Marion's sewing basket, and threaded a needle. Squaring her shoulders, Flora marched into the dining room.

The three men stood together at the end of the table, inspecting a brace of pistols. The air was thick with the scents of food and sweat. Spilled claret stained the table linens, red as blood. That would be a difficult stain to eradicate, Flora told herself with a weary sigh. But first things first. "Listen," she said.

The three faces turned abruptly toward her. Scott's and Campbell's were tight and pale, Cumberland's swollen with self-righteousness. "Listen," Flora said again, and walked across to the window.

Another ragged volley of gunfire drew a similarly ragged response from the nesting seabirds. Now that they were silent the men also heard the sounds. They exchanged looks of apprehension.

Flora opened one of the shutters. A distant fire tinted the night orange. Praying silently that God would forgive her her lies—they were for the greater good, after all—she said, "Cameron's clansmen have braved the Sound, Your Grace, and are hot upon your heels. As yet they are contenting themselves with sacking the village, but soon . . ."

"Barbarian rabble," stated Cumberland.

Allan would know that Cameron of Lochiel would never allow his men to plunder—at least not until their mission had been completed. But Allan was not here to say so. Flora said, "Before long someone will tell them that you are within these walls, Your Grace. A ship of the Royal Navy is only a few hours' walk away. I will take you there. But we must leave now."

"I shall only leave after I teach your impudent puppy of a cousin his lesson."

Flora made a demure curtsey. "The truth of the matter, Your Grace, is that Allan is no cousin of mine. He is one of our servants. I beg your pardon on behalf of my family, but surely you will understand our predicament, three women alone in the house and brigands abroad."

Cumberland gobbled indignantly. "He is no gentleman? And I shared my repast with him!"

"Under such circumstances, Your Grace need have no scruple about abandoning this affair of honor."

Outside a single shot was followed by the concerted shout of several voices. Flora clung to her bashful mien even as her mind raced ahead. What if men from the village, encouraged by liquor, decided to raid the house and drag Cumberland away? She hoped they did not know about the reward.

"Your Grace," Campbell said, "I beg of you, heed this young lady, your loyal subject, and leave this place forthwith. In disguise, if at all possible, as we were seen arriving here. Miss MacDonald . . ."

Flora never thought she'd find cause to bless a Campbell, but she did so now. "An excellent idea, Captain." She heard Marion walking back down the stairs and edged toward the door.

"Disguise?" demanded Cumberland. "Infamy!"

"Greater infamy," Scott said, "to be taken by such a rabble. They are not even regular soldiers! Why, they might return us to Edinburgh, there to kneel before the Pretender."

Flora spared a blessing for Scott as well. "I should think these . . . irregular soldiers would care less for your sword, Your Grace, than your person. Imagine the smile upon the Young Pretender's face when he sees your head spiked above the gates of Edinburgh Castle. He would not then regret losing the opportunity to accept your sword in surrender, for you would have made an even more profound surrender to him and his house."

From the village came the brave skirl of bagpipes. The scarlet hue drained from Cumberland's porcine face.

"I know you find your own safety of little moment, Your Grace," Flora went on in her meekest voice, "but as a prince of the blood surely you will grant this house protection from reprisals by wearing a disguise."

"Very well then," said His Grace, with little grace indeed. "What is this disguise you have settled upon?

"Come with me," Flora said. And to the two aides, "You must hide your weapons away. Just now we cannot afford to call attention to ourselves."

She shooed the duke toward the parlor as though he were a particularly difficult sheep.

Ord, Isle of Skye, April 20, 1746

The chill morning seemed as uncertain as the night, the light of the rising sun masked by cloud and murk. Flora leaned forward, half dozing in her saddle, then jerked awake at the sudden call of a flock of oyster catchers flying up from a field beside the road.

Several people dressed in their best walked by, no doubt on their way to Sunday services. "Good morning," said the patriarch with a tip of his hat.

Flora returned the greeting. Her maid, walking beside her as was the custom, did not.

Several steps farther on the man murmured, "Upon my word, that's the ugliest lass I have ever seen." His wife shushed him.

Flora tried not to smile. William Augustus, Duke of Cumberland, was not particularly handsome as a man. As a woman, his face would sink a thousand ships. It had not abandoned its scowl since they left Armadale. Now it creased even deeper, his constant complaints of a sore head from the previous night's intake of liquor and lack of sleep overwhelmed by mutterings of dignity denied and position perverted. Flora pretended not to hear.

She, Betty, and Marion had sewed an extra length of cloth onto the lower hem of Betty's old calico gown and added a quilted petticoat on top, to camouflage the change from one sprigged flowery pattern to another. A large cloak and hood after the Irish fashion helped to conceal the Duke's petulant features. Nothing could disguise his stride. His legs and feet, clothed in stockings, garters, and suitable shoes, moved in long ponderous steps, as though he wanted to proclaim to the world that he was not actually a woman.

If they were stopped and searched the pistols beneath his dress would give the game away. But he had refused to leave the house without them, coming so close to an inconvenient fit of rage that Flora at last acceded to his demand. She could only suppose that if he were searched thoroughly enough to reveal the pistols the fraud would be revealed in any event. She glanced around, her saddle creaking.

Campbell and Scott walked several paces behind,

wearing Donald's and her stepfather's cast-off clothes
covered by loose plaids. She had told them more
than once to walk proudly, as members of the clan,
not humbly, prepared at any moment to knuckle
their foreheads. Still the young men slouched along
in the manner that they no doubt expected of their
own tenants.

Flora looked ahead. There, the Cuillins were appearing through the murk. Their dark stone seemed more
storm cloud than rock, save for the line of razor-edged
peaks which etched the sullen sky.

Below the mountains lay Loch Eishort. And yes,
thank the Good Lord, an English ship rose and fell to
slow leaden surge of the waves. From a mast fluttered
the Union Jack, the emblem created by combining
England's flag with those of Wales, Scotland, and
Ireland—the latter as much a thorn in the English
side as Scotland itself. Now, Flora wondered, would
the Scottish saltire be removed from the brave red,
white, and blue banner?

The party made its way down a steep, muddy slope
to a rocky beach. The horse slipped and scrambled.
So did Cumberland. At one sloppy patch he went
sprawling, his skirts riding up to his plump, breeks-
clad thighs. Cursing, he gained the beach, splashed
through a tidal pool, and clambered upon a rock. His
emphatic gestures earned no response from the ship's
crew, although Flora caught the dull gleam of a tele-
scope trained upon them from the quarterdeck.

Campbell and Scott waved their plaids up and down.
Cumberland hitched up cloak and dress, produced a
pistol, and fired it into the air.

Flora's horse started at the sudden report. She reined

him in and peered toward the ship, hoping that the men's actions would not be interpreted as provincial insolence and thereby attract a cannonade.

Many men were now gazing over the ship's gun-wales. Officers gestured. Sailors lowered a boat. Others pointed weapons toward the shore.

"You have returned to your own," Flora told the duke. "I shall take my leave."

Captain Campbell stepped forward with a bow. "Please make our compliments to all those to whom we have given trouble."

"Indeed," added Lieutenant Scott, with a bow of his own.

Cumberland laid his meaty hand on Flora's knee. His wig had been left behind, and his hair hung lank around his face. His eyes, half concealed in folds of flesh, gleamed up at her. "If you should happen to find yourself in London, Miss MacDonald, I should provide you with a small establishment of your own and as fine an assortment of gowns as any female could wish."

She opened her mouth to offer a polite response, realized just what he was offering, and shut it again. A tug on the reins and she was free of his presumptuous hand, with the bonus that her horse's hoof pressed Cumberland's foot into the sand—not, alas, against a rock. He jerked back with a vicious oath.

"You are very welcome," she said to the other officers, and to the Duke of Cumberland she said, "I hope, Your Grace, that you will never find cause to appear in this part of the world again."

"God forbid, woman, God forbid."

Amen, Flora added to herself.

He turned toward the approaching boat, favoring his foot, but shook away Campbell's supportive hand. Ripping off his outer clothing, the duke stamped them in disgust into the sand and seaweed. No hope of returning the dress to Betty, then.

Flora urged her horse toward the path. Behind her she heard the boat's keel scrape against the sand, and the voices of Campbell and Scott identifying themselves and their superior. In return came the greetings of the ship's officer, and then something she had not expected to hear at all, laughter, quickly shouted down.

She gained the top of the hill, prodded her horse into a trot, and did not look back.

Armadale, Isle of Skye, April 20, 1746

Her mother greeted Flora at the door, the candle in her hand guttering in the wind. "Come sit yourself down by the fire. I'll tell Betty to bring bread, cheese, and porter."

In the parlor Flora found Allan waiting. Politely he stood up and offered her his chair. She folded her aching limbs into it and extended her icy hands toward the fire burning hot and fragrant above the stack of peats.

"I'm pleased to see you returned safely," he said.

"I fell in with a troop of MacLeods, and they escorted me home."

"Our—guest is now safely aboard ship?"

"Aye. He is that."

"And not grateful for our help, I daresay."

"Not especially." She did not tell Allan about the

duke's last offer, or else her cousin would have hunted him down and shot him where he stood. "And you? I trust you slept well?"

"Much too well. When I awoke the dawn was past. But when I hurried to make my appointment on the field of honor I found the door locked. Your mother would only open it when I gave her my word not to follow you." Allan shook his head. "There was no need to lock me in, Flora. If Cumberland chose to flee this battle, just as he fled the battle at the Spey, it is no reflection upon me."

"Very true."

"However, it would be better if we never told anyone that part of the story."

Flora considered the leaping flames reflected in Allan's eyes. Please God he would never realize that her entire plan had been intended to protect him from himself, even to denying his rank to the duke and his men. If she could hardly bear to see her dashing cousin humiliated, neither could she tolerate his anger. And he would be irrational enough to be angry, not grateful. "I shall never speak a word of it. Although I daresay no one will have enough interest in the story for me to speak at all."

"Like as not," Allan conceded. "Cumberland, I suppose, will return to the war on the Continent. A pity he proved unsuccessful in performing the task for which he was recalled to Britain. An enemy on its northern border will distract England from its task in Europe, to quell the power of France. But that need not concern us." Allan laid his fingertips gently on side of her face. "Now, Flora, I have been speaking with your mother . . ."

She leaned into his touch with a sigh as much
resigned as relaxed. In time she would marry him.
He was quite the handsome fellow, with ample
charm of manner and speech. But, more important,
he needed her.

From James Boswell's
Journal of a Tour of the Kingdom
of Scotland with Samuel Johnson:
Isle of Skye; September 13, 1773.

> Last night's jovial bout disturbed me
> somewhat, but not long. The room where
> we lay was a room indeed. Each bed had
> tartan curtains, and Mr. Johnson's was the
> very bed in which the duke was to have
> lain in Armadale, but which he abandoned
> in his flight.
>
> At breakfast we spoke to Miss Flora of
> her acclamation in Edinburgh, where the
> prince jested with her, chiding her for
> helping his enemy. She told him, she said,
> that she would have done the same thing
> for him had she found him in distress.
>
> It was not the escape that had destroyed
> Cumberland's reputation, Mr. Johnson
> opined, but his abandonment of the field,
> both at the Spey and at Armadale, where
> the field was but a village wedding. And
> his appearance before his sailors attired
> in women's clothing had only added insult
> to eclipse. "'Billy the Lily' Cumberland,"

said he with a chuckle. "I hear that during his retirement in Bath, where he confined his strategizing to the game of whist, wags were given to presenting him with lilies. He would then rant and rain curses down upon all present, until he was at last carried away by a burst blood vessel."

"If not for his royal connections he'd have faced court-martial, as did Cope," Kingsburgh suggested, whilst his wife sat demurely refreshing our teacups.

"The war upon the Continent might have been won had Cumberland returned there," I said, "instead of leaving France even stronger for the next conflict. It was in that struggle that young General Wolfe did well enough to save Hanover itself from France's grasp, even though he himself died in the hour of his victory. Just as well he never knew how his victory contributed to our present stalemate."

Mr. Johnson shook his head gravely, having always been of the opinion that had the English army been able to return from Germany then Charles would never had retained his separate throne. But, conversely, if England had been able to abandon the Scottish frontier, and its garrisons in Hanover, and those in Ireland as well—which, encouraged by Prince Charles's Catholic Emancipation act, took the opportunity to rise—then perhaps the Continental wars of the last decades could have been won.

Still, Mr. Johnson went on to speak of the present political situation, which meets with his approval: how the French ship bringing Prince Charles's father and brother to Scotland most conveniently—by English measures, at the least—sank in a storm, leaving the prince to take up the crown of Scotland as Charles III. How, finding himself with no heirs acceptable to any British person save for his rivals the Hanoverians, he wed the minor Austrian princess who became mother to his daughter, Charlotte, the Princess of Albany, who has recently wed in turn young George III of England.

I have heard that Charles himself, disappointed in his hopes of the British throne, now contents himself with drunken rages. Perhaps all his victory at the Spey wrought for Scotland was to spare it the reprisals of a victorious Cumberland—who can say? For now the same economic forces which worked to unite our two countries almost seventy years since are now working to unite them once again. Why, I myself was drawn to London to seek my fortune, as Mr. Johnson never fails to remind me, saying that the noblest prospect which a Scotchman ever sees is the high road that leads him to another country.

My heart was sore to recollect that Kingsburgh had fallen sorely back in his affairs, was under a load of debt, and intended to go to America. I pleased myself in thinking that so fine a fellow and his strapping sons would be well everywhere.

The MacDonalds could easily find occupation in the British Highland regiment lately raised by Lord North upon Queen Charlotte's entreaty, eager as she is to find employment for her countrymen. And eager as he is to remove her countrymen, doughty fighters as they are, from the borderlands. Such a regiment, Mr. Johnson has often said, could be most advantageously utilized in the service of the American colonies, which are now sorely pressed by the extension of French Quebec beyond the Ohio River. How eloquently colonial loyalists such as Adams, Henry, Franklin, and Jefferson plead for the intervention of their motherland in local affairs!

Mr. Johnson saluted our hostess with his teacup. "Yours is a name that will be mentioned in history, and if courage and fidelity be virtues, mentioned with honor. For your loyalty to the house of Hanover, despite the dishonor of its son, does you and yours nothing but credit."

Kingsburgh and his wife shared an enigmatic glance. "Ah," said he with a shrug, "how these tales do grow in the telling."

Miss Flora ducked her head modestly, and I detected yet another secret smile upon her countenance. I wondered at its origins, but she said nothing more.

Later Kingsburgh conducted us in his boat across one of the lochs, to where our

horses had been sent round. Taking our
leave of him, we rode on, speaking as we
journeyed of the man who would never be
king, carried over the sea from Skye.

Postscript:

Charles Edward Stuart did not listen to Lord George
Murray. He chose the worst possible stretch of ground
for his battle with Cumberland, Culloden Moor near
Inverness. His exhausted troops were massacred. The
Bonnie Prince fled, becoming "the prince in the heather"
of many a romantic tale, among them the story of Flora
MacDonald disguising him in the clothes of her (nonexistent) maid Betty and conducting him over the sea
from Uist to Skye.

William, Duke of Cumberland, earned his sobriquet
of "Butcher" by enthusiastically pursuing an ethnic
cleansing policy against the Scots. He returned to the
Continental wars, but in 1757 was dismissed for making a deal with France which compromised Hanover.
France was ultimately defeated, both in Europe and
in North America, where after Wolfe's victory at Quebec it ceded Canada to Britain. Without the pressure
of French colonies to the north and west, and with
increased taxation to help pay for the war, the English
colonies began to grow restive.

In the ensuing Revolution, Allan MacDonald and
his sons fought for the Crown, just as Allan had done
during 1745–46.

First, Catch Your Elephant

Esther Friesner

"Still snowin'?" A querulous voice rose high on the thin, alpine air from one of the many tents clinging to the flanks of the mountain.

The tent-flap shimmied in the piercing wind that had been blowing since before the ages when the gods first discovered how much fun it is to pull the wings off mortals. A sharp, brown nose peeked out only to be withdrawn again hastily into the comparative warmth of the tent.

"Gaaaah, stupid question," the proprietor of the aforementioned nose replied with little grace. "Yer an idjit fer askin'. An' I'm a bigger idjit than that for botherin' to check. 'Course it's still snowin'!

Been doin' bugger-all *but* snow since we left bloody Narbo!"

A third voice now joined the conversation. "I say, fellows, that's a bit of an exaggeration, what? Oh, we may be in for flurry or two, but it's not even winter yet. I say we should count ourselves fortunate, stiff upper lip, put on a happy face and all that. Our situation may be deuced uncomfortable, but we've soldiered through worse than this before. Crossing the Pyrenees wasn't a piece of cake, but we did it, and we fought our way across the Rhône, elephants and all, and it'll take more than these dashed Alps to keep General Hannibal's boys out of Italia. Why, before we know it, we'll being giving those Roman chappies a spot of Carthaginian what-ho they won't soon forget. Now let's all give three rousing cheers for good old General Hannibal and then what say we go scare us up a bit of breakfast?"

This time when the tent-flap opened, it was to accommodate the violent, swift, airborne passage of a tall, gangly young man in the full uniform of one of Carthage's finest Canaanite auxiliaries. He landed on his nigh-fleshless buttocks in a snowbank and was soon thereafter joined by his bedding, his mess kit, and the Baal-in-a-Box portable altar that his mother had insisted on packing for him when he first enlisted.

"And don't come back, y' pansy!" came the united cry from those remaining within the tent.

"Oh, I say," the unfortunate young man remarked, picking himself up out of the snow and brushing himself off. He began to gather up his scattered gear, muttering morosely all the while. "Bad show. Won't do at all. I shall inform the authorities, see if

I don't. Ought not to be allowed." He moved slowly, still sore from previous ejections from more than half a dozen other tents. When at last he'd recovered all his belongings, he trudged off in search of more convivial lodgings.

He was still searching when his snow-clotted footsteps brought him into that part of the Carthaginian camp where the officers dwelled. He could tell by the smell. A large military encampment was no bed of flowers, but at least this unspeakably cold weather did something to cut the stench. However, there was one smell peculiar to that part of Hannibal's camp housing the upper echelons that not even a glacier could mitigate.

"Argh! Phew! Ugh! Oh, *drat* those elephants!" the young soldier swore mightily. Then he recalled his dear Mamma back in Tyre and felt chastened for having used such language. Wistful thoughts of home blurred his vision as he plowed on, trudging through the piles of snow.

Had he not been so overpowered by teary nostalgia, he might have noticed that not every pile underfoot *was* snow.

His scream brought the whole complement of upper-echelon officers running to see what had happened.

"What in Tophet was *that*?"

"Astarte's left tit, don't tell me another bally elephant's gone over the brink!"

"Are you mad, man? Since when does a full-grown war-elephant scream like a little girl?"

"What, d'you mean you didn't have your elephants fixed before you joined up?"

"Fixed?"

"You know." The speaker made snipping motions with his fingers, then thought better of it and made them with both arms.

"How d'you fix an elephant?" someone else wanted to know.

"I wouldn't know, old man. How do you break one in the first place?" The officers all burst into guffaws of comradely laughter.

They were still pounding one another on the back while the young soldier managed to extricate himself and his possessions from their malodorous nest and tried to sneak away unseen. He'd had more than his share of humiliation for the day, and it was still early morning. He might have saved himself the effort. Even the lowest local godling whose earthly purview was nothing more than one lone, lightning-stricken pine tree could have told him that any man who manages to fall into a pile of elephant poo should take it as a definite promise of how good the rest of his luck is going to be.

"Who goes there?" A mighty bellow rang out through the crisp, clear air. It started three small avalanches in the immediate neighborhood and gave a nearby family of chamois a collective heart attack. Tall (by Carthaginian standards), muscular (by any standards), and overbearing (by all standards save his own), Hannibal of Carthage bestrode the narrow world like a colossus, even though his wide stance and heroic swagger meant granting the keen mountain winds open access to his wedding tackle. (Not that it mattered: Ever since the Carthaginians had taken to mountaineering, the enlisted men had gotten into the habit of throwing "Welcome Back, Stranger" parties for their

frost-shrunken short-arms each time they successfully answered Nature's call. All of the camp followers had quit in disgust early on in the great climb, when their clients refused to pay them a finder's fee as part of services rendered.)

The young man stopped in his tracks, cringing. Mamma had often told him how his dear, departed father, a soldier through and through, believed that the worst thing a fighting man could do was draw the attention of his superiors. Hugging his Baal-in-a-Box close to his chest, he closed his eyes and concentrated on becoming invisible.

It didn't work. A heavy hand fell onto his shoulder and spun him around. He stared into the blazing eyes of his supreme commander. "What's your name, boy?"

"Ma- Ma- Ma- Ma-" The young man's wholly inadequate chin bobbled like a blob of fat atop a seething stewpot.

"Stop bleating like a damn goat and answer the question!"

"Y- Yes, sir. Mago, sir."

"Mago, eh?" Hannibal rubbed his chin. "Got me a brother named Mago."

"Y- Yes, sir. Capital fellow, sir."

"Did I ask you?" Hannibal's wrath was terrible to behold, but at least it served one kindly purpose: Anyone caught in the full blast found himself about ten degrees warmer for it. Young Mago actually worked up a modest sweat just standing in the way of his commander's displeasure, though he knew he'd pay for it soon enough, and not just by having to chip icicles off his eyebrows.

"No, sir, you did not ask me, sir." Deciding that his

best bet was to salvage the morning's collected faux pas, Mago smartened up his attitude. "I apologize for having said anything, sir. In future I will not offer any opinion unless in response to a direct question from you or one of my superior officers, sir. I mean, from you or *another* one of my superior officers, sir, seeing as you are. Superior. And an officer. Of mine. Sir." He stiffened his spine, puffed out his chest, and for some unknown reason clicked his heels together. This latter gesture only succeeded in refreshing the miasma of pachydermal by-product still hanging over his person.

Hannibal frowned and covered his nose. "Boy," he said, "I don't know whether that stink's coming off of your sandals or your stupidity. I haven't heard so much mindless, senseless, time-wasting drivel since the last time I had to talk with a Roman diplomat. You're not a born Carthaginian, are you?"

"Sir, no, sir!" Mago's stomach plummeted with shame under his general's scorn, but he held fast to his snappy pose the way a drowning man might cling to a spar. "My father was a Canaanite, sir, and my mother's family came from Tin Island. Sir!"

"Tin Island?" Hannibal was at a loss, and he was a poor loser.

"An island in the western seas, sir, beyond the pillars of Hercules and a skosh to the north, famous for its tin mines," one of his lieutenants hastened to explain, sidling up to the general the better to murmur the information with as much discretion as possible. That is to say, not much. Since Mago's unlucky misstep, it seemed as though every man in camp had come forward to see what the to-do was all about.

Even some of the elephants were taking an interest from the vantage of their picket lines. "The tribesmen there are said to make excellent warriors. There are rumors that the great Carthaginian navigator, Himilco, once reached those shores, but he found the food so distasteful, the climate so damp, and the behavior of the tribesmen at their ritual ballgames so ghastly, that he determined to leave all future contact with those people to the Greek merchants."

"If that's so, how'd this boy's ma manage to get her a Canaanite husband?" Hannibal demanded.

"Love will find a way?" the lieutenant suggested hopefully.

"Aw, forget it." Hannibal spat mightily into the snow. "I don't got to deal with his ma. You, there! Maggot! What'd you think you were doing, blundering through the officers' part of camp? You lookin' for trouble?"

"Actually, sir, I was looking for a spot of breakfast."

Hannibal stared at him as though he'd sprouted a second head, this one with a visible chin. "Breakfast? Did I hear you right, Maggot? You want your *breakfast*?"

"Sir, yes, sir," Mago replied. "If it's at all convenient, sir."

"Well, I'll let you in on a little secret, Maggot: It's *not* convenient. And d'you know why? 'Cause we don't *have* anything to serve you boys for breakfast, that's why. What d'you make of *that*, Maggot?"

Mago was not paying full heed to Hannibal's sarcasm. His sense of self-worth was taking a ferocious belaboring under the general's insistence on mispronouncing his name and it left him somewhat distracted. It was a pity that his dear Mamma was not present to remind him that another of his late father's pearls of military wisdom was *Never give less than your utmost attention to a testy general, a rabid dog, or a willing barmaid. You never know which way they're going to jump on you.*

Had he been just a smidgen more mindful of his perilous situation, he never would have replied, "Sir, if that's the case, I do believe we're all in a bit of a pickle, eh, sir?"

"A pickle . . ." Hannibal chewed over the word as carefully as though it were the condiment in question. "Is that what you'd call it? Let me fill in a few pieces of the big mosaic for you, boy: Here I am, playing wet-nurse to all of you morons, the sorriest passel of lowdown, worthless sissies ever to escape being infant sacrifices to Baal Hammon back when it might've done us all some good. I herded your sorry asses all the way from Iberia, got you across the Rhône River, and did what I could so's you'd survive that royal butt-whupping the Allobroges were dishing out when they ambushed us—which, incidentally, was where we lost I don't like to think *how* much of our supply train. For the honor of Carthage, I forced you bastards to crawl halfway *up* the biggest, nastiest mother of a mountain range on the map just so's tomorrow we can all climb *down* the sumbitch and kick us some Roman ass on the other side. You might think that was enough for a natural man to accomplish, but is that what the gods have in mind for *me*? Oh, no! I got to do even *more*. I've got to feed all of you limp-lunged, lily-livered ladies, *and* our Gaulish tribal allies, the Insubres and the Boiis, *and* the war-elephants. Feed 'em what, you might ask, given what I just told you about our supply train? Well, I'm glad you asked, son, and I'm gonna tell you: I . . . don't . . . *know!*"

By this time poor Mago was seriously debating the advisability of breaking away from Hannibal's foam-flecked tirade and flinging himself over the edge of the nearest cliff, but he was so ringed around by avid onlookers that all his exit options were blocked. Silently he prayed to his Baal-in-a-Box for an end to Hannibal's diatribe.

He got it.

"And all *that*—" Hannibal was breathing hard now, and there was a dangerous look in his eye. "—every single last little bit of that assorted grief, duress, and top-level misery is what you, in your wisdom, call a fucking *pickle*?! Well, I'll give you a pickle you won't forget, Maggot! Now hear this: You're the new alimentation officer! Congratulations!"

"S- sir?" Mago's limbs began to tremble, and not from the cold. "I'm very conscious of the honor, sir, but, ah, wh- what exactly is an alimentation officer supposed to *do*, sir? Specifically?"

"Do?" Hannibal echoed, his steely eyes glittering with gleeful malice. "Not too much. Just be in charge of chow for this whole damned army, that's what. On pain of death. Got that, soldier, or do you need me to *demonstrate* the pain-of-death part? Well? What are you standing around like that for? It's almost breakfast time. You'd better get started." He turned smartly and took a few strides through the snow, then looked back to add: "Oh, and by the way, Maggot—"

"Sir?" the miserable new-made officer whimpered.

"—I *really* don't like pickles."

     ✦   ✦   ✦

Melqartpilles of Tyre heard the sound of wild weeping coming from the lee of one of the larger piles of elephant dung festooning the Carthaginian camp. He had a kindly heart and an inquisitive mind, did Melqartpilles of Tyre, both of which had conspired to contribute to his enforced midnight escape from that very city after the time he'd idly wondered whether a certain nobleman's beautiful daughter were still a virgin and, on discovering that she was, immediately decided it would be *un*kind not to do something about it.

He was the sort of man who couldn't help being kind, especially to the ladies. He was also the sort of man whose kindness extended to befriending the otherwise friendless, be they man, woman, or beast. He simply had a good, if indiscriminate, heart. Thus, while a sensible man would have heard the crying and promptly walked off at speed in the opposite direction, Melqartpilles (Mel to his friends) headed straight for the source.

I'll bet it's old Danel the elephant-keeper, he thought as snow crunched under his sandals. *There's been a real scarcity of fodder for 'em lately, and when they suffer, he suffers. That man cares more about those unwieldy beasts of his than he does about his own family! Of course, I've seen his family and the elephants are more attractive. And smarter. And a damned sight more fragrant.*

It was not old Danel crying, as Mel discovered when he rounded the dung heap: It was Mago.

"Mag?" Like most folk who knew Mago, Melqartpilles considered the man to be a cartouche-carrying twit, but he liked him anyway. And twit or not, when the elephant chips were down, Mago always acquitted himself heroically in battle. When the Allobroges had sprung their aforementioned ambush on Hannibal's men, it was Mago who'd thrust his shield over Melqart-pilles's head just in time to deflect a chunk of rock that had meant business. "What's wrong?"

"Oh, hullo, Mel." Mago wiped his nose on the back of his hand and snuffled sorrowfully. "Nothing much. I'm just a dead man, that's all. Dead before lunch, if I know good old General Hannibal. I expect him to call for my execution within the hour. Not the sort to let the work pile up, that one."

"Unlike Danel." Mel toed the pile of elephant poo distastefully. "We're occupying turf where you can't swing a cat without having it fall into a crevasse: Why can't he just commandeer a few of the Insubres or the Boiis or even our own men and have them shove this stuff over the side of the mountain?"

"Oh, you know Danel." Mago managed a wobbly grin. "He's that fond of the elephants. Can't bear to part with anything connected with 'em."

"In case you haven't noticed, *this* stuff is no longer connected. It's a wholly independent stench."

"Well, we do need to keep some of it on hand, donchaknow. For fueling the cookfires and all that rot."

Mel laughed. "I think we could spare *some* of it for landfill. Just walking here from my tent I saw enough of this stuff lying around the camp to cook a fifty-course banquet! You know what the men say about this campaign? 'Same day, different shi—'"

Mago was crying again.

Mel frowned. "This is still about that whole being executed before lunch business, isn't it? Weird timing. Why's Hannibal want to do it *then*?"

"Because he can't bloody well have me executed before *breakfast*! *Or* after it, for that matter, because there's not going to *be* any bloody breakfast and that's the reason why he's going to have me executed before lunch!" Mago buried his head in his hands and sobbed.

"Uhhhh." Mel scratched his head, well and truly perplexed. "I don't suppose you'd like to run that by me again? Slowly?"

Mago did so, between sniffles and sobs and the occasional ululation of grief. When he was done, Mel understood the situation but was no less confounded by it.

"That son-of-a-Roman-she-wolf! He's got no right doing this to you, Mag, old buddy. Can't say I'm surprised, though. He never treats the native Carthaginian troops this way."

"Really?" Mago had given up on wiping his nose and let the drips freeze where they would. "I heard something like that, but I thought it was just a nasty old rumor. One hates to believe one's supreme commander plays favorites."

"*Plays* favorites? He wrote the damn rulebook! Look, I know your mom's a foreigner, but both of our daddies hailed from Tyre so that *ought* to count for something with the old man. Without Tyre, there never would have *been* a Carthage, but do you think Hannibal thinks of that? Noooooo. You want to know where we stand in *his* estimation? Canaan-fodder!"

"Oh, I say." Mago clicked his tongue in a disapproving manner.

"It's true! We're a disposable quantity in Hannibal's army. The only favor he ever threw our way was giving us these snappy-looking red shirts to wear as part of our uniforms, and lately I'm not so sure it *was* a favor. Red shows up awfully clear against all this snow; might as well hand us over to the Allobroges wholesale for target practice. We're lower than the Carthaginians, we're even lower than the suburban Carthaginians from the Iberian settlements. Sure, we might outrank the Boiis and the Insubres, but they're *real* foreigners, bloody Gauls. The only consolation I've got is that as far as Hannibal sees it, *all* of us rank under the fucking elephants! And trust me, that's not a good place to be."

"All I wanted was a spot of breakfast." Mago was starting to crumple again.

"Oh, stop that," Mel snapped, out of patience. "It's not going to solve anything or save your hide. You look more pathetic than a puppy with a sore paw. Too bad you're not: Them's good eatin'."

"Yes, well, locating a source of 'good eating' is the only thing that *will* save me." Mago's tears dried quickly in the flames of pique. "I've got to feed a whole bloody army or die, don't I now? Ha, ha, what a lark. I'll just toddle down to the butcher's and order a few tons of bully beef, shall I, or perhaps a brace of rabbits and let nature take its course? I've got several thousand men to feed and nothing for miles around to feed them. I suppose I could try persuading General Hannibal to have the officers try eating a few of the enlisted men, but then who'd do any of the *real* work around here? Calling me a pathetic pup is certainly going to help me *so* much, I'm sure. If that's all you can do, I suggest we stop wasting each other's time and you be on your way. I shall look forward to seeing you at my execution, if you haven't made other plans. Good day to you."

Wrapping his dignity around him like a cloak, Mago strode off proudly. He only got about three strides away before Mel seized his arm and yanked him back.

"Mag!" he cried. "Mag, you're a genius! By all the gods, the solution's been right under our noses the whole time!"

"I *beg* your pardon? You can't mean you intend me to cook the enlisted men for the officers' mess? I say, that won't do at all. They're mostly gristle, you know."

"Right, gristle, whatever, shut up and follow me! If we're gonna make this work, the first thing we've got to get is someone who knows how to cook. Come on!" Dragging his friend along, Mel sprinted through the camp until they reached the perimeter whither Hannibal had consigned the Gauls.

It was the work of a moment for Mel to locate a rock tall enough to serve as a platform, clamber atop it, and send out a whistle loud and shrill enough to draw the attention of every warrior around. "Noble allies of Carthage!" he began. "I bring you word of a great danger that threatens us all. Our beloved general, Hannibal, has given charge of feeding our entire army to this man here." He pointed at Mago, who blushed like a temple virgin. "I call upon you now to come forward and help him in this task!"

There was a moment of silence, followed by the sound of one bold voice raised in the question on everyone's mind, namely: "And why should we do this thing, you silly Canaanite-person?"

"Why?" Mel echoed. "*Why?* Why, because our plan for providing enough food for everyone is more than one man can accomplish on his own. It demands *teamwork*!"

This information stirred the Gauls to new levels of indifference. Mel tried again:

"Because our plan won't be easy, but once you've pitched in and helped you'll be proud to know that we've separated the men from the Boiis!"

Some of the Gauls began to wander away. Others looked around for handy piles of elephant dung wherewith to express their true feelings. Mel made one last gallant sally:

"Because this man's mother came from Tin Island and if we don't help him out, he'll feed you one of *her* recipes!"

A rumble of dread shook the Gaulish encampment to the core. Some men present were actually seen to faint. Cries of "Avert! Avert!" assailed the heavens so mightily that for a time it seemed as though the Gauls were about to cause their own worst fear to come to pass, namely that the sky might fall upon their heads.

Well, their *second* worst fear, the first being Tin Island cuisine.

An instant later, Mel and Mago had more than enough warriors ready and willing to put Operation Frequent Nutrition into action.

Hannibal leaned back in his chair and picked his teeth, content. "Boys, I never would've believed it if I hadn't a-tasted it with my own eyes," he declared. "That was the damn finest breakfast I've had in a donkey's age. I gotta give you credit, Maggot: You may be a chinless, gritless, dumbass Canaanite, but sometimes you're almost as bright as a real Carthaginian."

Mel and Mago exchanged a wink before the latter replied, "Sir, thank you, sir. And I do appreciate the fact that you did not object to my conscripting the aid of some of our Gaulish allies."

"'Course not. You know the rules: Any warrior in this man's army who's acting under *my* direct order is not to be hindered in any way from the prompt and effective completion thereof." He sat up straight and ran one finger around the rim of his bowl, gathering up the last savory drops of gravy. "You can't beat breakfast for getting a man in the mood to fight a war. Like I was telling the Gauls, an army travels on its stomach. Hope they'll remember that. You know what them Roman sumbitches think makes a good breakfast? Bread and olives! Well, what can you expect from a bunch of spelt-heads who don't even know the value of war-elephants? Can't fight a war without war-elephants; never could and wouldn't want to. Like my daddy Hamilcar always used to say, just give me some war-elephants and stand back, because I'm about to go Mykenaean on someone's sorry ass!"

"Er, what exactly did he mean by that, sir?" Mago inquired timidly.

Hannibal shrugged. "Damned if I know. Daddy drank. But by Baal Hammon, that don't mean he didn't know how to get the most out of a war-elephant!"

"He's not the only one," Mel muttered.

A horrible wailing pierced the crystal air. An elderly man with a displaced gag hanging around his neck and assorted lengths of rope trailing from wrists and ankles came stumbling up to fling himself at Hannibal's feet. Mel shot Mag a look of intense alarm.

"I thought you said you knew how to tie a man up so he couldn't get loose for a whole day!" he hissed.

"Yes, well, I do, but old Danel, he— Oh, dash it all, he's *old*, isn't he? Rather why we call him 'old Danel,' donchaknow. I didn't feel right tying him up *too* tightly. Wouldn't want to hurt the old boy."

"But you didn't have a problem with the old boy getting loose before we'd have the chance to get out of town? Way to go, Mag. You didn't hurt old Danel but you sure as Shem killed *us*."

While the two Canaanites were exchanging these accusatory pleasantries, old Danel the elephant-keeper was unburdening himself of news from the pachydermal front. As he spoke on, Hannibal's brow grew darker and darker, his eyes more and more enflamed with steaming rage. A sound like boulders rubbing flanks in an avalanche arose from his slowly grinding teeth. He thrust himself out of his seat, leveled a finger at Mel and Mago, and at the top of his considerable lungs bellowed:

"You did what *with* my *war-elephants?"*

"Well, this is another fine mess you've gotten me into," Mago remarked to Mel.

The two of them lay spread-eagled in the snow in the middle of what once had been the Carthaginian war-elephant picket lines. The lone survivor of what the enlisted men were already calling Mago's Massacre stood some distance away, regarding them mournfully. (The Gauls assisting in the plan had deemed her too scrawny to be worth the slaughtering and besides, they'd run out of garlic.) By Hannibal's orders they were to be left there until dawn when, if the icy cold of an alpine night had not killed them, he'd vowed to finish the job himself.

"What are you talking about?" Mel shot back. "This is only the *first* mess I've ever gotten you into."

"Well, there's not going to be any more of them, are there? Because we're going to be executed for this one, aren't we?" Mago said bitterly. "So it'll have to do, won't it?"

"And whose fault is that? At least I was *trying* to help you save your lousy life at the risk of my own! Was there anyone *else* doing that for you, huh? I didn't think so. Hannibal gave you an impossible order because he wanted you dead but he also wanted you to squirm around a lot first. The only way you were ever going to get out of this man's army alive was if you escaped, but you didn't have half a hope of escaping while everyone knew you'd pissed off the general. Too many people were watching the trails, afraid that if they let you get away, Hannibal would nail *their* nuts to the tent pole. Ah, but if you somehow managed to *fulfill* that impossible command, the pressure would be off; you'd be just another Canaanite grunt like me. No one pays attention to our whereabouts unless we're in battle or in trouble. I told you, the plan was for *you* to tie old Danel up good and tight which was *supposed* to give us time to take a quick bow for scaring up breakfast, make our getaway before anyone stopped belching long enough to wonder *where* we got all that meat, slide down the mountains, head for the hills, and be halfway back to Canaan before anyone noticed we were gone! But would you follow through? Nooooooo. Goodie Two-Sandals has to take pity on an old man, has to tie him up *easy*. Baal

Hammon almighty, Mag, you're as soft-hearted as a Hebrew!"

"Oh, shut up."

"No, *you* shut up."

"Yo. Howzabout the pair o' yuz shaddup?"

The unheralded irruption of that third, alien voice was so startling that Mel and Mag would have jumped clean out of their skins if not for the bonds holding them pinned to the ground. They twisted their heads this way and that, searching for the source of those rough words, until at last they spied him. He looked like any other Canaanite conscript, though he wore his uniform somewhat awkwardly, as if he weren't quite used to it. His accent was another thing that didn't fit him exactly right.

"That's better," he said, coming closer and squatting down between the prisoners. "So. You the guys that cooked up General Bigmouth's elephants, huh?" He smiled, revealing bad teeth and breath that reeked of olives.

"Actually, the Gauls did the hands-on cooking," Mag replied. "Apparently there's some silly prejudice goin' around against my dear Mamma's Tin Island–style of cuisine."

"Tin Island cooking?" The man shuddered for an instant, then threw off the sick feeling and resumed his affable smile. "Anyhow, I just stopped by here to say thanks. Latest word down from HQ is that Hannibal's gonna scrub the mission and head for home."

"What?" Mago could scarcely believe the evidence of his own ears. This was understandable, considering how badly clogged they were with snow and other substances not pleasant to mention. "You mean he's taking the troops back to Iberia? Oh, I say, but he was ever so can-do about invading Italia. Why did he change his mind?"

The strange soldier's grin got wider. "Why do *you* think? Yeah, it's rich. All day long he's been pacin' up an' down, carryin' on about how it ain't really a war unless ya got enough war-elephants, no can do, fahgeddaboudit. All his advisors, they've been tryin' to convince him to go ahead, finish crossin' the Alps, invade Italia, but all he does is give 'em this real sarcastic look an' ask, 'Oh, so *you* think I can still invade Italia without war-elephants, huh? But *can* I? Can I *really*? *Can I?*' By Jupiter, if I hear 'Can I' one more time, I'm gonna—"

"I say!" Mago exclaimed as the man's choice of divine vocative registered on his half-frozen brain. "You're a bally Roman spy!"

The man leaned forward and casually slapped Mago across the face. "Why'ncha say it a little louder, chump? I think there's maybe a coupla Carthaginian guards up the mountain who didn't hear ya."

The slap had no effect on a face already rendered about as sensitive to pain as an icebound boulder. Transported with unthinking delight, Mag turned his head toward Mel and chirped, "This is splendid, simply splendid! We've discovered a Roman spy in our midst! Good old General Hannibal will pardon us, and free us, and maybe even give us a promotion, and—"

Mel sighed. "Aren't you overlooking one little thing, Mag, buddy?"

"What's that?"

"That knife he's got under your chin."

"What knife?"

"This one, bright boy," the Roman said, pushing the blade a little harder against Mag's numbed skin. "Feel *that*?"

"Sorry, old man," Mag said cheerfully. "Love to oblige you; not possible. Been out here all day in the bloody weather. Can't feel a thing."

"So howzabout you take my word for it. Listen to your friend, there. Sounds like he's the brains of the outfit. Right, Brains?" he said, addressing Mel.

"Whatever you want, Roman," Mel replied. "I wouldn't turn you in even if I could. As far as I'm concerned, we owe Hannibal nothing."

This response clearly pleased the midnight visitor. "That's what I like to hear. Yeah, you *are* a smart guy. Rumor says the whole elephant-on-a-bun caper was your idea. Okay, Brains, listen up: As a whaddayacallit, duly appointed repurresennative of the whole Senatus Popolusque Romanorum *schmeer* back home, I gotta tell ya, we truly depreciate how you put the skids under Hannibal, even if you didn't mean to. I mean, the guy's a total *pazzo, a* crazy. He goes home now, that gives us a little more time to get ready to welcome him when he does show up, knowwhaddaimean? And talk about welcome, you guys come to Rome with me, you'll get a welcome you'll never forget: land, money, plenty of favors from the big boys in the Senate, all the *vino* you can drink, maybe a little of the ol' *ave-vale* with the ladies if you get my drift and I think you do."

Mel put on the biggest, blandest, most sardonic smile he could manage without cracking his frosted face. "Gee, pal, that all sounds reeeeaaaally nice. Right about now, a visit to sunny Italia would hit the spot, and the spot I'm thinking of in particular is gonna need a whole *lot* of hits before there's gonna be any of that whaddayacallit with the ladies. But you know what? It's not gonna happen. And you know why? 'Cause the moment Hannibal finds out we're gone, he's gonna send the troops after us. Or do you think we can outrun the whole Carthaginian army?"

The Roman scowled. "I'm tryin' to help you, an' you make fun of me? What, do I amuse you?" He tossed his knife from hand to hand meaningfully.

"Hey, hey, hey, no, nuh-uh, not at all, nope, no, sir, definitely not, you betcha." Mel had never spoken so quickly even when trying to explain to one Tyrian lady's rather brawny husband that nude singing lessons were all the latest rage. "All I'm trying to say is that maybe we'd better, uh, think things through before we make a break for it, see? Find some way to keep Hannibal from following us. Because as mad as he is right now, he's only going to get madder when he finds us gone. He's one stubborn bastard, too. Why, I wouldn't put it past him to come after us mounted on *that* thing—" he nodded to where Hannibal's last remaining elephant stood "—just so he could execute us by having her crush our heads."

"Crush our heads?" the Roman repeated.

"By having the elephant step on 'em, yeah. That's it in a very squishy nutshell."

"Whoa. Now *that* sounds creepy. All we do back in Rome is crucify people." The Roman shook his head and muttered, "Man, you nutty Carthaginians, always two steps ahead of the game! We Romans better come up with something a whole lot scarier than crucifixion if we wanna stay on top. It's all about *respect*, see? I mean, if people can talk about Rome without they gotta change into a fresh loincloth after, we lose respect. We'll never take over the whole Mediterranean operation that way."

"Good gracious, Mel, you don't really think that General Hannibal would have old Bessie stomp us, do you?" Mago piped up. "I mean, look at her! She's on her last legs, probably won't make it off this mountain whether he goes home or changes his mind about pressing on into Italia anyhow."

"Trust me, Mag," Mel answered. "If there's one man who knows how to get the most out of an elephant, it's Hannibal. Even if he kills her, he'll make her help him catch us before she dies."

"Too bad we don't have any experience with the beasts, outside of how they taste, what?" Mago said, trying to jolly his mind away from thoughts of inevitable demise. "Win her trust, gain her affection, be like that odd chap back in Saguntum, the one who could get the beasts to do whatever he wanted just by whispering to 'em, somehow fix things so instead of hunting us down the old girl persuades General Hannibal to let us go and forget all about us."

"Hunh! What kind of herbs have *you* been putting in your stewpot? It'd never happen. Like our Roman friend here said, Hannibal's crazy, but I don't think he's crazy enough to listen to an elephant."

"Unless the elephant were a touch mad, too, I suppose," Mago remarked. "As my dear Mamma always used to say, the only thing a madman respects is someone madder than he. I believe the phrase was coined during a particularly strenuous ballgame where the opposing team won by chopping off the— Ow!"

"Sorry." The Roman shrugged and looked sheepishly at the bloodstained knife blade that had just slashed through one of Mago's bonds and a bit of his wrist as well. "Slipped." He quickly severed the rest of the thongs binding Mel and Mag, then helped them to their feet.

"Look, we honestly appreciate the effort," Mel said as he rubbed some feeling back into his legs. "But weren't you paying attention? We won't be able to get away. Hannibal will come after us. He will come after us with his one remaining elephant and he will have her crush our skulls because he is stubborn and determined and just plain crazier than a cross-eyed camel. *Do you understand that?*"

"Yeah, yeah, sure, sure." The Roman didn't look at all worried. "But like your friend here says, the only way to stop a crazy is to show him you're crazier than him." He reached under his cloak and tossed the newly freed Canaanites a pair of deadly-looking shortswords. "This is not a problem. C'mon. It's time we taught Hannibal a little . . . respect for the enlisted man."

Hannibal was deep in happy dreams of all the ways he would make that pair of elephant-eaters suffer for their crimes before he killed them. His one regret was that he could not do the same to their Gaulish helpers, lest he risk losing valuable allies. No matter. He would just have to take all the nasty, bloody, agonizing, creative tortures he would have used on the Gauls and transfer every last one of them to Melqartpillades and Mago. The best part of it all was that since the two of them had been lying out in the snow for so long, there wasn't as much risk of them bleeding to death before he'd had his will of them.

A childlike smile curved the corners of Hannibal's lips, but it quickly vanished as a panic-stricken voice outside his tent broke his sleep with the cry, "The prisoners have escaped!"

"Escaped?" he bawled, sitting bolt upright in the predawn blackness. "By all the gods at once, don't those Canaanite swine know there *is* no escape for them as long as I'm alive? Eshmunamash! Eshmunamash, get your ass in here and help me put on my armor. Eshmuna—! Damn, I *knew* I should've got me an aide-de-camp with a shorter name. Might as well start getting dressed myself, then go find that worthless—"

He was still mumbling imprecations as he struck a spark to the wick of little oil lamp beside his bed. The flame caught and flared. Light filled the tent.

Light danced and glittered in the glazy eye of the severed elephant head at the foot of the Carthaginian general's bed.

Hannibal screamed.

East of Appomattox

★

Lee Allred

Even a marble man has his limits. Perhaps they might not think so back home, but London was not Richmond. London was too damp and chill and Robert E. Lee too old to pretend otherwise.

He cleared his throat and called to the young office clerk on the other side of the wooden railing. "Young man," he asked, "might I have some hot tea while I wait?"

The clerk's only response was to duck his head and hunch himself over his paperwork.

Lee had expected as much.

The small wall clock struck the quarter hour. Big Ben, on nearby Westminster's clock tower, echoed a muffled reply through the thick walls of the squat Foreign Office building. For several minutes the only other sound in the room was the scratching of the clerk's pen nib. It was a small office, just big enough for the bench Lee sat on, the clerk's desk, and the wooden railing separating the two. A swinging gate in the railing allowed the clerk passage into the hallway, a side door near his desk to what Lee assumed was the office of whatever official the clerk served. From the looks of the rusted hinges, the door saw little use.

The clerk set down his pen and blew on his hands to warm them. Lee allowed himself a slight smile. This cramped, drafty excuse for an office was just as cold for a Londoner as it was for a son of gentle Virginia. Lee's smile vanished as a new current of cold air blew down the back of his neck. He drew the collar of his military cloak tighter.

A *military cloak*, thought Lee. He shook his head.

Ambassadors do not wear military uniforms. At least, not ambassadors from America—either of them—but Longstreet had insisted Lee do so. *General* Lee, after all, was still well thought of in London even five years after the war. The President had hoped *Ambassador* Lee would be just was well regarded.

Well, that only proved Longstreet was no more infallible than Lee was, regardless what any of the new history books said about Gettysburg. Lee and his uniform had fared no better in London than his predecessors. The British had shuffled Lee from one government office to another until he had at last been led to this forgotten hallway where now they studiously avoided recognizing his existence, let alone that of his nation.

He had sat here unattended to for hours. Now it was

nearly the end of the working day. He wondered if they would simply shut up the building for the night with him still sitting on this hard, cold, splintery bench.

Enough.

He took hold of his cane with his good arm and heaved himself up off the bench. He stepped over to the wooden rail and, leaning over, tapped the cane on the desk of the startled clerk.

"Young man, I do not fault you for doing what you clearly have been ordered to do. Your obedience is commendable in one so young. But as I am a guest—however an unwanted one—in your establishment, propriety, sir, common decency requires that you as host see to it that an old man with a bad heart does not die on the premises. Surely Her Majesty's government has at least the manners of a third-rate hotel. In short, sir, I am freezing to death!"

The rusty latch of the side door clacked open.

The boy's head slowly turned in its direction. Lee, however, pretended not to notice. He rapped his cane again. "I repeat myself, young man, in case my Virginian tongue falls hard upon your English ears. Might," he said slowly, pausing on each word, "I have some hot tea while I wait?"

The side door opened an inch or two at this, just enough to show Lee a glimpse of a portly red-haired gentleman. The man *humphed* in a deep voice and said gruffly, "Smedley, fetch some tea."

"B-but sir! You said—!"

"Fetch some tea, Smedley. The British Empire isn't about to fall merely because you bring an old man some tea. See to it, boy!" A pause. "*And see you do nothing more.*"

Smedley gulped and nodded. He scurried through the gate in the railing, past Lee, and down the hall out of sight.

Lee turned to speak to the man, but the door quickly shut and the door latch clacked into place. Lee returned to his bench.

Smedley returned shortly. He carried a wooden tray with a battered tea service. He placed the tray on Lee's bench without a word and fled back to his desk.

Lee shrugged and poured himself some tea. He squeezed a slice of lemon into his cup. The juicy spray carried in the room's draft, filling the cramped office with the smell of lemon.

Lemons.

Lee thought yet again of poor Jackson and as he did so Lee's arm twinged. The dull pain in his arm had started that horrible night at Chancellorsville. The pain sometimes turned his arm numb, leaving it hanging there useless. Doctors told him it was caused by a failing heart, but late at night Lee wondered. What did doctors know of the workings of Providence? Of restitution and of vengeance? Had Lee not uttered the words himself? *You have lost your left arm, but I have lost my right . . .*

Lee shook his head to clear it of the memory. Steam curled lazily up from his tea. He drank. The tea's warmth quickly spread through his tired frame. Once the cup was drained, he pushed the tray aside and began his wait again.

Lee's last campaign: his siege of London. The siege of Baltimore had gone easier, but an army fought beside him then. Now he had only himself.

Only himself and a God who had turned His back on

Lee. A God who now spoke to him only through the dead words of one who would never speak again.

Strange, Lee could never remember any of the glorious speeches of Southern politicians, but Lincoln's words? Lincoln's words, even those from discarded texts never uttered, texts now unread, unwanted—those words were chiseled upon Lee's heart.

Whether that nation—or any nation, so conceived and so dedicated—can long endure.

The North had lost Mr. Lincoln's War. But had the South truly won Mr. Davis's? Had it done so, would Lee be in London today? *The prayer of both could not be answered; that of neither has been answered fully. The Almighty has His own purposes.*

He turned his face away from the young clerk and wept the tears of an old man.

The clock chimed the end of day in the City. Neither Smedley nor Lee moved from his respective post. He could hear the bustle of the rest of the Foreign Office locking up for the night. No one came back to check on him. Soon the entire building was quiet, save for the ticking of the clock.

I imagine it is dark outside already, Lee thought. *The sun sets early in mid-October this far north.* London was farther north, even, than the tip of Maine.

Virginia, Lee forcefully corrected himself. Old habits died hard. The proper frame of reference was the northern tip of *his* nation. Maine had no more meaning for him now than had Nova Scotia or Newfoundland.

Yes, and keep telling yourself that, old man. Perhaps you—and the British—will one day believe it.

A new hour chimed. Smedley set down his pen and began to clear things away for the night. He trimmed the gaslights one by one. Before extinguishing the last one, he paused, then called out without looking back at Lee, "If there is anyone left in the building—and I'm not saying there is, mind you!—but if there is they might be wanting to leave before I trim all the lights. This old building's a right rabbits warren with the lights out, all right."

Lee grunted as he pulled himself up by his cane. "Speaking to men who don't exist, are we, young Smedley? A slippery slope, indeed. You might soon fail to remember that nonexistence of the person whom, of course, you aren't addressing."

Smedley blanched. Lee smiled as he stepped toward the hallway. "In the future young Smedley," he called over his shoulder, "perhaps a better approach might be, oh, to quote into the empty air the Gospel According to St. John, chapter nine, verse four."

"S-sir—?" Smedley asked, trying to swallow the word almost as soon as he'd blurted it out.

"Slipping already are we?" Lee smiled. He turned completely around. "The verse—or at least the latter portion—reads: 'The night cometh, when no man can work.'" He nodded toward the lamps. "Applicable, wouldn't you say?" He turned, took a step, halted, then turned around again. "As applicable to you as the verse's first part is to me: 'I must work the works of him that sent me, while it is day.'"

Lee's face hardened. The work of him that sent me. "I shall return again tomorrow," he added, not daring to show even a junior clerk his own doubts about the Cause. "And the next day and the next if needs must." Lee's doubts were his own; his duty belonged to his countrymen.

The side door latch clacked. The door opened a few inches, and again Lee could see the shadowy form of the red-haired man behind it. The man crooked a finger at Smedley. Smedley gulped and went as white as the foolscap paper he'd been writing on.

"Do not, I pray you sir, blame this boy for his slight misstep in speaking to me," Lee said. "Given his youth, he discharged his duty admirably."

The man only beckoned again at Smedley. Smedley quickly darted into the door, only to return a few minutes later, even more pale, if possible. He carried a large iron ring with a single rusted key. "Y-you are to follow me, sir," he said. "Mind you watch your step."

The Foreign Office after dark proved itself indeed to be a right rabbits warren. Smedley led Lee through one twisting hallway after another. Eventually they came to a great door latched and locked. It was obvious Smedley's key fit the ancient lock, but the boy made no move to unlock it.

"We are to wait here, sir," was all he'd say.

They waited.

Eventually Big Ben struck the half-hour. "Right, then," Smedley said. He fit the key into the lock and turned. The latch proved harder, but eventually he heaved it back. The great door swung open to the night air and London's impenetrable fog. "Please to step outside, sir."

Lee did so.

Smedley immediately swung the door closed behind him. "Sorry, sir," Smedley whispered just before the door slammed shut. "I was just doing what I was told."

Lee heard the lock click and the latch slid back into place, leaving him alone in the fog.

Even in the fog, Lee knew where he was. Downing Street. Across the narrow cul-de-sac sat the numbered doors that housed the British cabinet. Had he represented any other nation on the face of the earth, he could but walk up and knock on the doors and present his credentials. But since he did not, he made no move to cross the street.

Instead he waited. Whatever games the British were playing, Lee had no choice but to wait.

The wait was not long. A sulfur match sizzled and burned, lighting a hooded lantern. The soft light through the fog revealed a waiting hansom cab that stood hidden in the fog and shadows. The door of the cab opened. Inside sat the red-headed man from Smedley's office. Lee had expected as much.

Lee crossed the street. He stepped carefully over the cobblestones slick with fog damp. The cab's driver jumped down to help Lee into the cab. Lee sat himself across from the red-haired man.

Aside from being younger than Lee had first thought, the red-haired man looked nothing out of the ordinary. Heavy wool coat lined with fur at the collar, smart trousers, leather ankle boots, silk top hat, gloves—the man dressed like any of a thousand captains of industry in the City. Lee knew better. He had spent his life in the army, where he'd learnt to look past identical uniforms to judge the abilities of the men beneath.

"I believe you've taken rooms at Moreley's?" the man said to Lee. A statement rather than a question. Before Lee could answer, the man tapped the roof of the cab with his gold-handled cane. The cab started at once. It turned around in the cul-de-sac and pulled slowly past the numbered doors.

The man watched Lee's eyes as they passed the doorways and smiled. A diffident smile at best, Lee thought. As meaningful as a smile on a dog. No. A dog's smile at least had energy. This man, his voice, his whole bearing was one of . . . he searched for the word. Languor? Torpidity? No. Perhaps only simple boredom.

Do we bore you, sir? Is the Confederacy but a tedious, disagreeable chore, best done as quickly as possible, thence forgotten? Lee closed his eyes and saw again the dead of Sharpsburg. He forced his eyes open before worse memories came. You've no idea what our Cause has cost me, or what sums I'll pay for it still.

On reaching the mouth of Downing Street, the cab turned right on Whitehall instead of left toward Trafalgar Square and Moreley's—hardly a mistake even a tourist would make in a fog. The man quickly smiled at Lee's puzzled look. "Quite correct, General," he nodded. "We've turned the wrong way. I thought a prolonged chat might be agreeable to you."

"A meeting in your office, sir—one several hours if not days earlier—would have been far more 'agreeable.' Far more convenient, too."

Still smiling, the man shook his head. "Ah, but not for me, I'm afraid. Those weren't my offices; I have none, you see."

A corner of Lee's mouth turned up. "I suppose this is the part in your little drama where I ask who you are."

"Will you?"

Lee shook his head. He'd played these games during the War. "No, sir. I see no point to it." The man underestimated Lee, but then he was used that; being underestimated had served him well in the past. "I suspect your answer would be . . . suspect at best."

The man nodded with obvious satisfaction. "Quite so. In fact, had you asked, I should have been very much disappointed in you."

The man slumped forward. He rested his ample chins on the gold handle of his cane as he seemed to think over his next words. "But in as much as you have *not* asked my identity, I believe that I shall answer your unasked question as fully as it is in my power to do so."

He pursed his lips. "I am not connected in any way to Her Majesty's Government, you understand. I do not represent the Crown, I hold no office, no portfolio. In short, sir, I do not exist."

"I hardly think so, sir. After spending a few days in your charming city as a man who doesn't exist, you can be sure I know the difference."

"Well played." The man smiled. "Your president was quite right, you know, in sending you. I cannot think of another of your countrymen with whom I'd even bother. Most diplomats, frankly, are hardly worth the effort. Crashing bores." The man's face brightened. "But you, sir? 'The Napoleon of our age,' the soldier who won his county's independence through sheer force of will? No, you interest me, dear General."

"*My* interest, sir, is in the successful discharge of my duties."

"Something you find difficult to do speaking to a

man without a name, I imagine." The man leaned back. "I cannot give you my surname, of course. Nor my Christian name—too singular by half. And, 'Michael,' a more common form for my poor name, strikes me too much of Milton's fallen orator. 'Which way I flie is Hell; my self am Hell.'" He smiled. "No, while the snake may have the best lines, I do not think, given what we must talk about this evening, that using that particular name would prove the best course."

He thought for a moment. "Ah. Perhaps a more agreeable compromise might be 'Croft.'" He smiled. "Yes. What a pleasant solution. Yes, you may call me Croft." Somehow he actually found the energy to chuckle. "'A small portable filing cabinet' is just the name for me."

Lee gave a sour smile. "My mission nears completion, then. I hoped, sir, for a cabinet meeting—and it appears that I have one now."

"Oh, I assure you this is much better. My younger brother is somewhat rashly prone to say I *am* the Government." Croft shrugged. "Rather, I have become a shortcut, a convenience in difficult situations."

And our Confederacy is one such, thought Lee. His arm began to ache again. He rubbed it absentmindedly. "Let us begin down that shortcut then, shall we? Tell me, Mister . . . Croft. Why is it your government no longer recognizes our Confederacy?"

Croft smiled blandly. "Whatever do you mean? The British government has recognized you. Lord Palmerston did so shortly after your brilliant victory in Pennsylvania. Made a lovely little speech about it, too, about how England had its Runnymede, but the South had their General Meade."

"Your government has since done everything in its power to disavow that recognition!"

Croft fingered the black velvet curtains as he stared out the window. "Hmmm. The fog seems to be lifting somewhat. Strange how fog lifts and falls for no discernible cause." He turned to Lee. "And what reason have you been given for this supposed . . . intransigence by Her Majesty's government?"

"Officially? None." The British government wasn't even talking to the Confederacy enough to admit it wasn't talking. Nor enough to deny it.

"That then implies you've an 'unofficial' reply, would it not?"

As if this charade tonight wasn't. "What was passed on to us through a neutral third party—unofficially, of course—"

"Of course."

"—was the recent rapid turnovers of your government."

Croft nodded slowly. "Much truth in that, I'd dare say. Palmerston, Russell, Derby, Disraeli, and now Gladstone. We've gone through five governments in as many years. Five since your Gettysburg. Things have been rather muddled of late." He sighed. "I've found it most . . . tedious."

Lee snorted. "Too 'muddled' to even spend the few minutes it would to take to accept my ambassadorial credentials? Unlikely, sir. Unlikely."

Croft only smiled. "You've not met Disraeli, then. The sobriquet 'Dizzy' is no mere onomatopoeia."

"I tire of your games, sir. One would think that in staging this elaborate rendezvous, you would at last be intent on providing answers. Well, sir! Provide them!"

A moment passed as Croft looked Lee up and down, measuring him against some secret scale. "Very well," he said at last. "You wish to know why the British government is so reluctant to continue to treat with yours." He shook his head. "Hardly any cognoscitive effort is required, my dear General. One need merely speak that one singularly ugly little word."

Lee knew full well which word Croft meant. That hateful, shameful word Lee could no longer bring himself to speak.

Croft spoke it for him, all but hissing it:

"Slavery."

For the first time, the lethargic Croft showed fire, a fire in his eyes Lee was all too familiar with: He had seen it in the eyes of the Northern abolitionists before the war.

Nothing would extinguish *that* blaze. Nor did Lee, down in the recesses of his soul, truly wish to try. Duty, however, impelled him to. How many times would he be called on to defend the indefensible?

"May I remind you, sir," Lee said, choosing his every word carefully, "that the internal affairs of a sovereign nation, particularly one on the other side of a vast ocean, are of no concern to Britain, either to her government or to her subjects."

Yes, Lee thought. *Self-determination's a principle I can defend—just as long as I do not think through that principle's ultimate personal ramifications.* "And," he continued "may I also remind you that your government recognized the Confederacy despite our peculiar institution. If it was not a concern then, it should not be a concern now. Nothing has changed."

"Perhaps that lack of change *is* the problem," Croft shot back. "General Lee, I've read your view on the 'servile question' as your political parties refer to it in senatorial debates—"

"The South, sir, has no political parties," Lee spoke with pride. The evils Republicanism and Whiggerydom had brought were one taint, at least, from which the South had freed itself.

"My apologies." Croft smiled wider. A crocodile smile. "The *factions*, then, of your government's undivided whole." He fingered the curtain for a moment. "You favor a gradual emancipation—but an emancipation nonetheless. Rather more in line with your President Longstreet's views than that of the Yancy-Rhett faction controlling your senate." He let go the curtain. "Of course, not even the *Charleston Mercury* dares term you a 'black Republican.' Not yet."

Lee knew they had started calling Longstreet that. Lee had spent his trip across the Atlantic wondering, was he being sent by Longstreet to shield Lee from the coming storm? Or by Rhett to get rid of a troublesome marble man. No matter. By now, anyway, the Louisiana crisis should have all blown over. Southern politics seemed to be the art of overreacting. "My personal views don't matter. My government's views do."

"We differ on that, too, but let it pass for now. What 'government views' would you have Whitehall know?"

"That the matter is our business, not yours."

Croft's smile was gone. "You repeat yourself," he said, his voice rising.

"Only because you won't listen the first time." Lee's voice also rose. "I cannot state the Confederacy's position strongly enough."

"The truth of an opinion doesn't depend on how strongly it is stated."

"I suggest, sir, that you then apply that maxim to yourself, because you, sir, are *shouting*." And so was Lee. He took a deep, calming breath.

The carriage pulled to a stop along the banks of the Thames.

Croft grunted. "Tempers run hot. Perhaps some cool night air? I've something of interest to show you at any rate, General."

Lee had of course heard of the great Victoria Embankment project. To actually see it, even dimly through a thinning fog, was something else again.

Croft insisted they step out of the cab. He led Lee to a good vantage point on Westminster Bridge.

What game is Croft playing now? Lee imagined he'd soon find out. He was beginning to understand how McClellan must have felt.

Croft pointed out the seawall (a mile and a half long, Croft said, but Lee could see only a small length of it in the light fog) that held back the Thames five hundred feet from its natural riverbank. The exposed riverbed had then been gouged out and a strong foundation laid. Scaffolding and the beginnings of masonry walls sketched out the substructure's eventual shape. Lee could even see the track bed where the underground railroad would run.

Underground railroad, frowned Lee. Was there ever any escaping the stain of slavery?

Croft was waiting for Lee to say something. Very well. Honey words over something as innocent as this cost little. "Most impressive," Lee nodded. "I understand that when this is finished, a great boulevard will be built over this excavation. Shortly after my arrival I saw your city's other great project, Queen Victoria Street. I must say, though, that carving a street through a city is far less impressive than carving one from a mighty river."

Lee expected Croft to nod or speak or do something, but Croft still just stood there waiting.

"There is some purpose," Lee asked, "in your showing this to me?"

"Some small purpose, yes." Croft nodded. Lee did not like that smile Croft wore. "Tell me, do you know the primary purpose of this whole project? Not the street. Not the underground railroad. But the real reason for the Embankment?"

Lee shook his head.

"Sewage, General Lee. Simple, plain foul sewage. The Embankment is nothing more than a great covered sewer designed to carry waste ten miles east to Barking. As things stand now, it's all just dumped into the Thames here at this very spot. Right in Westminster. Right in the heart of Empire."

Croft removed his hat and brushed it with the cuff of his coat. "One could argue that . . . excreta . . . is a very private affair indeed, one of no consequence to the larger community. If—"

Did the man think Lee stupid? Did he think Lee a McClellan? Lee held up his hand. "No need to belabor it. I grasp your analogy." He paused. "But do you?"

"Eh?"

"Have you fully followed your own analogy—and this sewer—to its termination?" Lee gestured in the direction he assumed Barking to be. "The sewage will still eventually be dumped into the Thames. If not here, then at Barking. You've merely delayed its disposal . . ." His voice faltered and trailed off. Croft had led Lee by the nose as easily as Lee ever had led McClellan.

"Yes, General. Sooner or later, it must be disposed of. Your Confederacy is merely delaying that."

The carriage clattered across Westminster Bridge and turned north along the bank of the Thames opposite Westminster. Croft sat quiet, the fire in his eyes extinguished as if snuffed out by the chill air off the Thames.

Lee sat quiet, too, but his fires began to burn all the brighter. Even if doubts about the Cause were never really very far away, regardless of what Croft said or did, Lee's duty would always remain standing. Unbreachable. Unflankable.

Or would it? He had stood unbreachable, unflankable the very day those doubts had started: that day so long ago when General Scott offered him command of the Union Army. Lee, his duty clear, had turned Scott down and gone off to fight for Virginia. He wondered. Had Lincoln, his commander-in-chief, asked in person would Lee have still refused?

Yes, Lee admitted to himself. Virginia had called. She had beckoned to him, and he had followed her, rendered deaf, dumb, and blind by her call. He could not hear what Lincoln had so desperately tried to say to him, to Virginia, and to the rest of the South. Not until afterward, when he had read Lincoln's words in the cool, calm air of peace did he realize too late that Lincoln had truly sought to prevent the war. And the South had—*Lee* had!—made war rather than let their nation survive.

And the war came.

The carriage recrossed the Thames on Waterloo Bridge and headed down Fleet Street toward the Strand and Trafalgar Square. He could hear men and boys hawking newspapers, but couldn't understand their thick, impenetrable accent. He supposed it was the equivalent of the American cry of "Extra, extra!"

Croft pulled the cab's thick velvet curtains closed. "I thought it interesting your using that particular verse of scripture tonight with young Smedley."

Lee found himself almost amused at Croft's oblique approach. First sewers, now scriptures. Croft was not so much trying to flank Lee as to pin down the flanks before swinging hard against the center. *That is what I wanted to do at Gettysburg before Longstreet showed me the better way. I would have lost my war, just as Croft will lose his tonight.*

"I take it," Croft said, "that you are familiar with that particular chapter in St. John?"

"The healing of the blind man."

"The healing of the man blind from *birth*."

Not oblique at all, but as clumsy as Joe Hooker. "Please spare me the lecture about how the Confederacy was born blind—"

"'I must work the works of him that sent me,'" Croft recited, "'while it is day: the night cometh, when no man can work.'" He looked at Lee. "Your Carpenter spoke those words to bring light. You, General, speak them to bring darkness."

Lee spoke not for several heartbeats. Then in a

low, measured voice he said, "*Never* speak to me like that again, sir. *Never*."

"Isn't it true?"

"The devil can quote scriptures for his own purposes, Mr. Croft. The Northern abolitionists did."

" 'Both read the same Bible and pray to the same God, and each invokes His aid against the other.' " Croft smiled at Lee's surprise. "Yes, General," Croft said, as if reading his mind. "I'm quite familiar with Mr. Lincoln's farewell address. Not too many people are, though, are they? Not surprising, considering he never delivered it. Of course, given your part in the affair, you know all about that."

Long and slow, like a teakettle, Lee's breath hissed out. "My . . . part, as you put it, Croft, was that of trying to prevent what happened."

"You failed."

What could Lee do but nod? After Gettysburg, after Baltimore, his army had marched into Washington. Mobs from Baltimore had reached it first. Before Lee could stop them, the mob dragged a bruised and bloody Lincoln out of the White House. Screaming that Lincoln would never preach to them ever again of Emancipation or of Union, they—

"Tell me, General," Croft asked. "When you saw what was happening, did you rein back your horse? Or did you spur it on so that you could join in?"

A curse escaped Lee's lips. Tears streamed down his cheeks; he tried covering his face with his trembling hands. "It wasn't like that, I tell you—"

"What was *he* to you?" Croft mocked. "Not any of your concern, surely—*their* governance of *their* own president."

Lee raised his face. "He was *my* president, too."

Croft didn't even need to smile. Too late, Lee tried to choke back the words already uttered.

"That he was," Croft said. "That he was."

The cab came to a sudden halt. "Trouble up ahead, guv'nor," the cabby called out.

Croft seated his top hat firmly on his head and opened the door. "Shall we get out?"

They had stopped just short of Trafalgar Square. The fog had nearly lifted. Lee could see Nelson's column flickering in torchlight. A mob had gathered at the entrance of Moreley's, the one that faced the square. They carried torches and placards. And something else, something horribly else.

Croft, however, casually ignored the growing mob and started to point out the four new statues at the base of Nelson's column. "Oh, do look," he said pleasantly, "Landseer's finally gotten his lions in place, although they do appear to be backwards."

Lee glared at him. "Are they yours?"

"The lions?"

"The mob. Is this just part of your game tonight like Smedley and the carriage ride?"

"Oh, that mob's real, all right—"

"You knew about it in advance, though didn't you?"

Croft only smiled. "Wonderful thing, the transatlantic cable. At times it can seem to bestow prescience, even omniscience. Once the news hit the papers tonight, it was obvious what would happen." He nodded at a new commotion in the crowd. "I say, isn't that effigy meant to be you?" Torches began to set the gray-coated figure ablaze. "It appears you've finally been recognized in

London after all." He nodded to the driver who jumped down and opened the door. "Perhaps we'd better drive on. They may decide to burn a more realistic effigy."

"What is this all about?" Lee asked as he climbed back into the carriage.

Croft settled back in his seat. "I doubt it'd be safe to take you around the back of Moreley's—or any other hotel for that matter, my dear General. And *my* club is out of the question as well—Diogenes may well claim to be hanging out his lantern for an honest man, but I doubt very seriously my club is really in the mood tonight to receive one. Especially one in a Confederate uniform. No, we'd best skip Clubland and Pall Mall altogether. We must jump my rails tonight." Croft rapped the roof of the cab. "Northumberland and around," he called. To Lee he said, "We'll give Bobby Peel a chance to tidy things up. In the meantime I have a friend who lives nearby. We'll just pop in to see him while we wait."

The cab turned around. Lee pulled open the curtains. Torchlight threw shadows across his face. The shadows danced and deepened as the carriage slowly crept away from the mob.

"What is this all about?" Lee repeated.

Croft reached out and gently pulled the curtains closed again. "The night cometh, General," he said in a faraway voice, "when no man can work."

Croft pulled a carefully folded telegram from his waistcoat and handed it to Lee.

Rhett and Yancy had finally gotten their way; the Confederacy had passed the amendment to outlaw unilateral emancipation by a state.

Croft then handed Lee another telegram. "It would appear Louisiana has found more profit in trade with Britain and the North than in slavery. They've passed an emancipation act in defiance. The Confederacy simply can't allow that, can it? 'All one thing or another,' as you said. Your own governor of Virginia is calling for troops to put down the Louisiana secession. The Confederacy must and shall be preserved. So much for state rights and sovereignty."

Lee let the telegrams fall to the floor. And with it, his Cause, his home, his world. A just, and a lasting peace, among ourselves, and with all nations. In the end, the South had achieved neither.

Croft bent down and picked the papers up. "The Foreign Office knew this was only hours from happening. It was just a matter of keeping you out of touch with both Richmond and Fleet Street until it did." He slipped it back in his pocket. "You saw the mood of Britain back there. The British government will recognize the new Pelican Flag Republic by morning. I'm sure the North won't be far behind us. The Confederacy is over, General. If it does nothing, it slowly disintegrates one state at time. If it fights, it faces not just Louisiana but Britain and the North as well."

"Overwhelming odds never stopped a Southerner from doing his duty before." A hollow boast and Croft had to know that.

"And what 'duty' is *that*?" sneered Croft. "The last time you claimed your duty lay in protecting your state from an outside government. You betrayed your oath as an officer, betrayed everything else you held dear all for Virginia. Now Virginia does exactly to Louisiana what you claimed the North tried to do to Virginia."

Duty. "I told you my personal views don't matter. I represent my government, not myself."

"If you would but speak for yourself, your nation would follow. Virginia would follow her marble man anywhere. Resign your post, condemn your government's actions."

Lee shook his head. He knew his duty.

Croft snorted. "There sits Duty like a stone wall."

"You do not know the South."

"No. But I know men."

"You'll never convince them. You'll never convince *me*."

"I've no need to. Your sense of duty will see to it for me."

Lee turned away. "I'll not justify myself to you."

"'Which way I flie is Hell; my self am Hell. And no place for pardon left.' No," Croft said with a slow shake of his head, "there's only one person to whom you need to justify your actions. Only one who can restore your sight."

The carriage pulled to a stop on Downing Street at the very spot where it had all begun. Smedley met them at the forgotten door to the Foreign Office. He led Croft and Lee back through the maze of halls to the cramped office, past the bench, through the gate in the wooden railing, and on through the side door.

In the flickering light from a tiny fireplace sat a huddled form under a rough cloak. The man looked up at their approach. His gaunt, craggy face stared up at them, the face of Abraham Lincoln.

Lincoln spoke no greeting.

How could he? The mob had cut out his tongue.

Lee shrank back, but there was no place to run from Lincoln's eyes. *Which way I flie is Hell.* Lee's heart pounded as if it would burst; a sharp, sudden pain pierced his right arm.

Croft turned to Lee, his face twisted with hate and disgust. "You want scripture? I'll give you scripture: 'If thine enemies fall upon thee; if they tear thee from the society of thy father and mother and brethren and sisters; if the very jaws of hell gape open the mouth wide after thee, he hath descended below them all. Art thou greater than he?'"

Lincoln shook his head and held up his hand to Croft. *Leave us,* he seemed to say.

Milton's serpent must have had that same curled snarl to his lips after offering the fruit in the Garden. Croft stepped back into the shadows, supremely confident he had brought down the Eden dream of Southern Arcadia, a paradise lost.

Lincoln looked back to Lee with eyes ancient in holy pain. Those very words of Lincoln's chiseled upon Lee's heart now flew up unbidden from Lincoln's still, unmoving lips. *The mystic chords of memory will yet swell.*

"I tried to save you," pleaded Lee.

We are not enemies, but friends.

"I did everything I could."

We must not be enemies.

Lee's knees buckled. He grabbed a chair for support. "What would you have of me?" he cried.

You have no oath, Lincoln's eyes answered. *You have no oath registered in heaven to destroy the government, while I shall have the most solemn one to preserve, protect, and defend it.*

I had the same oath, Lee screamed to himself,
*and I betrayed it. And for what? The Cause? Tell
this man about the telegrams. Tell this man about
Louisiana and how tonight you must now betray your
precious Cause itself.*

Lee turned from Lincoln only to see Croft's smug
face, his lidded eyes hurling silent accusations. Was
Lee's duty truly nothing more than vain pride?

Which way I flie is Hell, Milton's serpent smirked,
*and no place for pardon left but by submission and
that word Disdain forbids me.*

Lincoln rose from his chair. His thin, frail body
unfolded as he stood, towering over Lee. With the
halting shuffle of the aged and infirm, Lincoln stepped
slowly across the room to Lee. He placed those massive hands on Lee's shoulders.

*We are not enemies but friends. Let us strive on
to finish the work we are in; to bind up the nation's
wounds—to all which may achieve and cherish a just,
and a lasting peace, among ourselves.*

"I cannot." *That word Disdain forbids me, and my
dread of shame.* "You're asking me to turn against my
own people, against Virginia." *He hath descended below
them all. Art thou greater than he?* "I cannot."

Lincoln turned from Lee. He stepped toward the
window, as if to say as he had before the war—*In
your hands, my fellow countrymen and not in mine,
is the issue.*

Lee took one halting step toward him. "You trusted
in my sense of duty once and I failed you! I'll only
fail you again." Pain raced upward along his arm.
He shrunk back. "Do not ask this of me!" *Art thou
greater?*

Duty. Lee tried to cling to his only lifeline, but this time it held him not afloat, but pulled him down, ever farther down. *Duty—duty to what? To whom? The works of him that sent me?* What kind of works were betrayal and dishonor and slavery? What kind of master demanded such works?

What kind of servant obeyed?

What kind of man was born so blind he could not see it?

"Help me," Lee whispered.

Lincoln slowly turned, his eyes brimming. *With firmness in the right. As God gives us to see the right.* He reached his long arms wide and embraced his former enemy.

Lee shook in pain. His chest burned, his heart raced fearfully. He could hardly breathe. And yet, for the first time in years he felt at peace. He suddenly realized it was in this room Lincoln had written the words that could heal his nation. It was in this room Lee could write the words that could heal *his* nation.

Our nation.

Croft stepped up with pen and paper. Lee at last saw him for what he truly was: not a serpent holding forth the fruit of knowledge, but a friend cradling a precious gift, offering Lee not a bargain for his soul, but a sacrifice to save Virginia—and himself.

Lee looked at the squalid, shabby room of exile, looked into Lincoln's pain-filled eyes of true Lost Causes, looked at the price he, too, would have to pay.

"I will pay that sum," Lee said.

He reached for the pen.

Murdering Uncle Ho

★

Chris Bunch

I was quietly running F Company, 5th Special Forces (Airborne), Lai Khe, in what had been South Vietnam, when Bull Simon called on the scrambler phone to ask if I wanted to get killed.

Naturally, I accepted immediately.

At the time—April 1969—I was simultaneously the youngest lieutenant colonel in the Army, and at the absolute bottom of said Army's shit list.

Both events came from the same cause:

I had been John F. Kennedy's favorite Green Beret.

Naturally, when Kennedy's hand-picked successor, Hubert Humphrey, got his head handed to him by Nelson Rockefeller in the '68 elections, and Kennedy was sent off in disgrace to Hyannisport, I was doomed. If I'd had a brain, I would've quietly arranged a nice soft assignment, teaching ROTC at a women's college maybe, until my time ran out, then found an honest job mugging drunks somewhere.

Instead, I volunteered to go back to Vietnam, back into the nightmare that wouldn't end until we pulled out, hollowly proclaiming "victory," in 1987.

All of this deserves a bit of explanation.

In 1963, I was a comfortable junior at Georgetown, majoring in international relations.

I probably shouldn't have gone to Georgetown at all, because it developed a taste for politics in me, without adding the ability to compromise and equivocate any good politician or statesman must have.

Like most Americans, I'd heard Kennedy's immortal "Ask not what your country can do for you, but what you can do for your country" speech, and determined my place of service would be in the State Department.

My father, a career officer who'd gone to work for "State," actually the CIA, after being badly wounded during the Korean War, snorted in dismay. He considered State, in his words, "a bunch of worthless pussies who couldn't find their dick with both hands and a White Paper."

But the Army wasn't for me. I somehow thought I was above marching from here to there with mud up my ass.

Then Kennedy went to Dallas, in November 1963. Three men hired by extreme rightist H. L. Hunt and a cabal of his equally crazed Texan cronies tried to assassinate him, almost succeeded, and my world changed.

Suddenly, pushing red-ribboned papers around the world didn't do anything for me. In spite of Hunt's giving the right wing a bad name, the Republicans were stupid enough to nominate ultraconservative Senator Barry Goldwater, and Kennedy was returned to office in the biggest margin in US history.

They say that he believed he then had a mandate from Heaven, as the Chinese say, and could do whatever he chose.

In 1964, I graduated from Georgetown, and immediately joined the Army.

That was just in time for Kennedy to overreact to the intelligence disaster in the Gulf of Tonkin, and subsequent pinpricks against US "advisors" in South Vietnam, just as he'd overreacted to Berlin, the Cuban missile crisis, and the Dominican nonsense.

But this time, he didn't get away with it.

A Brigade Landing Team of Marines went ashore in Da Nang, Special Forces were built up throughout the country, and a brigade of the 82nd Airborne Division was sent to Bien Hoa as a fire brigade.

I barely noticed.

I was one of a herd of young warriors, sure there was about to be a war, a real war, and we wouldn't get to Vietnam before the gooks were hammered into oblivion.

It's interesting to note that less than ten members of my Officer's Candidate School class are still alive.

The war *did* wait on us.

I finished OCS, got my butter bars as a second lieutenant, and went to Jump School and Ranger School.

Kennedy announced the reformation of Rangers as full units, companies, then a full battalion, based at Fort Benning. I got assigned there as soon as I got my tab.

Now there was a full-scale troop buildup, throughout the Army.

"Everyone" knew what was coming.

Everyone except the rulers of North and South Vietnam.

The Marine base at Da Nang was hit hard, with over five hundred casualties, and that was it for Kennedy.

Plans for the invasion of North Vietnam went on the front burner.

There were leaks, of course, and diplomats from various nations came and went at the White House.

But Kennedy and his saber-rattling team would not listen to any calls for reason, for caution, for moderation, not until "the Communists are taught their proper lesson," as his brother Robert said.

We trained, and trained, and trained, and then, in endless shuttles of civilian 707s, we went to Vietnam, endless rows of tents, and more waiting for the Word.

I was a first lieutenant, executive officer of Bravo Company, First Ranger Battalion (Airborne) when the C130s finally loaded sticks of jumpers at Ton Son Nhut Airfield, outside Saigon, and droned north for the invasion of North Vietnam in May of 1965.

We kept well out to sea, as if keeping a secret, past the demilitarized zone, and then the huge formation of planes, escorted by flight after flight of fighters, were off the coast of North Vietnam.

None of my Rangers even pretended sleep, not even those who'd seen combat in other wars.

This was it, this was the big one, this is where we

would stop pissy-assing around and break it off in Ho Chi Minh's butt.

Just below Haiphong Harbor, the formation split. Elements of the 101st were to jump into Haiphong and secure the harbor for the Marine landing teams headed toward shore.

The rest of us, Rangers and 82nd Airborne, went toward Hanoi, North Vietnam's capital.

My company, and two others, had been given a rather grim mission. We were to jump into almost the middle of Hanoi, just south of Ho Tay Lake. Our target was only known as a "military district," and no one really knew how many regulars of the Democratic Republic's army we'd face.

After we'd subdued these regulars, we were to head west, along the lakeside boulevard, and support other Rangers attacking North Vietnam's capitol building. We hoped to catch Ho Chi Minh and other governmental leaders at home, which, our briefers said, would end the war in a single masterstroke.

It didn't work out like that.

"*Stand up,*" the jumpmaster shouted, and doors on either side of the C130's ramp came open.

"*Hook up,*" and our static lines were clipped to the lines, clips facing inward.

We shuffled forward, stumbling under almost a hundred pounds of weapons and gear.

"*Make equipment check.*"

"*Sound off for equipment check.*"

The light next to the door was bright red.

Outside, it was a gray dawn, and below us was Hanoi, gray, sprinkled with lakes. I hoped to hell I wouldn't land in one.

"Stand in the door."

We were as ready as ready could be. Men were pressing hard against my back. We were to go out as tight and fast as we could, to keep the stick from being scattered all over the city below.

"Ready . . ."

The jumpmaster listened to his headphones, then straightened.

"GO!!"

He slapped me on the shoulder, and I was out into the slipstream, hands on my reserve, head bowed. The blast took and spun me, and I was falling. The static line came taught, yanked my backpack open, and the chute deployed. It cracked me like a whip, and I jolted hard.

I looked up, saw all those lovely unblown panels of my parachute perfectly deployed.

To one side of me was the huge Red River, in front and to my left, West Lake.

They'd dropped us right on target.

Above droned other planes, and the sky was full of parachutes. Parachutes and the greasy smoke of antiaircraft fire. I saw a 130 get hit, go into a bank, streaming paratroopers, and crash into the middle of a housing area. A missile flashed up, was gone, and a pair of jets dove down toward its launch site.

We'd been dropped low, only eight hundred feet, to give the enemy gunners as little time to shoot as possible.

Below me, the ground loomed up, brick walks, and, thank God, a bit of grass.

I slapped the release on my GP bag, full of ammo for one of my machine gunners, and it dropped to the end of the line.

I came in hard, rolled as I'd been taught, and came to my feet, dumping my chute, harness and reserve.

I had my newly issued M16 cradled in my arms, and carried a Light Antitank Weapon, the so-called "cardboard bazooka."

Plus a Randall knife strapped to my leg and a somewhat unauthorized Bill Jordan Special, a cut-down, modified Ruger .44 Magnum pistol.

And I still felt naked, hearing the *snap-crack* of rifle fire, and the chatter of machine guns.

There were other troops landing, some slamming in hard on the bricks, and someone shouted pain.

A machine gun chattered, and green tracer spat across the open area, too close to me.

They'd told us to save the LAWs for "hard targets," which I'd decided would be anyone shooting at me.

I cracked it open, aimed at the barracks the MG fire was coming from, and squeezed down on the firing mechanism.

Nothing happened.

I cursed the damnably unreliable LAW, just as someone rolled up to the window and flipped a grenade in.

There was a blast, and the window blew out, and the machine gun stopped firing.

I was shouting orders, and my noncoms were screaming, and we were on some kind of line, charging the barracks, smashing into them, killing anything that moved.

I don't remember anyone trying to surrender.

If they did, they weren't likely to be lucky.

Not that day.

Troopships with armor and legs—non-airborne troops—were supposed to be coming up the thirty-five miles from Haiphong to reinforce and quickly relieve us. Both Rangers and paratroops are intended as shock troops—go in, hit hard, take casualties, and then get out.

It didn't work that way.

We fought from that military area for two days as troops in mass, then scattered determined elements kept coming in at us.

It turned out we'd been facing Ho Chi Minh's personal security element, about a battalion—five hundred men—strong. All that saved our young asses is that these Regulars were a bit out of practice, and that we'd surprised them.

The Rangers at the Palace fared even worse, getting almost obliterated. Ho Chi Minh and the other members of the hierarchy were long gone when the palace finally fell, nothing more than a mass of rubble.

The problem was, nobody had figured the Viets would fight so hard. It took two days to take Haiphong and clear the Red River. The resistance was the same sort Americans would have made if someone invaded the Chesapeake River and made for Washington.

By the time elements of the First Infantry Division arrived, our company of 250 men was down to 75 effectives, and I was company commander.

We weren't relieved, but ordered to swing toward the river, and help the 82nd take the Old Town, which was very strongly defended.

The People's Army was waiting for us.

The fighting was now the ugliest of all: urban warfare, with civilians trapped in the middle.

The bloodlust was gone from us all, and we tried to make sure we were only killing soldiers.

But that wasn't always possible. The Viets fought hard, holding positions to the last man, almost never surrendering. Hanoi was starting to look like pictures I'd seen of Berlin at the end of WWII.

It may have been a week, it may have been two, but finally we were slowly pushing the Viets back into the Red River.

Then the remnants of a regular battalion struck, trying to head west, for Hanoi's outskirts. I'd gotten some replacements, but had taken more casualties. I had about eighty soldiers when they hit us.

They pushed a wedge between two of my platoons. I called for air support, but, in the smoke and drizzle, none of the fast movers could get in.

A colonel was on my PRC25, saying we had to hold.

But we couldn't, and I felt we were about to break. Even Rangers can't hold forever.

But I remember we now had artillery support, air-lifted 105s.

The Viets were on top of us, and my only option was to call in fire on our own positions.

We had a few seconds to find cover; the Viets had none as the rounds screeched into the dusty, rubbled street we fought from.

The third volley got me, lifting me and punching me through a shop wall.

I landed on something soft, realized I was hit but still alive, and stumbled out.

Here and there, tattered, dust-covered, bearded, staring, my men came out of the shatter.

They looked god-awful . . . but they still had their weapons, and still were fighting.

It was the Viets' turn to hesitate, then break, going back, in stumbling runs, the way they'd come.

I made sure they were retreating before I allowed

myself to look at my shattered leg, my torn chest and arm, saw a tank with a white star on its turret rumble toward me, decided I'd done enough for one day, and went down.

I don't know who put the Viets' banner across my chest as they carried my stretcher to a waiting medevac chopper. I think I'd like to kick his ass, for that was one of the biggest causes of my future troubles. All I had was the banner, and, all bullets expended, my .44 Magnum.

I went out to a hospital ship, where amazingly nobody stole either my flag or pistol, and then to Camp Zama in Japan, then back to Walter Reed, where they started putting me back together.

The war wasn't going well, and "Sam Richardson's Last Stand" was just what the media, and the American public wanted.

There were already thirty thousand dead, twice that wounded, and Kennedy was forced to call up the reserves.

They wanted me to take the Congressional. I refused. I'd met men who'd won that medal and knew damned well I'd done nothing but what I was supposed to be doing, and that's not what they give that little necklace for.

They were getting me ready for my third operation at Walter Reed, and I was already anesthetic-silly when the President of the United States came calling.

In swept Kennedy, flanked by more generals than I'd seen pictures of in the Pentagon, plus, of course, a scattering of press types.

I guess I did something dumb, like try to sit up at attention. I was in the presence of one of my heroes, and a real legend.

"Relax, Major," Kennedy said, with that famous grin that'd brought him who knows how many votes.

"Uh, sir, It's 'lieutenant.'"

"Not anymore. You were made captain while you were still on the ground in Hanoi, and I just took the liberty of jumping you up a grade."

I may have moaned, thinking how that would play with my fellow officers. Kennedy must've thought I was in pain.

"Maybe this'll make you feel better," he said, holding out a hand without looking back. A general put a box in it, then another. He gave me the Distinguished Service Cross, which is just below the Medal of Honor, and a Purple Heart.

I stammered thanks.

Kennedy moved beside me, let the photogs have their shots.

"Plus," he said, "when you get better, I want you as one of my aides."

I managed a "yessir," then events got to me, and my mind went away.

The papers, of course, loved it:

PREXY NAMES RICHARDSON
TO PERSONAL STAFF
LAST STAND HERO TO
ADVISE KENNEDY

And so forth.

I was recuping well, and my father came to see me.

"Congratulations, I suppose."

"I didn't know what else to do, sir."

"No," he agreed. "Not much you can do when

the gods reach out. But you might be in for some problems."

"I've already gotten some grief," I told him, "from some of my friends."

"That, too," my father said. "But I was thinking more of something I learned a long time ago. If you like the circus, don't sit so close you can smell the elephant shit."

I didn't understand, not for some months. By the time I did, it was too late.

I hated Washington. Going to Georgetown, which supposedly educates you in the realities of power, I should have known better. But I didn't. The only people who went there wanted something. Preferably for nothing.

I can't remember anyone who fulfilled Kennedy's orders to "ask not . . ." All the bastards did was ask . . . and take.

And the Kennedy brothers were no different than anyone else.

I saw, very quickly, that mad gleam of power in JFK's eyes, and realized he would do anything to keep or increase his authority.

I also despised his personal morality. Kennedy, it was said truly, would fuck a snake if someone held its head. He had no qualms about cheating on his wife, at any moment of the day or night if he could find a hall closet to slip his latest bimbo into.

He lied to the people of America, justifying it with "When the time is right, they'll be told. But not yet." Which meant, as far as he was concerned, never.

His brother the attorney general was even worse, keeping his own overweening ambition concealed in the pretense that all he wanted to do was help his brother.

I never forgot what my father told me, that one of Robert Kennedy's first jobs was as one of the unutterably evil Senator McCarthy's lawyers.

I was, indeed, too close to the elephant.

I applied for a transfer back to the real Army several times, but was always refused. Kennedy said he "needed me."

I should have known I was his token war hero, especially after he called me into his office, and told me I was headed for Fort Bragg.

"For what, sir?"

"Since the Green Berets are mine, I think it would be a good idea to have one around me."

"But—"

"On your way, soldier."

And so I went. And found something wonderful.

I'd deliberately chosen paratroops, and then Rangers, not because I wanted the little tabs and devices on my uniform, but because I wanted to be a warrior among warriors.

In Special Forces, I found warriors far more dangerous, more qualified, than I could have dreamed of.

They treated me, naturally, as just another White House dickhead.

I kept my mouth shut, and soldiered hard.

I wanted approval from these men, and I didn't get it.

But I returned to Washington with my beret, and a determination to get myself back to Vietnam, in any capacity so long as it was with SF.

The progress of the war helped.

It was not going well at all.

We held Hanoi, just like we held all of the other major cities in North and South Vietnam. But what of it?

Ho Chi Minh, his Communist party, and his army sank into the marsh of the countryside. Ho went back up the Red River, back into the mountains on the Chinese border, just as he'd done when the French tried to hold his country after WWII.

From there, he fought his war.

We garrisoned the cities, and tried to hold the roads.

And the Communists fought back. Not "fairly," as if there's such a thing in war.

But from the ditch, from the jungle, always at our back.

When we got arrogant, or careless, his Regulars, or the main force Viet Cong in the south, or even the local guerrillas, would appear, strike hard, and vanish.

Enraged, we struck back, bombing villages we thought were "hostile," or even declaring entire districts free-fire zones. If those areas weren't hostile before the helicopter gunships or the B52s or the fighter-bombers came over, they certainly were afterward. To ensure the people we were supposedly helping fight Communism hated our guts, we sent through battalions of legs, who thought any gook was a Commie, and probably deserved to be dead.

The puppet government we supported in Saigon was only interested in looting and control. Their best troops, the Army of the Republic of Vietnam paratroops and Rangers were used as palace guards.

Kennedy seethed, increased the draft, and had, by 1967, over a million Americans in country.

And the war raged on.

University students protested the war, and these protests were slapped down by Attorney General Kennedy. He made the famous statement that "protest in a time of trouble is treason," and the prisons filled up with middle-class Americans, who were given the option of jail or the military.

The pretense Kennedy maintained that he actually gave a damn about civil rights was shattered, and cities exploded into riots. His vice president, Senator Johnson (D.-Texas) snarled, saying Kennedy had promised to build a better society, and instead was wasting his, the party's, and the country's substance in a country no one could find on a map.

Kennedy ignored him, and so Johnson and Kennedy finished their terms not on speaking terms, and Johnson wasn't given the traditional chance at the presidency, but rather that hoggish toady, Hubert Humphrey.

As the 1968 elections neared, the always-sophisticated Communists mounted a scattered offensive in cities across Vietnam. The offensive failed, but Kennedy insisted on further increasing the draft, and sending another million men overseas.

That was enough for the voters. The extreme conservative Republicans were ignored by their party for a change, and the Republicans ran moderate Nelson Rockefeller, who destroyed the Democrats.

Naturally, one of the first things Rockefeller did after taking office was to put the draft into high gear, and send another million men into the war.

But that was in his first one hundred days, when

it's very hard for a president to do anything wrong in the public and media's eyes.

One of Kennedy's last acts, before he left office, was to jump me again in the promotion lists to lieutenant colonel.

That would further destroy my chances of just fitting back into the Army.

But I stayed in, and pulled a few strings.

I figured if I could get back to Vietnam, not only would I maybe be helping my country, but I could save my career by staying well out of sight.

The C Team of 5th Special Forces, named F Company, I ended up in charge of was at Lai Khe, a few hundred heroes who did everything from advising the ARVNs, to pulling intelligence missions up to the border, running A Team camps in the middle of nowhere, to all the other strange missions the Green Hats got.

If I thought being in the elite would keep me from this time of troubles my country and Army were going through, I was quite wrong.

The tour of duty had been increased to two years, over the previous eighteen months, so soldiers weren't constantly rediscovering fire. These draftee and non-special operations soldiers spent their time either huddling in the oversized, overcivilized base camps, or else timorously sweeping the jungle. Every now and again, a column of US soldiers would encounter, generally on their terms, the Viets. There'd be a brisk firefight, or sometimes a knock-down brawl, and then the Viets would vanish back into the bush, into the mountains, leaving us to lick our wounds.

We certainly weren't losing the war . . . but more important, we weren't winning it, either. I wondered what would have happened if Bobby Kennedy hadn't used the draft and punitive federal legislation to kill any semblance of a peace movement, like the US had during the so-called Philippine Insurrection.

For many people, their tour in Vietnam was nothing more than sweaty boredom, never seeing the enemy, and only encountering him . . . or her . . . when a convoy they happened to be riding on was ambushed, or a friend on perimeter guard was sniped, or what they read in *Stars and Stripes,* the service newspaper.

I met Arthur "Bull" Simons in a rather strange way. He was running the supersecret Study and Observations Group, with the rank of a one-star general. Special Forces never got a lot of rank allocated, enlisted or commissioned, even when they were Kennedy's darlings. It wasn't until the escalation that Simons saw his star, the only one he'd ever get. At the time, the head of all Green Berets was a one-star, Bill Yarborough, and, again, it took the buildup before he got a second one.

Simons was a legend. He'd been described once as the "only soldier who actually hates people." Maybe he did, but he also took damned good care of his crews, as they ran illegal crossborder reconnaissance into Cambodia, Laos, and even, I was told, into China itself.

He was about as frightening a man to look at as you could imagine—a bit under six feet, about two hundred pounds, built like a boulder. His face was lined, hard, and he had a nose like a hawk.

He'd been a Ranger in WWII in the Pacific, active in clandestine warfare after that.

Naturally, when he came down to Lai Khe, wanting to personally oversee a rather special mission I still don't know the details of into Cambodia, he hated my guts. I was not only one of the "pussies" who'd swarmed into SF looking for that trick combat patch on the right sleeve, a beret, and some war stories, but a political bastard as well.

I kept my mouth shut and did everything he wanted.

His team, actually three recon teams slammed together, went across the border, and the shit closed in on them.

They were trapped, about twenty klicks into Cambodia, in the area known as the Parrot's Beak. Simons wanted gunships and liftouts to save them.

Somehow the US ambassador to Cambodia heard about their plight, and ordered nothing could be done to embarrass the US. His order was echoed by the general commanding III Corps, my personal boss. Simons's men were to be abandoned to escape and evade on their own. Which meant die in place.

I took a deep breath and ordered my own helicopter resources into the air, went across the airstrip to the local gunship company, who owed me, and got their B-model gunships in the air.

As I gave the orders, for the first time in a long time, maybe since Hanoi, I felt a great weight lift. The hell with orders, the hell with the chain of command, and the hell with my career. I was finally doing something that was right.

I ordered my Mike Force, evil Chinese mercenaries called Nungs you could absolutely trust, unlike the ARVN Special Forces and army, to insert and get the SOG people out. I pulled on my combat harness, threw some magazines for my old Schmeisser machine pistol into a pack, and went with them.

It was hot, it was heavy, it was bloody, and it isn't the story I'm trying to tell.

By the next dawn, we brought out all of Bull Simons's thugs. Four were dead, but we extracted the bodies, and *all* of our own casualties, including the Nungs.

Simons brought his command and control Huey down on the strip at Lai Khe as I landed and stumbled out, wanting only a beer, to make sure my wounded were taken care of, eighteen hours sleep, and finding out what little of my career was left.

He got out of his bird, and I saluted him.

He looked me up and down, not even a smile on his face.

"I guess I was wrong," was all he said, and he went back to his ship and headed back for Nha Trang, one of SOG's headquarters.

Somehow, maybe because the SOG mission was most secret, and approved at "the highest levels," I stayed a light colonel, in charge of my unit, and nobody said anything. If there was a distinct chill when I went to III Corps headquarters in Saigon, what of it? Special Forces were never the favorites of the Regular legs.

Time passed, and I was relatively content. I wasn't doing anything to win the war in particular, but I wasn't losing it, either, unlike some others.

Things continued to get worse, culminating with a sapper raid against the Republic's palace in Saigon that managed to not only kill a host of ARVNs and civilians, but the serving president and prime minister of South Vietnam as well.

President Rockefeller had the unpleasurable experience of approving General Duong Van "Big" Minh as emergency head of state. Big Minh had served once before, proven his incompetence, and been set aside. But he was, I guess, to the powers in Washington, the only game in town.

Three weeks after the echoes of the Saigon catastrophe were dying, I got the call from up north, from Hanoi, from Bull Simons.

"You looking for action?"

"Always, sir," I said.

"Then grab your shit and get up here. I've got a hot one that'll prob'ly get us both massacred, and I could use a light colonel to run my reaction force."

"Doing what, sir?" I asked.

"Not even on a scrambler, Richardson."

"What about my company?"

"Turn it over to your exec. It's approved, upstairs. Way, way upstairs. You'll be on TDY for at least two months. Or maybe forever."

He told me where to report. I packed a duffle bag full of my favorite weapons, two bottles of Johnny Walker, and a couple changes of socks, and grabbed the first flight down to Saigon, then from Ton Son Nhut north to Hanoi.

I reported to a certain room in the airport terminal, and an unmarked jeep took me, and three other Special Forces types Simon had volunteered, into the city.

Hanoi was not only a city in ruins, with the only new construction either the slap-up pressed-beer-can shacks the Vietnamese entrepreneurs specialized in, or military prefabs.

The people looked at us coldly, then away. Even the beggar kids stuck out their hands without a grin, without any chatter, as if we owed them.

Everyone knew us for the enemy.

I felt with a shiver we didn't belong here and never would.

The jeep took us to the Metropole Hotel. That had once been the hotel for the elite, back when the French were here. Now it was a safe house for CIA and other disreputable sorts like Special Forces.

Simons was waiting to brief us.

The mission was quite simple: Intelligence had somehow—I wasn't told how—found out where Ho Chi Minh, his main general, Vo Nguyen Giap, and the main command structure of the Communists were.

Bull Simons proposed to take a fifty-man team in after them.

"Assassination?"

"Don't ever use that word," he said, and there wasn't a smile on his face or voice. "We're to take Uncle Ho into custody. If he resists . . ." Simons shrugged his massive shoulders.

"Can I ask who approved this? Just out of curiosity, sir?"

"No," Simons said. "You can't. But I'll tell you there isn't any higher authority for us. And that doesn't mean Westy, either."

There were only two men above General William C. Westmoreland, Commanding General of all US Forces in Vietnam, Admiral Harry Felt, in Hawaii . . .

And President Nelson Rockefeller.

I knew enough, maybe more than I should.

Simons moved us from the safe house to a villa outside Hanoi, while the fifty men trickled in.

I wondered if the Bull had gone quite mad picking me, for the men that came in were true legends:

men like Dick Meadows, who'd snatched more prisoners with his recon teams than most American line battalions; Jerry "Mad Dog" Shriver, a man with the coldest eyes in the world, who seldom changed his clothes, and slept with a suppressed greasegun on his chest; David "Babysan" Davidson, who looked just like his nickname, who'd spent one out of five days of his life in Vietnam; Bob Howard, the most decorated soldier in *all* of America's history; supersniper John Plaster, others.

I complained to Simons that maybe I was out of my league, and he gave me a wintry smile.

"Look at it this way, Richardson. I need me somebody who won't go pulling an Audie Murphy, and will cover my ass, or my flanks, and not go yodeling forward like a Custer."

"Thanks, sir. I think."

I thought that if this mission were a disaster, it would be years before Special Forces would be able to rebuild its strength.

But failure wasn't on the agenda.

And then there were fifty of us. All of us were Americans, except for ten hand-picked Montagnards, Rhades. All of them had served in our camps for years, and were as trusted as any roundeye.

NOFORN, as it was said. No foreigners, who might just have loose lips or, as we'd found on occasion, those whose real loyalties were with Ho Chi Minh.

We got some details on where we would be going: a big cave complex, very, very near the Chinese border.

"So there'll be no room for fuckups," Simons said cheerfully. "If you happen to go and get killed, try to look like a dead gook."

He still didn't tell us the name of the caves, or their exact location.

We trained hard, and fast, for everyone knew of operations that had great intelligence and looked good, but by the time people quit farting around and went to the field, the bad guys were long gone.

We couldn't find, or build, a duplicate of our target, so we concentrated on just learning how the others operated, how they thought, since none of us were familiar with the others' style.

That meant running patrols, big patrols, sweeping south of Hanoi. There were more than enough Viets in the jungles and paddies to make the training most realistic. We took half a dozen casualties in firefights, inflicted far more. Replacements came in, and we kept training.

We would fight in ten-man teams, another new thing, and so we practiced fire and maneuver, again and again and again.

Others built satchel and link charges, and everyone spent a lot of time on our improvised ranges, going through immediate-action drills to counter an ambush, firing everything from pistols to the two little 60mm mortars we'd take in as our artillery.

We would, if the shit hit the fan, be able to call in Air Force and Navy fast movers, fighter-bombers, but we were, Simons said, out of range of "real" artillery. "Except for the bad guys, of course," he added.

There was a problem with insertion—if we flew out of Hanoi, every Viet who could look up would report our half dozen helicopters.

Simons decided we'd go in by sea. He got big HH53 Sikorskys and their pilots, from the Air Force. "Twice our minimum requirement," he told me. "Fucking choppers break a lot."

When we got the go, we'd fly out to waiting carriers off Haiphong, the carriers would steam to a certain point, and we'd take off again. The HH53s, normally used for rescue purposes, were fitted for midair refueling. We'd refuel, go in on foot from a landing zone. The choppers would return to the carriers.

When . . . if . . . we made contact, they'd immediately take off from the ships and fly in to a certain point, refuel, and then come get us.

"Which means we could be on the ground getting killed for a while," Meadows said.

"You have a problem with that, Captain?" Simons demanded.

"Not at all, boss," Meadows said. "Just trying to figure out how many magazines to take."

And then the bad things started happening.

I was very glad I was out in the bush, running up and down and back and forth. When I creaked back in, there was a message to report to Colonel Simons. Immediately. Which meant before a shower, a beer, or even a balls-scratch.

"You are very damned lucky, Colonel," he growled.

"Why so, sir?"

"Because you've been out there in the tules for a while, so you can't be the rat-fink."

"I beg your pardon, sir?"

"Somebody's leaked," Simons said, and explained.

Somebody had talked at the wrong time and in the wrong place.

William C. Westmoreland had shown up in Hanoi, expressing interest in how "his" Special Forces were doing. Worse, also interested and in Vietnam on a "fact-finding mission," were two hard right-wing Republican politicos: Richard Nixon, who'd somehow avoided disgrace in the aftermath of the Kennedy attempted assassination; and John Connolly, once a Democrat, who'd milked the fact that he'd been in the limo with Kennedy in Dallas as far as he could, then jumped parties, looking for a national office.

Neither of them, I knew, was to be trusted in the slightest.

I supposed the ticket, in three years, would be Richard Nixon for president, Connolly for veep. They were smoking funny cigarettes—America doesn't elect losers, like Nixon was after Kennedy won in 1960, and everyone distrusts a fence-jumper, figuring a man who'll sell his own out once will do it again, if it benefits him.

But if President Rockefeller had ordered Ho Chi Minh's assassination, which was very definitely against presidential policy (in spite of Kennedy's obsession with Fidel Castro), that would make good fodder for the Republican Right.

Especially if it failed.

"Not me, boss," I said, getting only a little pissed. That sort of directness was just Simons's way.

"No shiteedah, Richardson," the Bull snarled. "I just wanted you to know what's going on . . . and not tell anyone, and I mean anyone. We got enough to worry about.

"We'll be going in in seventy-two hours. The operations order'll be available tomorrow morning.

"We're under a complete security hold. No MARS calls, no in-country phone calls, no visits, no visitors, and any last letters will be censored and not in the mail until we're in the boonies."

I left, wondering what kind of war it was where the commander of all in-country troops wasn't told about an operation. All wars are political, of course. But this one was too damned much like that for my liking.

But it was the only one I had.

We cleaned already spotless weaponry, sharpened already razor-edged knives, and wrote those last letters.

The basic weapon we carried was the CAR15, the stubby-barreled version of the M16. There'd been argument, finally settled by the Bull, on whether we should carry CARs or AK47s. The issues were reliability, lightness, ease of resupply, and so on and so forth. Simons had said we'd go for the CARs, because when somebody popped a cap, everyone would know whether it was a black or white hat.

I didn't get involved in the argument. I knew better than to try to lug my Schmeisser. It was a good weapon, but it did fire 9mm pistol rounds, which are pissing in the wind in a real firefight.

Other basic weapons were the M79 grenade launcher and cut-down Chinese RPD machineguns (called by them the Type 56). We went with the RPD because it could be lightened far more than the standard M60, and was more reliable than the SEAL's favorite Stoner.

The three snipers on the team carried accurized, semiauto scoped M14s, less accurate than the normal M70 Winchester bolt-action rifles, but capable of delivering a higher rate of fire, which Simons considered important, since he hoped to gun down Viet bigwigs in clumps.

Other than that, we carried a grabbag of 12-gauge

pump shotguns, personal handguns, grenades, and explosives. Plus everyone carried at least one LAW.

I was carrying enough crap already, but added an old-fashioned suppressed High Standard .22 automatic to my pack. Other people, especially Jerry Shriver, also carried silenced pieces.

Our commo was one AN/PRC-77 per team, but the radios would only be used when we were closing in, or if we ran into trouble or on extraction. The US didn't believe those little brown bastards in the jungle could intercept, let alone read, transmissions, and ignored ambushes that proved things different.

But we knew better, having learned that the hard way. So we'd keep radio silence as long as we could.

For an emergency, we also carried search and recovery radios, small transistorized units used to bring in pickup.

Our weaponry may have varied, but the rest of our equipment was standard. For ammo pouches, we used canteen carriers, which would lug more magazines than the issue items. In our rucks, we carried changes of socks, and standard patrol rations, which was a pack of Minute Rice, coupled with yummy add-ons like pilchards, Hong Kong crabs, strange-looking canned meat, and other items you had to be a while in the jungle to appreciate.

Instead of wearing any sort of camouflage fatigues, we wore standard fatigues we'd blotch-sprayed with flat black paint, a standard SOG modification. On our feet were normal jungle boots, and we wore floppy hats.

The 'Yards wore black pajamas and Cong hats, enough to fool any enemy we encountered for hopefully one magazine blast.

We assembled in midafternoon of the third day, ready to go.

Simons's briefing was fairly short.

He showed us the target, and there were mutters of dismay. It was, indeed, just on the Vietnam-China border, and was called Hang Pac Bo. In peacetime, if there was ever going to be anything such in this part of the world, it might have been a tourist attraction.

Flanking the map were huge aerial photo blowups.

"Don't fuck up and wiggle north," Simons said. "We don't need to be meeting any Chinese." He smiled as much as he ever did, nodded at Meadows. "Dick's already made enough enemies on that side of the border."

The contour lines on the big map were close together. We were going to be humping some steep mountains, as predicted.

Simons issued every man a map, and we studied them as he went on.

"We'll insert here," Simons said, tapping the big map. "Just on the far side of this little village called Tra Linh. It looks like there's some kind of secondary east-west road here, that leads close to the caves. We'll keep south of that road . . . if it even exists . . . and move to the far side of this road, here, that goes into this other little village, Ha Quang.

"Call it two days' march.

"Assuming, which is a big assumption, we aren't blown by then, we'll then slide our way to the caves and look for trouble.

"We chanced an overflight of the caves with a drone a week ago, and it looks like there's at least two companies of NVA Regulars on guard. We'll try to move through them, or, failing that, beat the shit out of them hard, then go after Uncle Ho."

Mad Dog Shriver snorted.

"They'll hear us coming, boss. There's no way we'll be able to sneak into Ho Chi Minh's bedroom without somebody blowin' reveille. Best we just think about kicking their ass out of the way from the get-go."

"You're probably right," Simons said.

"But you gotta have dreams, Jerry," somebody said, and everyone laughed.

"If we go in the shitter," Simons said, "I mean really in the shitter, we'll try to break contact and reassemble somewhere down here, around Na Giang, although that might not be possible, and we'll pick an alternate Romeo Pappa en route.

"If we *absolutely* go in the shitter, and have to run like hell, we'll break up and exfiltrate, and then there'll be a pickup over here, in Cao Bang. If things go that bad, there'll be a couple of companies of Marines go in and take the airstrip there, and wait for survivors.

"Or maybe not. We'll play things by ear, depending on how they go.

"Again, don't exfiltrate into China unless you have to. The Agency isn't worth shit getting people out of there, like we all know. I think there's still a few OSS guys stuck in Yunnan somewhere."

Again, there was laughter.

"That's it," Simons said. "Everything else is SOP, like we rehearsed it. We'll know more, have more on the ground.

"You've got the rest of the day to look at these photos. I've outlined what I think the route maybe should be. Anybody with better ideas . . . see me in my office.

"Oh yeah. Some romantic damned fool gave the operation the code name of Eastern Sunrise."

A few people groaned.

We spent the rest of the day memorizing the photos. It looked steep, unoccupied, and grim.

But that was the sort of thing we were paid to do.

Nobody had any better ideas than the Bull, so the next day, we assembled our gear, made final checks as three Jolly Green Giants came in, and boarded.

The flight down the Red River to the sea was quiet. None of us were brooding, but rather intent on what we'd do on the ground, how we'd move, and such.

We landed on the carriers off Haiphong, and Air Force service people swarmed the Jolly Green Giants, giving them final servicing. There were four more already aboard ship, our backups and cover.

The ships steamed north for a few hours.

The ship's PA system went off: "All Sunrise raiders . . . all Sunrise raiders . . . man your birds for takeoff. Man your birds for takeoff. And . . . good luck and God go with you."

I didn't think God spent much time on the battlefield, but there were those who went over to one of the waiting chaplains for prayer or confession.

And then we were in the air, and headed back toward land and Uncle Ho.

Some of us pretended unconcern, and faked dozing.

The cover for the Jollies was they were making a border flight, keeping well enough away from the line to prevent diplomatic complaints. If all went well, they'd follow the border to its intersection with the Red River, well to the west of our planned LZ, and back down the river to Hanoi.

The first bird aborted after only twenty minutes of flight, turning back toward the carriers.

All this I found out after the mission was over.

Just after we lost the Giant, we fueled from a pair of specially modified C130s.

Then the Giant's loadmaster went down the line, signaling five minutes to go.

The three HH53s carrying our raiders dipped toward the ground, and the loadmaster slid the door open.

Outside reared heavily jungled mountains, with a few narrow valleys with tiny rivers running through them. Once, twice, I saw cleared jungle near a mountain top, and a scatter of huts and fields.

Then we were going in, and over the wind rush and the roar of the engines I could hear weapons being loaded.

The LZ was an abandoned rice paddy, just ahead.

The pilots flared their ships, without bringing them down to leave marks that could be seen later.

We were on our feet, packed as closely together as any jump formation, shuffling forward, and then out the door.

I bent my knees, squelched into mud, and then was moving, staggering under almost eighty pounds of pack and weapons, away from the '53, and going down on one knee into a perimeter.

The three helicopters lifted away, to rejoin the others. With any luck the dropoff wouldn't have been seen by any Viet watchers, nor the slight change in engine noise noticed.

The birds were gone, and my ears stopped ringing, and again I was caught up in the silence of the jungle.

We waited for another few minutes, and then we could hear bird noises, monkey chatter.

Nobody started shitting, shouting, or shooting, so we'd evidently inserted without being seen.

Without needing any words, we formed up in two columns, and started north, following a creek that tumbled, chuckling, through a wide ravine.

It was deadly hot, the height of the dry season. Everyone managed to "slip" into the creek as we climbed, and some even to fill their canteens.

At the front were our Montagnards. With them were Shriver and Davidson, unquestionably the best point men we had.

The columns went up the ravine to a high pass. We could see, to our right, Tra Linh, so our pilots had put us down where they should've.

We went down the mountain's far side, and on through jungle until the word . . . hand signals, not even whispers . . . came back to where I was at the head of my reaction force that we'd found the road.

We moved away from it half a klick back into jungle, found a deer trail, and headed west.

It's almost impossible to describe jungle movement to someone who hasn't seen and done it.

The pace is incredibly careful—as slow as two hundred meters a day, slower if you're anticipating contact. That's a step a minute.

If you're on point, you're watching ahead of you, your eyes flickering to the side, then in front and down, looking for boobytraps.

You make sure there's no wait-a-bit vines with their thorns to hold you back, no red ants lurking in those bright green trees to cascade down the back of your neck or, worse, into your moustache if you're vain enough to wear one.

Your foot comes up, moves forward, comes down, toes and ball of the foot first. Weight is put on very slowly, and if, God forbid, there should be any movement, you're ready to leap back and go flat before that mine can detonate.

Slowly you put your full weight down, eyes moving back and forth.

If you see, hear, sense nothing, you lift your other foot, and bring it forward, taking another step, making sure you didn't drag any brush with you that could leave marks.

Behind you was your slack man, watching for something you might miss. Sometimes he carried a grenade launcher, loaded with antipersonnel darts, or a machine gun. Somewhere back of him would be a man with a compass, since the maps were antique and wrong at best.

You couldn't walk point very long, so you'd rotate back, to slack, and the march would continue.

Of course, you never, ever used a road, a human trail, or used machetes to cut your way along. All of those were deathtraps for the inexperienced or lazy.

We moved fairly quickly, about a kilometer an hour, using animal trails when we could.

At the end of the column, behind my reaction force, were the tailgunners—men most skilled in fieldcraft, with Bob Howard in charge, making sure we left almost no evidence of our passage.

Grunts learned to move quietly enough, in small enough units, to occasionally surprise the enemy.

Special Forces prided themselves on being able to move so quietly they surprised monkeys.

Our column moved under a bird dozing on a limb, that didn't wake up with a squawk until half a dozen troopers had gone by.

One problem we had was the number of men on the operation. Fifty, as infantrymen had discovered, was enough to get in big trouble if a decent-sized enemy force, a company or stronger, discovered you. Conversely, it's hard for fifty to move through the jungle without being discovered.

But that was the only option Bull Simons thought was possible.

As we moved, we passed a low knoll. It was pointed out, and that would be our RV . . . where, if we were hit at our RON—remain overnight—position, we'd try to reform.

We moved on.

In deep jungle and high mountains, day vanishes in an instant. The sun was just starting to vanish when word came down the column, pointing left, to where a hill rose. We went on about another few hundred meters, then arced back.

We took positions, by teams, on that hill. We'd bypassed it initially to make sure we weren't being followed.

We weren't, and so we found fighting positions, in teams around the hill.

My team laid out its immediate reaction drill, in case we were hit during the night, and put out claymore mines. These were small wedge-shaped chunks of plastic that could be either command-detonated, as were ours, or set with trip wires to blast some six hundred steel pellets straight out when tripped. It was stamped FRONT TOWARD ENEMY, just in case it had been issued to an utter dummy.

A troop found me, just as I was contemplating my rice, about to make dinner, and told me the Bull wanted to see me.

I followed him to just below the hillcrest, where Simons had set up his command post.

Simons told me, and the other team leaders, what he wanted, in his grating whisper, which I swear carried as far as the average drill sergeant's bellow.

The next day, after midday meal, my reaction force was to take point. Simons thought we'd reach the approximately north-south road that led to the caves about that time, cross it somewhere below the hamlet of Ha Quang, and then, when we reached a tiny river about a klick beyond, turn north to the caves.

When we closed on the caves, Simons's attack element would flank us to the east, and then strike the caves as we found targets.

If they were able to "seize" Ho Chi Minh, or any other of the Communist hierarchy, they'd fall back through us, I'd engage whatever Viet forces were in pursuit, then break contact and we'd take that disused road until things felt dangerous, then move into the jungle back toward our DZ.

It sounded nice, simple, and workable.

But it didn't work out that way.

It almost never does in combat.

Simons had just finished when one of his radiomen slithered over.

"Sunrise Control, sir."

Simons took the handpiece, listened.

"Sunrise Six, this is Sunrise Control," the tinny voice said. "No skinny for you. Report, over."

Simons used squelch code, clicking his handset button twice. That meant "Received, over." Three would have meant "In contact, shut up, they're close."

"Sunrise Control, out."

Neat and clean, the way things are supposed to be.

It was getting dark when I found my way back to my position.

I unhooked my harness, put on mosquito lotion, wistfully thought of being able to take off my boots, and set my M16 in front of me.

Then I mixed my Minute Rice with water in the pouch, opened a can of something by feel, dumped it in the rice. I dosed everything with Tabasco, unquestionably one of the few secret weapons the US had in that war.

It turned out to be the famous mystery meat.

Men who'd gone through the Royal Tracking School in Malaysia swore it was orangutan. But there weren't any of the big apes in Vietnam.

Others said it was local monkey.

Cynics thought it was the infamous "monkey meat" the Foreign Legion ate in the '50s that some cost-conscious quartermaster had gotten his hands on.

I knew it wasn't water buffalo, since I ate that fairly regularly.

Gourmets had no place in the Green Berets.

I ate without thinking about what I was doing, leaned back against my pack, and went to sleep.

My team was within hand's reach of me.

Simons, feeling confident, had ordered only a one-third alert, which gave everyone a good night's sleep, off and on.

I stood last watch, together with Staff Sergeant Jenkins. Before dawn, we tapped everyone awake, took quiet shits if we had to, packed anything we'd taken out of our rucks, ate more rice and whatever, brushed our teeth, and were ready to rock and roll.

By daylight, we were moving off the hill.

Simons's estimate was right. Around midday, we reached the north-south road. It was a little too well tended to make anyone happy. Point elements went across, then everyone went down and tried to think like a bush, as a squealing noise and rumble approached.

It was a Russian PT76 tank, with its hatches unbuttoned, but its crew looking very, very alert.

It went on past, and came back fifteen minutes later.

It was just then the thought came: America, like France, had been accused, quite correctly, of taking these "gooks" less than seriously. That was one of the biggest complaints Special Forces had about the regular Army.

Yet here we were, attempting to assassinate a head of state, with nothing more than fifty crazies with machine guns. Would we have tried to kill Stalin, Hitler, de Gaulle with such a pissant force? Of course not. We would've dropped the entire 82nd Airborne in their laps.

Talk about contempt for the enemy...

I forced the thought away. We were too close, too hot, to allow any negatives. And besides, it was far too late.

We crossed the road, then crept north.

The jungle was thick, uncut, and the land was rough, mountainous.

My map said we were close, very very close, when the signal came back down the line: "Richardson up."

I moved past my crouched men to the Montagnards, who were on line along a ridge crest.

Babysan Davidson beckoned to me, and I slid up beside him.

He pointed, and I used a bush to peer downslope.

Below me were the caves.

And what looked like the entire Vietnamese Communist party leadership.

Here and there were the entrances to the caves. Hidden under trees or carefully camouflaged were low huts. The grounds were as immaculate as the White House, yet still clearly jungle. No overflight using conventional visuals would have seen anything.

There were guards here and there and, in front of one cave, another parked tank.

There were Soviet jeeps, and several antiaircraft guns.

The day was hot and still.

I chanced binoculars and saw, below me, dignified men walking about. It could have been the steps of the Capitol Building on a sleepy summer day, with senators and representatives digesting their lunch, and planning speeches.

And now we would kill them all.

I slid back in line, brought my troops up, and chanced using my radio.

"Sunrise Six Actual Up."

Simons crawled up a few minutes later, his bodyguard and radiomen behind him.

Babysan waved him to the crestline, showed him what I'd seen.

Simons came back, with one of the few smiles on his face I ever saw.

His plan was going perfectly.

He picked up the handset, whispered commands into it.

Behind me, men started moving toward the flank.

Then Babysan started waving furiously at me. I crawled up, Simons behind me. He was pointing, miming binoculars.

I found my bush, looked through it in the direction Davidson was pointing.

I saw Satan, or anyway the man most Americans thought was his embodiment.

It was a frail old man with a long, wispy beard, being helped by an aide, in deep conversation with two much younger men. Trailing the three were a host of aides.

Ho Chi Minh.

Our target was right there in front of us, no more than two hundred meters away.

Simons was beside me, hissing into his radio, "Snipers up! Goddammit, snipers up!"

And then the shit hit the fan.

Bull Simons's other radio, on command net, crackled, "Sunrise Six, Sunrise Six, this is Charlie Golf. Approaching your area. Request sitrep, over."

Watching Bull Simons try to keep from exploding in all directions might have been funny.

Somewhere else, not here.

"Who in the roaring blazing fuck is Charlie Fucking Golf?" he managed.

I had no idea, and then we heard the roar of a helicopter.

An HH53 blazed overhead. Not one of the dirty, flat green Giants that we had, but a finely waxed, gleaming machine that was fit to carry presidents.

I knew the bird. I'd seen it in Saigon.

It was General William C. Westmoreland, Commanding General, MAC-V's own chopper. And now I knew who Charlie Golf was. Commanding General. Someone must've picked it as a call sign we might recognize.

Simons ran off a string of obscenities. The radio droned back, blithely.

"Sunrise Six, this is Charlie Golf. Pop smoke at your location, and prepare a Lima Zulu. Over."

We were about to kill Ho Chi Minh, and this stupid frigging Westmoreland wanted to do a white-glove inspection or something.

It actually wasn't quite as stupid as it sounds, as I found out, years later. It took that long for things to be declassified, because of what a disaster that day was.

Even the declassified data is spotty, but it seems that someone in Washington talked about some kind of supersecret, ultraclassified mission being planned.

Richard Nixon and John Connolly, who I correctly thought were planning a run at the presidency in 1972, decided now was the occasion to get in on the act, either critically if it failed, or in bed with it if we succeeded.

Evidently they did not know exactly what President Rockefeller had ordered. By the time I investigated it was clear the mission had been planned by the CIA, and ordered directly by Rockefeller, bypassing all conventional lines of command.

Westmoreland, not knowing what was going on up north, and getting angrier by the minute at being bypassed, flew to Hanoi with the two politicians and, by relentless grilling, found out where our team was headed and its mission.

I don't know if he would have ordered us to stop, or what made him fly north from Hanoi, especially with Connolly and Nixon. Evidently he didn't know exactly where Ho Chi Minh was supposed to be, or anything more than the area we were moving in.

No one knows, even, who ordered smoke, and a landing zone cut. It might have been an overzealous staff officer, listening to, most likely, Connolly.

Westmoreland was too professional . . . I think . . . for that, and Nixon too cagey. Not to mention cowardly.

Regardless, we lay on that hilltop, frozen in shock.

The Viets below us weren't.

That summer calm was shattered, as if someone had pitched a rock into a hornet's nest.

Alarms rang, and troops began doubling here and there.

Two men had Ho Chi Minh by the arms, and were hurrying him to the shelter of a cave.

I have no idea where the snipers were.

But someone had to do something.

I slid my LAW off my chest, remembering its total unreliability, pulled the pin and slid the tube forward. The iron sight flipped up automatically, and I aimed.

I squeezed down on the firing mechanism, and nothing happened.

The sights were off that small man, only a few

meters from safety. I started to correct, and the goddamned LAW fired.

The rocket, wisping smoke, shot out and down, passing over Ho Chi Minh's head by at least two meters, and
struck a commo truck thirty meters distant. It exploded,
and the truck bucked and burst into flames, just as Ho
Chi Minh and his entourage vanished into safety.

I was staring down, almost in tears at my miss,
and so I didn't see Westmoreland's helicopter sweep
overhead, not one hundred meters off the deck, no
doubt drawn by the smoke which the pilot might have
thought was our ordered marker.

Some people said it was an SA-2 missile that was
launched, which I doubt, given its range requirements
for arming. More likely it was a heavy machine gun
or maybe even a lucky shot with an RPG.

Whatever, something took the big Sikorsky through
the canopy, and exploded. The helicopter bucked, rolled
on its side, and dropped. About ten meters above the
ground, an explosion boiled through its fuselage, then
it struck, and another explosion sent bits of aluminum
and . . . other things . . . through the air.

Simons, quicker than us all, was on his feet.

"All right," he shouted, and I think his voice carried
across the nearby border. "India Alpha. Shoot their
dicks off, then we're moving out. By teams!"

Down below, a pair of PT76s rumbled into life.

Three LAWS spat from the flank, hitting them in
their lightly armored sides. Two exploded, the other
boiled smoke, and spun to a halt.

We fell back, down the hill.

"To the road," Simons shouted. "The hell with
being careful!"

We obeyed, shooting as we moved. We were undoubtedly doomed, but the reflexes of our training took over.

We went down the road, almost to that hamlet of Ha Quang.

Mortars thudded, and people went down. If they still moved, someone had them back on their feet, and carried them. Medics tried to treat them as we moved.

If they were dead, they were abandoned, with sometimes a grenade, its pin out, tucked under them as a hasty boobytrap.

Just before the village, Simons was standing at the junction of that almost road.

"Down this way," he ordered.

I stopped my reaction force there, spread them out.

"Goddamit, Richardson—"

"Move your ass, sir," I shouted. "I've got my orders."

A momentary grin came and went, then he grabbed his handpiece, was calling for our lift ships.

I counted twenty-five men running past me, leapfrogging their way. There were ten men with me.

Babysan and Mad Dog Shriver hurtled past, behind their Montagnards.

A solid wave of infantry boiled down the road, and machine gunners opened up. One of the gunners grunted, flopped over, and I had his RPD.

The Viet infantry was hesitating.

M79s thunked, and grenades exploded in their midst.

I put a drum from the RPD into the mass, and they broke and ran.

Then we were moving, following the others toward safety.

Artillery slammed in somewhere, obviously being fired blind.

A mortar team came around a bend, spotted us, and ducked into cover.

One of the 60 gunners dropped four mortar rounds on top of them, and that was something we didn't have to worry about.

We were moving fast, but not fast enough.

The Viets were closing, and now their mortars were killing and wounding men around me.

Simons was shouting something on the radio, and a mortar thunked in, I swear next to him. Simons flung his hands up, fell, and my heart stopped. If he was dead . . .

One of his radiomen was down as well, and then Simons, drooling blood from his limp arm and shrapnel wounds on his face, staggered to his feet.

Dick Meadows was there, and somehow had the enormous Bull over his shoulder, and the main column was moving back.

We held as long as we could, men going down, wounded men barely able to stand shooting back, then we retreated.

Shriver was beside me, a bloodstained grin on his face.

"Gonna be a *hell* of a last stand, won't it, sir?"

I hoped I managed a smile back, then a round spanged into my RPD, and it was dead.

I grabbed an M16, saw a pair of Viets no more than a hundred meters away, shot them down.

I heard Shriver shouting to me, and saw him, with his Montagnards, crouched around a pile of logs, an ideal position.

There were ten of us who stumbled to the position.

Viets came up the road, and were shot down.

A wave of them came out of the brush, and were gunned down.

I called for us to fall back again, and we were up.

A machine gun chattered, and two of the 'Yards dropped. Bob Howard grinned, waved at me, moved back, after the others.

Then there was a shouting mass of Viets on us, and I had my Randall in one hand, my pistol in the other.

I slashed one Viet's throat, pushed him into another, shot him in the chest.

I saw Jerry Shriver snap-shoot two men, then he went down. A moment later, a grinning, shouting Viet stood, holding his blood-dripping head.

I shot him in the face, and then one of the Montagnards chattered an RPD burst into the knot, somehow missing his fellows and us.

We were moving again, and I was throwing grenades.

A bullet hit me in the upper chest, but I could still run.

Time blurred, and I cursed my pistol for being empty, threw it at an oncoming Viet, and someone else shot him.

Then there wasn't anybody to shoot, and behind me I heard the roar of helicopters.

Our Jolly Greens, against orders, didn't come in at the LZ near Tra Linh and wait, but came looking for us.

Then the birds were on the ground, and Jenkins was helping me aboard and we were airborne.

Twenty-four of us made it back to Hanoi, all of us wounded.

It was the greatest disaster in Special Forces history.

We mourned our dead, while the rest of the Army mourned Westmoreland, and America mourned Connolly and Nixon.

For a time, the operation was an utter secret, and various lies were told about how the commander of all forces in Vietnam had gotten killed.

But Senator Teddy Kennedy, who'd never been thought of as the soldier's friend, stood tall in the Senate, demanding an explanation and medals for what he called "America's finest warriors."

I don't know about myself, but I knew damned well he spoke the truth about the others.

More Congressional Medals of Honor, sixteen, were hastily given out than in any other battle in American history. Bull Simons, Dick Meadows, Bob Howard and others got theirs at the White House. Babysan Davidson, Mad Dog Shriver and others received theirs posthumously.

I also got one, which I again felt I didn't deserve.

But this time, I accepted the award.

The war dragged on.

Ho Chi Minh died that fall, mostly of old age, and it made our mission seem senseless, since Vo Nguyen Giap and Pham Van Dong replaced him with never a lost step.

Our mission was an utter catastrophe.

Study and Observations Group never recovered from the loss, and was broken up. Nor did Special Forces ever really recover, in my opinion.

But I'll never be able to remember that day without hearing a whisper from Shakespeare:

"And gentlemen . . . now a-bed
Shall think themselves accursed they were
   not here,
And hold their manhoods cheap whiles
   any speaks
That fought with us . . ."

The following is an excerpt from:

HELL HATH NO FURY

BY
DAVID WEBER
& LINDA EVANS

Available from Baen Books
March 2007
hardcover

CHAPTER ONE

Commander of One Thousand Klayrman Toralk sat upright in the personnel carrier strapped to his circling command dragon's back, despite the buffeting wind of the beast's passage, so that he could see clearly over the edge of the windshield. The sight was impressive, he admitted, watching critically while the final few transport dragons, scales glittering with gemlike intensity in the last light of day, settled like huge, multihued insects onto the handful of islets clustered in the middle of so many endless miles of swamp. Unfortunately, "impressive" wasn't exactly the same thing as "well organized." In fact, the words which came most forcibly to mind were "awkward as hell."

And the reason the maneuver looked awkward was because it *was* awkward, he thought sourly. Despite his deep respect for his immediate superior, this entire operational concept could only have been put together by a ground-pounder. Any Air Force officer would have taken one look at the topographical maps and informed his superior roundly that he was out of his mind. Crowding this many transport and—especially—touchy, often ill-natured battle dragons into such a constricted space violated every precept of peacetime training regulations and exercise guidelines.

Too bad Ekros never heard about all those regs and guidelines, Toralk thought. *Or maybe he did. After all, how could even a demon make sure that whatever could go wrong did go wrong if he didn't know exactly what he was screwing up?*

The thousand chuckled with a certain bare minimum of genuine humor. Yet even as he did, he knew that if

Commander of Two Thousand Harshu hadn't pushed him—hard—on this, he would have told the two thousand it was impossible. Fortunately for Arcana (if not, perhaps, for the tender sensibilities of One Thousand Toralk), Harshu wasn't particularly interested in the artificial safety constraints of peacetime. He wasn't overly hampered by excess tactfulness, either. But he *was* completely willing to absorb a few casualties, among his dragons as well as his troops, to get Toralk's attack force into position with its beasts sufficiently well rested to maximize their combat radius.

And it looks like that poisonous little prick Neshok was right—barely—about whether or not I could fit them all in, Toralk conceded.

The last of the transports landed a bit short of its intended island, and a towering, mud-streaked fountain erupted as the huge dragon hit the water. Fortunately, it was shallow enough that the beast wasn't in any danger of drowning or miring itself in the muck, and the levitation spell kept its towed cargo pod out of the water while it floundered ashore. Of course, Toralk had no doubt that if he'd been a little closer, he would have heard an interesting chorus of yells and curses coming from the infantry inside that pod. It might have stayed out of the water, but that hadn't kept it from bouncing around on the end of its tether like some sort of insane ball. And all of that water and mud the dragon's impact had thrown up had had to go somewhere.

Toralk grinned behind his goggles, despite his tension, then shook his head and leaned forward to tap his pilot on the top of his flight helmet.

"Yes, Sir?" The pilot had to raise his voice to be heard, but not by very much at this ridiculously low speed.

"Let's set it down, Fifty Larshal," Toralk said, and pointed at the larger island at the center of the half-dozen congested, swampy hummocks which had been chosen for his forward staging points.

"Yes, Sir!" Larshal said, and the command dragon lifted onto its left wing tip, banking more steeply as it circled down towards the indicated perch.

Toralk gazed into the west, where the embers of sunset still glowed on the horizon. This particular bivouac wasn't going to be much fun for anyone, he reflected. Maybe that would be for the good, though. Men who were thoroughly pissed off after spending a wet, muddy, bug-infested night not sleeping were likely to show a little more . . . enthusiasm when it came to shooting at the people responsible for them being out here in the first place.

*   *   *

Hulmok Arthag was an unhappy man.

Someone who didn't know the platoon-captain well might have been excused for not realizing that. Or, rather, someone who didn't know Arpathian septmen well might have been excused for not realizing Arthag was any unhappier than usual, given how little an Arpathian's expression normally gave away.

He stood under the forest canopy—thinner than it had been when the Chalgyn Consortium survey crew had been slaughtered, just over two months ago—and gazed into the predawn darkness, longing for the empty plains of home. Life had been harder there, but it had also been much less . . . complicated.

"Copper for your thoughts, Hulmok."

The platoon-captain turned at the sound of Platoon-Captain Dorzon chan Baskay's voice. The Ternathian cavalry officer looked improbably neat and clean—not to mention well-dressed and freshly shaved—for someone who spent his nights sleeping in a tent in the middle of the woods with winter coming on. Arthag had sometimes wondered if there were a special Talent for that, one that was linked by blood to the families which routinely produced the Ternathian Empire's diplomats. Not that chan Baskay had ever wanted to be a diplomat, whatever the rest of his family might have had in mind for him.

Which just goes to show the shamans were right. No man can outrun his fate, Arthag reflected with the faintest lip twitch of amusement.

"I don't know if they're worth that much," he told the Ternathian after a moment.

"I'm pretty sure they are," chan Baskay responded. Hulmok raised one eyebrow a fraction of an inch, and chan Baskay shrugged. "I've heard all about your 'instinct' when it comes to picking people for your command. And while I'll admit you've got a remarkably good gambler's face to go with it, it's pretty clear to me that something's jabbing that 'instinct' of yours as hard as it's jabbing every single one of mine."

"Really?"

"Hulmok, they've been talking to us for a month now," chan Baskay said. "In all that time, they haven't said one damned thing except that they want to talk, instead of shoot. And they've been throwing grit into the machinery with both hands for the last week and a half. Which, you may have noticed, exactly corresponds to the point at which I finally got formal instructions from the Emperor. You think, maybe, it's pure coincidence that they got even more obstructionist as soon as *I* stopped sparring for time?"

"No." Arthag shook his head. "No, I don't think that—not any more than you do."

The two men looked at one another. Chan Baskay's expression showed all the frustration and anger he couldn't allow himself to display across the floating conference table from the Arcanan diplomats, and Arthag's very lack of expression showed the same emotions as both of them contemplated the Arcanans' last week or so of posturing. Rithmar Skirvon, the senior of the two Arcanans, had hardened his negotiating posture noticeably. His initial, conciliatory attitude had all but completely evaporated, and he seemed determined to fix responsibility for the initial violence of the clash between his people's troops and the civilian survey crew on the dead civilians.

That was a pretty significant shift from his original attitude, all by itself, but it was obvious to chan Baskay that Skirvon's instructions were exactly similar to his own in at least one regard. Neither side was prepared to give up possession of the Hell's Gate portal cluster to the other under any circumstances. Chan Baskay hadn't found it necessary to be quite as . . . confrontational as Skirvon, since Sharona currently *had* possession of the cluster, but he could at least sympathize with the Arcanan on that point.

What he couldn't understand was why Skirvon seemed actively intent on forcing a breakdown in the talks. He wasn't simply stonewalling, simply withdrawing into an inflexible position which he could always have blamed on instructions from his superiors. Instead, there'd been a whole series of insults, "misunderstandings," and "lost tempers" coming from the Arcanan side. And by now, chan Baskay no longer needed Trekar chan Rothag's Sifting Talent to tell when Skirvon was lying. All he had to do was check to see whether or not the Arcanan's mouth was moving.

"Hulmok," he said after a moment, his eyes unwontedly somber, "I've got a really bad feeling about what's going on. But that's all I've got. I don't have a single concrete thing to hang my worry on. So, if you've got something specific, I damned well need to hear

David Weber & Linda Evans

it before I sit back down across from those bastards in a couple of hours."

Arthag considered the Ternathian for several moments, then shrugged very slightly.

"I do have a Talent," he acknowledged. He wasn't entirely pleased about making that admission to anyone, for several reasons, but chan Baskay was right. "It's not one of the mainstream Talents," he continued, "but it's run in my bloodline for generations. We've produced a lot of shamans because of it."

"And?" chan Baskay prompted when he paused.

"I can't read minds, and I can't always tell when someone's telling the truth, the way Rothag can. But I can read what's . . . inside a man. Tell whether he's trustworthy, honest. Recognize the ones who'll cave in when the going gets tough, and which ones will die on their feet, trying. And—" he looked directly into chan Baskay's eyes "—the ones who think they're about to slip a knife into someone's back without getting caught."

"Which pretty much describes these people's school of diplomacy right down to the ground, assuming Skirvon and Dastiri are representative samples," chan Baskay snorted.

"I'm not talking about double-dealing or cheating at cards, Dorzon," Arthag said somberly. "I'm talking about *real* knives."

"What?" Chan Baskay stiffened. "What do you mean?"

"I mean that little bit of 'lost temper' yesterday afternoon was carefully orchestrated. I mean that when Skirvon demanded that *our* people apologize for provoking it, he'd rehearsed his lines well ahead of time. I mean that the lot of them are pushing towards some specific moment. They're not only working to a plan, Dorzon—they're working to a *schedule*. And the thing that's driving me mad, is that I don't have any idea *why* they're doing it!"

Chan Baskay frowned. Commander of Fifty Tharian Narshu, the senior officer of Skirvon and Dastiri's "honor guard," had exploded in a furious tirade over a trivial incident between one of his soldiers and one of Arthag's PAAF cavalry troopers the day before. The Arcanan officer had actually "allowed himself" to place one hand on the hilt of his short sword, which chan Baskay was positive had to be deliberate posturing on his part, rather than a serious threat. After all, Narshu had to know what would happen if his outnumbered men wound up matching short swords against H&W revolvers.

But by the same token, an officer in Narshu's position had to be equally well aware of his responsibilities as part of the diplomatic mission . . . and if *he* wasn't, then certainly the diplomats he was there to "guard" were. Yet Skirvon had reprimanded Narshu in only the most perfunctory manner, even though both Arcanan negotiators must have been conscious of the example their escort's CO was setting for the rest of his men.

"How confident are you of that, Hulmok?" he asked after a moment. "The schedule part, I mean?"

"I'm not as totally confident of it as I'd like to be," Arthag admitted. "If these were Sharonians, I'd be a hundred percent certain. But they aren't." He shrugged ever so slightly. "I keep reminding myself that it's remotely possible I'm misinterpreting something. After all, it's only been two months since we even knew they existed. But still . . ."

Chan Baskay nodded again, wishing his stomach muscles weren't tightening the way they were.

"One thing *I'm* certain of," he said slowly, "is that they don't have any intention of actually negotiating any sort of real resolution. For one thing, they're still lying their asses off about a lot of things."

"For example?" Arthag raised his eyebrows again.

"Exactly how Shaylar died, for one thing," chan Baskay said grimly. "And these repeated assurances about their eagerness to reach some sort of 'mutually acceptable' disposition of the portal junction, for another."

"And about who shot first?" Arthag asked.

"No." Chan Baskay grimaced. "On that point, they're actually telling the truth, according to Rothag. They don't have any better idea of who shot first than we do. And oddly enough, they also seem to be telling the truth when they insist that the officer in command at the time tried to avoid massacring our survey crew."

"I think maybe Rothag better have his Talent checked," Arthag said bitingly.

"I know, I know!" Chan Baskay had the air of a man who wanted to rip out handfuls of hair in frustration. "I've Seen Shaylar's message myself. I *know* chan Hagrahyl stood up with his hands empty and got shot down like a dog for his pains. But they insist that wasn't what their officer wanted, and Rothag's Talent insists they're telling the truth when they say it."

"They may *believe* they are," Arthag snorted. "But if they do, it's because the bastard lied to them about what happened out here."

"Maybe." Chan Baskay shook his head, his expression half-exasperated and half-hopeful. "I keep wishing Shaylar had managed to contact Kinlafia sooner." He grimaced. "That sounds stupid, I know. The fact that she managed to reach him at all under those circumstances, much less sustain the link through what happened to her and all of her friends . . . Gods, it was nothing short of miraculous! I can't even imagine the kind of guts it took to hold that link. But we didn't actually See or Hear anything until after chan Hagrahyl went down."

"But we know what happened, anyway," Arthag pointed out. "Darcel—Voice Kinlafia—was linked deeply enough to know that from the side traces. Besides, she *told* him so."

"Granted. But she Told him, and she Showed him her *memory* of chan Hagrahyl going down with his hands empty and the crossbow bolt in his throat. That's not the same as Seeing it happen for ourselves. We have what she told Kinlafia, but we don't have anything before the actual event, don't know if there was something Shaylar didn't see herself, or saw but didn't recognize, or didn't realize it had happened at all, in those few seconds we didn't actually See."

"I'm sorry, Dorzon," Arthag said after a moment, "but I can't think of anything which could possibly change what happened or why. And even if I could think of anything now, it's too late for it to have any effect."

"I know. I know." Chan Baskay gazed off into the depths of the forest. "But they're still insistent that they didn't want any of this, that what happened was against their standing orders to establish *peaceful* contact with any new human civilization they encountered, and Rothag's Talent insists they're telling the truth about that. Which presumably means it accurately represents their government's long-term policy, no matter how badly things have gone wrong on the ground. To be honest, that's the only hopeful thing I've heard out of their mouths yet! Unfortunately, it's outweighed by everything else . . . especially what *your* Talent is telling you."

"Well," the Arpathian said slowly, "what do you plan to do about it?"

"Gee, thanks," chan Baskay said. "Drop it on *my* plate, why don't you?"

"Well, you *are* senior to me," Arthag pointed out reasonably. "My promotion was only confirmed last week. And you're the official diplomat around here, too."

"I know." Chan Baskay drummed the fingers of his right hand on his thigh for several seconds, then shrugged.

"The first thing is to have Chief chan Treskin Flick a dispatch to Company-Captain chan Tesh. I'll tell him what we're worried about, and ask him for instructions. And the next thing is probably to have Rokam pass the same message back to Company-Captain Halifu for relay up the line to Regiment-Captain Velvelig."

Arthag nodded. Chief-Armsman Virak chan Treskin was the Flicker who'd been assigned to relay messages to chan Tesh's senior Flicker, Junior-Armsman Tairsal chan Synarch. Petty-Captain Rokam Traygan was chan Tesh's Voice, but despite everything, they were still desperately understaffed with the long-range telepathic communicating Talents out here. Traygan had originally been slated to hold the Voice's position at Halifu's portal fort in New Uromath. In light of the situation here at the Hell's Gate portal, he'd come forward to replace Darcel Kinlafia when the civilian Voice headed back to Sharona with Crown Prince Janaki. Fortunately, the Portal Authority had managed to scare up a third Voice—Petty-Captain Shansair Baulwan, a fellow Arpathian—to hold down Halifu's fort, and they were working hard to get still more Voices forward. But for right now, at least, there was absolutely no one else to spare in Hell's Gate or New Uromath, and it was critical that chan Baskay have the shortest possible message turnaround time . . . and the greatest accuracy and flexibility when it came to relaying diplomatic correspondence. So they'd ended up assigning Traygan to him and Baulwan to Halifu, at the critical inter-universal relay point, while chan Tesh (who was in the potentially stickiest position of all) made do with written messages relayed through the Flickers. It was clumsy, but until they could get more Voices deployed forward, it was the best they could do.

"And in the meantime?" the cavalry officer said after a moment.

"And in the meantime," chan Baskay replied with a grim smile, "we do the best we can. I'm inclined to trust your Talent, even if these aren't Sharonians. So, pass the word to your people. I don't want them going off half-cocked, but I don't want them taken by surprise if these people are working to a schedule and they decide to push further than they have."

"Swords and crossbows against pistols and rifles?"

"If that's all they have, that's one thing." Chan Baskay shook his head. "On the other hand, it's been a month now, and we need to be careful about letting familiarity breed contempt. So far, they haven't produced anything man-portable that looks like some sort of personal super weapon, but for all we know, they've just been waiting for us to get accustomed enough to them to let our guard down."

"Point taken," Arthag agreed. "I'll talk to my people."

"Good. And when they get here this morning, I want you handy. Close to Skirvon, as well as Narshu."

*   *   *

As he climbed down from the back of the completely unaugmented horse the Sharonians had "loaned" him for the trip from the swamp portal, Rithmar Skirvon found himself wishing he'd been in the habit of spending more time in the saddle. Whatever the rest of him thought of his current assignment, his backside didn't like it at all. And the miserable nag his "hosts" had provided didn't make it any better. He suspected they'd deliberately chosen one with a particularly unpleasant gait just for him.

434 David Weber & Linda Evans

He pushed that thought aside as he handed his reins to one of Fifty Narshu's troopers and started across the now-familiar clearing towards the Sharonian negotiating party. Deeply drifted leaves rustled about his boots like bone-dry dragon scales, and the air was cool and bracing, particularly compared to the hot humidity from which Skirvon had come.

Despite that, his "hosts" didn't look particularly happy to see him as they waited under the towering forest giants' multicolored canopy, and, as he contemplated what was about to happen, Skirvon had never been more grateful for all his years of experience across the bargaining table. For that matter, his taste for high-stakes card games had served him in particularly good stead over the last two or three weeks, as well. His face was in the habit of telling other people exactly what he wanted it to tell them, and while he'd developed a certain wary respect for Viscount Simrath, he was confident the Sharonian diplomat didn't have a clue what was coming.

Of course, he reminded himself as he reached the floating conference table and his waiting chair, *there's always the possibility that I'm wrong about that.*

But, no, that was only opening-day nerves talking. If the Sharonians had suspected the truth, they would certainly have reinforced their "honor guard" here at the conference site. For that matter, they wouldn't have passed Skirvon and his diplomatic party through the swamp portal at the crack of dawn this morning, either.

Face it, Rithmar, he told himself as he settled down in the chair across the table from Simrath yet again, *your real problem is that you're scared shitless.*

His lips quirked ever so slightly at the thought as he waited for Uthik Dastiri, his assistant, to sit beside him. That, however, didn't make it untrue, and he reminded himself once again that this entire ploy had been as much his idea as Hundred Neshok's. In fact, Skirvon had probably done even more than Neshok to sell the concept to Two Thousand Harshu. Somehow, though, he hadn't quite envisioned his own direct participation in sufficient detail when it had sounded like a *good* idea.

Mul Gurthak is so going to owe me for this one, he thought. *He may be in the Army, but I'm damned well not drawing combat pay!*

He watched Viscount Simrath and Lord Trekar Rothag sitting down opposite him and suppressed a sudden urge to pull out his chronometer and check the time.

"Good morning, Master Skirvon," Viscount Simrath said, as courteously as if he didn't realize Skirvon had been deliberately stalling for at least the last two weeks.

"Good morning, Viscount," Skirvon replied, as courteously as if he really thought Simrath didn't realize it.

"I trust we may be able to move forward, at least a little bit, today," the Sharonian diplomat continued. Under the formal rules and schedule they'd agreed to, it was his turn to control the agenda for the day.

"Progress is always welcome, My Lord," Skirvon conceded graciously.

"I'm pleased to hear that. However, the fact remains that I'm still awaiting your response to the points I made to you following the receipt of my last message from Emperor Zindel," Simrath said pleasantly. "In particular, I note that you continue to insist that the Union of Arcana must receive title to at least half the portals contained in this cluster. A cluster, I remind you, which is in Sharona's possession and which was first surveyed by the civilian survey crew which your troops massacred."

"I'm afraid I must disagree with you, Viscount," Skirvon said in his most respectful tones. "You appear to be implying that Arcana has taken no cognizance of Sharona's insistence on retaining total possession of this cluster—despite the fact that it's still to be established who actually fired the first shot, and the fact that our total casualties have been much higher than your own. In fact, we *have* taken cognizance of that insistence. Our position may not have changed," he smiled the empty, pleasant smile of a professional diplomat, "but rejection *of* your emperor's . . . proposals is scarcely the same thing as not responding *to* them."

The Ternathian noble leaned back in his chair—the floating chair, provided by Skirvon—and folded his arms across his chest. The leaves whispering windsongs overhead were growing thinner by the day, Skirvon noticed as a shaft of sunlight fell through them and illuminated the tabletop's rich, polished grain and glittered brilliantly on the translating personal crystal lying between him and Simrath. Those leaves remained unfortunately thick, however, and a part of him wished Two Thousand Harshu had decided he could wait just a little longer.

Which is pretty stupid of you, Rithmar, when you've been pushing him just as hard as you dared from the beginning.

"Master Skirvon," Simrath said, "I'm at something of a loss to understand Arcana's motives in sending you to this conference table."

"I beg your pardon, My Lord?"

"Officially, you're here because 'talking is better than shooting,' I believe you said," Simrath observed. "While I can't disagree with that particular statement, ultimately, the shooting is going to resume unless we manage to resolve the issues between us here, at this table. So it strikes me as rather foolish for the two of us to sit here, day after day, exchanging empty pleasantries, when it's quite obvious you're under instructions not to agree to anything."

Despite himself, Skirvon blinked. He was ill-accustomed to that degree of . . . frankness from an opponent in any negotiation. After all, two-thirds of the art of diplomacy consisted of wearing down the other side by saying as little as possible in the maximum possible number of words. The last thing any professional diplomat truly wanted was some sort of "major breakthrough" whose potential outcome lay outside the objectives covered by his instructions.

More to the point, however, Simrath had observed the rules of the game up to this stage and taken no official notice of Skirvon's delaying tactics. So why had he chosen today, of all days, to stop playing along?

"In addition," the viscount continued calmly, "I must tell you that the distressing number of . . . unpleasant scenes between members of your party and my own do not strike me as being completely, um, *spontaneous*, let's say. So I have to ask myself why, if you're so eager to negotiate with us, you're simultaneously offering absolutely nothing new, while either encouraging—or, at the very least, tolerating—extraordinarily disruptive behavior on the part of your uniformed subordinates. Would you, perhaps, care to enlighten my ignorance on these matters?"

Skirvon felt a most unpleasant sinking sensation in the vicinity of his midsection.

Stop that! he told himself sternly. *Even if they've finally started waking up, it's too late to do them much good.*

At least, he damned well *hoped* it was.

"Viscount Simrath," he said in his firmest voice, "I must protest your apparent charge that the 'unpleasant scenes' to which you refer were somehow deliberately

contrived by myself or any other member of my negotiating party. What motive could we possibly have for
such behavior?"

"That *is* an interesting question, isn't it?" Simrath
smiled thinly. It was a smile which never touched his
gray eyes—eyes, Skirvon realized, that were remarkably cold and clear. He'd never realized just how icy
they could be, and it suddenly struck the Arcanan that
Simrath was not only extraordinarily tall, like most of
the Ternathians he'd already seen, but oddly fit for
a diplomat. In fact, he looked in that moment like a
very tough customer, indeed, and remarkably little like
someone who spent his days carrying around nothing
heavier—or more deadly—than a briefcase.

"What, precisely, do you wish to imply, My Lord?"
Skirvon asked with the air of a man grasping a dilemma
firmly by the horns.

"I wish to imply, Sir," Simrath said coolly, "that it's
never actually been your intention to negotiate any
sort of permanent settlement or mutually acceptable
terms. For reasons of your own, you've seen fit to initiate these negotiations and to keep Sharona talking. To
this point, I've been willing to play your game, to see
precisely what it was you truly had in mind. However,
neither my patience, nor Emperor Zindel's tolerance, is
inexhaustible. So, either the two of us will make significant progress over the next twenty-four hours, or else
Sharona will withdraw from the talks. We'll see," if his
smile had been thin before, it was a razor this time, "how
you prefer shooting once again, rather than talking."

Skirvon felt Dastiri stiffen at his side. Despite the
Manisthuan's espousal of *garsulthan*, or "real politics,"
Dastiri's skin had always been thinner than Skirvon's.
Fortunately, the younger man appeared to have himself
under control, at least for the moment. Which was

actually about as much as Skirvon could say about himself, if he wanted to be honest. He managed to keep himself from looking over his shoulder at Commander of Fifty Narshu, but it wasn't the easiest thing he'd ever done.

"That sounds remarkably like an ultimatum, My Lord," he said.

"Does it?" Simrath cocked his head to one side, as if carefully considering what Skirvon had said, then shrugged. "Good," he said in an even cooler tone. "After all, that's what it is."

"The Union of Arcana is not accustomed to bending to ultimatums, My Lord!" Skirvon's response came out harder and more clipped than he'd intended.

"The perhaps you should seek to profit from the novel experience, Master Skirvon," Simrath suggested. "Or, of course, if my plain speaking has sufficiently affronted you, you can always withdraw yet again to . . . how *was* it you put it the other day? Ah, yes! Withdraw to 'allow tempers to cool,' I believe you said."

Skirvon was astounded by the sharpness of the anger Simrath's words—and scornful attitude—sent jabbing through him. He felt his expression congeal, his nostrils pinched in ever so slightly, and the slight flicker in Simrath's eyes as the Sharonian obviously observed the physical signs of his anger only made that anger even sharper.

At that moment, Skirvon would have like nothing better than to stand up and storm away from that table. Or to snatch an infantry-dragon out of some outsized pocket and blast the smiling aristocratic bastard across from him into a smoldering corpse. Unfortunately, he could do neither of those things . . . yet.

"My Lord," he said through gritted teeth, instead, "I must protest the entire tone of your comments and your apparent attitude. As I say, the Union of Arcana unaccustomed to bending to ultimatums. However," he made himself inhale deeply and sat back in his own chair, "whatever your own attitude, or that of your government, may be, *my* instructions remain unchanged." *Which*, he reflected, *is actually the truth*. "As such, I have no option but to continue my efforts to achieve at least some progress in resolving the matters which bring us here before anyone else is killed. I will continue to pursue my duty, but not without telling you that I most strongly protest the insulting nature of this exchange."

"If the insult is too great," Simrath said, almost indifferently, "please feel free to withdraw. Otherwise, I trust, you'll at least stop insulting my intelligence by simply repeating the same, worn out, and completely pointless positions again and again and again."

* * *

Dorzon chan Baskay watched the Arcanan diplomats' faces darken with anger. The younger of them, Dastiri, had never been particularly hard to read, and his anger at chan Baskay's confrontational language sparkled in his dark eyes. Skirvon was obviously older and more experienced than his assistant, but despite that, he was nowhere near as good at concealing his emotions as he clearly thought he was. And the fact that even though Skirvon was as furious as he obviously was, he'd swallowed not just the content of chan Baskay's words, but the deliberately insulting tone in which they'd been delivered, as well, told the cavalry officer quite a lot.

Unfortunately, chan Baskay wasn't certain exactly what that "lot" was. The fact that Skirvon hadn't stormed away from the table in yet another of his patented temper tantrums was interesting, though. Whatever these bastards were up to, Skirvon clearly *needed* to be here this morning.

Which, coupled with Hulmok's observations, doesn't precisely fill me with joy.

He didn't so much as glance in the Arpathian o[...] direction, but he did withdraw his gold fountain[...] from his breast pocket and toy with it. He turned it [...] for end, watching it gleam richly in the morning sunlig[...] He had no doubt that the Arcanans would interpret it [...] another insolently dismissive gesture on his part. Tha[...] didn't bother him particularly, but it wasn't the real [...] reason for it, and the corner of his eye saw Arthag's tiny nod as the Arpathian acknowledged his warning signal.

"I deeply regret that you've apparently so completely misconstrued and misunderstood my efforts, My Lord," Skirvon told chan Baskay through stiff lips. "Since, however, you seem to have done so, by all means explain to me precisely what sort of response to your emperor's terms you would deem a sign of 'progress.'"

* * *

"For a start," chan Baskay told Skirvon in an only slightly less indifferent tone, "you might begin by at least acknowledging the fact that our current possession of this junction—paid for, I might add, with the blood of our slaughtered *civilians*—means we are not, in fact, negotiating from positions of equal strength. We need not even discuss sharing sovereignty over this junction with you. We already have it. As Sharona sees it, Master Skirvon, it's your job to convince us first, that there's any logical or equitable reason for us even to consider giving up any aspect of the sovereignty we've secured by force of arms, and, second, that there's any reason we should trust your government to abide by any agreement you manage to negotiate."

Skirvon ordered himself not to glower at the arrogant Sharonian. That sort of blunt, hard-edged attitude was far more confrontational than anything he'd seen out of Simrath to this point, and he wondered what had prompted the change.

tle, too late, you prick, he told Simrath
ask of his eyes. *All I have to do is
for another hour or so, and then . . .*
My Lord," he said after a moment. "If
upon rejecting my government's efforts to
me arrangement based on something other
brute force, I suppose I have no choice but to
t your proposal on your own terms.

"As you say, Sharona is currently in possession of
this junction. I would submit to you, however, that it
would be a grave error to assume that that happy state
of affairs—from your perspective, at least—will continue
indefinitely without some indication of reasonableness
from your side. My government has stated repeatedly,
through me, that talking is better than shooting. That
doesn't mean shooting couldn't resume if our legitimate
claims are rejected on the basis of your current military
advantage."

Skirvon sat forward in his chair once more, hands
folded on the rock-steady table floating between him and
Simrath, and looked the Sharonian straight in the eye.

"In all honesty, My Lord," he said with total candor,
"given the fashion in which you've just spoken to me,
and spoken about my government, a resort to military
force isn't totally unattractive to me. I suspect, however,
that your masters would be no more pleased than my
own if that should happen. So—"

Rithmar Skirvon went on talking, making himself pay
no attention to the steadily ticking seconds and minutes
flowing away into eternity.

—end excerpt—

from *Hell Hath No Fury*
available in hardcover,
March 2007, from Baen Books